To my friend Petra Jíšová,
who told me a story about a wish in a bottle,
that grew into this novel . . .

anything that isn't this

CHRIS PRIESTLEY

HOT
KEY
BOOKS

First published in Great Britain in 2015 by Hot Key Books
Northburgh House, 10 Northburgh Street, London EC1V 0AT

A CIP catalogue record for this book is available from the British Library.

ISBN: 978-1-4714-0464-1

1

This book is typeset in 10.5 Berling LT Std using Atomik ePublisher

Printed and bound by Clays Ltd, St Ives Plc

www.hotkeybooks.com

Hot Key Books is part of the Bonnier Publishing Group
www.bonnierpublishing.com

Preface

The Duel

'Choose your weapon,' said the old general, coughing into a silk handkerchief and striking the handsome young cavalry officer in the face with his white leather glove.

'I choose . . . Time,' said the younger man with a sigh, settling himself down in the long grass under the bright morning sun and closing his eyes.

Francis Palp, from *The Ghost Tram and Other Stories*

Chapter 1

Frank looked down at his plate. The vegetables, once perhaps an appetising and inviting shade of green, had been boiled to the point of translucency. The potatoes were dust grey and dry like masonry rubble. There was a piece of indeterminate meat that looked as though it had been pickled in formaldehyde for a century or two. He stabbed it with his fork and it deflated flatulently.

'I'm not hungry,' he said.

He put his knife and fork down.

'But it's your favourite,' said his mother with a cheery grin.

'Er . . . No it's not,' said Frank, pushing the plate away.

'Are you sure?'

'It's not my favourite.' Frank folded his arms.

'Well, whose favourite is it?'

Frank's mother looked round the table, from Frank to his sister Petra, to Frank's father and then back to Frank, but no one responded. The electrical hum that was always present in the apartment grew in volume and Frank winced as it growled in his ear.

'I was sure it was someone's favourite,' said his mother. She frowned a little with the effort of trying to recall.

'Favourite or not,' said Frank's father gruffly, between noisy mouthfuls, 'eat up. You mustn't waste good food. We'd have thought a meal like this was a feast in the War.'

'We would,' agreed Frank's mother.

They sighed, smiling at this shared reminiscence of hardship. Frank muttered and jabbed a chunk of potato with his fork and put it in his mouth. It tasted of nothing at all. It just dustily coated his gums and tongue. He swallowed it with difficulty and prodded the watery vegetables suspiciously. He dropped his cutlery on the table.

'Look, I'm sorry but I can't . . . I can't eat with him staring at me,' said Frank.

'Who?' said his mother.

'Him!' said Frank, pointing his finger towards a tall young man in a dark grey, creased and ill-fitting suit standing in the corner of the room near the standard lamp, peering over the top of a small notebook in which he was scribbling.

Frank's parents exchanged awkward glances and then looked at Frank's sister, who in turn looked at Frank.

'You can't mean the Student,' said Petra eventually, with a forced chuckle.

'Yes,' said Frank. 'I *do* mean the Student. I can't eat with him watching and, you know, spying on me and taking notes all the time. Why doesn't he just eat with us?'

'He couldn't write then, could he?' said his father.

'That's my point,' said Frank. 'I mean –'

'But he's probably just doing some homework,' said his mother. 'They have so much homework to do.'

'Homework?' said Frank.

'Well, he is a Student, dear,' said his mother.

'Student of what?' said Frank, sitting back and folding his arms again. 'What's he a student of?'

Again, everyone around the table exchanged nervous glances. 'More potatoes, my love?' said Frank's mother, tipping a spoonful onto his plate.

'He's . . . He's doing it again,' said Frank, pointing at the Student.

'Shhh, Frank,' said Petra.

'Don't be rude,' said his mother.

'How is that rude?' said Frank exasperated. 'How am I rude? It's not fair!'

'Don't talk to your mother like that,' said his father crossly, casting a surreptitious glance at the Student and then looking down at his plate – his thin, white centre-parting in his thin, black hair like a knife cut, split to the skull. The throbbing hum went up a notch in volume and intensity.

'But –'

'Shhh!' said Petra.

'Why?' said Frank.

'Don't be silly, Frank,' said his mother.

'I'm not being silly,' he said.

'Frank,' hissed his sister, looking sideways.

Frank followed Petra's eyes and saw his father staring at him from under his eyebrows. The electrical hum grew louder still. The lights in the room began to dim, then flare up and dim again, seemingly in time with the flaring of his father's nostrils. The hairs of his moustache were trembling.

Frank's father was not a big man, but somehow he could dominate any space. His mood was voracious, omnipotent – it became the mood of the room. It was as if he was some kind of wizard who controlled the air about him. Frank was usually very careful to keep a weather-eye open for any storm that might be brewing, but sometimes he didn't care. Sometimes he had a self-destructive urge to fly a kite and see if the lightning struck.

'Eat your food!' said his father. 'And mind your own business!'

Frank scowled and sighed and looked at the Student, who was smiling to himself as he wrote.

'Stop looking at him,' whispered his mother. 'He doesn't like it.'

'*He* doesn't like it!' replied Frank exasperated. 'He's in our apartment!'

Frank's mother smiled as though she was just about to have her photograph taken. The electrical hum intensified so much, the fork on Frank's plate rattled. He could feel his stomach tremble too, but he could not bring himself to give in just to keep the peace. Peace was another trick of the Grey.

'And I'm sure he is most welcome,' she said, speaking the words at dictation speed.

'He's spying on us!' said Frank, looking accusingly at the Student, who refused to make eye contact with him. 'You know it and I know it.'

'Don't be silly, Frank,' said his mother nervously. 'The Student is our lodger, that's all.'

'Then why is he taking notes all the time?' shouted Frank.

'Notes?' said his father, loosening his tie. He was sweating now, his face red. 'He's not taking notes. What would he have to take notes about?'

The student scribbled furiously in his notebook, his tongue sticking out of the corner of his mouth.

'He's doing it now!' said Frank. 'Look at him!'

The student scribbled something in his notebook, and dropped his pencil. It rolled across the floor towards them. Everyone stared at it on the floor, and then Frank's father leant down, picked it up and handed it back to him.

The lead had been broken by the fall to the floor, so the student took a large penknife from his pocket and began to sharpen it. No one spoke. The only sound in the room was the *shupp . . . shupp . . . shupp* of the blade shaving the pencil into a point again. He put his penknife away and put his notebook back up to his face and they began to relax.

'I bet he makes most of it up anyway,' muttered Frank.

The Student wrote something, crossed it out and then wrote something else.

11

'So,' said Petra, ever the peace-maker, resting her hands on the table, 'tell me about the Big Day, Father.'

Frank scowled at the Student, who ignored him and looked at Petra wide-eyed, pencil poised. It was all right for Petra, thought Frank. She had married and moved out. She didn't have to hear about the Big Day every five minutes.

'Oh, it's very exciting, isn't it, dear?' said Frank's mother brightly. 'I can hardly think of anything else!'

The Ministry did not generally celebrate the past, only very selectively. The Ministry did not want its citizens making unfortunate comparisons. 'A man who looks backwards will never see tomorrow' was the message on one of the Ministry's posters. Like many of the supposedly uplifting messages from the Ministry, it sounded more like a threat.

The Big Day was to be an exception to this cult of looking forward. The Big Day in November was going to be a rare celebration of pre-Revolutionary heroism and, more to the point, it was going to celebrate the pre-Revolutionary heroism of Frank's father. It was to take place at the scene of that heroism – the Castle.

Frank's father exhaled deeply and seemed to calm as quickly as he had become enraged.

'It is a great honour,' he said, putting his hands together and talking as though he was giving a speech to small children or the very old. The hum quietened to a purr. 'It's a great responsibility. It all needs to go like clockwork – and it will, if I've got anything to do with it.'

Frank's father smiled and winked at Frank's mother, who placed her hands on top of his.

'I just don't see why he has to spy on us,' said Frank.

'Go to your room!' said his father, banging his hand down on the table and making the Student jump and drop his pencil once again.

Frank scraped his chair back, scowled at the Student and stomped to his bedroom, slamming the door behind him. Petra bent down and picked up the pencil, handing it back to the Student.

'Thank you,' said the Student.

'You're welcome,' said Petra.

Chapter 2

Frank had been thinking about the Grey a lot recently. He hadn't even noticed it when he was younger, though he was sure it had always been there – or at least been there for so long it may as well have been always.

When he was little he had played, happily mostly, in the playground at the back of the apartment. There had been a ragged gang of kids of varying ages and they had played old games learnt from older siblings and devised some of their own.

Over time, other youths moved in and took over the swings and the roundabout, drinking and smoking. They wrecked the place, stripping everything to its metal bones until the swings were just a bare frame with dangling, amputated chains, and the roundabout a scratched central hub, standing like a bollard, too damaged to spin.

Gradually, one by one, the local children moved away or were kept inside by parents worried they would be led astray by the youths. Only Frank and Dawn Calypter, a girl who lived upstairs in Frank's apartment block, were left.

Dawn was the same age as Frank. They had played together since they were old enough to walk. They had grown together, to roughly the same height and skinny build – though there the similarity ended.

Frank's face was long; Dawn's was square. Frank's eyes were brown; Dawn's were blue. Frank's hair was a wiry clump, bullied into having a side parting; Dawn's was straight and black and usually in an untidy bob. But there was one thing about them that was exactly the same.

One day, when they were both four years old, for reasons neither of them could recall, Frank had thrown a stone at Dawn and hit her in the face, splitting her upper lip. Without pausing to cry, and with Frank staring at the blood that was already oozing from the wound, Dawn picked up the stone he'd thrown and threw it back, hitting Frank in the face, splitting *his* upper lip. They then both wailed their heads off. They had been left with identical thin, white scars on the right side of their upper lips.

This clash did not dent their friendship. If anything, it sealed it. Frank and Dawn created a little imaginary world from the barren remnants of the playground, lost for hours in the dramas they created. Or they would wriggle under the high chicken-wire boundary to explore the war-damaged houses that still stood nearby back then – despite having been forbidden to do so by their parents.

This vivid world they made was a shelter and defence from the Grey, though Frank did not know it then. It formed a bubble around them, shutting out everything and everyone that did not please them. But eventually they too left the playground.

Frank and Dawn went on to the same school, where they would talk occasionally – but only occasionally. The intense friendship they'd enjoyed seemed to belong in the now-deserted playground, and in that lost imaginary world and nowhere else. Without children, the playground became a sad and sinister place. The Grey claimed it as its own.

Frank had realised long ago that most people didn't see the Grey. It was too big. The Grey was so huge, in fact, it was impossible to get more than a glimpse of it. It was everywhere – in the spaces between things, in the shadows, in the fog, in the air they breathed. Frank had noticed it first when he was about ten. There was no special incident, no flash of light. One minute it had been as invisible as infrared, the next there it was in all its oppressive horror.

It seeped into you. It became part of you – or, more importantly, you became part of it. Because that's what the Grey was, really: the sum of all greyness, of all mediocrity and dullness. It was a crushing weight and yet it was also a formless, aching emptiness.

The Grey settled on people from above and it crept up on them from below. It invaded their pores when they slept, it crept into their minds when they made love. The Grey took away difference and replaced it with sameness. It sucked the life out of life itself.

And all this happened without a scream or whimper because it happened in such small incremental steps that it was barely noticeable. Most people never even knew the Grey existed.

Frank had tried to tell other people about it – his mother, his friend Roland – but he had been met with confusion by his mother and deep suspicion by Roland, who clearly thought Frank was either crazy or telling a joke at Roland's expense. Either way, he and Roland were no longer friends and the Grey remained.

To Frank it felt as though they were all trapped under dusty glass, like insects pinned to a mouldering board, yellowing labels next to them written in sepia ink; exhibits in some dark corner of a forgotten museum. They could change nothing – affect nothing.

Of course he had not been able to totally rule out insanity; how could you rule out the possibility of being deluded? That was the whole thing about delusion. He had been thinking more and more about that possibility, in fact.

But having spent a few hours questioning his sanity and the certainty of everything he knew, Frank decided that this line of thought was just another way the Grey had of keeping you in check; another way of making you feel powerless.

Chapter 3

Something must have jostled Frank because he opened his eyes and found himself standing on a busy tram. There was a sudden jolt and lurch to the left, and his face collided with the window, squashing his nose against the glass. He had clearly fallen asleep standing up. Again.

He seemed to spend half his time straddled between sleeping and waking these days. He wasn't entirely sure which was which, or which truth would disappoint him most: to think this dismal dream was the best his imagination could come up with, or that this soulless puppet show was the real world.

Frank was returning from one of his regular Saturday shopping trips with his mother. She insisted on shopping in the fruit and vegetable market across in the Old New Town rather than their local one in the Old Town because she said the quality was so much better, but Frank could see no difference: the food seemed equally as limp and measly in both places.

Frank hated going on these shopping expeditions, but felt unable to refuse. His father would shout at him if he did, and then, to make matters worse, start shouting at his mother

18

for allowing Frank to walk all over her. But it was not as though he was doing anything more important, and now that his sister had left home, his mother did need help with the bags. But still.

Every person in the packed tram apart from him was a middle-aged woman who looked just like his mother, dressed in the same shapeless grey coats and headscarves. They either made a point of ignoring him, or peered at him suspiciously. Why would a seventeen-year-old boy be on a tram with his mother? They probably thought he was a Student.

The tram rattled and screeched as it turned a sharp bend, pushing all the passengers together. Frank was reluctantly squeezed inside a clenched fist of bosoms and ample behinds.

Frank's mother was engaged in a conversation with a woman he did not recognise, but as soon as he caught her eye, his mother grabbed him by the arm and pulled him towards her through the throng.

"This is my son, Frank,' said his mother. 'Say hello, Frank.'

Frank said hello. The woman smiled and looked him up and down as though she was planning to buy him.

'He has plenty of hair,' she said finally, clearly struggling to find anything at all to say.

Frank's mother reached up and put her hand to his head, stroking his hair. Frank pulled his head away with a grimace.

'He's a good boy,' said his mother.

The woman nodded, a sceptical curl to her hirsute upper lip. Frank took no offence. He knew he wasn't a good boy too. Not to say that he was bad. He wasn't actively one thing or another.

'We're looking forward to the Big Day, of course,' said Frank's mother.

The Big Day! Would they ever shut up about the Big Day? It was months away. Frank's mother waited for the woman to pick up on this, but she did not take the bait.

'To think that my husband is going to be presented to the King,' she said.

'Yes,' said the woman, taking another sour, sideways look at Frank.

Frank's mother shook her head, smiling. 'The King,' she said. 'Imagine that.'

Frank stared out of the window as they turned into Perseverance Boulevard, which ran alongside the river on the opposite bank to the Old Town. The gloom made a partial mirror of the glass and Frank thought again how dull and unsatisfactory his nose was.

Then, appearing just between his left nostril and eye, walking across his cheek, was Olivia Pulvillus. The tram stopped at lights and Frank pressed his face against the glass and stared as she climbed up the steps, searching for her keys, unlocked the door and disappeared inside.

Frank had to stop himself crying out. Mirror-Frank had long ago pointed out that every man needed an Everest: every man who intended to make anything of himself needed a mountain to climb, an ocean to cross, a continent to discover. Olivia Pulvillus was Frank's undiscovered continent.

Undiscovered by him, at any rate.

Olivia sat at the next table to Frank in History. She had the most beautiful nose: long and slender and very slightly arched. She had pale hair that sparkled like silver wire when she moved her head, and when she laughed a small mole on her throat trembled up and down, up and down. Frank could look at it for hours. He could look at her for hours. There was nothing in the world he would rather look at.

They had spoken barely a word to each other and yet Frank was sure that Olivia was crucial to the better Frank he was determined to be. She was unaware of this fact – or of Frank, for that matter – but that too was a challenge Frank welcomed. Or if not welcomed exactly, certainly accepted.

The tram rattled away from Olivia's long apartment block – a cream-coloured building in the Empire style, pale as Olivia's skin. Ironically the building was actually older than Frank's apartment in the Old Town. This was because much of the Old Town had been heavily shelled during the War and the Revolution that followed.

A very particular thrill ran through him. The tall woman standing nearest to him seemed to sense the flesh-coloured nature of his thoughts and curled her lip in disgust. But Frank didn't care.

Spotting Olivia outside school was perhaps the best thing that had ever happened to Frank, although he struggled to remember one single other good thing with which to compare it. Not a lot ever happened to Frank or his family and mostly it was either dull or bad or both.

In point of fact, nothing much ever happened at all, ever, anywhere, as far as Frank could see. He watched the news and it was the same old mix of threat and tedium night after night. It was like everything exciting had already happened and there was nothing left over except insipid mimicry of the past.

But this sighting of Olivia – this was the kind of sparkly, vivid thing that only happened to people in the old books Frank loved to read. This was quite literally – literarily – wonderful. This was extra-extraordinary. This was a flash of clear blue light in this twenty-watt world.

The tram moaned plaintively as it turned, rattling across the junction and moving onto Fortitude Bridge, the oldest of all the bridges across the river, lined with massive statues of giant, soot-blackened angels.

A huge barge floated downstream loaded with scrap metal, so low in the water that it looked as though it would sink at any minute. It left a shimmering, greasy wake, like the slimy trail of a snail.

A group of Civil Servants were gathered round a young man at the base of one of the angels. They seemed to envelope him like an amoeba. Frank pressed his face against the filthy glass window, straining for a clearer view, but the tram was already turning. Frank turned to look at his fellow passengers but they had either not noticed or were pretending not to have noticed. It amounted to the same thing.

Frank used to point these things out when he saw them but he soon learnt that no one wanted that. They didn't want the trouble. They did not want to see it. If he told people – even other kids at school – about something he had seen, they would look away or tell him he was being paranoid.

'This place . . .' muttered Frank.

His mother scowled at him. The tram rumbled back into the Old Town and into Resolution Avenue where Frank and his mother got off at the stop beside the old record store, posters

for the Big Day slathered across its boarded-up windows.

There were stops nearer to their apartment, but after this one the fare increased and so they always walked the last quarter of a mile, weighed down with bags of potatoes and turnips.

Everyone in this stretch of Old Town walked in the same distinctive manner – weighed down or not: hurriedly and hunched over as though through a heavy rainstorm. And indeed it did start to rain as Frank and his mother walked down the street.

And the reason why everyone walked like this? Well, that was because of the Sniper.

Ever since the end of the Revolution there had been stories of a sniper up on the rooftops of Resolution Avenue, armed with a rifle, refusing to accept the struggle was over, picking people off in the streets below. No one knew what side he had been on, or how or why he chose his targets. That was all part of the Sniper's mystique. The Sniper had taken on a supernatural quality. Or perhaps he had always been supernatural. Perhaps he had always been there – since before the Old Town, even.

Frank wasn't sure he believed in the Sniper but that didn't stop him flinching at a pigeon fluttering above him, or clenching his teeth together so hard it made his jaws ache. Sometimes he was sure he saw, out of the corner of his eye, the twinkling glint of a telescopic sight.

The Sniper added to the gloom in the Old Town. In another place, in another time, this threat of impending death might have instilled a carefree joy – a thankfulness for every moment lived, savoured in the knowledge that it might be the last. But not in the Old Town. Not there. Not then.

Because the people of the Old Town were not by nature joyful people. If they had ever been, all signs of it had been erased or smothered. Life for them had become a kind of burden and the bearing of it without (too much) complaint had become a point of pride. 'Things could be worse,' they said. 'Be thankful,' they said.

But always in a voice that suggested nothing of the sort.

Chapter 4

Frank attended the Ministry School in the Old New Town. It had been purpose built after the Revolution to school all the children of the city, save for the children of the New New Town, who had their own school down by the river.

It was a soulless building, more like an office block or a factory than a school. There were warehouses down by the railway tracks with more character and charm. Added to which, it was stuffed full of people Frank despised. But none of that mattered now, because he knew where Olivia Pulvillus lived!

He might never be able to speak to Olivia at school, not in the way he wanted to speak to her. How could he? There was no privacy at school; no place for that kind of delicacy. No subtlety. No nuance. No colour. The Grey was all-powerful at school.

Frank's goal there was to be invisible, to remain unnoticed, and this goal was, for the most part, achieved. Which would have been fine were it not for the fact that he secretly burnt with indignation that his uniqueness was not acknowledged.

All around him, mediocrity flourished. A joke was funny, a comment considered clever, not by virtue of its quality or content, but by the accident of whose mouth it dribbled from.

Frank's favourite part of the school was the library. It was just as dull as the rest of the school architecturally, but at least it was full of books and – usually – empty of the people he hated.

Frank would come to the library most lunchtimes and breaks and whenever he had a free period. He would do his homework there, researching it and writing it. It was easier to do it there than at home.

But he would also spend a lot of time just randomly flicking through books, particularly ones with photographs of the Old Town and the way things were before the Revolution. He could stare into those images for hours.

Frank was sitting at a table in the library doing just that a few days after spotting Olivia Pulvillus's apartment block, when who should walk into the library but Olivia herself. This seemed particularly auspicious to Frank as he wasn't sure he had ever seen Olivia in the library before.

Frank raised the book in front of his face so that he could surreptitiously peep over the top every now and then. He caught tantalising glimpses of her through gaps in the bookshelves when she stood browsing the art section.

Eventually Olivia pulled a large book from the shelf and Frank ducked down as she walked over to a table at the far end of the room and sat with her back to him. She picked up her bag, taking out a notebook and pencil case. She rested her head on one hand and leafed through the book with the other.

Frank could stare at her now with impunity. His vision seemed to telescope, zooming in on her hand as it slid round the nape of her neck, as his own hand longed to do, and on the fall and rise and fall of her slender shoulders as she breathed, the light playing across the –

'Frank!'

'What?'

'Snap out of it,' said Dawn, clicking her fingers. 'I thought you were having a seizure.'

'Oh,' said Frank, putting his book down and turning a page. 'Hello, Dawn.'

She sat next to him and looked across at Olivia.

'We don't often see Olivia in here,' she whispered.

'Olivia?' he said.

Dawn raised her eyebrows and stared at him, smiling. Frank frowned and ignored her.

'Oh, no – wait,' said Dawn. 'I remember now. She's doing something for her mother. She owns that huge clothes shop in Old New Town. Olivia is helping her change the look of the place – you know, make it more modern. She was asking my opinion and I told her there were a couple of books in the library she might like to look at. Amazingly she seems to have taken my advice.'

Dawn looked around the room. 'I'll miss this place when we leave,' she said. 'The library, I mean.'

Frank nodded. 'Me too.'

'So many great art books,' said Dawn. 'Most of them you can't even get any more. Even if I could afford them, which I can't.'

'It's weird to think we won't ever see it again, isn't it?' said Frank. 'I mean, it's not like I . . .'

27

Frank's sentence trailed off because he saw that Olivia was walking towards them. She glanced quickly at Frank and then spoke to Dawn.

'Sorry,' she said. 'I've left something in my locker. Do you think you could just watch my stuff, Dawn?'

'Of course,' said Dawn.

'Thanks,' said Olivia. 'You're a pal.'

Olivia glanced at Frank again, and then walked out of the library.

'When you want something, I am,' muttered Dawn.

'What?' said Frank.

'Nothing,' said Dawn. 'Let's go and have a nose at what she's up to.'

'No!' said Frank. 'Well . . . OK.'

They walked to Olivia's table and Dawn picked up her bag and opened it.

'Dawn!' said Frank. 'Stop that.'

Dawn laughed.

'Don't be such a prude, Frank,' said Dawn. 'It's not like I'm going to steal anything. I'm only being nosy.'

'Well, you shouldn't,' said Frank. 'She trusted you to look after it.'

'Ha!' said Dawn. 'I'll bet you anything you like she took her purse with her.'

'Even so.'

'Do you ever worry that you're too reckless, Frank?' said Dawn.

'Very funny.'

'Looks like she's designing a logo for the shop,' said Dawn.

28

Olivia's notebook was open and at the top of the page was written, in carefully written capital letters, the words YOUNG PULVILLUS, each letter written with a different coloured pencil. Olivia always wrote her headings like this.

'Young Pulvillus?' said Dawn, raising an eyebrow. 'That's the big idea?'

She picked up Olivia's pencil case and sighed.

'Do you have any idea how much these cost?' she said. 'Coloured pencils?'

'Not really,' said Frank.

But he knew that all colour was expensive. That was why there was so little of it about – especially in the Old Town. The Ministry did not actually come out and say it, but it was happy to give the impression that it considered colour to be elitist. Which of course meant that only high-ranking Ministry Men and their families felt able to use it or could afford it.

'It's not fair,' said Dawn.

'No,' agreed Frank. 'But then nothing is.'

Dawn groaned loudly.

'What?' said Frank.

'Don't you get sick of it though?' she asked.

'You know I do,' said Frank.

Dawn slumped down at the table, waiting for Olivia to come back. She rested her head on one hand and sighed.

'I'm going to push off,' said Frank.

Dawn didn't seem to be listening, but he didn't want to be there when Olivia returned. He didn't want to talk to her here, with Dawn. He'd rather not talk to her at all.

'Bye then,' he said to Dawn.

'Yeah,' she said. 'See you, Frank.'

Frank returned his book to the shelf he'd taken it from and headed for the door. He looked briefly back at Dawn, who was rooting through Olivia's pencil case. He shook his head. He had never seen Dawn as someone who would ever be jealous.

Frank set off along the corridor and turned a corner to find Olivia ahead of him, talking to a boy called Scape. He came to a halt and pretended to be looking at the noticeboard, casting surreptitious glances at them whenever he could.

Frank hated Scape. He hadn't always hated him. Mostly he had merely disliked him intensely, but lately Frank could feel himself actually twitching with a suppressed desire to beat Scape over the head with something quite large and heavy.

But Frank was a coward and Scape was pretty tough – or at least fearless, which can often amount to the same thing. Frank had seen him fight a boy in their first year of school. Scape had banged the back of the boy's head repeatedly on the pavement until he was dragged off.

Not that this was how Scape would have come across to the casual observer. In fact, it was his cocky, easy-going charm that annoyed Frank most of all. Scape seemed to have absolutely no trouble talking to girls, and girls actually seemed to enjoy his attentions. That annoyed Frank too.

And here was Olivia doing the same. Laughing at Scape's stupid jokes and giggling every time he touched her. Not that Frank could hear what they were saying, but Scape's jokes were always stupid. And he was always touching girls. They didn't appear to mind. Frank was sure that if he touched a girl's waist the way Scape was sliding his hand around Olivia's, they'd slap his face and scream.

Olivia was pushing Scape away, but she was laughing as she did it. Eventually they parted and Olivia headed towards Frank, who turned to the noticeboard and studied the leaflets intently until Olivia had clip-clopped by.

Frank had not really been concentrating before, but now he realised he was staring straight at a little flyer advertising careers at the Ministry.

'We need smart kids like you,' said the headline. A neatly dressed man in his thirties pointed out of the photograph, his grin pearly white, his shirt crisply ironed, his hair neatly cut and slicked back.

Across his forehead, with a thick black pen, someone had drawn a penis and testicles, long hairs sprouting out of them. Frank would have bet a good deal of money that Scape was responsible. He hurried away before someone thought it was him.

Chapter 5

Frank's favourite possession – except perhaps his grandfather's old typewriter – was his bicycle. Without it he would have felt trapped. He always felt better riding his bike. Always.

Not that he ever went very far, but that wasn't really the point. Just getting away from the Old Town – from his family, his apartment block – for half an hour felt so good.

The Old Town was an island. It was a great lozenge of land in the middle of the mighty River Drear, connected to the Old New Town on the west bank and the New New Town on the east, like a huge barge moored to the banks by a variety of bridges of varying antiquity.

The many-arched and ancient Fortitude Bridge, the bridge

Frank was using to cross to the Old New Town, was the oldest. The giant angels that rose up along its length had no doubt once inspired feelings other than dread, but centuries of smoke and fumes had blackened them and wars and revolutions had grotesquely re-sculpted their features.

It was seen as a miracle that the bridge survived both the War and the Revolution, but not without cost. Bullets had punched ragged holes in the angels, sheered off noses and severed fingers. Bomb blasts had bitten into faces and ripped through wings and robes. They were fallen angels now, tormented creatures of hell.

They had always terrified Frank, ever since he was a boy. He used to have nightmares about them stepping down from their huge plinths and striding round the city, their broken wings twitching, their huge, sooty hands reaching out to grab anyone foolish enough to get within reach.

But most of all it was their faces that frightened him; their raddled, ruined non-faces. What had no doubt been beautiful features when first designed, had been distorted by time and history into the glowering, snarling, lolling faces of ogres and monsters. Mouths and eye sockets gaped and strange new orifices bloomed on throat and chest.

Frank resented the fear he felt even from within the confines of a tram – and so rebelled against it by using the bridge despite it, because of it, and to damn it to hell. It was easy to be brave if you were already lion-hearted. It was so much braver for a coward to show courage. Or so Frank told himself.

Having said all that, he would never have actually walked across the bridge as he saw some do – no, not for anything. Just like only stupid people seemed to be capable of happiness, so too did only stupid people not have the imagination to dread those stone giants. Frank could, when he steeled himself, manage to cycle across it as he did now, so long as he did not look up at their terrible faces.

Frank had learnt at school how his distant ancestors had chosen the island site for its strategic benefits and how a great city had grown up, once the heart of a great empire – an empire now all but forgotten.

The island was as high as it was long – a craggy clump – and the Old Town was clustered barnacle-fashion around its edges, clinging to the lower reaches of the rocky outcrop on which perched the Castle.

The Castle had evolved from a small fortification and, over the millennia, leaked out over the Old Town like lava from a gargoyle-encrusted volcano until it had ceased to be clear where the Castle stopped and the Old Town started.

It had also eaten into the rock itself. It was worm-ridden – a veritable ants' nest of tunnels, with portholes in the flanks. Cannons used to poke out of these windows in olden times, like the gun ports of a mighty ship, but now they were barred with rusting metal grilles – nests for pigeons and bats.

At the eastern edge of the Castle there was a small courtyard open at one end with a wall and then a sudden drop to sharp rocks below. This courtyard had been the scene of a last-ditch defence of the Castle in the War by a group of soldiers led by Frank's father. Because of this, Frank's father, who now worked for the Ministry, had been given the honour of being presented to the King on the Big Day.

The Castle still had a kind of religious significance to the

34

people of the Old Town. It was the fixed point of their world; a place of certainty and immutability. The legend of the Invisible Lizards illustrated this perfectly.

The Invisible Lizards were supposed to live in the Castle, on the rocks and in the tunnels. No one knew how old the story was, but every child grew up knowing that if the Invisible Lizards were ever to leave the Castle, the city would fall and all would be lost. They could not see the Lizards, of course, but they drew comfort from knowing they were there.

The Castle wasn't really a castle at all now. It was a memory of a castle. Enclosed within its mighty, ancient walls, there was a honeycomb of utilitarian office buildings, all corridors and fire doors, that housed the Ministry where Frank's father worked – one of the many drones in the government hive.

Frank had never been inside the Castle. No one was ever allowed past the gates unless they worked there – not even the family of those who worked there. He had once been desperately curious to know what was behind those huge buttresses when he was young, but now found that he had no interest at all.

It was because Frank knew what it had become in reality, this great spired and crenelated crown. It was a castle turned office block. It was a thrilling tale stripped of embellishment; all romance drained out of it, vampire-like, by the Grey.

Now safely across the river, Frank stopped and leant against the railings of the riverside walk and looked back across the water to his home among the anonymous blocks at the base of the Castle. It looked better from here. Everything looked better from far away.

Except Olivia.

Frank had been unable to get her out of his mind ever since spotting her from the tram. His imagination was now in orbit around that bright and beautiful star. She was perhaps the only bright thing there was. But what to do about it?

Frank had a plan. As soon as he had formulated it, he felt better. He would create a New-Frank from the tattered Half-Frank who had sleepwalked through life thus far.

This New-Frank would be worthy of Olivia. But he had to earn her affection, earn her love, her respect. He had to put some distance between himself and the Frank of school. Invisibility had been fine for that Frank; it had seen him through some bad times. But now he had a reason to step out of the shadows.

He couldn't just walk up to Olivia's apartment block and knock on the door. Frank chuckled to himself at the preposterousness of that idea. He needed confidence, not rejection.

Frank was sure that if fate existed at all, then his fate and Olivia's were bound together somehow and he would prove it if it killed him. He would reveal what was already there, like a sculptor revealing the statue inside a block of marble.

He would cycle to her apartment. On each visit he would allow himself three passes, up and down. If she did not appear during that time, then he would accept it and ride away, to return the next chance he had and repeat the process. He would allow himself ten – no, twenty – separate visits in total. If it was meant to be, as Frank was sure it was, then she would come out and they would meet as though by chance.

Frank was suddenly struck by the importance of this new pact with himself; this contract with destiny. He felt nervous. He felt dizzy. He decided that he would go and see his grandfather first and begin this new regime of cycling past Olivia's apartment on the way home.

Chapter 6

The Old Cemetery reared up over the narrow cobbled lanes around it. It was a great hump-backed hill of the dead, a necropolitan version of the Old Town, dug and filled, re-dug and re-filled, over centuries until the ground had risen up to be level with the balconies of the buildings around it. A black bubo studded all over with tombstones, like a mouldering orange pricked with cloves.

On top of this bone hill, at its highest point, was a tall and ancient tree, its cracked and wrinkled bark blackened like the headstones around it, its branches reaching up and grabbing at the filthy grey sky. The roots of the trees clambered over and between those headstones, and maggoted down into the bone-filled earth below like an inverted family tree. Through every grave the pale roots wormed, wrapping themselves round skull and femur, rib and tooth.

Despite being called the Old Cemetery, the graveyard was actually in a dark corner of the Old New Town. It had been built across the river from the original Old Town but a New Town had built up around it, girding it on all sides. Now those very buildings of the Old New Town were themselves old and grey, scarred and bruised, and a New New Town had been built on the opposite bank.

The crusted, flaking iron gate groaned as Frank pushed it open but only partially, as the hinges tightened, meaning Frank had to squeeze through the gap, only just managing to scrape past the rusty metal latch. It seemed to open less and less each time, and Frank sometimes wondered if he was the only person who ever went there. He certainly never saw anyone else there.

His grandfather's grave was right at the top of the hill at the foot of the tree. It was a high headstone, made of granite, as were all those around him. They were solid things, appearing more ancient than they were, tiny shards of quartz twinkling in the shadows of the chisel cuts.

Frank liked to lie down here, surrounded by these tall headstones, hidden from the street outside, looking up at the black lattice of tree branches above. It was one of the few places he felt himself, or what he thought might be himself.

A small flock of ravens took flight and flapped lazily off in the direction of the Castle. Frank looked at his grandfather's headstone, his name carved in the stone.

'Grandfather?' said Frank.

Frank said it quietly. Partly because everyone knows it's wrong to speak loudly in a graveyard, but also because he didn't want to startle his grandfather.

'Grandfather?' he said again.

Frank always had to say it at least twice.

'Eh?' said a dusty voice. 'Is that you, Frank?'

Of course it was Frank.

'Yes, Grandfather,' he said. 'How are you?'

'Oh, mustn't grumble,' he said.

Frank could hear him stirring, shifting his position to get more comfortable. He yawned.

'What sort of day is it?'

Frank looked up again. His grandfather liked detail.

'The sky is grey – a cold and pale grey like you see in shadows across snow. There's only one cloud. It has the shape of a lion's head, its mouth open. There's a breeze and some of the highest twigs in the treetop are fidgeting.'

Frank could sense him nodding appreciatively. His grandfather said that he savoured words now. They'd replaced food for him since he died.

'How's your father getting on?'

'He's getting ready for the Big Day.'

'Ah yes,' said his grandfather. 'Of course. My son was always

one for being organised. I have no idea where he got that from. And your mother? How's she?'

'She's well,' said Frank. 'Much the same. Still cleaning up at the Castle. She gets tired. Falls asleep in front of the television most nights.'

'And how about you?' said his grandfather.

'Oh, you know . . .'

'Have you spoken to that girl yet?'

Frank already wished he'd never told his grandfather about his feelings for Olivia. Every time he came now, his grandfather asked him about her and every time he did Frank would have to say:

'No.'

'Faint heart never won fair maid,' he said.

Again. There was no way Frank was going to tell him about his plan to actually meet Olivia. No – when he had actually met her, then he'd talk about it.

'I know, Grandfather,' said Frank. 'But you don't really understand.'

He snorted.

'Of course,' he said. 'Because I'm old and dead I don't know anything.'

'You know I don't think like that,' said Frank.

There was a sniff and a shrug.

'I know, lad,' he said finally. 'You're a good boy.'

A cat moved through the tombstones.

'I worry about you,' said his grandfather.

'I know you do,' said Frank. 'But I'm fine. Honestly.'

What was 'fine' though? Frank didn't know.

'You're sixteen,' he said.

'Seventeen, Grandfather,' said Frank.

'Well, then. Things are going to change.'

'What kind of things?' asked Frank.

But he knew what he meant.

'I'll still come here and see you. Don't worry. Even when I'm fifty-seven.'

'No you won't,' said his grandfather, but so quietly Frank didn't hear him.

The twigs above Frank's head whispered together and it was the only sound. It was hard to remember they were in a city of living people all going about their lives. Bankers were counting money; street cleaners were cleaning streets. Frank's father was in the Castle; his mother would be coming home from the shops after work. School bells would be sounding soon for the end of the day.

'Why aren't you in school?' said his grandfather.

Sometimes Frank wondered if he could read his mind. Maybe you could do that when you died. Maybe you could read people's minds.

'School is finished, really. We've had our exams. You know it's my last year, don't you?'

'Of course,' said his grandfather. 'I'm not senile.'

Frank smiled.

'Do you know what my favourite subject was when I was at school?'

'Was it History?' Frank asked.

'Yes it was,' he replied.

His grandfather had told him this many times before.

'History is the most important subject there is, Frank,' said his grandfather. 'People will tell you it's Maths or Science or some such, but it's History, take it from me.

'It's where I learnt to be a writer. History is full of stories. They get told over and over, and changed and adapted. History is the fossilised remains of storytellers – the fossilised remains of you and me.'

Frank's grandfather loved to tell stories. Frank loved to listen to them. His grandfather had been a writer when he was alive. But his work was seen as too bourgeois for the Ministry and it had been suppressed. You couldn't buy his books anywhere, even in the second-hand shops. He had been edited out of history. He wasn't even allowed to be a fossil. It made Frank angry and sad.

'There was a country to the east, many years ago,' began his grandfather, 'where the king commissioned the greatest sculptor of the age to make a giant portrait head of himself in stone.

'It was gigantic and he set it on a hill to the north of the capital on the main route in, so that visitors would be forewarned of his greatness and travellers reminded of what marvels they were leaving behind.

'Of course,' continued his grandfather, 'the king died, and, as is so often the case with great kings, his son and heir was weak, and before long the empire collapsed and the country was invaded by its enemies.

'On being enthroned as king, the conquering invader commissioned another sculptor to alter the features of the giant head until they matched his own.

43

'Now, owing to the fact that this sculptor was not as skilful as the original one, and the new king's features being rounder than the first's, a great deal of the head had to be lost to facilitate this change.

'The new head was still gigantic, of course. It still stood as a marker on the main trade route out of the capital, and the city actually became more affluent under this new ruler. The city grew; it spread.

'By the time he died, the conqueror was much loved by the people and when his son came to the throne there was some resistance to his refashioning the head to match his features, but he managed to persuade the populace, erroneously, that this had in fact been the late king's dying wish – that this refashioning be done whenever a new king came to the throne.

'And so it came to pass. The day after each coronation, a sculptor would be set to work on remodelling the head to fit the new monarch.

'Centuries went by and, after much re-sculpting, the head was actually life size and had to be placed on a plinth in the market square of the new town that had spread out of the capital and into the surrounding valley.

'The tradition continues to this day, apparently. The head is now in the basement of a dry cleaning store, the city having built up and over the site.'

'Can you still see it?' asked Frank.

'Oh, yes,' said his grandfather. 'The work is very fine – very fine indeed. But it is impossible to see with the naked eye. They will rent you a magnifying glass for a small fee.'

Frank smiled to himself.

'For a small fee,' he repeated.

'What was that?' said his grandfather.

'Nothing,' said Frank, getting to his feet, remembering Olivia suddenly. 'Listen, Grandfather, I've got to go.'

'Frank?' said his grandfather, plaintively.

'I'll see you soon,' called Frank over his shoulder. 'Promise.'

Chapter 7

The end of term was in sight now. Teaching had effectively come to an end after the exams of the previous month. There was a curious atmosphere of redundancy in the school for those like Frank who were leaving.

The teachers who were solely concerned with those in their final year had changed their natures in a subtle way. They walked about the school with a lighter step – and were resented by the teachers who were still battling with the lower years.

To those concerned with their last days, the school had become a collection of memories and nothing more. Frank found the whole thing more than a little unsettling.

Frank would never have said that he actively liked school, but actually the classroom was one of the few places where he did feel some sense of belonging, some sense of a point to life.

Frank liked to learn, in the main, and he liked the metronomic routine of the school day. If life was a repetition of days, over and over again, then it may as well be days lived in a place of learning, surrounded by books, as anywhere else.

So he felt a little lost now. He didn't like this new way the teachers had – as though they had already washed their hands of him. He preferred the old business-like relationship he had with teachers; he took it as a mark of respect, even if none was intended.

He didn't want to chat to them or share a joke. What little credit he had for being a diligent, if unremarkable, student now evaporated and school became, like so much else in life, a popularity competition – a competition Frank was always going to lose.

Time seemed to have broken its gears. Life that already seemed to move at the pace of a dead snail had slowed even further. Pointlessness had added a new layer of tedium to existence. Frank yearned for the end of term. If school was dead, then why not bury it and move on?

Frank answered questions fairly regularly in class, although not enough to appear eager, but outside of class he said as little as possible that might hint at an urge to fit in. He did not want to give anyone the satisfaction of ignoring him or excluding him.

But on this particular day, Frank found himself among a group of students who, whilst not in any way friends of his, were, at least, not actively hostile to him. Frank felt relaxed enough to contribute occasionally to the conversation.

A couple of these students were discussing a Ministry Young Citizen book they'd been reading called *Into the Outzone*, which featured the adventures of a time-travelling ghost and a robot vampire. Frank recognised the title though he hadn't read it – nor had he any intention of so doing. He wasn't interested in the book or the author, but he did have an interest in time.

Still, had Olivia not walked to stand nearby, he probably would not have become involved at all. Instead, he raised his voice in the hope she might hear and imagined himself talking to her alone. And with that thought, his confidence grew.

'What about if you could travel into the future?' said a girl called Paula. 'And see how things had turned out? Wouldn't that be amazing?'

'Er . . . We . . . But that's just it,' said Frank, glancing round at Olivia, who was looking for something in her bag.

'What?' Paula said.

'You can't travel into the future,' said Frank.

'I know,' she said. 'No one can travel in time. I just mean, imagine if you could.'

'But what I mean is,' said Frank, 'time travel to the future must be impossible. It can never be done.'

'Why not?' said a boy called Gaster. 'I mean, if you could travel into the past?'

Frank smiled. He was enjoying himself. 'I'm not saying that's possible either. But it's different, isn't it?' he said.

'How?' said Gaster.

'Because the past has happened,' said Frank. 'It's . . . It's there behind us. Like a road we've already gone down. If we look backwards we can see where we've been. But if we look forwards . . .'

'We see into the future,' said Alula.

'We *imagine* the future,' said Frank. 'Because the future isn't there yet.'

'What?' she said with a frown.

But Frank could see she was actually interested in what he was saying. Olivia was listening too, he could tell. He was fairly certain.

48

Frank felt some strange bond between them now that he knew he had stood only yards away from where she ate and slept. It was as though he and Olivia shared a secret – when in fact this secret was itself a secret kept from Olivia.

'How can the future be there?' said Frank, waving his hands around. 'Even an hour from now? A minute? A second? Think about it. Has it already happened somehow? Are we on a timeline and things ahead have already been decided? Is the future waiting for us? Are the people we're going to meet standing around – like actors in a play – waiting for us to walk onstage. Are we –'

'What the hell are you talking about?' said Scape, sitting down next to Alula.

'Nothing,' muttered Frank. 'I was just explaining that –'

Scape clamped his hands over his ears.

'Don't start telling me,' he said. 'I don't want to hear your mad crap.'

Everyone laughed. Olivia laughed. Scape started talking and she listened to him instead even though what he was saying was the most banal nonsense. Frank listened too for a while, just to be closer to Olivia and to show he was a good sport, even though he wasn't, but after a while he got up and left, unnoticed.

Frank thought a lot about Time. His face felt like it was squashed up against the now, like there was a sheet of frosted glass barring his way to the future, only visible as a vague smudge, more dream than promise. He looked back at the others and could not understand why they were so content, so cheerful.

Chapter 8

The following Saturday, Frank found himself once again walking home with his mother, laden with shopping. It always seemed an age to Frank before they arrived at the metal entrance gate of their apartment block, and another age before they unlocked it and walked across the courtyard to the lobby.

That long, hunched-over walk along Resolution Avenue . . . It felt to Frank like he'd been holding his breath the whole time from getting off the tram, waiting for the Sniper's bullet to punch a full stop in his skull. Part of him had sometimes even wished its arrival, but not now.

He always felt a head rush when, at long last, he pulled the gate open for his mother. His teeth finally unclenched with a click and his jaw ached with the spent effort as he let the gate clang shut behind them.

The courtyard was quiet apart from the sound of washing being taken in from the balconies above them and the patter of raindrops on their clothes and bags, the snarl of their shoes on the gravel.

The garden in the centre was just a collection of dry leaves and bare twigs now. Mrs Clavus used to look after it, but she had died six months before and no one wanted to take over.

In the midst of all the dead plants was Maxilla the tomcat. He lay there with his good eye open, flicking his tattered ear and the tip of his tail. He was jet black apart from a white heart-shaped patch on his spine. He was the victor of many battles – a warrior cat. Anyone foolish enough to even try to stroke him would feel his wrath.

The courtyard had been full of cats at one time, but they had all but disappeared. Only Maxilla and two or three others remained. Mrs Cremaster did her best by putting food out for them, but they seemed to leave in the end all the same. Soon there would only be Maxilla – and he didn't need her charity. He was the best rat catcher alive.

Frank put his shopping bags down on the tiled floor of the lobby, flexing his fingers, which had by now been squeezed

white and distorted by the bite of the narrow handles.

He shook them to get the blood flowing again, but all that did was make them sting as though they were burnt, and he winced and cursed under his breath. His mother ignored him and walked on towards the stairs.

Frank muttered and picked the bags up to follow her when he noticed that the metal cantilever gate to the lift was standing open. It was never open. It was always locked. It was always locked and they did not have the key – no one they knew did. He walked over and tried the lift door – that too was open.

'Mother?' pleaded Frank. 'Please, just this once – can't we use the lift? Look, it's open!'

The word 'lift' seemed to hit his mother in the back like a dagger. She flinched and skidded to a halt, her shoes squeaking on the tiled floor. She turned to face him – her eyes wild, her teeth clenched – and, throwing her bags to the floor, she stormed back towards him.

Frank's mother had the mildest of manners ordinarily and this change in her was terrifying; nightmarish, even. Although he was a good foot taller, Frank took a few steps back and raised his arms in defence, so sure was he that she was going to hit him – even though she never had. Instead, she stopped in front of him and shook her head, staring up at his face.

'How many times have I told you?' she said. 'Never, ever, use the lift. NEVER!'

'But –'

'NEVER!' she yelled – so loudly that Frank flinched and took another step back, the words still echoing round the lobby.

With that, his mother turned with another indignant squeak of her shoes and headed off towards the stairwell. Frank watched her go, mouthing silent curses.

'What are you doing?'

Frank leapt back and turned to the sound of the voice. It was Mr Spiracle from the ground floor. The old man was crazy and Frank's mother said Frank should have more understanding. But Mr Spiracle's craziness seemed so often to be directed at Frank.

'I said, what are you doing?'

'Nothing, Mr Spiracle,' said Frank. 'I'm not doing anything. Just coming back from shopping with my mother. Goodbye.'

'Why are you looking at the lift?' asked Mr Spiracle, narrowing his eyes and leaning forward.

'I . . . was . . . I was just looking, that's all,' said Frank. 'I live here too.'

Mr Spiracle was a tall man, a lustrous mane of white hair atop a very high forehead. His face was gaunt – cadaverous, even – but the most disquieting things about him was his eyebrows. Not just the fact that they were as black as his hair was white, or that they were inordinately bushy – although they were both those things. No, it was the fact that they had a life of their own.

Even then, as Mr Spiracle peered at Frank, only one of the eyebrows seemed to heed the call to frown; the other was wandering up his furrowed brow towards his hairline, as if it were a wild animal making for the cover of woodland.

'I . . . you know . . . I just noticed it was open,' said Frank. 'It's dangerous. Someone might fall. It's normally locked.'

'I'm watching you,' said Mr Spiracle as the eyebrow disappeared into his white hair.

'Why? Why are you watching me?' said Frank. 'I'm not even doing anything.'

Mr Spiracle stared at him. The remaining eyebrow crawled off slowly, in search of its mate.

Frank headed towards the stairwell.

'I'm watching you,' repeated Mr Spiracle.

Chapter 9

Frank slowed to a stop, resting his foot on the kerb, and paused to look at Olivia's apartment block. It was set back from the road and the river behind a small garden of pale gravel and clipped box hedges, all behind a tall, black, wrought-iron railing topped by golden spikes.

A long path led from each gate in this railing through the gravel to a short flight of steps leading to a large door. Bell pushes down either side of it were labelled with the names of the apartment dwellers. The door was huge and above it was a large glazed panel showing spokes bursting from the head of a bronze lion.

How different it was here. These buildings had been ravaged by the same battles that had obliterated most of the Old Town, but when the Old New Town buildings were rebuilt, it was as faithful copies of the ones destroyed or damaged. Here, the highest-ranking Ministry Men lived. In the Old Town, the holes in the old maze of medieval houses were filled by stark concrete and glass apartments blocks.

Frank's apartment was better than many. It didn't have too many floors. It had a communal courtyard.

But grim was the norm. Grey was the only colour. Even this blatant double standard did not make the people of the

Old Town angry. Pragmatism was a badge of pride. They just shrugged and said, 'Well, if you were them, wouldn't you do the same?'

The Old New Town was like a different world. Only a river breadth away and yet it may as well have been another country. Here the streets were wide and straight and well-lit. No one stooped here. There was no Sniper on the roof. People stopped and chatted in the street.

Perseverance Boulevard was one of the best addresses in the city. Only Diligence Hill was better, being that much further from the river and the choking fogs.

Frank felt odd just looking at them and glanced around to check he wasn't being watched by Civil Servants, but even the Civil Servants who patrolled this area seemed calm and relaxed in comparison to the fidgety packs they were in the Old Town.

He had developed a kind of relationship with the building over the weeks he had been cycling there - more of a relationship, in fact, than he had ever managed to develop with Olivia herself.

The building seemed to have a personality of its own. More and more, it seemed to Frank to be deliberately and cruelly obstructing him in his quest. It withheld Olivia from view and refused to release her at the appropriate time.

Even the architecture of the building seemed to taunt him. A series of bare and pert-breasted cream caryatids supported the balconies on the second floor, their arms raised above their heads. Their shadowed, downturned faces had more than a passing resemblance to Olivia – as did their breasts – although Frank could only speculate in that department.

Frank pushed off and pedalled himself past, the building flickering by through the black metal railings like an old movie, or magic lanterns show, in perfect rhythm to the tittering of his spokes.

He cycled slowly, getting slower and slower, deciding that this was not really changing the rules of his pact with fate. Frank would have said he did not believe in fate or God or indeed anything. But in his heart he knew Olivia was some kind of door or key, at least, to something else.

Now, on his first of three passes, he was absolutely, childishly certain that Olivia would emerge from the main door of her apartment building. He felt it in every fibre of his body. He knew what she would be wearing. He knew how the light would play on her hair. He knew every minute detail.

And yet she did not emerge.

Even on the second pass Frank was still pathetically hopeful and he almost crashed his bike when the door did in fact open, but only to reveal a stout and elderly gentleman and his ancient dog. He mumbled heartfelt obscenities as he carried on his way.

When the third and final pass was done, he stood for a short while, staring at the building with what he hoped appeared to be a quiet dignity and determination but which, to the casual observer, may have seemed more like tearful dejection and bitter resentment.

Frank was being tested, he knew that. That, after all, was the point. If there was a point. If he gave up, or even showed any weakness of resolve at all, it would be all the proof destiny needed that he wasn't worthy of Olivia's love.

And Frank was sure it was love. Love. LOVE.

It was true, he did spend much of his time thinking about what Olivia looked like naked, and the relative softness of various parts of that nakedness, but that was because this was a grown-up love, not some silly hearts-and-flowers schoolyard love. This was passion, all-consuming: the love of a man, not a boy.

The thought of the thought of the naked Olivia fired his blood again and he felt that manly passion now, squeezing uncomfortably against his bike saddle as he cycled away. It was painful, but that discomfort was at least something. Without it, he would be numb like everyone else.

Chapter 10

One of the very last ordeals of school to be overcome was the careers interview with Mr Prothorax, the deputy principal of the school. No one really understood the purpose of these interviews, as a school-leaver's job prospects were almost solely determined by the job their father did.

Frank sat outside the office with a queue of others, waiting for his name to be called. It was the same office, he vividly recalled, that he had sat outside as a small boy waiting to get inoculated, sobbing to himself with fear, Roland trying to cheer him up. He had a shiver as he remembered that terror of needles. The shame of crying and the way everyone refused to make eye contact with him as he left that office still stung after all these years.

He could hear the muffled sounds of the classrooms further down the empty hallway. Through the window in front of him he could see across the courtyard to the dining hall where he would sit and have lunch later. His stomach growled expectantly at the thought.

The exams might be over but the results would not be known for weeks. He hoped he had done reasonably well. He wasn't a great scholar, but he wasn't a poor one either. He was sure he was a lot cleverer than the spoilt Old New Town kids he was surrounded by. Their private tutors could cram them full of knowledge but Frank knew he had a kind of cleverness that was harder to quantify.

He was probably clever enough to go to university, had his parents been able to afford it. Only the top Ministry Men sent their children to university and whilst his father was getting his moment of fame with the Big Day, he was not in that league.

The fate decreed to him by the Ministry and by his father's position in it, was some low-level desk job at the Castle where he might, if he simply got on with whatever mundane task he was allocated, one day have an office of his own and possibly even his name on the door.

The work he did would be mind-numbing and tedious, but he would have the satisfaction that it would somehow, in ways he would never be told, link up with the tedious work of others and make sense to someone, somewhere. He would be a drone, but in the service of the hive.

The door opened with a whine and Mr Prothorax poked his enormous, bulbous, balding head through the crack. He looked like the bare ball joint of a leg bone jutting out of a coffin.

He called the name of the boy to Frank's right and the boy got up and disappeared into the office. Frank could hear the conversation as a set of low murmurs without being able to detect a single word.

Frank stretched out his legs and then pulled them back in, trying to get the blood circulating again. He closed his eyes and was surprised at how sleepy he suddenly felt. Boredom was exhausting. He felt like he'd been drugged.

His mind wandered to Olivia, as it always did now, fleshly magnet that she was. He was so drowsy though that even this thought seemed like too much effort. His eyelids began to droop. The school sounds began to fade. He could hear the distant ticking of a clock.

Frank actually jumped when the door handle rattled and the boy reappeared to walk away down the corridor. A few moments later, Mr Prothorax's bald head poked out once again.

'Palp,' he said. 'Come in.'

Frank dutifully got up and followed him into the office. Mr Prothorax sat down at his desk and beckoned for Frank to sit opposite. Mr Prothorax put his glasses on and lifted up a set of papers, flicking back and forth. Frank began to feel sleepy again and stifled a yawn.

'Frank Palp,' said Mr Prothorax, nodding. 'Frank Palp . . .'

Frank was not sure whether he was meant to say anything in response so decided he would just sit there and wait for Mr Prothorax to ask him a direct question, which, after a few moments, he did.

'Well then, Palp,' he said, lacing his fingers across his chest and looking over his glasses. 'What do you want to do with your life?'

His voice betrayed the signs of having asked this question many times that day. They both knew that it was almost rhetorical.

'I don't know, sir,' said Frank.

'Don't know?' said Mr Prothorax, smiling and taking off his glasses. 'I'm sure you have some idea.'

Frank shifted in his seat and stroked his chin, trying to look as though he was trying to think of something.

Mr Prothorax drummed his fingers on the desk.

'You're a bright boy, it seems – when you want to be – but you do lack concentration,' he said, his smile widening. 'You have perhaps been allowed to drift. School is more forgiving of this than the outside world, Frank. You need to sharpen up a little, eh?'

'Yes, sir,' said Frank.

Mr Prothorax nodded.

'I see you are fond of reading,' said Mr Prothorax, consulting his notes.

He said the word 'reading' as though Frank had been described as enjoying running naked or sword-swallowing.

'Yes, sir,' said Frank.

'Well, reading is all well and good, Palp,' said Mr Prothorax, leaning back in his chair, 'but it's not mathematics, is it?'

'No, sir,' said Frank.

'Or physics?'

'No, sir,' said Frank.

Frank was wondering if Mr Prothorax was going to list all the things reading was not when Mr Prothorax suddenly clapped his hands together.

'You need some direction, Palp,' said Mr Prothorax. 'Do you see? Direction!'

'Sir?'

'What would you like to do, eh? What sort of job do you think you are suited for?'

Frank struggled to respond. He struggled to see the point of responding.

'Come along,' said Mr Prothorax. 'You must have given it some thought.'

'I don't know, sir,' said Frank.

He really didn't. He had no idea. Not even a vague one. He was sure he had once had dreams about what he might do, as all children do before the Grey smothers them, but whatever they were had disappeared into that fog a long time ago.

'Well, what about the Ministry?' said Mr Prothorax.

Frank knew that Mr Prothorax would eventually suggest the Ministry – and not just because his father, mother, sister and brother-in-law all worked there, but because pretty much everyone in the city worked for the Ministry one way or another. If there was one thing Frank was sure of, he did not want to work for the Ministry.

'Maybe, sir,' said Frank. 'Yes. Perhaps.'

Mr Prothorax sniffed at this lack of enthusiasm.

'What if we put "the Ministry" on the form for the moment? Just so there's something there? Hmm? You can always change your mind later.'

Frank nodded and Mr Prothorax smiled, contented, put on his glasses and carefully wrote the words on Frank's form. He studied his work with a satisfied smile as though it had been a delicate pencil drawing of a skylark.

'Excellent,' he said. 'You see. You're already showing some direction, Frank. Well done.'

'Thank you, sir,' said Frank as he stood up to leave.

'Good luck with the exam results,' said Mr Prothorax.

'Thank you, sir,' said Frank.

'And good luck for your future at the Ministry – if that's what you decide, of course,' said Mr Prothorax, holding out his hand.

'Yes, sir. Thank you, sir,' said Frank, shaking the offered hand. It was cool and moist and revoltingly soft. It was like grabbing hold of an empty suede bag.

The rest of the queue looked up briefly as Frank stepped out, but on seeing it was Frank, they all looked down again, none of them disguising the disinterest on their faces. Frank's stomach clenched slightly, but he took strength from the fact that he would probably never see most of these thick-necked dullards again.

This moment of bravado did not last. By the time he reached the end of the corridor Frank was almost hyperventilating. In truth, he felt that he had already reached the pinnacle of his life and, having crested the hill, he was now slithering down the other side, picking up speed all the time.

And who knew what was at the bottom.

Chapter 11

Frank woke up and realised he was in the cemetery. He wondered for a moment if he was dreaming, but no, he was really there. Or as really there as he was really anywhere. He must have nodded off.

'Grandfather?' he said, as he sat upright, stretching, knocking his head on a gravestone.

'Frank,' said his grandfather. 'You're awake.'

'Almost,' he said, rubbing his head. 'My arm's gone dead.'

Frank realised what he had said and opened his mouth but closed it again, realising it was better just to pretend he'd never said anything.

'What's the weather like up there?' said his grandfather.

Frank looked up, squinting, at the branches above him.

'It's dull,' said Frank. 'But it's not cold any more. Summer's finally here and it's not raining. Yet.'

'Is there a wind?' said his grandfather.

'Not really,' said Frank.

'I always hated the wind,' said his grandfather. 'It's a windy town the Old Town. A cold wind too, even in the summer, when it came from the north or from the east. It goes straight through you.'

'It does,' said Frank.

'I never liked the climate of the Old Town,' said his grandfather. 'It's a strange thing, isn't it, that so often we are born into a place that does not suit us?'

Frank had never thought about it before. Was anyone suited to where they lived?

'At least you got to travel,' said Frank.

His arm was coming back to life and he flexed it back and forth.

'A little,' said his grandfather.

Frank was very jealous of the fact that his grandfather had travelled. No one else in his family had ever been anywhere – but no one else in his family seemed to care.

'Before the Revolution it was easier to travel,' said his grandfather. 'Before the War people used to travel a lot, if they were of a mind to. Travellers used to come here too – lots of them.

'You young people can't imagine what it was like then. It was very different. There were cafés full of intellectuals huddled in heated debates about art and politics and life. You could get drunk just on the chatter.' But Frank could imagine what it was like because he had read books from that period. He could imagine it but he could not imagine being there.

'You sound like you preferred it, Grandfather,' said Frank. 'Life before the Revolution.'

'No,' said his grandfather. 'I did not prefer it. There were many things that needed to change. The Imperial Police were every bit as bad as the Ministry Men, let me tell you. But there was hope then. People forget that. When you have no hope you convince yourself that hope is a myth.

'We knew things needed to change and we were hopeful they would. We dreamed of it and worked to make it happen. Working for change makes you feel like change is closer. Working for change is actually a kind of change.'

Frank knew what he meant. No one believed there might be anything better now. Pragmatism had become a kind of religion. This was how it had to be because this was how it had to be. To think otherwise was unpatriotic.

'During the time of discovery and conquests,' said his grandfather, 'a set of adventurers stepped ashore on an undiscovered land. They planted the Imperial flag. They planted a colony and this colony grew and grew until, in time, every inch of the wilderness was tamed and every acre farmed or mined or quarried or built upon.'

Frank shook his head.

'We always ruin everything, don't we?' said Frank. 'I wonder if there's any really unspoilt land anywhere any more.'

'It's in the nature of man to devour whatever is available, Frank. We are rapacious.'

Frank nodded. It was true.

'It wasn't until after the colony became independent,' continued his grandfather, 'that they discovered the terrible truth about the land they now called their own.'

'What was it, Grandfather?' asked Frank, frowning down at the leaf litter at the base of the gravestone.

'Scientists discovered something incredible whilst looking for something else entirely – as is often the case with science, as it is with love.'

'What did they discover?'

'They discovered that the land had in fact been inhabited the whole time.'

'But how?' said Frank. 'Were the inhabitants invisible?'

'In a manner of speaking, yes,' said his grandfather. 'They discovered that there was a rich and complex ancient civilisation there, but that it was minuscule, with buildings the size of grains of sand.

'In fact, the beach they had landed on was this civilisation's largest and most wondrous port – a city destroyed by the boots of those adventurers as they wandered back and forth the first day they landed.

'This miniature metropolis contained elaborate and sophisticated architecture and public spaces, theatres, villas and sculptures. It was a city to rival any on the planet, from any age.

'The scientists searched for any survivors from that tiny world, but centuries of occupation had clearly destroyed all hope of that. They had, unknowingly crushed an entire world – an entire people – wiping it from history.'

'What did they do when they found out?' said Frank.

'Well,' said his grandfather, 'many other civilisations have been erased through time, of course, without guilt or remorse from the conquerors, but this was different. The fact that it was an accident made it feel more of a crime. Odd, isn't it?

'When the news broke, people talked of little else. At first they hunted vainly for survivors. It caused a great depression among the population such that they became lethargic and listless.

'Industry collapsed. Shops emptied. Schools closed. Society shut down. People began to emigrate back to the motherland.

This emigration picked up pace until the population was not sustainable.

'The island is deserted now. The buildings are collapsed and overgrown. Doors loll open like the mouths of the dead. Birds fly in and out of glassless windows. Soon even these ruins will decay and there will be no sign that humans ever lived there. Save for the microscopic sculptures and facades of that long-forgotten miniature city on the shore.'

Frank took this image in. He felt himself pull back and away from the ruins of the miniature city until they were unrecognisable, and then did the same with the new city built unwittingly above it, until that too seemed like grains of sand.

He felt like he would have carried on going, drifting further and further away in his imagination until everything was indistinguishable from the general fog of the Grey, had not the image of Olivia appeared, like an angel, to save him, to anchor him.

'I have to go, Grandfather,' said Frank.

'Of course,' said his grandfather. 'Of course you do.'

Chapter 12

The last day of term finally arrived and the principal, Mr Notaulix – a tall, bearded man with the intonation and self-righteousness of a preacher – gave a long, faltering speech to the assembled pupils about how the school had done all it could to prepare them for the rich and varied life ahead of them. They must go on now to be good citizens, hardworking employees, loyal husbands and wives, caring parents.

There was some giggling at the word 'parents' but it was not met by the usual fierce combative glare; rather, it was collaborated with and gently encouraged by a smile none of them had ever seen before, a smile Frank would have imagined impossible on such a dour face.

This weird, unlikely display of goodwill from the principal only served to make Frank feel more detached. He had never felt more of an outsider than when he stood there on that last afternoon watching girls hugging tearfully and boys slapping each other manfully on the back.

He was genuinely surprised by the levels of emotion on display. He felt a curious pang of jealousy. He was suddenly envious of this ability the others had to find some meaning in what was surely meaningless. But what would be the point? A year from now they would walk past each other in the street without recognition.

'Well, that's that,' said Dawn, stepping up beside him in the courtyard at the end of the day. 'Onward to the world of employment.'

'What did you say to Prothorax?' said Frank.

'I said I wanted to be a painter,' said Dawn with a chuckle.

'Really?' said Frank. 'What did he say to that?'

'He suggested working in one of Ministry paper mills upriver from the New New Town,' said Dawn.

Frank shook his head.

'It's actually not such a crazy idea,' said Dawn. 'I'd get free paper offcuts and the pay isn't bad. How about you?'

'The Ministry, of course,' said Frank.

'But you hate the Ministry,' said Dawn.

'It wasn't my idea,' said Frank.

'But you'll have to do something. Eventually.'

Frank ignored her and looked away to where Scape and others were laughing and shouting.

'Look at them,' said Frank in bafflement. 'Just look at them.'

Dawn chuckled again.

'They do seem even more content with themselves than normal,' she said.

'I hate them,' said Frank

'No you don't,' she said.

'Yes I do,' said Frank. 'So do you.'

Dawn looked back at them as if considering this idea.

'No,' she said, shaking her head. 'I don't hate them. I don't care about them enough to hate them.'

'Well, you should,' said Frank.

'Oh?' said Dawn. 'You're very bossy today. Are you getting in training for life at the Ministry?'

Frank scowled. He was angry that Dawn thought she could make fun of him. To make matters worse, Dawn seemed to take Frank's annoyance as further encouragement to tease him.

'Don't be such a grouch,' she said. 'Why let them bother you?'

'Don't pretend they don't bother you, Dawn,' he said. 'Because I know they do.'

'Sometimes,' she agreed. 'Not always. But not if I can help it. Not today.'

'Well, they annoy me,' said Frank.

Dawn sat down on the low wall beside them.

'You should be glad. After the party you won't have to talk to any of them again if you don't want to.'

'The party?' said Frank.

'Yes – the party,' said Dawn. 'Don't pretend you don't know.'

Frank did know. There was an end of school party the following night, but he had no intention of going. He'd assumed Dawn wouldn't be going either.

'I'm not going,' he said.

'Why not?' she said. 'You should come.'

Frank stared at her as though she was insane.

'Why would I? Why would I socialise with these people? I'd be a hypocrite.'

Dawn laughed.

'For goodness' sake, Frank,' she said. 'Don't take everything so seriously. It's a party. It's free. There'll be music and dancing.'

'I'm not going,' said Frank.

'This is because you can't dance, isn't it?' said Dawn, punching him on the arm. 'Doesn't matter. I can show you.'

'I can dance,' said Frank defensively.

Dawn raised an eyebrow.

'I can,' said Frank. 'You don't know everything.'

'When have you *ever* danced?' said Dawn.

'When have *you* ever danced?'

'Me?' said Dawn. 'I love dancing. I dance all the time.'

And she started to dance. Right there. Right in the courtyard by the fire escape. Dancing to some tune in her head, eyes closed, arms snaking, hips rocking. When she opened her eyes, Frank was gone.

Chapter 13

Just like that, school was over. Frank was surprised to find that there was not the massive, momentous difference between the one state and the next – between Schoolboy-Frank and Graduate-Frank. They seemed, on the face of it, almost identical, except that now Frank could concentrate exclusively on bringing about a meeting with Olivia.

His parents were, it was true, already dropping hints about the need for Frank to look for employment and Frank's father left him in no doubt he thought that employment ought to lie at the Ministry.

Frank struggled to see an alternative himself and so he tried not to think about it, and pretended instead that this was just the end of term, rather than the end of school. He was on holiday – at least until his exam results were in.

Frank had agreed to meet his father to go to the barber's. It was the last thing he wanted to do but at least it might be a distraction. Frank had been going to the same barber with his father ever since he could remember. It was a dingy cave of a place over by the cemetery.

The walls were wood-panelled, stained nearly black, and the chequerboard floor tiles were so tarnished with old wax there was practically no difference between black and white. The windows were coated with a yellow film that cast the whole room in an amber light.

But the sinks, the mirrors, the brown leather chairs were immaculate. Here the enamel and chrome shone and sparkled as the scissors snipped and the razors scraped on leather straps.

On the walls was a framed barber's certificate from the Ministry and several framed pictures – the King in his crown and robes, the President, a crudely painted picture of a lake and mountains covered in snow, and a sepia-tinted photograph of younger Mr Prementum, the barber, in uniform.

Frank's father read a newspaper. Frank looked at the pile of magazines on the table. Girlie mags peeped out from under the ones about fishing or farming – a nipple here, a lipstick smile there. Frank reached his hand forward, ostensibly to pick up a magazine about the wonders of industry, but really to uncover one of those smiling, bare-breasted girls.

'Next!' said Mr Prementum as the till drawer pinged open and the previous customer paid. Frank leapt back as though burnt by a fire.

'You go, Frank,' said his father, frowning at him.

'The usual?' said the barber as Frank took his seat and he wrapped a towel round his shoulders.

Before Frank could reply, his father said, 'The usual.'

The barber nodded and smiled and Mirror-Frank smiled back. Mr Prementum had lost an ear in the war and wore a metal replacement. It was attached to his head by two leather straps and was made of tin. Mr Prementum would tap it to acknowledge that he had heard a customer – even though of

course he could hear nothing through that ear. It was an irony that never seemed to lose its amusement for Mr Prementum.

Mr Prementum took his work very seriously. He combed and snipped with the skill and concentration of a surgeon, finessing and finessing until he was moving from single hair to single hair, taking fragments from them it would have taken a microscope to see.

Then – and only then – did the razor appear. Even Mirror-Frank looked a little nervous at this. Many years before, when Frank was only a little boy, Mr Prementum had cut Frank's ear with the razor. Frank wondered if his hand betrayed some desire for revenge on those who still had both their ears.

Both Frank and the barber remembered this incident vividly and Mr Prementum, who was not a great one for words, always tapped his metal ear with his razor and winked at Frank before he began. This was clearly meant to put Frank at ease, but always sent a shiver of queasy anticipation through his groin.

Mr Prementum would scrape away at the nape of Frank's neck for a while and then, after taking a deep breath, begin to scrape around Frank's ears. The noise was one that Frank found excruciating. He desperately wanted to retract his head into his shoulders but was terrified any movement at all would cause Mr Prementum to slice his ear.

The relief when it was all over was evident on both their faces when Mr Prementum, with more than a touch of triumph, would hold up the mirror and show Frank the back of his head. Frank would nod and Mr Prementum would put his lips together and begin to whistle a long and complex piece of music, all of it out of tune. Then Frank's father would pay – always giving him a tip – and that would be that.

'How did the careers talk go, son?' said his father as they walked home. 'You never really said much about it.'

'All right,' said Frank. 'You know . . .'

He had never liked talking about school and had always held out hope that his parents would pick that up immediately from his tone and end their questions there. Was it too much to hope that the questions would end now he'd left?

'What did they suggest?' said his father.

'They suggested the Ministry,' said Frank flatly.

What more was there to say? What else were they ever going to suggest? A life in the circus? A cowboy? A ballet dancer? His father smiled.

'There you are then,' said his father proudly. 'You see?'

Frank said nothing. What was there to see? The fact that the Ministry provided nearly all the jobs for anyone with decent exam results did not mean Frank belonged there. He refused to accept that. He would never accept that.

'Yes,' said Frank, hoping that would be that.

His father was not willing to let it drop.

'There are worse jobs than the Ministry, let me tell you,' said his father, frowning a little now. 'My grandfather worked in the mines north of the mountains. Twelve-hour shifts, all of it underground. And I know you don't want to hear about the War but –'

'I know,' said Frank.

'And your uncle Peter,' he continued. 'Your mother's brother. He worked in the shipyards. Lost an eye to a flying rivet.'

'I know, Father,' said Frank. 'I've heard these stories before.'

'Stories?' said his father. 'They aren't stories. I'm not your grandfather, you know. These are true. You need to know them and learn from them.'

Frank nodded. His father was breathing harder now.

'What you have against the Ministry, I will never know,' he said gruffly. 'It's put food in your belly and clothes on your back your whole life. You should be grateful.'

Frank sighed.

'It's just not what I want to do,' said Frank.

'What do you want to do?' said his father, his voice getting tighter and tighter. 'Sit around all day reading books?'

'No,' said Frank, although that didn't sound so bad. 'I just want to do something more with my life than work at the Ministry.'

'More than your old man,' said his father.

'I didn't mean that,' said Frank.

'Yes you did,' he said.

Yes he did

They walked on in silence for a while and gradually his father's mood began to improve again.

'Anyway,' said his father, 'at least you'll look smart for the party tonight.'

Frank had no idea his father was even aware there was a party.

'Your mother told me,' said his father. 'Obviously she didn't hear it from you. Petra bumped into Dawn Calypter from upstairs. Poor kid. Her father is a right –'

'I'm not going,' said Frank.

His father nodded.

'I was never one for parties myself, either,' he said, putting a hand on his son's shoulder.

This did not really come as a great surprise to Frank.

'I never really saw the point. I never could stand all that dancing.'

'But Mother liked to dance, didn't she?' said Frank.

'Your mother?' said Frank's father. 'Yes, I suppose she did. She was a good dancer, as it happens. That was a long time ago. But that doesn't make any difference to us men, eh? Parties are for women really, aren't they? They love all that dressing up and carry on.'

His father winked and slapped him on the back as if a new bond had been formed between them. Frank instantly decided with a shudder that it was, after all, absolutely imperative that he go to the party.

Chapter 14

The end of year party was early in the evening so that there would be no problem for the partygoers to get home before the curfew siren.

Frank arrived and immediately looked at his watch. He had intended to go early so that he could leave early, but he had worried about appearing keen, so had cycled past and then round and around for half an hour, before chaining his bike to a railing and walking back.

By the time Frank got to the school gates, there was a steady stream of his peers going in, laughing and shouting. The elite were arriving in cars, waving to those already there as though they were Ministry movie stars, and the crowds clapped as though they actually were.

Frank almost turned on his heels to beat a hasty retreat when Dawn appeared in front of him. He almost didn't recognise her. She was wearing make-up – deep red lipstick and a thick black eyeliner that made her eyes look twice as big. Her hair was different too. It was neater, sharper edged. She looked older. Frank couldn't even see the scar on her mouth because of her lipstick.

'Frank!' she said excitedly. 'You came.'

'Yeah,' said Frank, smiling weakly and peering at a group passing by. 'But I think I've changed my mind. I'm not really in the mood. Sorry.'

'Don't be silly, Frank,' she said, grabbing his arm. 'You're here now.'

'But –'

'No,' said Dawn. 'I'm not listening. Come on.'

Frank looked at the couples streaming past them.

'I don't have a date,' he said.

'Me neither,' said Dawn. 'What if we went in together?'

Frank frowned.

'Calm down,' said Dawn, raising an eyebrow. 'We're not getting married. I just mean that we can go in together. Just to fit in, for once. How about it? We can do what we want inside.'

Frank thought about this for a moment, then nodded.

'OK,' he said. 'Why not?'

Dawn laced her arm through his and they headed towards the door.

'You look nice, by the way,' he said.

'Thanks, Frank,' said Dawn with a grin.

They gave their tickets to Mrs Elytron, the Biology teacher who was on the door, and walked inside. It was dark and it took a few moments to adjust their eyes.

Frank let his arm hang loose and Dawn took the hint and let go of him. Frank began trying to pick out individuals from the crowd. Or at least he tried – and failed – to pick out the only one he was really looking for: Olivia.

'Let's get a drink,' said Dawn, and Frank nodded, following along behind as music suddenly blared out.

There were two teachers at the bar – a couple of trestle tables covered in a plastic sheet – no doubt to ensure there was no repeat of the previous year's trouble when a large amount of cheap Ministry vodka had somehow been added to the fruit punch.

It took a while to get served but eventually they stood, backs to the wall, looking at the room. It was filling up – or rather, though it was getting busy, all the people so far chose to keep to the edges, leaving the centre free.

A voice came over the speakers, followed by a squeal of feedback.

'All right!' it said. 'Who wants to have a good time?'

A half-hearted cheer went up.

'I said, who wants to have a good time?'

This time the cheer was louder, if still a little sarcastic, and laced with laughter. Frank peered into the far corner and saw Mr Prothorax with a microphone, tugging at the lead. Scape yelled, 'Get on with it!'

Frank noticed some activity as a group of men clattered on stage holding instruments. After a few bangs and twangs, they started to run through a repertoire of some of the hits from the Ministry Music Show on television. It was the kind of music Frank loathed but he was in a minority as usual because the crowd applauded and whooped, spreading out onto the dance floor. Frank closed his eyes. He could feel the thump of the bass in his stomach.

'Come on,' said Dawn after a few minutes. 'Let's dance.'

She tried to pull him towards the dance floor.

'I don't dance,' said Frank, doggedly resisting. 'I told you.'

'Sure you do,' said Dawn.

'No, I don't!' yelled Frank as the music suddenly stopped.

83

There was a smattering of giggles. Dawn shook her head at him before walking away onto the dance floor and, as the music started up again, dancing on her own.

Frank walked back to the bar even though he had barely started his drink. He looked at the clock – he'd only been there twenty minutes. It felt like hours. Why the hell had he come?

He put his half-finished drink on a ledge and queued up for another just to waste time. The girls in front of him giggled and pointed at the dance floor, which was now full. But there was no sign of Olivia. Frank couldn't even see Dawn any more.

He could see Scape though. He was leaping around like he was trying to put out a fire with his feet, whooping and yelling. He put his arms round two of his friends and they threw themselves about the dance floor with a berserk abandon that seemed more angry than joyful. Or at least it did to Frank.

He was so distracted he hadn't even realised, until that moment, that one of the girls in front of him was Olivia. She was wearing a pale dress, clearly expensive, low at the back, her hair brushing this way and that against her smooth skin as she talked to her friends. She turned sideways and flashed her exquisite profile, with her long imperial nose.

Frank was mesmerised. He tuned out the music entirely and focused in on the hair waving back and forth like seaweed in the ocean, like barley in a summer breeze. He wanted more than anything to grab her, turn her round and kiss her, but he also knew he was absolutely incapable of it. He was incapable of even asking her to dance.

She turned her head, talking to the friend to her left. Frank watched her lips moving and focused in on them, tuning out all the other noise in the room until he could hear her voice. She was talking about her birthday, planning what they would do. Frank made a mental note of everything he heard.

But Frank could not hold that level of concentration. The noise of the room roared back into his consciousness like a train into a station and he felt hemmed in all of a sudden. He was jostled and shoved by Scape's braying group of boys who were clearly somehow drunk already. Frank pushed them away and left the queue, wandering towards the toilets for some respite from the din.

'How's things, Frank?' said the boy standing next to him at the urinals.

Frank turned, catching an unwanted glimpse of the boy's hand and much of what he was holding.

'Hello,' said Frank. 'Roland. It's been a long time.'

'Well,' said Roland, 'we've seen each other most days, Frank. We just haven't talked.'

This was true. There was an unexpected edge to Roland's voice.

'Why did we stop talking?' said Frank, trying to sound casual as he zipped up his fly.

Roland washed his hands, pulled down a length of towel and dried his hands.

'You turned into a bit of a prick,' he said. 'That's why. Don't you remember?'

Roland said this in such a mild and good-natured way that simply made it all the more savage. It was a knife so sharp that Frank did not even realise he was bleeding until after Roland had left the room and the door had clattered shut behind him.

Frank went to the sink and washed his hands mechanically. He looked up and Mirror-Frank was staring back, shaking his head, a wry smile on his face.

'What?' said Frank.

Mirror-Frank made no reply. He didn't have to.

Frank dried his hands and pulled open the heavy door, letting the music flood in. The dance floor was a mass of writhing, bouncing silhouettes. Olivia was in there somewhere, he thought bitterly.

He turned disconsolately towards the exit. The music pulsed, seemingly pushing him towards the door with each beat. He had never felt so unnecessary or so bitter at the thought.

A hand reached out and grabbed his arm as he opened the exit door and he turned, imagining that somehow it might be Olivia – but it was only Dawn.

'Where are you going?' she said.

'Home,' said Frank.

86

'Why?' she said.

Her face was flushed with dancing. She was still moving to the beat, bobbing up and down almost imperceptibly. Frank wondered if she was drunk too.

'I just . . . I'm not in the mood,' he said, turning away.

'For goodness' sake, Frank,' said Dawn sharply. 'You're always moaning about this place – that nothing ever happens. That everyone is dull and boring. So when something does happen, enjoy it.'

'I don't mean stuff like this,' said Frank, screwing up his face and looking back at the crowd. 'I mean big stuff. You know . . .'

'No,' said Dawn, frowning and folding her arms. 'Like what? What are you looking forward to? War? Another Revolution? Famine? Pestilence? What, Frank?'

'I don't know!' said Frank. 'Not this, all right?'

Dawn stared at him for a moment and then turned to walk back to the dance floor, disappearing into the darkness and the dancers. Frank stood for a moment staring back into the room, then headed off to his bike and cycled home.

Chapter 15

It was an hour before curfew, a week later, when Frank propped his bike against the railings of the hosiery shop on the corner of Steadfast Street. It was dark, a big sickle moon lying back on the pinnacles of the Castle above him, giving it thin, glowing horns. The street lamp nearby was throwing shadows of the railings across the pavement and shining on the cobbles still damp from the earlier downpour. Frank waited.

The dark streets were deserted. Or they seemed deserted. Frank knew they were never really as empty as they seemed. Civil Servants were always around, even if you didn't see them.

Frank stared into the shadows, searching for any sign of movement. He was sure that he saw nothing at all, but every time he shifted his gaze to somewhere else, he was equally sure that something was watching him – something inside the darkness he had been convinced was empty.

Frank shook his head and wandered over to stand opposite the steps leading up to the railway bridge that crossed the river from the Old New Town to the Grand Station in the Old Town. Not that anyone really travelled by train any more – only Ministry Men and the military.

Frank had read about the old days of the Grand Station, when it was the terminus for one of the great railway journeys of Europe, with fine restaurants and cafés clustered around it. But it was more of a faceless depot now, the gilded facade long gone.

Frank waited and waited, wondering if it was just a waste of time. Then all at once there they were, silhouetted from the arc light above: climbing up the steps and onto the planked wooden walkway that ran alongside the tracks, separated by the huge black criss-cross of girders. Frank pressed himself back into a doorway, into the shadows, watching.

He recognised Olivia straight away, even in that electrical twilight. Undiscovered she may have been, but he had mapped that continent so many times in his imagination. He knew its every promontory, every inlet.

It was Olivia's birthday. He had heard Olivia set the time for this whilst standing behind her in the queue at the party. It had made it worth going for that alone. Frank crossed the street and edged up the steps for a better look as they moved out of view.

Frank knew what they were doing in any case. It was something teenagers did when they reached eighteen. They wrote a wish, put it in an empty Liberation Beer bottle and dropped it into the river from the railway bridge.

This wasn't anything Frank ever planned to do when he reached eighteen. What was the point? Even if he was superstitious, there was no bottle big enough, nor paper long enough, for the list of things he would wish for. Where would he stop? There wasn't a single thing about his life he wouldn't change without a second's thought.

Frank had a sudden realisation that without school, all casual sightings of Olivia had come to an end. He felt a coldness in the pit of his stomach as he realised it was possible he might never actually see her face again.

Frank heard the distant rumble behind him and saw the figures gather excitedly. This was the last piece of the ritual. By tradition, the bottle had to be dropped as a train crossed the bridge. Otherwise it just wouldn't count, apparently.

The revellers on the bridge heard it coming too and whooped. Frank winced at the sound of their voices. He could distinctly hear Scape, and he hated Olivia's friends. They were the kind of people who didn't even know they were Grey when they were full of it. He wished they were being dropped into the river instead of the bottle.

The train arrived, more loudly than Frank had expected. It shook the girders of the bridge and rattled the boardwalk and Frank's ribs, and above its rumble he could hear the cries of Olivia and the others as she dropped the bottle. Leaning over, he saw a tiny fleck of white in the black water where it struck the surface.

The group leapt up and down and hugged each other and chanted something Frank could not make out before heading back towards the Old New Town, their shadowed shapes converging into one many armed and legged creature that broke out into a run and scuttled off into the dark like an insect.

Frank hurried away from the bridge as they returned, running across the road and taking up his place once more in the shadowed doorway. They spilt down the steps, laughing and shouting and heading off to who knew where.

Once they'd gone, Frank walked up the steps and along the boardwalk to the spot where Olivia had dropped the bottle. The railing was still warm from their touch and he could smell their perfumes, their cigarettes. He closed his eyes and imagined himself beside her as she leant over the railing.

When he opened them, he was looking down at the river. The water was black and viscous, like oil. Lights from Perseverance Boulevard reflected in it, but even the reflections were greasy, slippery things, sliding over the surface like luminous eels.

The breeze turned and Frank caught a whiff of the river's rotten stench. The river began in the mountains, crystal clear and pure, and then, bit by bit, it was contaminated and polluted until it became this foul, slow-moving slug, slimy and stinking of chemicals and death.

It did not seem a fitting repository for wishes. It looked cold and bleak and was more suited to the suicides who regularly threw themselves into its polluted waters. They were dead in seconds.

Suicides were hushed up, of course, and not acknowledged at the Ministry. The Ministry decreed contentment and nothing other than contentment could or would be tolerated.

But Frank had seen, with his own eyes, two bodies fished out before the Civil Servants arrived to bag them and take them away. That was the real river for those who understood it – a place where hopes and the hopeless alike were taken under and extinguished.

Frank looked up at the Castle's spiked crown, a deeper, colder black against the night sky. It had a vertiginous quality to it: to look up at it was to imagine it tumbling down on top of you, burying you, skewering you with its barbed and broken pinnacles.

Frank went back for his bike and rode off towards his apartment block. It was the last half-hour before curfew now and the streets were empty. The trams had stopped, the cafés were closed, the shops shuttered up and the Old Town silent. It was his favourite time.

Frank's dynamo lit up the street ahead as rain began to fall once again, making the cobbles shine like scales on a snake. The tramlines glistened, arcing this way and that.

He pedalled harder and harder, his heart pounding, the dynamo blazing brighter and brighter, whining against the wheel rim, lighting up the streets and sending a flickering cobweb of shadows across them from the tram cables overhead.

'Olivia!' he shouted, and the very sound of her name was like a charm.

Chapter 16

Back at the apartment, Frank chained up his bike and walked through the deserted courtyard to the lobby. Mrs Cremaster's door was open a crack, her bony, desiccated fingers on the handle, her eye glinting in the shadow.

'Hello, Mrs Cremaster, how are –'

The hand swiftly retreated and the door clicked shut. An unpleasant smell was wafted towards him on the draft of its closing and Frank winced and shook his head before walking on.

'Hey, Frank.'

It was Dawn, carrying two rubbish bags. They hadn't spoken since the party.

'Dawn,' said Frank. 'You OK?'

'Yeah,' she said. 'You?'

Frank smiled and shrugged.

'Sorry I dashed off at the party,' he said.

'You missed a good night.'

'Really?'

'What have you been up to?' she asked. 'It's almost curfew.'

'Is it?' said Frank, trying to sound nonchalant.

Dawn smiled at him.

'This wouldn't have anything to do with Olivia, then?' she asked.

Frank could feel himself blushing.

'What?' he said. 'Ol . . . Olivia? Olivia who?'

'Olivia Pulvillus,' said Dawn. 'From school. Remember? The one whose chest you were always staring at.'

'What?' said Frank, with more of a squeak than he had intended.

'Calm down, Frank,' said Dawn. 'Your secret's safe with me. I've seen you hanging about outside her apartment block a couple of times now. You'll get yourself arrested if you're not careful. You know the kind of people who live there.'

Frank's throat went dry.

'I don't know what you're talking about,' he said. 'Why would I be hanging about outside her block?'

'Knowing you, Frank,' she said with a sigh, 'I'm guessing that you haven't got the nerve to simply ask her out like a normal person would and are hoping to "accidentally" bump into her.'

Frank frowned. Dawn clamped her hand over her mouth.

'Oh, no,' she said. 'You are!'

Dawn laughed and then put her hand over her mouth again.

'How do you even know where she lives?' said Frank.

'She invited me to a party once.'

'You?'

'Yes!' said Dawn. 'Me.'

'I'd better get in,' he said, scowling. 'Goodnight, Dawn.'

Dawn smiled and headed out into the courtyard.

'Night, Frank,' she said over her shoulder.

Frank ignored her and walked towards the stairwell.

'Who's there?' said a voice in the shadows.

'What?' said Frank, backing off and peering.

'Oh, it's you, is it?' said Mr Spiracle, emerging into the yellow gloom of the lobby.

'Mr Spiracle,' said Frank, nodding and carrying on towards the stairs.

Mr Spiracle's arm shot out with surprising speed and his hand clutched Frank's by the bicep. The grip was firm and painful.

'Where have you been?'

'What?' said Frank, snatching his arm away. 'What's it got to do with you?'

'One day you'll poke your nose in where it's not wanted and then you'll see,' said Mr Spiracle.

'See what?' said Frank. 'What are you talking about?'

Mr Spiracle smiled a sinister, knowing smile. A gold tooth twinkled like a star in the blackness of his mouth. One of his eyebrows reared up and swayed about.

'You'll see the truth,' he said.

'About what?'

But Mr Spiracle was already retreating backwards into the shadows. Within seconds Frank struggled to see him, even though he knew he was there.

'About what?' he repeated.

But there was no response. Frank crossed the lobby and into the stairwell, taking the stairs two at a time, eager to escape the attentions of Mr Spiracle.

'Where have you been?' said his father when he walked in, the lights already pulsing to the beat of the electrical hum. Frank could feel the tension fizzing in the air.

'To take a book back to a friend,' he said. 'I told you.'

'For this long?'

His father spoke quietly but coldly. Frank did not meet his gaze. Frank's father scowled and opened his mouth to speak but was interrupted before he could. The Student smiled and scribbled in his notebook.

'Hello, little brother!'

'Petra!'

Frank hugged his sister and she held a hand to either side of his face.

'Have you grown again?'

'I don't think so,' he said, looking past Petra to where his father sat, still scowling menacingly.

'Yes,' she said, looking him up and down. 'Definitely. Hasn't he, Mother?'

'What was that?' called his mother from the kitchen.

'Frank!' shouted Petra. 'Hasn't he grown?'

'Next Wednesday,' called Frank's mother.

Petra shook her head. The curfew siren sounded outside and the electrical hum grew louder still.

'You'll get caught out after curfew one of these days,' said his father. 'And don't think I'll be coming to get you out of jail. I can't be seen to get involved.'

Frank's father looked over towards the Student, who had crept a little closer, but the Student did not look up from his notebook.

'What about Petra?' said Frank. 'How come she's here after curfew?'

'Petra is staying over,' said his mother. 'Just for tonight. She'll sleep on the foldaway bed.'

'She would be very welcome to take my bed,' said the Student.

'Ha!' said Petra. 'I'm not sleeping in the same room as Frank! But thank you.'

The Student smiled and coughed.

'We're not talking about Petra,' said Frank's father. 'We're talking about you.'

'He's sorry, aren't you, Frank?' said his sister.

Frank frowned. Petra widened her eyes and nodded towards their father. The Student stared at Frank expectantly, his pencil hovering over the page. Frank sighed.

'Yes . . .' he said. 'Sorry, Father.'

His father stared at him, clearly expecting more.

'I . . . I should have been back sooner,' said Frank. 'I'll make sure I am next time.'

'Well then . . .' said his father, mollified for the moment.

'Sit down, sit down,' said Frank's mother, coming into the room with a bowl of potatoes.

They sat down and more food was brought in. His mother and sister served the food and they began to eat and talk.

Frank's sister did most of the talking. Frank was very fond of Petra and listened intently for a while, but he found himself drifting away back to the bridge and to Olivia and her bottled wish. What was it? he wondered. What would someone like Olivia wish for?

'Frank,' said his mother. 'Frank!'

Frank sat up, startled.

'What?'

'Eat up, or you'll never be big and strong.'

Frank scowled. His sister laughed and Frank smiled despite himself.

'How was the end of school party?' Petra asked as she poured herself another glass of water.

Frank shrugged.

'You know,' he said. 'Not my thing.'

'Oh I loved mine,' said his sister. 'It was the best night of my life.'

'Really?' said Frank.

'Not better than your wedding night, I hope,' said Frank's mother.

'Mother!' said Petra, blushing.

Everyone laughed and Petra joined in. The mood seemed to lighten. But Frank noticed that Petra grew quiet after that. She was staring into her glass as though she could see the party contained within it. Her face wore an expression Frank had never seen before. Even the Student stopped writing to look at her.

'They didn't have that sort of nonsense in our day, did they, dear?' said Frank's father as the conversation returned to talk of the party.

'No,' said Frank's mother sadly. 'No, they didn't.'

'I danced and danced . . .' murmured Frank's sister.

Now everyone looked at her as she slowly put her hand to her face and began to cry.

'Petra,' said her mother, getting up and hugging her. 'There, there, my love. Everything will be all right in the end. You'll see.'

'I'm fine, Mother,' said Petra, sniffing. 'I'm being silly.'

Petra pushed her hair away from her face and smiled weakly. The Student carried on looking at her, pencil poised. Frank frowned at him until he too, blushed and began writing, head down, face hidden by his book.

'Please,' said Petra. 'Everyone just carry on, I'm fine. Say something.'

Frank looked back at his sister as his mother began to tell them about a programme she had heard on the radio about potted plants. Petra was looking down wistfully, lost in her memories again.

After dinner, Frank and Petra cleared the table. Petra washed the plates while Frank dried them.

'Did something special happen that night?' asked Frank. 'At your end of school party?'

She sighed and shook her head. Frank grinned.

'Are you sure?'

Petra turned and looked at him, tears in her eyes.

'I can't explain it,' she said. 'Please . . .'

'I'm sorry,' said Frank. I didn't mean to –'

'I can remember dancing – not with anyone in particular, just a group of us, girls mainly. I remember looking round and we were all so young and so beautiful – even me in those days – and happy and . . .'

She picked up another bowl and started washing.

'But now . . .' she said, looking down at her leg.

Petra had caught her foot in a tramline two years before and fallen badly. The leg had broken and had never been the same since. The foot was now permanently turned in and she walked with a stick and a heavy limp.

'I'm sorry,' said Frank.

'It's no one's fault,' she said. 'Or at least, no one's but mine.'

'Does it hurt?' he asked.

She shook her head.

'Only in here,' she said, patting her breast and putting a handprint of soap suds on her jumper.

She laughed and flicked suds at Frank. Frank carried on drying but almost dropped the plate he was holding when he turned to find the Student standing right next to him, staring at Petra.

'Will you stop creeping up on people!' said Frank.

Petra turned and saw the Student standing there and smiled at him. And the Student smiled back.

After they had washed up, they rejoined their parents in the lounge to watch television. Frank sat down on the sofa next to his mother and sister.

'Budge up, Frank,' said his mother, nudging him in the ribs with her elbow. 'Let the Student sit down.'

Frank grumbled but was not allowed much choice in the matter as his mother beckoned him over and he sat down next to Frank.

Frank didn't really like being this close to the Student. To sit this close was to accept him and Frank did not accept him. He tried to move his body so that none of it was in contact with the Student's.

His father sat in his own armchair, and switched on the television, and got up to slap it several times on the top of the box until the picture stopped rolling over. They sat in its queasy glow, their shadows looming behind them on the walls.

The programme started. It was the daily Ministry Talent Show. Any Ministry worker could enter and show off some supposed talent. The excitement this elicited from both the prospective performers and the audience was a source of utter bafflement for Frank.

'Look at that!' said Frank's mother in genuine amazement as someone began juggling flaming torches.

'Juggling has to be the most pointless thing in the world,' said Frank.

'Shhh,' said his mother.

'Seriously, what is the point of it?' continued Frank. 'Why spend all that time learning something so completely useless?'

'Anything is useless if you want to say so,' said Petra. 'Singing, dancing – anything.'

'It's different though,' said Frank. 'Singing and dancing are things that lots of people do. We can join in with that if we want to. Juggling isn't. We're just supposed to stare in wonder. Anyone can do it if they could be bothered but –'

'Frank,' said his father without taking his eyes from the screen. 'Your mother wants to watch without a commentary from you.'

Frank folded his arms and sat back into the sofa.

'Look!' said his mother. 'That's Mrs Coxa's boy. He can eat glass, you know. Imagine that!'

Frank stood up suddenly.

'I'm going to turn in,' said Frank in what he hoped was a voice that signified his disdain for both the programme and their viewing of it. 'Goodnight.'

'Goodnight,' they replied without looking round.

Frank looked at the Student spreading himself out to fill the space he had vacated, and shivered a little. They'd be happier if he was their son, he thought. He seems more at ease here – more at home.

Chapter 17

Frank lay on his bed, picked up a book and began to read but after a couple of pages he realised he wasn't taking it in. He could hear the sound of laughter coming from the lounge. He tried to start again but gave up after a few more pages and put it down. He was finding it harder and harder to clear his mind and let someone else take over.

He moved across to his desk and put a sheet of paper in his typewriter. After a moment's thought, he began to type.

Clack–clack–clackedy–clack–clack–clack–thud–clackedy–clack–clack–ping!

Shhhhhhhup.

Clack–clackedy–clack–thud–clack–clakcedy–clackedy–

thud—clack–clack–ping!

Shhhhhhhup.

There was a knock at the door and Petra walked in. Frank froze in mid-typing posture, index fingers poised. She closed the door behind her and sat on the end of the Student's bed.

'Still can't type properly, I see,' she said.

'I'm fine the way I am,' said Frank.

'What's the matter, Frank?'

'Nothing,' he said. 'Nothing's the matter.'

'You seem . . . tense,' she said.

'Do I?' said Frank.

She looked at him for a long time.

'Are you still mooning around after that girl?' she said.

Frank wondered for a moment if she had spoken to Dawn and then he remembered that he had, on a visit to his sister's apartment the month before, briefly told her about Olivia. He hadn't meant to, but Petra had a way of putting him at ease and it had just slipped out.

'Leave me alone, Petra,' said Frank. 'I'm fine.'

'What's her name? Ottla?'

'Olivia,' said Frank. 'I really don't want to –'

'Any luck yet?' she said with a smile.

'No,' he said. 'Look –'

'Why don't you just ask her out?' said his sister.

Frank turned round with a sigh.

'You don't understand.'

'No, I don't,' said Petra. 'Enlighten me.'

'She's from the Old New Town,' said Frank.

'So?' said his sister.

'She mixes with all those Ministry kids,' he said.

'You're a Ministry kid,' said Petra.

Frank shook his head.

'You know what I mean – kids whose fathers are actually important.'

'Frank!' said his sister, frowning.

'What?' he said. 'I'm only telling the truth. I never said I wanted to be one of them. I don't. I hate them.'

'You're a snob, do you know that?'

'What?' he said, putting the book down. 'I'm not a snob! I'm the opposite of a snob – whatever that is.'

'Ha!' said Petra.

'What's that supposed to mean?'

'Come on, Frank,' she said. 'At least be honest.'

'I'm not a snob,' said Frank. 'How am I a snob?'

Petra sighed.

'I'm not,' said Frank. 'I don't want to be rich. I'm not interested in money. Well, not money for the sake of it. I just want more from life than Mother and Father want. Don't you ever want more?'

'Of course,' she said. 'I'd like a bigger apartment, one with a balcony overlooking a park, and –'

'No,' said Frank, slapping his hand down on the bed. 'Not that kind of more. Don't you ever want things to be more . . .'

He struggled to find words that he felt his sister would understand.

'What?' said Petra, wide-eyed. 'You sound like a child.'

'Why is it childish to want something better?' asked Frank sulkily. 'It's like pretending to be content is the same as actually being content. I'm not going to pretend.'

'Why do you want to be miserable all the time?' said his sister.
Frank put his hands to his head.

'I don't want to be miserable,' said Frank. 'Why would I want to be miserable? If I'm miserable it's because I don't want to be miserable.'

'Well, you don't seem to want to be happy,' said Petra.

'I want to be happy,' said Frank. 'I just don't want to want to be happy. I don't want to want it. I want to *be* it.'

Petra smiled and shook her head.

'Do you ever listen to yourself?' she said with a chuckle.

But Frank didn't want to be mollified.

'How can anyone be happy in this place? I mean, really. Come on. Look around you. Look at how we live. No one with an ounce of intelligence could be happy with a life as dull as this. But that's the point, isn't it? Only stupid people are happy.'

Petra frowned.

'So everyone's stupid except you?' she said.

'I didn't say that,' said Frank. 'Are you saying everyone except me is happy? Are you happy? You don't look it. You didn't look it at dinner.'

Tears sprang to Petra's eyes again.

'You're selfish, Frank,' said his sister. 'You anger Father and then it's Mother who has to deal with it while you shut yourself up in here doing whatever it is . . .'

She looked at the typewriter.

'What are you writing anyway?' she asked.

'Nothing,' he said, pulling the sheet out and hiding it under a book.

'What do you mean "Nothing"?' she said.

'It's a short story,' said Frank.

His sister raised her eyebrows.

'What about?'

Frank shrugged.

'Can I read it?'

'No,' said Frank.

'Why not?'

'I just don't want you to read it,' said Frank.

'You think I won't understand it?' she said.

'I didn't say that,' said Frank.

'Because I'm too stupid? Like everyone else?'

'What?'

Petra opened the door to leave.

'I hope you do something exciting with your life, Frank,' she said. 'Because if you don't, I think you'll carry on blaming us for everything.'

'I don't blame you,' said Frank.

'Yes, you do,' she said. 'And it's not fair.'

Petra left, closing the door behind her, and Frank kicked out at his chair, knocking it over. He pulled the sheet of paper from under the book, crushed it into a ball and threw it across the room.

Chapter 18

Frank couldn't sleep. Petra's speech niggled away at him – as did the image of her tear-filled eyes as she was leaving. Petra was the only one of them whose opinion Frank remotely cared about. He closed his eyes when he heard the Student's hand on the door handle and felt the glow from the hallway light on his eyelids as he came in.

Frank felt bitterness rising up again. When would he ever have any privacy? It was bad enough that he had to put up with him spying on the family all day long, but he also had to share this tiny room with him. Frank had nowhere he could call his own.

The Student gave Frank the creeps. He could not have been much older than Frank but the suit and tie he habitually wore made him look like a freakishly young-looking middle-aged man. And besides, Frank was sure the Student went through his stuff when he wasn't there.

Not that he had much stuff to go through.

Frank kept his eyes clamped shut, dreading the idea that he might catch a glimpse of the Student getting undressed. He hadn't always been able to avoid that sight. Just the memory of his pale and shiny skin and yellowing underwear made him nauseous.

Eventually he heard the springs creak and twang on the Student's bed, followed by yet more scribbling in his notebook. What was he writing? Was he writing about Frank? About what position he slept in?

A few minutes later and he could hear the Student wheezing in his sleep. There was an unpleasant rattle at the end of the wheeze, as though he had rusty wire caught in his lungs. Frank recoiled. Whatever it was it didn't sound good and it was probably catching.

Frank turned onto his back and stared at the ceiling. There was a thin, jagged crack running from one corner to the other and a family of tiny spiders were emerging to scurry back and forth.

Frank took a deep breath and closed his eyes again. He tried to shut out the wheezing and the spiders and the Grey and concentrate on Olivia, but it was hard work. He imagined her back on the bridge, but alone this time.

He was there too. He walked up beside her and she turned, smiling as he approached. She didn't resist as he put his arm around her under her open jacket, letting his fingers slide across the bare flesh just above the waistband of her jeans.

She pressed her hip against his as they both stood leaning over the railings, a beer bottle each, a wish in each bottle. The train arrived and began to cross, but the rumble of the train was not quite right. There was a whine and a clatter to it.

Frank opened his eyes and sat up in bed. Was he waking into another dream? No. The Student was still wheezing. He pushed back the covers and knelt on his bed, throwing the curtains round him and looking out of the window at the empty, darkened streets outside.

At first he could see nothing except the vague difference between the skyline and the sky, between jagged rooftops and chimney stacks and gable ends and the starless night.

But slowly, as Frank's eyes adjusted to the gloom, he began to make out the shuttered windows and darkened doorways of the apartments on the other side of the street, of the closed storefronts and locked kiosks.

Then to the east there was a flash, like distant lightning. It lit up the tiles of the roof two streets away and blackened the silhouettes of the nearer buildings. Moving lights threw angular shadows across the walls, which rose and fell as the light source changed position.

Again the flash. A clear blue-white. It was a tram. It could not be anything else. But no public trams ran after the curfew siren. None would run for hours. No, it could only be one thing: the Ghost Tram. And yet how could it be?

Frank's heart quickened. He had heard of the Ghost Tram – everybody in the Old Town had – but he had always assumed it to be a story. It was said that the Ghost Tram was a feral tram, driverless and empty. It roamed the streets at night. No one knew where it came from or where it went but if it stopped for you, and if you climbed aboard, then you would never, ever, ever, be seen again.

Frank could hear it now. What he had taken for more wheezing from the Student was in fact the sounds of the tram slithering among the sleeping streets. He could hear the *shhh* of its wheels on the polished rails and the clank of the couplings, interspersed with the occasional electrical hiss and fizz.

Then he saw it – a brief glimpse of the pantograph sliding along the cables between two tiled rooftops and then a flash of the brightly illuminated carriage windows as it rounded a bend.

'It's not good to look at the Ghost Tram.'

The Student was awake.

'You've seen it?' said Frank, without taking his eyes away from the window.

Another faint burst of tramlight illuminated the scene.

'Once,' he said. 'Just a glimpse at the end of an alleyway near my uncle's house. For an instant only.'

The Ghost Tram was already moving away, the bursts of light growing fainter like a dream, melting away into blackness. The sound went first and then the light and then it was as though it had never been there. Frank shrugged off the curtains and looked at the Student.

'Do you think it's true what they say?' said Frank. 'That if you get on you're never seen again?'

The Student did not reply. Frank looked back to the window.

'I thought it was made up,' murmured Frank. 'Where does it come from? Where does it go?'

'No one knows,' said the Student.

'Someone knows,' said Frank with a sneer.

'It's not Ministry,' said the Student.

'Everything's Ministry,' said Frank.

'Forget it,' said the Student, turning over and pulling the blanket over his head.

'Forget it?' said Frank. 'I've just seen a myth. How often does that happen? How often does anything happen?'

'Even so,' said the Student. 'For your own good.'

'You didn't forget it, did you?' said Frank.

The Student made no reply, just wheezed as though deflating. Frank got back into bed. It felt cold and hard, like wet sand. He squirmed into the mattress, trying to get comfortable, finally laying on his back.

He thought about the Ghost Tram and its sinister progress about the city. He wondered if it had stopped for anyone that night as it glow-wormed through the streets. Were they being carried away to who knew where? Were they screaming and banging on the windows, or were they sitting calmly, waiting for their fate?

These thoughts made Frank feel even colder and he pulled the blanket up to his nose. He felt the Grey pressing down on him, squeezing his chest and forcing him down, down, into the mattress, the springs growling beneath him.

He opened his eyes but the room seemed as dark as the inside of his eyelids. He thought of Olivia again. She was a firefly thought in this gloom and she grew in luminescence as he flicked through all the images he could remember of her. These images were not actual, not real memories, but memories of dreams, dreams of memories – recollections of imaginings.

Unreal or not, they were vivid. Frank saw Olivia standing in the room – although it was not his tiny room but a much larger one – loosening her clothes one by one and letting them fall to the floor until she stood completely, unashamedly naked.

Frank saw her walking towards him, smiling, lifting up the blankets and climbing into the, now much larger, bed beside him. He could feel the warmth of her body pressing against him, skin to skin. He could feel her hand moving down his stomach –

'Are you masturbating?' said the Student.

'What?' said Frank, jolting out of his trance, Olivia's warmth disappearing in an instant. 'No!'

The Student scribbled in his notebook.

'What the hell are you writing?' asked Frank.

The Student said nothing.

'You'd better not be writing that,' said Frank. 'That I'm . . . you know . . .'

The Student said nothing, but his pencil whispered across the page.

'What are you writing now?' hissed Frank.

'Nothing,' said the Student.

'Then why is your pencil making a noise?' said Frank.

'I'm writing poetry,' said the Student, wheezing a little.

'In the middle of the night? In the dark?' said Frank.

'It's very sad poetry,' said the Student.

Chapter 19

Frank slowed down on Perseverance Boulevard as he passed Olivia's apartment building, trying hard not to turn his head as he glanced towards the front door. If he looked directly at the building it would refuse to cooperate, he knew it. It was that kind of a building: spiteful. The scene passed by at the edge of his vision. He willed her door to open.

But nothing.

He cycled to the corner of Endurance Plaza and then turned round to come back. Again he slowed as he passed the gate and the path leading up to the front door; slowed and slowed and slowed as much as he could without actually stopping.

Again, nothing.

That was Frank's third and last pass. He was always sorely tempted to go on a fourth, because he couldn't help holding a sneaking suspicion that Olivia always emerged thirty seconds after he left – but without some kind of system he would be there all day cycling back and forth and back and forth, and what happened if someone saw him? This was a building full of Ministry bigwigs after all. He could be reported. Maybe he already had been.

What happened if Olivia saw him from her apartment? What if she was in her room and just happened to look out of the window to see him cycling past time and time again. His ploy would be obvious. He would look an idiot. She would despise him.

The discipline of restricting his visits made him feel like it was a trial. It imbued it with gravitas. It meant he would be worthy when he finally cycled by and she stepped out and they met

She wouldn't know who he was straight away and Frank would have to remind her and she would laugh and Frank would laugh and then he would ask if this was where she lived and she would say yes and Frank would tell her he lived over in the Old Town.

He would ask her where she was going and she'd say no place special and Frank would ask if she minded if he tagged along because he was only there to see his grandfather in the cemetery – and after all, he could wait.

Olivia would laugh at this joke but blush a little, wondering if she really ought to be laughing at a joke about Frank's dead grandfather. She would be touched that he was visiting the cemetery. She would smile a crooked smile.

They would walk along the embankment by the river. She would ask about Frank's grandfather and Frank would tell her all about him and how strange it was they had not bumped into each other before because he visited his grandfather every week . . .

Of course, the details of this meeting changed at every imagining, but the thrust was always the same and the feeling that coursed through Frank's body was always, always the same. He felt better. He felt that only this meeting could make him good and stop him from being the dull pinned-down and labelled insect that he was the rest of the time.

But the meeting would just have to wait. And that was fine. Almost fine. Not fine at all, really. But tolerable. Just. It would happen when it was meant to happen. Frank had become very fatalistic of late. He ascribed this to a greater maturity.

He took a deep breath, and with one last look towards Olivia's apartment, he headed off towards the Old Cemetery, arriving there a few minutes later and chaining his bike to the lamppost outside the wet fish shop opposite the cemetery gates.

He bent down to tie his shoelace and noticed a little girl of perhaps five or six standing close by with her mother – a skinny, anxious-looking woman with thin, greying hair draped across her shoulders like cobwebs.

The little girl was eating a vanilla ice cream in a cone. It was warm and the sun was making an effort to leak through the downy clouds. A wasp began to hover beside her and she whimpered and tried to swat it away. It was joined by two more.

'Leave them alone and they will leave you alone,' said the mother. 'How many times have I told you?'

The little girl gulped back sobs and tentatively poked out her tongue as more wasps appeared and began to land on the ice-cream and crawl over it.

'Just ignore them,' said her mother crossly as the girl whimpered.

A wasp landed on the girl's cheek and Frank saw her eyes widen in terror.

'You'll get yourself stung!' hissed her mother.

Frank muttered under his breath. The mother stared at him suspiciously, daring him to interfere. Frank looked away, shaking his head. It was no concern of his how she treated her daughter. Anyway, there was a huddle of Civil Servants up the hill, about a hundred yards away. Frank was sure they had been looking at him. The last thing he wanted was to cause some kind of a scene.

Frank looked at his watch and then away towards the river. The Ministry Men moved away, much to his relief. When Frank turned back to the little girl, her face was completely obscured by wasps – all except one wild staring eye. Frank could not bear to look at it and crossed the street to the cemetery gates.

Frank walked up through the gravestones to the crest of the hill and into the shadow of the tree, between the great wrinkled tentacles of its roots, and squatted down beside his grandfather's grave. He traced his fingers across the etched letters of his name, the moss that grew there soft to the touch.

He called quietly to his grandfather and was answered after a moment or two.

'Frank?'

'Yes – it's me.'

'How is your father?' said his grandfather, stirring under the earth.

'Still obsessed with the Big Day,' said Frank. 'Other than that, much the same.'

'Obsessed?' said his grandfather. 'Is he really obsessed? My son does not seem the type to become obsessed by anything.'

'Everyone seems obsessed by it, actually,' said Frank.

He shook his head.

'Everyone but you?' said his grandfather after a pause.

'Everyone but me,' said Frank.

'Is it so bad?' said his grandfather. 'To have some excitement for a change?'

'I wouldn't have thought you'd fall for that kind of thing, Grandfather,' said Frank.

'Gagh,' said his grandfather. 'You'll find that when you're dead, you change your mind about quite a few things. It gives you a whole new perspective.'

'But it's not real excitement,' said Frank.

'For them it's real,' said his grandfather.

Frank shrugged.

'Maybe. Their lives are so dull, they jump at the chance to get worked up about the least little thing,' said Frank.

'But not you,' said his grandfather.

'I can't pretend to be excited if I'm not,' said Frank.

His grandfather said nothing in response. The silence sounded critical.

'Why do people prefer pretence?' said Frank. 'Why is it better to pretend to like something than to be honest? Why is it better to pretend to be happy? Only stupid people are happy.'

Again, his grandfather was silent.

'Grandfather?' said Frank. 'Are you still there?'

'Yes.'

'Are you all right?'

'I'm dead, Frank,' he said.

There was a small pause and then Frank heard a wheezing chuckle. Frank wasn't amused.

'I don't understand all the fuss,' said Frank. 'It's not like he's a real king. He has no actual power.'

'Ah, but they're the most powerful of all,' said his grandfather.

'Who are?'

'The kings with no power.'

'How?' said Frank.

'Well, a king who rules by right expects loyalty and can

demand it,' said his grandfather. 'But a king who has the loyalty of his people when he no longer rules by right – well, think how much more powerful he must be. He cannot demand their loyalty and yet he has it.'

'I suppose . . .' said Frank, unconvinced. 'But then why do the Ministry give him a chance to take centre stage at the Big Day in November? Aren't they scared of him? If he's so powerful?'

'It's because they're scared of him that they feel they have to accommodate him,' said his grandfather. 'But they fear him, Frank. They fear him and they hate him.'

Frank thought about this. He could not imagine the Ministry being scared of anything. Surely they controlled everything?

'Nothing can be controlled fully,' said his grandfather, reading his thoughts. 'The urge to control is the most self-defeating of all urges. The father tries to control his son, the priest his flock, the government its citizens. But it is all doomed to failure. The more they try to control, the more they instil the desire for rebellion.'

'They could govern fairly,' said Frank. 'How about that?'

He was thinking of the Ministry. He was thinking of his father.

'They could,' agreed his grandfather. 'But when all you want to do is to control, you see fairness as weakness. The desire for control is all.'

Frank looked off towards the Castle.

'There was once a country to the north where they executed their king,' said my grandfather. 'They held a trial and one after another, witnesses appeared and condemned him for his crimes against the people.

'In reality his crimes were small in comparison to those who had instigated the coup against him, but such details are easily forgotten in the excitement of revolution.

'The highest court in all the land – a court that had sworn its allegiance to the king on many occasions, and which had been his faithful and cruel servant – sentenced him to death.

'The king was taken to the vast square in front of the Winter Palace, the scene of many of the most celebrated executions in that country's long history, and there his head was struck from his body by a masked swordsman especially imported from the desert provinces where their swordsmen are renowned for their power, accuracy and heartlessness.

'When the king's head was struck from his neck, however, there was not the roar of approval the new regime had hoped for. Nor was there the riot or revolt they had feared and prepared for. Instead, the onlookers were silent, and seemed possessed of a deep and overwhelming melancholy.

'The executioner grabbed the head by the hair and showed it to the crowd in the time-honoured fashion. But this display was greeted by silence – even among the children, who are normally so bloodthirsty on these occasions. After a few moments they all shuffled away.

'Things did not improve in the next few days either. This gloom emanated outwards like a plague from those who had attended the execution until, one by one, the whole population was infected.

'All industrial output ground to a halt as workers either did not turn up at all or stood idly about if they did, staring at their boots or at the wall, shaking their heads despondently.

Classrooms stood empty as teachers lost the will to teach, children the urge to learn. Even the military started to be affected.

'In the end the junta had to bring the king back.'

'But they'd beheaded him,' said Frank, confused.

'They came to the conclusion that a headless king was better than none, and so it proved.'

'They put the headless body back on the throne?'

'Yes,' said Frank's grandfather. 'There was a countrywide day of celebration. The king was more popular than ever.'

'Without a head?' said Frank.

'Yes,' said his grandfather. 'Everyone agreed that in this new incarnation he seemed kinder, more thoughtful, more in touch with the people.'

Frank chuckled.

'What happened to the head?' he asked after a moment.

'Ah,' said his grandfather. 'I'm glad you asked. That was the only down side. There were constant rumours that the head was gathering followers in a neighbouring country and was plotting a triumphant return to reclaim the throne . . .'

Chapter 20

Frank stopped by the Battered Bookstore on Righteousness Avenue on his way home. It was his favourite bookshop in the city. It was the only one where pre-Revolutionary books were sold, rather than the Ministry-approved fiction that was the norm everywhere else. He had found some real treasures there.

This was pretty much the only place to find old books at all. The Ministry had shut down all the public libraries years before, saying that in times of austerity they were a luxury the state could no longer afford.

All new books were published by the Ministry and it also insisted on vetting every old book periodically to ensure that none of the content was 'unhelpful to a sense of citizenship'.

The Revolution had been led by intellectuals, so the Ministry could not quite bring itself to actually destroy books. Or not completely; not openly, not directly. They weren't book-burners. There had been long debates about what should be done. In the end it was decided that they would replace every cover with a plain brown one and take the last twenty pages out of every old book before allowing them to be sold as pre-Revolutionary examples of bourgeois wrong-thinking.

Why twenty and not fifty or five pages was never explained. Neither was it explained why taking the last pages made the book safer. This vandalism really had only one end – to make these books annoyingly unreadable for most people. But not for Frank. It made the books frustrating, yes – but it would take more than that to put him off completely. He saw it as a resistance to the Grey.

Frank pulled a book out from the shelf. He always – without fail – checked to see if the Ministry's ghouls had somehow forgotten to remove those pages – but they never had. Efficiency was the defining feature of the Grey. He sighed.

'Hello, Frank,' said Mr Trochanter, peering round from a set of shelves in the centre of the shop.

'Hello,' said Frank.

'That was a heart-felt sigh,' said the bookseller.

'I always think I'll find one that hasn't been butchered,' said Frank.

'I've never come across one, Frank,' said Mr Trochanter. 'Not in all my years in the book trade. They are very diligent at the Ministry.'

Frank frowned.

'Just once I'd like to know how that author intended the book to end.'

'But on the other hand, you are free to make your own ending,' said a voice behind him.

Frank turned to see a tall man with a long but friendly face standing behind him.

'Sorry?' said Frank.

The man smiled.

'Apologies for interrupting,' he said. 'I was just pointing out that with the last pages gone, you were released from the tyranny of the storyteller.'

'The tyranny of the storyteller?' said Frank, laughing. 'I don't see it that way at all.'

'What way do you see it?' said the man, stepping forward and looking at Frank.

Frank could see straight away he was a Ministry Man. High-ranking too, judging by his suit. He was immaculately dressed and groomed, with a precisely shaped slate-grey moustache.

'Sorry, sir,' he said. 'I'm sure you're right.'

Frank put the book on the counter and headed for the door. The man stepped in his way, stopping him without actually making contact. Frank's heart clenched like a fist.

'Don't run off,' said the man amiably. 'I'm genuinely interested. Honestly. We are alone, I assure you.'

Frank looked to Mr Trochanter but he was busying himself behind the counter. Besides, he knew the Ministry Man was not talking about Mr Trochanter.

'Well,' said Frank, swallowing hard, 'I . . . I see a story as the journey . . . and the ending as the destination. The getting there can be fun – you know, in itself – but I still want to get to where I'm going. That is, I want the author to know where we're going.'

The man nodded.

'Perhaps if more writers understood that,' he said. 'They might ensure that this destination was a hopeful one.'

'Hopeful?' said Frank. 'How do you mean?'

'Don't you think that readers – especially young ones like yourself – deserve hope? Shouldn't a story leave them with hope?'

'Not false hope,' said Frank.

'Should it not be optimistic, then?' continued the man with a smile. 'Why write a story that upsets people? Or depresses them? Or leaves them frustrated, filled with impotent rage? Particularly young people. What is the point of that?'

Frank shrugged and tried to weigh up the Ministry Man. He seemed to be one of those people who spoke very concernedly about young people without betraying the least affection for them.

'I don't think stories have to have a point,' said Frank. 'Not like that.'

The man smiled benignly back at Frank.

'But the Ministry goes to great lengths to publish books every year, aimed specifically at your age group,' said the man. 'A great deal of research has gone into those books.'

'I know,' said Frank, raising an eyebrow.

The man smiled again.

'You do not like the Ministry books?'

'I . . .'

The man nodded to indicate that he understood Frank's reluctance to criticise the Ministry.

'You prefer to read books with the last pages missing? Please – I'm interested. The Ministry books are very popular.'

'I know,' said Frank. 'Every one of them is a bestseller.'

'You don't approve of popularity?' asked the man.

'I don't disapprove of it,' said Frank. 'I don't approve of it. I don't really care about it at all, I suppose.'

'I see,' said the man. 'Suspicious, then? You are suspicious of popularity. You think perhaps that if something is popular, it must be trying too hard to please?'

Frank took a deep breath and paused before replying.

'I'd rather read a book by someone who cared about what they wrote – even with the last pages gone – than someone just writing what he was told to write or what he thinks I want to read.'

'You don't think a writer should think of his reader?' said the Ministry Man.

'No,' said Frank with a chuckle. 'I want to read stories by writers who don't care if I read their books at all.'

The man nodded but not in a way that made Frank think he agreed.

'May I?'

The man indicated that he would like to see the book Frank was buying. Frank handed it over. The man flicked through.

'You like stories of a fantastical nature,' he said, smiling.

'Not just those,' said Frank defensively. 'But yes – I do, I suppose.'

'As you know, the Ministry encourages the young to read stories about real people in real situations,' said the man. 'The Ministry encourages books that confront real issues that our citizens will have to deal with.'

Frank laughed.

'I know,' he said.

The man did not laugh with him, but still his smile was kindly.

'Oh,' said Frank nervously. 'You . . . You were serious. Sorry. I mean – those books are fine if you like that kind of thing, I suppose.'

'But you don't?' said the man.

Frank sighed. He knew he probably should just keep quiet, but no one had ever asked him about his taste in books. This man was the first person to ever show the slightest interest.

'I just want my mind to go in other directions than straight forward,' said Frank.

'Yes?' said the man.

'I want it to go . . . I don't know – sideways, you know?' said Frank. 'I can't explain it.'

'You've explained it very well. Sorry to take up your time.' The man handed the book back to Frank.

'You are at school?' asked the man.

'I've just left, sir,' replied Frank.

'An exciting time,' said the man.

'Yes, sir,' said Frank.

'May I ask what your plans are?' he asked.

'I'm still undecided, sir,' replied Frank.

'Really?' said the man. 'Then may I give you my card?'

He reached into his inside pocket and took out a small silver case with the royal crest of the raven and eyeball etched into its cover and opened it, taking out a small card with a name – Mr Vertex – and telephone number written on it in neat script.

'Thank you,' said Frank, putting the card in his pocket.

'Please,' said Mr Vertex. 'Call me. I think I have work you would find very interesting.'

'I don't know,' said Frank, smiling awkwardly.

'No pressure,' said Mr Vertex. 'Just think about it. Will you do that?'

Frank smiled.

'Yes, sir,' he said. 'Of course.'

Chapter 21

Clack–clackedy–thud–clack–clackedy–clack–clack–ping.

Shhhhhhrup.

Clack–clackedy–clack–clack–clack–thud–clakedy–clack–clack–ping.

Shhhhhrup.

Clack–clacl–clackedy–cla–

Frank pulled the paper out of his typewriter, peered at the words, screwed it up into a ball, tossed it into the bin with practised ease, and then fed a clean sheet onto the roller. He loved that noise the roller made as it welcomed the new page.

He typed his name and he typed the title and then he sat back staring at the words: *The Ghost Tram.* He looked at it for while before slowly edging forward with his finger poised over the keys. Then the door opened and his mother walked in. The Student stood up as she did so.

Frank had forgotten he was even there. It was as if he just materialised out of the dust motes floating in the air. He coughed and gripped his chest, slumping back down onto his bed.

'That's a nasty cough, dear,' said his mother, looking concernedly at the Student.

'Mother,' said Frank. 'You could at least knock.'

'Why?' said his mother, looking at the Student. 'It's not like you have a girl in here. Or is she under the bed?'

She looked at the Student and they both laughed, the Student's laughter turning into wheezing and coughing. They waited for him to finish, noisily swallowing his phlegm.

'Very funny,' said Frank after a moment. 'It's just polite. I'm trying to work.'

'Work?' she said in a tone Frank did not appreciate.

'Yes – work,' said Frank. 'I'm writing.'

His mother leant forward, squinting.

'The Gho—'

Frank snatched the paper from the roller and scrunched it up. The Student picked up his notebook and began to write. The effort seemed to exhaust him.

'Oh dear,' said his mother. 'Not going well?'

'Did you want something?' said Frank.

'Yes I did,' she said. 'I would like you to take some food to your father.'

'But –'

'No buts,' she said. 'He's stuck up at the Castle again doing preparation work for the Big Day.'

'What is he doing?' said Frank. 'It's not for months yet.'

'You know what he's like,' said Frank's mother. 'But he needs his food. Come on. We don't ask you to do much. And it's not like you're doing anything more important.'

Frank saw the quick glance she gave to the bin full of crumpled paper.

'Why can't the Student go?' said Frank.

'The Student can't go running errands for us,' said his mother. 'The things you say, Frank. Sometimes I think you deliberately go out of your way to –'

'All right, all right!' said Frank, putting his hands to his head. 'I'll go.'

Frank turned off at the Old Square and cycled towards the Castle. The road curved one way then the other, and became narrower and narrower and steeper and steeper until Frank had to stand up and lean forward and use all his strength to move at all.

The windows of the houses on either side became smaller and more widely spaced until eventually the road was towered over by massive walls that were the buttresses of the Castle proper, which now loomed over him like a threat in architectural form.

At the final bend there sprouted a flight of blackened steps that themselves, once again, steepened and narrowed, curling out of sight. Frank chained up his bike to a set of railings and began to climb on foot.

The steps rose up through an archway under a building and on the other side separated into three. Frank took the central one, which ducked under another building and out into a small, enclosed courtyard.

The steps continued again on the other side. The route was narrower but with steps twice as high so that Frank had to haul himself up using the ancient handrail. The buildings the stairway wormed its way through used to be houses, but were Ministry offices now – or deserted. It was hard to tell which were which.

Over his head swung ancient signs showing all manner of animals and symbols, mythological beasts and so on, the meanings of which had long been forgotten, but they were

said to mark the premises of the alchemists and magicians who lined the Castle Steps in days gone by.

They had been in the employ of the Emperor who kept them in the hope that they might develop a weapon to defeat his enemies or discover the means to turn base metals into gold. But all kinds of stories had circulated about what they really got up to in their laboratories – generating homunculi and raising the dead.

Gasping for breath, Frank finally staggered to the top of the last flight of steps and stood before the enormous, bronze, spiked entrance gate, flanked on either side by gargantuan statues of men fighting with mythical beasts, the stonework blackened like everything else in the city, but their weapons shining gold. Not real gold, naturally – that had been melted down by the Emperor long before.

The guards on the gate stood sternly beside their sentry boxes, huge peaked hats on their heads, their fur-trimmed coats at least a size too big, made to look even bigger by the boxed, padded shoulders. They grabbed their guns as he approached, but they all knew him.

'Just bringing sandwiches for my father,' said Frank.

The guard stepped forward with professional grimness and stomped to attention in front of Frank, took his papers and inspected them, looking from the photograph to Frank and then back to the photograph as though he had never seen him before and suspected the papers to be clever forgeries.

With a derisory sniff, the guard handed the papers back, stomped his boots, swivelled and set off towards the sentry box where he relayed Frank's words in a series of almost unintelligible barks, punctuated at the end with another crunching stomp of his boots.

The sentry saluted and then picked up a heavy black phone, cranking the numbers on the dial with some difficulty owing to his thick gloves. After a moment he mumbled something into the mouthpiece and slammed it down. Frank rocked back and forth on his feet, still catching his breath from the climb.

After a wait of only twenty minutes, Frank's father's secretary, Miss Tylida, came mincing across the courtyard behind the guards, the ticking of her heels echoing back and forth, an enormous shadow of her slanting across the Castle walls as she walked in front of one of the sentry searchlights. She swung her hips as she walked so that each step was in front of the other in a narrow, straight line. She could have been on a tightrope.

The guard came back to Frank, stamped and held out his gloved hand. Frank handed over the bag of sandwiches. The guard stomped, the studs of his boots sparking on the cobbles, swivelled, marched towards Miss Tylida, stomped (she always jumped), saluted and handed over the sandwiches. Miss Tylida nodded in thanks and waved at Frank, who waved in response. Then the guard marched back into position and Frank set off down the Castle steps.

Frank was just about to start the descent when a silhouetted figure loomed towards him, backlit by the glow of streetlight. It looked like a praying mantis encased in amber. Frank recoiled, stumbling against a wall.

'Is that young Mr Palp?' said a voice, quiet and well-bred.

The man stepped forward and light washed over his face.

It was the man from the bookshop. The Ministry Man. Frank recognised him but struggled to remember his name.

'Mr Vertex,' said the man, holding out his hand with a smile.

'Of course,' said Frank. 'How are you, sir?'

'I'm very well,' he replied. 'Are you working at the Ministry now?'

'No, sir,' said Frank. 'I was just bringing sandwiches to my father. He's working late.'

'That's very commendable,' said Mr Vertex. 'Your father must be very proud to have such a thoughtful son.'

'I suppose . . .' said Frank. 'I don't know.'

'Well, I won't keep you,' said Mr Vertex. 'Remember, I think I could find some interesting work for you here.'

'Yes, sir,' said Frank. 'Thank you, sir.'

Mr Vertex tipped his hat and set off towards the sentry boxes. Frank smiled at the idea that such a high-ranking Ministry Man would remember who he was. A lot of the teachers would struggle to remember his name by now. Frank was mildly troubled by that thought and shut it away.

If climbing the steps was an effort then descending was a different kind of trial. If anything, the steps seemed taller and steeper going down, and the fact that they leant so acutely downwards to allow rain to run off, meant that it was hard not to stumble and begin to run. Frank knew that were this to happen, he would never be able to stop until he reached the base of the hill – one way or another.

Frank was always pleased to get back to his bike. Pushing it down the hill, he felt more in control, more stable. The bike was a support – and it had brakes.

But this time, he felt different. He stood looking down at the impossibly steep cobbled street, spiralling away from him into the darkness, and felt like it was pulling him in. He got on his bike. He took a deep breath and pushed himself off.

Not that he needed to. Almost immediately he was going faster than he could have believed possible, clinging on to the handlebars for dear life, knowing that too tight a squeeze on the brakes would see him thrown, somersault-sprawling, bloody head over smashed heels, onto the waiting cobbles.

The wind stung his eyes as he flew downwards as if he was in a vortex, descending into a cobbled maelstrom, sucked down, down. The bike shook on the cobblestones and it rattled every nut, every cog, every bone and tooth. It seemed to scramble Frank's brain too. His vision became blurred and he felt light-headed.

His wheels spun so fast that his dynamo glowed like a lighthouse beam, blasting out a white glare so bright that Frank had to squint to look at it. It created a great bubble of luminous whiteness that pulled him on down the hill. Brightness. Darkness. Danger. Life.

When at last he reached the base of the hill and the incline began to flatten out, he pulled his breaks, gently at first, but tighter and tighter until he was squeezing them full force to stop himself flying out into the main road and under the tram that honked its horn in warning.

Looking back, panting, sweating, the street seemed to Frank nothing more than that – not especially steep, not especially special. The Castle was just a distant bruise on the horizon, as insubstantial as the storm clouds behind.

Chapter 22

At the weekend Frank cycled in front of Olivia's apartment block, passing for the third time without luck. He had been certain it would happen this time.

He had seen her so clearly in his head – the tight black jacket she would be wearing and the way she would flick her hair aside as she left the door, the sound of her boots on the gravel. She had been slightly less surprised to see him this time. She recognised him but was confused by his being out of context until he told her they sat near to each other in History and she said, 'Oh – of course!' and laughed and touched his arm.

He had said a couple of things that clearly amused her a lot and then they walked together along the shore until they reached the bridge and there, under its shadow, they fell into each other's arms.

'Hey!' shouted the old man, raising his umbrella like a sword.

'Sorry,' said Frank, startled from his waking dream.

'Shouldn't be riding on the pavement!'

'I know,' said Frank. 'I'm sorry.'

The old man shook his head and wandered off, muttering. Frank stood for a moment, straddling his bike, and looked back to Olivia's apartment building. For the first time some hope seemed to ebb away from him.

'What the hell are you up to?' said a voice behind him.

Who was it? Frank didn't know anyone this side of the bridge apart from . . . He turned. It was Scape.

'Nothing,' said Frank.

Scape stared at him, head cocked on one side. He laughed unpleasantly.

'Look at you,' he said. 'Always creeping about, aren't you?'

Frank shrugged and lost his footing on the kerb, his shoe slipping into the gutter. Scape laughed again.

'Relax,' said Scape. 'What do you think I'm going to do?'

Frank shrugged. He hadn't thought about it. Who the hell knew what Scape was going to do? Who cared?

'What brings you to the Old New Town, Palp?' said Scape, sounding proprietorial all of a sudden.

'Nothing,' said Frank. 'My grandfather's buried up at the cemetery. I'm visiting him and –'

'All right, all right,' said Scape. 'I didn't ask for your life story.'

Scape pushed his fringe back. Why was he still standing there?

140

'Anyway . . .' said Frank.

Frank started to walk away. Scape put out an arm and blocked his way. Frank's stomach lurched.

'What's the hurry?' said Scape.

'No hurry,' said Frank. 'I just . . . I just need to get on.'

Scape laughed. Frank hated him being here. Hated him contaminating this world. He belonged at school, to the past.

'Listen to you,' he said. '"I just need to get on." You sound like an old woman.'

Frank nodded, happy to agree if that would end the conversation.

'What have you got to do anyway?' said Scape. 'What are you really up to? You can tell me.'

'Nothing,' said Frank. 'I'm going to see my grandfather, like I said.'

'Oh – really?' said Scape.

'Yes,' said Frank. 'So . . .'

Scape stretched, groaning loudly. Frank stared at the ground, hoping Scape would get bored and go away.

'What are you doing – for work?'

Frank shrugged. Why was Scape still talking to him? This was possibly the longest they had ever been in each other's company. Certainly it was the longest time they had ever been alone together.

'What did you tell old Prosnorax at the careers interview?' said Scape. 'You must have told him something.'

'The Ministry,' said Frank.

Scape laughed.

'No kidding?' said Scape. 'Me too.'

Frank had to stop himself smiling at the idiocy of Scape seeing this as some kind of amazing coincidence. Almost everyone at that school would say the same thing.

'Course, your father's involved in the Big Day, isn't he?' said Scape. 'Amazing.'

'Yes,' said Frank.

Was that what all this was about? Why the sudden interest in what Frank or his father was doing?

'Why didn't you say anything about it at school?' said Scape.

Frank shrugged.

'I'd have been bragging about that all the time,' said Scape. 'You even get to watch in the Castle, don't you?'

Frank nodded. Scape whistled.

'Imagine that. Lucky bastard.'

'Yes,' said Frank. 'So I'm –'

'Maybe we'll be in the same department,' said Scape. 'At the Ministry. It's possible.'

Frank nodded. It was possible. That was one of the many reasons why working at the Ministry was such a dreadful thought. All these people he had just escaped from would reappear at the Ministry.

'I'm not even sure that –'

'Come on, Frank,' said Scape. 'What else are you going to do? Join the army?'

A gang of boys had marched off to sign up on the last day of term. Frank was surprised Scape hadn't been among them.

'Those aren't the only two options,' said Frank.

'Really?' said Scape. 'Tell me about the others, Palp.'

'Look, I've really got to go,' said Frank, turning his back on Scape. 'Sorry.'

'Sure,' said Scape. 'See you around.'

See you around? See you around? Why on earth would either of them want to see each other again if it could possibly be avoided?

Chapter 23

Frank cycled to the cemetery. The leaden sky was like a great, filthy, leaking sponge. *Drip, drip, drip.* Was summer already ending? The iron gate seemed even more reluctant to open than ever. Frank shoved it and shoved it, and the bottom of it ground into the path with a nerve-jangling screech. He was lucky he was so thin – and even then he found it a squeeze.

The tree above him scratched and twittered as a breeze trembled the topmost twigs and the sparse clumps of leaves. It was dark in the cemetery – darker even than normal, and dark as night in the streets around. The headstones were like ebony chess pieces, dumped in a heap ready for a game.

Frank had a collapsible umbrella with him and he opened it and balanced it on the top of his grandfather's gravestone and the one nearby, ducking and sitting underneath, using a folded newspaper to sit on. The rain pattered onto the black nylon with a vaguely disapproving tut.

'What's that?' said his grandfather.

'It's raining, Grandfather,' said Frank. 'It's hitting an umbrella.'

'Ah. So. What news?'

Frank took a deep breath. 'Well,' he said. 'I'm not sure there is any.'

He was determined to say nothing about Olivia – or even think about her in case his grandfather really could read minds.

'How are you finding life after school?'

Frank shrugged.

'I don't know,' he said. 'Nothing much has changed. I still haven't got a job, so it just feels like I'm on holiday.'

'Will you follow your father into the Ministry?'

'Not if I can help it,' said Frank. 'I don't really want to work there.'

'Where do you want to work?' said his grandfather.

'I don't know,' he said. 'But not there.'

What was this? First Scape and now his grandfather. Why did everyone suddenly give a damn about where he was going to work?

'There's no shame in working,' said his grandfather eventually.

'I know,' said Frank.

Although surely it depended on what you did. There was shame in some work, wasn't there?

'I used to work,' said his grandfather. 'I worked in an office at the Castle myself – although it was not called the Ministry then, it was called the –'

'The King's Office,' said Frank. 'I know, Grandfather. But that was different.'

'In what way?'

'Because things weren't so . . . so . . .'

Frank waved his arms around.

'If you mean "boring",' said his grandfather, 'believe me, it was boring. Mind-numbingly boring. You young people didn't

145

invent boredom, you know. It was just a way of paying the rent, no more.'

'But it meant you could write,' said Frank. 'It was a means to an end.'

'Yes,' said his grandfather. 'It was. I told myself that constantly. At each fresh humiliation, at each new level of pointlessness, I told myself that I was different from the others there.'

'And you were,' said Frank.

'Maybe,' said his grandfather.

'So you're saying I should work at the Ministry, but just think of it as a way of paying the bills?' said Frank. 'So that I can write?'

'I'm not telling you to do anything,' said his grandfather. 'My days of telling people what to do are long behind me, Frank. I'm dead.'

'I know,' said Frank.

Frank sighed and looked at the drips forming on the edge of the umbrella. The water gathered and grew heavy, hanging down until finally it broke away and fell to the ground. *Drip*.

'There was a man from a town near the mountains,' began his grandfather. 'He owned a factory making machine parts. He was a tough, friendless man; a hard boss, quick to fire anyone he thought was not doing their share of the work. But, unusually for his kind, he had a clean conscience and each night fell immediately into a deep sleep.

'But no sooner had he done so, he sat up in bed, swung his legs round and stood up. The man was still fast asleep, you understand, but he was a somnambulist: a sleepwalker. Like your uncle Rudi.'

'Uncle Rudi was a sleepwalker?' said Frank.

'Oh yes. He was a terrible sleepwalker all his life. Him and his wife – your aunt Frieda.'

'They were both sleepwalkers?' said Frank.

'Of course,' said Frank's grandfather. 'That's how they met.'

'Sleepwalking?'

'Yes,' said his grandfather. 'They came from the same village in a long wooded valley to the east. They would both rise from their respective beds to go sleepwalking. One night they met in the local square by moonlight and, well, love took its course, as love will.'

Frank tried to imagine them sitting in the moon shadows like ghosts, falling in love. He smiled and shook his head.

'But what happened to the man?' asked Frank. 'The man from the factory?'

147

'Oh, well,' said his grandfather. 'That was intriguing. Every night the man would get up, get dressed in a crisp white shirt, black tie, grey suit and drive through the empty streets to the factory of his main competitor where he clocked on to work the night shift.'

Frank chuckled.

'I love you, Grandfather,' he said.

'And I love you, Frank.'

Chapter 24

As Frank entered the lobby of his apartment block, he was aware that the silence he found himself enveloped in had followed in the wake of some noise he could not place. Then he noticed that the cables of the lift, visible above the door, were still trembling. It had just been used, he was sure of it.

The lift itself was not there. The lift was always there. But now it wasn't. Frank walked to the doors and put his hand on the metal handle. It vibrated. He felt it tremble through his fingers and up his arm. He saw the wires and cables settling back into place. He looked up but could see nothing.

'The Ministry might want to know about your interest in the lift,' said a voice behind him.

It was Mr Spiracle again. He stepped forward out of the shadows. His eyebrows were joined together, as though kissing each other, and made an unbroken strip across his forehead.

'What?' said Frank with a sigh. 'Why? I'm not interested in it. I just heard something. I'm allowed to look.'

'You're always hanging around,' said Mr Spiracle. 'Always sniffing around things that don't concern you.'

Frank lost his temper and took a hand out of his pocket, clenching his fist. As he did so, a small card fluttered to the tiled floor. Mr Spiracle ignored Frank's clenched fist and stooped to pick it up.

Mr Spiracle staggered back as he read the name on the card and he held it out to Frank with a shaking hand.

'I was joking,' he said, his voice trembling. 'You understand that, don't you? I . . . You . . . There is no need to . . .'

'I'm sick of you threatening to report me. I haven't done anything,' said Frank, taking the card from him.

'Report you?' said Mr Spiracle, laughing nervously. 'Why would I do that?'

Frank had never seen Mr Spiracle laugh. It wasn't a pleasant sight. He stared at him, baffled, and put Mr Vertex's business card back in his pocket. Mr Spiracle made a small bowing motion and retreated into the shadows, like a cockroach scuttling back into the skirting board.

Frank headed for the stairs, climbing two at a time. He opened the door to his apartment and his sister was standing in the hall, getting ready to leave.

'Hello, Frank,' she said, giving him a hug. 'I'm just on my way out.'

'Petra has been shopping with me,' said his mother. 'We've bought you a new coat.'

'What kind of a coat?' he asked suspiciously.

'You can't be fussy,' said his sister, 'when you won't come with us to shop.'

'Why can't I go on my own?' asked Frank.

'Because you'd buy something ridiculous and ridiculously expensive, that's why,' said his mother.

'Where?' said Frank. 'Where would I buy something

150

ridiculously expensive in this town? Is there some outrageous boutique I don't know about?'

Frank's mother brought the coat out, dusting it down.

'There!' she said, ignoring him. 'Even you can't complain about that.'

'What's that supposed to mean?' said Frank. 'I don't complain. Not any more than anyone else, I –'

'Shhhh, Frank,' said his sister. 'I've got to get back. Try it on. I picked it myself. You'll need a smart coat soon.'

'Why?'

'Everyone needs a smart coat,' said his mother.

'Do they?' said Frank.

'Of course they do,' said his mother. 'Supposing someone dies.'

'Ah,' said Frank. 'Of course. I wasn't thinking.'

'Stop being clever, Frank,' said his mother.

'Stop being clever,' repeated Frank. 'That could be our family motto. Perhaps I should get a tattoo.'

'Shut up,' said Petra, 'and try it on.'

Frank did as he was asked. The coat was at least one size too big. The sleeves covered his hands and he could have wrapped it round himself like a bathrobe.

'Doesn't he look smart?' said his mother.

'It's enormous,' said Frank. 'I look like I've shrunk.'

'Oh, you'll grow into it,' said his mother.

'How?' said Frank. 'How will I grow into it?'

'You're a growing boy,' she said.

'I'm seventeen,' he said. 'How much more growing do you think I'm going to be doing?'

151

'Your uncle Willem was still growing when he was thirty,' said his mother.

'Uncle Willem is *still* growing,' said Frank. 'It's all the pies he eats.'

'Take it off,' said his mother, ignoring him. 'You'll spoil it.'

'So now I can't wear it,' said Frank. 'It's too good for me. You should take it back.'

'Be quiet, Frank,' said his mother.

Frank took the coat off and shook his head in despair.

'I blame you,' said Frank to his sister as his mother took the coat away to hang it up.

'Me?' said Petra. 'You should have seen the one she was going to buy. If anything, you owe me.'

'Why does no one think I might have my own taste in coats?'

'Taste in coats?' said his mother. 'Since when did you have a taste in coats? We're not the sort who have a taste in coats. What nonsense.'

'I didn't say I did,' said Frank. 'I just said I might. I might have my own taste in things. Different from yours. Why is that so hard to imagine?'

'We couldn't afford to be so choosy during the War,' said his mother. 'We were grateful for whatever we had. No one is grateful any more.'

Petra nudged Frank in the ribs.

'Ow!' said Frank.

Petra nodded towards their mother. Frank sighed.

'Of course I'm grateful,' he said. 'Thank you.'

'You're welcome, I'm sure,' said his mother, pursing her lips.

The Student scribbled away in his notebook, his breath whistling like wind through dry grass. Frank stared at him but said nothing.

In the end, he walked away to his room, lay down and imagined what Olivia must look like naked. His imagination washed over her, back and forth, like a wave washing over a rock, flowing over every inch of her, inundating her.

He got up, loaded a sheet of paper into the typewriter and began to type.

Clack–clack–clack–clack–clackedy–clack–clack–clackedy–clack–ping.

Shrupp.

Clack–cla–

But it was no good. He could not think in words. He could only think in pictures and all those pictures were of Olivia. She had taken over his mind, taken possession of his imagination. Like a cuckoo chick, the thought of her pushed all other thoughts out of the nest and just grew and grew and grew.

Chapter 25

It was the last week of August. Results day had finally arrived and Frank stood on the balcony looking at the apartments opposite, trying not to think about it. Trying not to think about not thinking about it.

He had cycled past Olivia's apartment time and again, but never with a glimpse of her. Other people came and went, but never her. He had seen some of her neighbours so many times he must be starting to draw attention to himself. He was almost out of his allotted opportunities.

But more than that, Frank was starting to feel a little ridiculous. What had seemed like a sign of his persistence had lately seemed like a symbol of how desperate and pathetic he actually was. He had thought it would make him feel better, but it made him feel worse. Every single time.

There was a faint breeze blowing the washing hanging from the many clothes lines draped from balcony to balcony.

These clothes were the only trace of colour in the scene but even they were so muted by wash after wash that the view was still like looking at a faint, old photograph, once tinted, but long since faded. The Grey, the Grey.

Frank thought of the people behind those clothes. He realised

all of a sudden how little he knew about most of the people in those apartments, despite living here his entire life.

He started thinking about Dawn. She was the only one he ever saw from his childhood days, and he hardly ever saw her now. Petra had told him she had started work at a paper mill. He heard her walking about sometimes in the evenings, in the apartment upstairs. He heard her parents mainly. Her father was mostly away, but they always fought when he was back. Dawn's mother was drunk whichever.

Frank could see the vague shapes of people moving about in the apartments across the courtyard, between the shutters and past the balconies. He heard a woman singing in her kitchen. He heard rubbish being thrown in the dumpster down below.

'What time are you going to get your results?' asked his mother, appearing in the doorway.

'There's no hurry,' said Frank, turning round.

'Why?'

'The grades won't go down if I take my time.'

'Or up,' she said. 'Stop trying to be clever.'

Frank smiled. His mother was twisting a tea towel between her hands, pink from scrubbing.

'I thought you'd be excited,' she said.

'Sorry,' said Frank. 'I'm not.'

He turned back, unwilling to extend this conversation. His mother continued.

'Nervous then,' she said. 'Worried.'

Frank shook his head and sighed. He turned back to her.

'No,' he said. 'I don't feel anything, actually.'

'You must feel something,' said his mother tightly. 'You are silly sometimes.'

Frank opened his mouth but thought better of it and closed it again. What was the point? She stepped out of his way as he came back into the apartment.

'I just don't see how you can't want to know,' she said.

Frank shrugged.

His mother flicked the tea towel and it slapped the doorframe. 'Oh you do make me angry sometimes!'

'All right! I'll go this afternoon,' he said, putting his hands up in surrender. 'For crying out loud.'

'Why not go this morning?' said his mother.

'What difference does it make?' shouted Frank in exasperation. 'What difference does any of it make? Whether

I go this morning or this afternoon – or never? I'm not going to university. We can't afford it – we all know that. What point is there in getting good results?'

Frank's mother nodded, tears welling in her eyes.

'Well,' she said. 'I see. Of course.'

Frank immediately felt guilty. It wasn't his mother's fault they couldn't afford for him to go to university, he knew that. He did.

'Sorry,' he said.

'No,' said his mother with a weak smile. 'You're right.'

But Frank could tell she was on the verge of crying and he could not bear to see her cry. He wanted to hold her but could not make himself step forward, make his arms reach out.

His mother walked away, but after a few steps stopped and turned back.

'If I'd taken them,' she said 'I'd want to know. I'd want to see how I'd done. That's all. The War interrupted my schooling and we never got back to it after. I never took any exams so I don't know what it's like to do them and not care. I can't imagine it, you see. I'm not clever like you, Frank.'

Frank closed his eyes and hung his head.

'All right,' he said. 'I'll go and get the results now.'

His mother grinned and opened her arms to embrace him. She grabbed him in a bear hug and squeezed him.

'Now then,' she said. 'Was that so hard?'

Frank turned on to Fortitude Bridge. The Grey seemed especially powerful as he started to cross. A fog was rising up from the river and coiling itself around the bases of the angels, draped and clinging to the rough stone like a pale chiffon scarf.

Frank cycled on, determined not to look at them, but horribly aware of them as always. Halfway across, the chain came off his bicycle and Frank cursed as the pedals locked and he juddered to a halt on the cobbles. A tram bellowed its horn at him, as he quickly pulled his back wheel out of its path.

He dragged the bike onto the pavement and leant it against the base of an angel. He crouched down and pulled at the chain, cursing as his fingers quickly became coated in filthy black grease.

Frank rocked the pedals back and forth until the chain caught on the cogwheel, and stood up, wiping his hands on the wall and then on his coat.

It had become almost silent. The bridge was free of traffic. The fog had thickened and Frank could barely see the other side of the bridge. He looked up and saw that the angel above him was likewise obscured.

But then, while he watched, the fog momentarily parted and the angel lurched suddenly into sharp focus. The effect was startling – horrifying, even. It seemed as though the angel moved towards him, its shattered black face looming over him.

Frank jumped on his bicycle and bounced off the kerb, rattling over the cobbles, head down, face almost resting on his handlebars, until he was well clear of the bridge and the fog and the angels.

His heart was pounding in his chest and his breath came in short gasps that occasionally came out as whimpers. He looked back at the angels, seemingly floating on the fog there as though seated on clouds.

Frank turned onto Perseverance Boulevard, casting a swift glance at Olivia's apartment but telling himself that this pass did not count. Although, as he cycled past he wondered what would happen if she suddenly appeared at the door. Would it be within the rules of the game to stop and talk to her? Would that be allowed? He decided it would. Of course it would.

But Olivia did not appear.

Frank wondered if he would see Olivia at the school and that thought lightened his mood as he cycled past her apartment block, but by the time he reached the school gates his mood had darkened once again.

The Grey was close and stifling that day. Frank could actually feel it on his back as he cycled, felt it brushing against his face like cobwebs. He was gasping by the time he got off his bike and chained it up.

Most of the students had come in earlier it seemed because the school was almost empty. Frank was glad. This place was in the past for him now and it seemed wrong to even be here – the last thing he wanted was to actually speak to anyone.

Frank walked through the quadrangle to the office, knocked on the door and walked in. As he did so, there was the sound of something falling over and Mrs Lamella, the school secretary, appeared from a store cupboard adjusting her blouse and putting her glasses back on.

'Ah,' she said. 'A late-comer.'

Her lipstick was smudged.

'I've come for my results,' said Frank, feeling the need to say something.

'What was that?' she said, as she opened the filing cabinet drawer.

'My results,' said Frank.

'Of course,' said Mrs Lamella. 'Name?'

She knew his name.

'Frank Palp.'

'Frank . . . P–P–P–P–Palp . . . Ah – here we are.'

Mrs Lamella pulled out a brown Ministry envelope and handed it to him.

'Thank you,' said Frank, turning to leave.

'Not so fast, young man,' she said.

'Sorry?' said Frank.

'I need you to sign this,' she said, pushing a form towards him. 'Otherwise you might say you hadn't picked them up and, well, I'd be in trouble, wouldn't I?'

160

'Why would I say I hadn't picked them up?' asked Frank, taking the pen he was handed and signing his name.

'I have no idea,' said Mrs Lamella. 'Only you know that.'

There was another sound of something falling. This time accompanied by a hiss of pain. Mrs Lamella froze, smile fixed, and did not move again as Frank left the office. As he walked back across the quad, he turned, and looking through the dusty window, caught a glimpse of Mr Prothorax squeezing himself out of the cupboard.

Frank cycled away until he found himself at the corner of Perseverance Boulevard and came to a halt at one end of Olivia's apartment block.

Frank stood for a while, straddling his bike, holding the envelope. He looked back towards the school, then off at the cemetery, around to the Castle, and finally at Olivia's apartment. Tears welled in his eyes. He knew that opening this envelope was the end of something.

He slid a finger under the pasted flap and ripped through the paper. There was one single sheet with his name at the top and a list of the grades below. He read them one by one. They were neither a disappointment nor a surprise.

Maybe the future was waiting for him after all. Maybe it was there, ready to ambush him in all its grey mediocrity. Is that why Frank had never been able to see it before – not because it wasn't there, but because it was no different than the present? That thought was unbearable.

All of a sudden the letters and numbers of his grades seemed like a judgement on him. They were not the results of anyone special, as he had always believed himself to be; they were the results of the very average person he was in reality. There was no secret alter ego. There was no Super-Frank. There was just Frank.

He coughed, choking on the tears that were now rising, and he lifted his face to the glowering sky and stared into the great, grey void, looking for some kind of sign he knew, even as he looked, he would not find.

He had been sure that he didn't care at all and his feeling of desolation was all the more pronounced for being so unexpected. It grabbed him in its jaws and shook him until he felt that he might be ripped apart. His head was spinning. He felt sick.

He tried to think of Olivia, imagining that her image would be some kind of shield, but as quickly as he imagined her, the picture of her was shattered into a thousand fragments and carried away on the same grey tidal wave of despair as everything else.

It was a moment of revelation. Not one that came with a blinding flash of pure white light. This one was more like the pulling aside of a drab, tattered curtain to reveal something sad and wretched in the shadows.

Frank realised now that his obsession with Olivia had simply served as a distraction. Everyone was right – even Scape was right: there was no avoiding reality. Olivia couldn't protect him from that. Even if he had bumped into her – what then? He cringed with embarrassment that he had ever let himself believe in such nonsense.

Frank wheeled his bike back across Fortitude Bridge. The angels held no fear for him now. At the base of each one he punched out and connected with the plinth, making an audible thud. The first one hurt, but by the time he had reached the fifth he did not feel it at all, even though he was dimly aware that he had taken the skin from his knuckles.

He stopped and stared at his hand but he felt none of the dramatic power he had hoped for. He cursed as he realised he was still carrying on with the delusion that his actions meant something. He had hoped it would be raw and visceral, but it just seemed fake. Pain flooded in over his hand as though it had been doused in petrol and set alight, but even the pain could not make him feel important.

Whatever he said or did, he could not shake off the feeling that all his words, all his actions, were second-hand – that they had already happened, or that they were happening now but to a character in a book, not a real person.

Frank stood staring up at the soaring rebel angels, daring them to come to life, reach down and crush him in their crumbling, soot-stained hands. But they did not move.

The angel opposite had lost its face entirely and was now just a featureless flat oval. Her – his? – wings looked like rips in the substance of Frank's world, revealing a void of infinite darkness beyond.

That un-face seemed to stare down at Frank and it was the bleakest gaze his eyes had ever met. It was like looking into the face of Death's own death. It seemed to go straight to his soul – to peer into his soul and see nothing. The face was a mirror of his own emptiness. He felt scooped out, hollow.

Frank felt a queasy tightness in his gut. He felt suddenly racked with embarrassment and cycled home, filled with shame and confusion, rain and tears dripping down his face.

Chapter 26

Frank chained his bike up in the courtyard of his apartment block. Already a new calmness had come over him. He smiled sadly at Maxilla the tomcat.

'Hello, Max.'

Maxilla narrowed his eyes at him and hissed. Frank hissed back, and the cat got up and walked away sullenly, head down, ears back, his white heart patch rocking back and forth. Frank's legs felt like lead.

'Bad day?' said Dawn, who was sitting on the bench, arms around her curled-up legs, hugging herself. He hadn't even noticed her.

'Dawn,' he said. 'What are you doing out here?'

'My father's back,' said Dawn as though to her own feet. 'They're yelling at each other and seeing who can drink themselves unconscious the quickest.'

'Sorry,' said Frank.

Dawn shrugged. Frank took a deep breath and after a moment sat down beside her. He didn't say anything for a while because he had a sudden panic that if he tried to speak he would cry, and if he cried he might not be able to stop. Dawn seemed to sense this and it was a long time before she spoke.

'Results a bit disappointing?' she asked quietly.

Frank let out a snorted laugh.

Dawn waited for him to carry on but he said nothing more. He just stared ahead, chewing on the inside of his lip.

'What's the matter, Frank?' she asked, turning and laying her hand on his arm. 'I've never seen you like this.'

He laughed again.

'Really?' he said. 'You've never seen me miserable?'

Dawn smiled.

'Miserable, yes,' she agreed. 'You are pretty much always miserable – but not sad. I've just never seen you sad.'

Frank choked back tears.

'Is that what you think?' he said. 'That I'm always miserable?'

'Sorry,' she said. 'Come on, I was just –'

'I don't mean to be,' said Frank. 'I don't want to be. I don't choose to be.'

'I never said –'

'Do you remember when we were little? How we used to talk about who we'd be when we grew up?' said Frank.

'Yes,' said Dawn. 'Of course.'

It was a few moments before Frank could continue, and when he did, he stared towards the far wall of the courtyard as though watching a movie. Dawn followed his gaze as though she almost expected to see it too.

'You were going to be a painter,' he said. 'And I was going to be a great writer. Remember?'

Frank chuckled drily and shook his head. He felt so much older than he had been that morning. The thought of that Child-Frank amused him now.

'I was going to be a *great* painter,' corrected Dawn. Her own smile had cooled now, along with her voice.

Frank carried on, ignoring Dawn's tone.

'I suppose everyone must be like that when they're kids,' said Frank, coughing as his voice faltered.

'What do you mean?' said Dawn.

He turned to face her, his eyes shining.

'Everyone must dream when they're kids. Of being something special.'

'Why does it have to be a dream?' said Dawn.

'Because it does,' snapped Frank. 'And it's a waste of time and a waste of energy.'

Dawn shook her head.

'No, Frank,' she said. 'Don't.'

'I just . . .'

He shook his head, unable to find the words for a moment.

'All my life I've thought that something would just . . . would just happen,' said Frank. 'I didn't know what it would be. I felt like it would be something special. I thought that I deserved that somehow. It turns out that I don't.'

'Listen to you,' said Dawn. 'Your life has hardly started.'

'I know,' said Frank. 'I know.'

These intended words of comfort had made Frank even more bitter. A tear rolled down his cheek as he shook his head.

'Don't give up hope, Frank,' said Dawn, reaching out to him, putting his hand in hers.

She smiled kindly but Frank refused to catch her eye.

'What's the point of hope if the hope you have is a lie?' said Frank. 'Better to have no hope at all than false hope.'

'You don't believe that,' said Dawn. 'I know you don't.'

'I do believe it,' said Frank matter-of-factly.

He turned to face her now, eye to eye.

'I do believe it.'

'You have to have hope,' said Dawn.

'Do I?'

Frank turned to face her. She just didn't get it. She just couldn't see what had happened. She thought she was still talking to Old-Frank.

'I'm not like you, Dawn,' said Frank, wiping his face and sniffing.

'Oh?' she said, positively cold now. 'And what am I like?'

'I've seen you,' said Frank.

He felt composed now.

'You've seen me what?'

'You know what I mean,' said Frank with a sigh. 'You say you don't have any time for the people we used to laugh at but you do when it suits you.'

Dawn frowned.

'Is this because I danced at the school party?'

Frank sighed. This was becoming boring. He stood up.

'You were right,' said Frank in a tired voice, his eyes half closed. 'Better to accept life as it is.'

'I've never said that,' said Dawn.

'Well,' said Frank with a shrug. 'In any case. I just see things clearer now.'

'Good for you,' said Dawn, turning away.

Frank looked at her for a while. The day before he would have sat back down, desperate for Dawn to understand exactly what it was he was talking about, but he seemed to have shed that urge. He knew Dawn would never understand and he accepted it. That urge to be understood was another skin he had shed.

'Bye, Dawn,' he said, and walked to the stairs.

Frank took off his coat and entered the lounge where his parents were watching television with the Student.

The Student turned to face him, all pale grey and bones too near the surface, like the frame of a tent pushing at the canvas from inside. Frank actually flinched. The Student's skin glistened in the glow-worm light of the television, his eyes heavy-lidded.

'Father,' said Frank, looking away from the Student with a barely suppressed shudder.

'Yes,' said his father, without taking his eyes off the screen.

'I've decided that you're right. It's time I got a job,' said Frank. 'At the Ministry.'

Frank's father turned slowly to face him. The laughter on the television echoed round the room. The Student picked up his notebook and pencil.

'Well,' said his father. 'Everybody has to in the end.'

Frank smiled.

'I know,' he said. 'I'm sorry – sorry about all that stuff I said. I was just being silly – childish.'

'Was?' said his father. 'And what are you now?'

The Frank of the day before would have been annoyed by his father's tone of voice, but today he was happy to join his father in mockery of that silly, childish Frank.

'Have you applied?' said his father.

'Tomorrow,' said Frank. 'I'll apply tomorrow. I've got my results now, so –'

'How did you do, sweetheart?' said his mother.

'OK,' said Frank. 'I did fine.'

He handed her his results.

'There,' she said. 'You see. Such a clever boy.'

'You won't regret it, son,' said his father.

Frank nodded. Then his father and the Student both turned back towards the television. Frank walked to his room, took his coat off and threw it on the bed. He stared at Mirror-Frank.

'Come on,' said Frank. 'Say it.'

Mirror-Frank did not move or say a word.

'I know you think I'm a hypocrite,' he said. 'Well, I don't care.'

Mirror-Frank remained silent.

'I don't care,' said Frank.

Mirror-Frank turned and walked away.

Frank didn't even bother pretending to be asleep when the Student came in, but rolled over to face the wall as he got undressed. The Student clicked the light off and lay on the bed.

'Listen,' said Frank.

'What?' said the Student, his voice tired and distant, as though he was speaking from inside a box.

'That suit of yours,' said Frank.

'What about it?'

'It doesn't fit,' said Frank.

'It's all I can afford,' said the Student defensively. 'It's not polite to –'

'Shhh,' said Frank. 'I'm not having a go at you. I have a new coat that's a size too big. Trousers too. How about we swap?'

The Student didn't reply. Frank could tell he was mulling it over.

'Yes,' said the student with a cough. 'Why not? If it would be useful.'

'I just need a suit for an interview,' said Frank. 'Once I get a job then I can buy my own. It's a good coat. You'll be warm. When you go out, I mean. You do go out, don't you?'

The Student nodded.

'Can I ask you a question?' said the Student. 'Would you mind?'

'No,' said Frank. 'Go ahead. Although I'm surprised there's anything about me you don't know already.' 'When you apply to the Ministry . . .' he said.

'Yes?' said Frank.

'Can I ask if you are planning to work with . . . Mr Vertex?'

Frank frowned.

'You know Mr Vertex?' asked Frank.

The Student licked his lips.

'Mr Vertex is a very important man at the Ministry,' he said. 'Once he was kind enough to take a special interest in me.'

'How did you know I knew him?' asked Frank.

The Student coughed, but said nothing.

'You went through my pockets,' said Frank.

The Student shrugged.

'I'm sorry,' he said. 'It's what I do. It's not personal.'

Frank took a deep breath. 'Ah – it doesn't matter,' he said.

'How did you meet Mr Vertex, may I ask?' said the Student.

'I met him in a bookshop.'

'Ah,' said the Student, nodding. 'He does have a special interest in books. But . . .'

'But?' asked Frank.

'Perhaps it might be better for you to let your father introduce you to the Ministry,' said the Student. 'He would be very proud to do so. The Ministry always looks favourably on the children of employees.'

Frank smiled.

'You like him, don't you?' said Frank. 'My father.'

'Yes,' said the Student. 'Of course.'

'Why?' said Frank.

'Why do I like your father?' asked the Student.

'Yes,' said Frank. 'He doesn't seem very likeable most of the time – and I'm his son.'

The Student looked taken aback.

'But he takes such an interest in what you do,' said the Student.

'Does he?' asked Frank. 'Really?'

'Of course,' said the Student. 'You're not always around to hear it. But it's all in my notebooks. I could let you look if –'

Frank shook his head.

'No,' he said. 'That would be too weird.'

'Then you'll have to take my word for it,' said the Student.

At that he started coughing and Frank waited for him to calm himself and continue but the coughing did not stop. Frank didn't know what to do. He leant over and patted the Student on the back as he had seen people do in such situations. It did not seem to make any difference.

'I'll get you some water,' said Frank and left the room to fill up a glass in the bathroom.

By the time he had returned, the Student was now only wheezing, lying on his back, clutching his chest with a pained expression.

'Sit up,' said Frank. 'And drink this.'

The Student slowly did as he was told, taking the glass and sipping.

'I think you need something hot,' said Frank. 'I'm making you some tea.'

'No,' said the Student. 'I'll be fine.'

'I'm making you some tea,' said Frank.

The Student looked at him.

'Why do you care?' he said.

Frank shrugged.

'I don't know. You're keeping me awake with all that spluttering,' he said.

The Student smiled and nodded, coughing as Frank left the room. As Frank walked down the corridor towards the kitchen, his mother opened the door to her bedroom.

'Frank?' she whispered. 'What's the matter?'

'Nothing, Mother,' said Frank. 'I'm just getting the Student some tea. He's not well.'

She smiled.

'Well, aren't you kind?' she said. 'I thought you were sleepwalking. Your uncle Rudi was a sleepwalker, you know.'

'Yes,' said Frank. 'I know.'

Frank made a cup of tea and brought it back to the Student, who was sitting up now. Frank handed him a couple of pills.

'Take these,' he said. 'They'll help.'

The Student did as he was told. He sipped his tea and looked at Frank. There was clearly something troubling him.

'Frank,' he said. 'Please let your father introduce you to the Ministry. I don't think you would like working for Mr Vertex.'

Frank sat down on his bed and nodded.

'All right,' he said. 'Stop going on. Drink your tea.'

Chapter 27

Frank sat back looking up at the cemetery tree, high above him. Its naked branches seemed to go on for ever, dividing and subdividing into infinity, disappearing into the cloud that was so low it appeared caught in the twigs like sheep's wool in a hedge. He shouldn't have come. He wasn't really in the mood.

It was cold and Frank couldn't get comfortable. He had put a book down to sit on, but he was worried about resting his jacket against the headstones. A spider made its way along a flimsy thread, scurrying, pausing, scurrying again. Frank turned his jacket collar up and shivered.

'Is that you, Frank?' said his grandfather. The voice sounded muffled and damp and Frank might have mistaken it for the rustling of leaves had he not been listening for it.

'Yes, Grandfather,' he said, watching the spider climb up onto a gravestone and scuttle away. 'It's me.'

'You sound faint, Frank,' he said.

'Do I?'

'What?' said his grandfather.

Frank sighed, feeling guilty that he was already wishing he hadn't come.

'Frank?' said his grandfather.

'Yes!' said Frank, a little more forcefully than he had intended. 'I'm here, Grandfather.'

There was a moment of silence and Frank shifted uneasily.

'Grandfather?' said Frank, closing his eyes. He hugged himself against the damp chill.

'I'm going to ask Father to introduce me to the Ministry,' said Frank, shivering. 'I'm finally getting a job.'

'Ah,' said his grandfather. 'He will be proud. You sound . . . tense. Is anything the matter?'

'I'm not tense,' said Frank.

He was. He was tense.

'Well, I hope the interview goes well,' said his grandfather. 'I'm sure it will. I remember when –'

'You don't mind?' said Frank.

'Mind?' said his grandfather. 'Why would I mind?'

'Because . . .'

'It's not for me to tell you what to do, Frank,' said his grandfather. 'I'm old. I'm dead. You must decide these things for yourself.'

'But I thought you hated the Ministry,' said Frank.

'I've told you that I worked there,' said his grandfather. 'Why are you behaving as if it was a secret I kept from you?'

'I'm not,' said Frank.

'Do you want my disapproval?' said his grandfather.

'No . . .' said Frank.

But he did. He saw that now. He wanted to be told he was a disappointment. He wanted someone to say he was a disgrace – that to work there was a betrayal of everything he'd always said. He wanted someone else to say all this, because he could not say it himself.

Another silence.

'Maybe you could tell me a story,' said Frank.

'If you want me to,' said his grandfather.

'Of course I do,' said Frank, stifling a yawn. 'Please.'

His grandfather took a deep, sibilant breath that sounded like the dust falling on dry skin. Listening to it, Frank felt disconcertedly like he too was falling through the air, draining away like sand in an hourglass.

'There was a country on the other side of the mountains,' said his grandfather, 'where they found a way of taxing dreams.'

'Taxing dreams?' said Frank. 'How?'

'Oh, I don't know the specifics,' said his grandfather. 'I'm not a scientist. But they came up with a way of doing it, you can be sure of that.'

'But how did they tax them?' said Frank.

'Questions, questions. Well, they taxed them like they tax anything else, my boy,' he said. 'A certain percentage of every citizen's dreams were forfeit to the state. I can't remember the exact percentage.'

176

'And how were they collected?' said Frank.

Frank thought he could hear his grandfather grinding his teeth.

'There was a special apparatus in every bedroom,' said his grandfather.

'Special apparatus?' said Frank.

He surprised himself with the sceptical tone of his voice.

'Yes,' continued his grandfather, not noticing or ignoring it. 'As soon as the sleeper began to dream, the mechanism whirred into action. It would record the dreams, calculate the amount due and harvest it without the sleeper even knowing. It was quite painless, they say.'

Frank sighed.

'But what was the point?' he said. 'What happened to all those dreams that were collected?'

'I'm afraid this is where the story goes very wrong,' said his grandfather. 'They were meant to be stored in a vault – a special, secure vault, built specifically for this purpose – but of course it was only a matter of time before its security was compromised.

'The job of guarding the dreams was not well-paid and had little in the way of interest or distraction. The keepers began watching the stolen dreams. The authorities tried to stop it, but once they had started, the urge was too great.'

Frank nodded.

'And it got worse. The keepers realised what an asset they had in their possession. They began to borrow the dreams – for their own personal use at first, but a thriving black market in the harvested dreams began to appear over time.

'Of course, you could not know in advance what kind of dream you were going to get. It could be a complicated dream involving childhood memories – meaningless to anyone but the original dreamer, or it could be a pornographic dream of such unbridled debauchery that all but the most degraded imagination would struggle to cope. They could be nightmares – terrible, terrible nightmares. Although some people wanted those more than any other.'

'Why?' said Frank.

'Because they wanted the thrill, ' said his grandfather. 'They wanted to feel terror. Fear makes you feel alive.'

Frank nodded.

'The whole of society became hooked on these dreams,' said his grandfather. 'From the highest to the lowest, as cheap copies were made and distributed. The dreams were distorted and degraded each time they were copied, of course, and soon even the most benign dream took on a nightmarish edge.'

'What happened in the end?' asked Frank

'These confused, damaged dreams spread through the whole of society – dreams so fractured and enigmatic that even the most optimistic dreamer was corrupted or demoralised by them.

'Life came to a halt. No work was done. Travellers remarked at how men deserted their wives and mothers their children. The whole country collapsed. It is a place of ruin and decay to this very day.'

Frank shook his head.

'Your stories often end this way, don't they?' said Frank.

'Eh?' said his grandfather.

'Your stories,' said Frank, rubbing some life back into his leg. 'They are so . . .'

'Yes?'

'So . . . weird.'

There was a long pause.

'I thought you liked that,' said his grandfather.

'So did I,' said Frank.

'I see.'

'Sorry,' said Frank. 'Don't get me wrong. I have really loved them. I'm just saying that they aren't very realistic.'

'They are to me.'

'It doesn't matter,' said Frank. 'Forget I said anything. I didn't mean to upset you.'

Frank waited for his grandfather to respond but he didn't. Frank thought he heard something but it could have been a worm tunnelling or the soil settling.

Chapter 28

Mr Prementum looked at Frank in the mirror and nodded as he placed the cover over his shoulders and cranked the chair up a couple of notches. Mirror-Frank raised a quizzical eyebrow.

'The usual?' said Prementum, his comb already tugging at Frank's hair.

'No,' said Frank.

Mr Prementum continued as though Frank had said nothing.

'No,' repeated Frank.

Mr Prementum stopped and looked at him in bafflement, turning his good ear towards Frank.

'Not the usual?' he said. 'But Mr Palp always –'

Frank turned round in the chair and looked Mr Prementum in the face – something he realised he had almost never done – and seeing his un-mirrored face with the tin ear on the other side, made it feel like looking at a twin.

'I know,' said Frank. 'But I want something different.'

The barber looked nervously towards the empty chair where Frank's father would normally sit.

'Shall we wait for you father to –'

'No,' said Frank. 'He's just popped to the bank. He told me he'd meet me here when he'd finished.'

'But –'

'It's my hair,' said Frank. 'I know my father normally says what I'd like and I know you were in the army together and everything, sir, but . . . well, I want it like this.'

Frank fished out a crumpled photograph from a magazine and handed it to the barber, who looked at the photo, then at Frank, and then nodded with a smile.

'Of course,' he said, tapping his tin ear and winking.

When he had finished, Frank looked at the mirror and felt for the first time in a long time that there was nothing there but his reflection. Mirror-Frank was gone for good. New-Frank looked back. Better-Frank.

His hair was shorter now and most of the mass of curls had been cut out, apart from at the front, where they reared up and thrust out over his forehead. Mr Prementum had, on his instructions, applied a little hair oil and his hair now shone with a lustre it had never had before.

With the hair removed from above his ears, Frank's face looked older and tougher. His lifelong habit of looking up through his eyebrows disappeared in an instant.

There was a new, hard edge to his features. He would never be good-looking, he knew that, but at least he did not look pathetic any more. His new look suited his new mood. He now looked more like he felt – and that felt good.

'What the –' said Frank's father when he looked over his newspaper.

Frank had seen his father come in without taking more than a fleeting glance over towards Frank and Mr Prementum. He stared at Frank as though not fully recognising him.

'I didn't want to look like that any more,' said Frank 'I need a new image.'

'A new image?' said his father. 'A new image? We don't have images. We're not the kind of people who have images. Who do you think we are?'

'For the interview,' said Frank. 'I need something more . . . more grown up.'

His father's frown softened a little.

'At the Ministry,' continued Frank.

'Well, I suppose you do look a bit smarter, come to think of it,' said his father. 'But I don't know what your mother's going to say.'

His father put the newspaper down and went to pay, still glancing back at Frank confusedly.

'Father?' said Frank as they walked away from the barber's. 'There's something I want to ask you.'

His father stopped.

'And what might that be?' he said.

'I wondered if you might – that is, I wondered if you would, you know – recommend me to the Ministry?' asked Frank.

Frank's father face slowly collapsed into a wide grin, his moustache stretching with it.

'Well, of course,' he said. 'I thought you were never going to ask.'

Frank smiled sheepishly.

'My father introduced me,' said his father. 'They like that up at the Castle. It sets the right tone. They see it as a family up there. And between you and me, what with the Big Day and everything, it won't do your prospects any harm either.'

'Grandfather introduced you?' asked Frank.

It was a curious image.

'That's right,' he said. 'I know you only think of him as writing those weird stories of his, but he worked there before the Revolution and after. He had to pay the rent and feed me and your grandmother. She worked there too, actually. That's where they met.'

'Really?'

'Ask him,' said his father.

They carried on their way, walking a little closer to each other, Frank noticed, than they usually did.

'Why don't you ever visit him?' asked Frank.

'We said everything we needed to when he was alive,' said Frank's father. 'We never got on. We never understood each other. Never really tried, I suppose. That's how it is sometimes.'

His father turned to him and smiled sadly. Frank nodded, waiting for his father to continue. But he said nothing more and they carried on their way with barely a word until they arrived back at the apartment building.

Frank's mother burst into tears when she saw him. At first Frank thought it was because he had chopped off too much of his curly hair, but then he realised it was because she recognised the moment: the end of his childhood. The end of all that.

Chapter 29

Frank handed the sentry the letter inviting him to interview. The sentry peered at it, scanning each line solemnly, then he turned on his heels and marched to his superior, who did the same with the letter until he nodded. The sentry clicked his shiny black boot heels, turned to Frank and waved him through.

Frank felt a strange rush of excitement as he walked through the gates and on towards the Great Archway, when only seconds before he had been suppressing an urge to run away as fast as he could.

Finally walking through the Great Archway was a genuine thrill – something he had wanted to do since he was a small boy. But of course this was simply the first of many arches, many arcades and courtyards.

The Castle was like a series of boxes, one inside the other, each more complex than the last. It was a maze of corridors to match the maze of tunnels that ran below it. This was why he handed a coin to one of the many Guides who stood about at the entrance to the first courtyard.

The Guides earned a good living making sure that visitors arrived at their destination. They knew the corridors and stairwells of the Ministry like the faces of their own children. What might seem like an identical corridor to the visitor – wax polished floor, flickering strip lights, pale grey walls, dark grey fire doors – was unique to the Guides.

Those foolish enough to think they might manage without their services soon rued this penny-pinching. It was said that more than one visitor had been lost for good, mistakenly wandering down into the tunnel complex below, never to be seen again.

Frank followed hard on the heels of his Guide, who walked at a disturbingly brisk pace, hunched over, a bald patch smack in the centre of a mop of lank hair. Frank panicked every time the man disappeared round a corner, sure that he would be gone for good when Frank himself rounded it.

But the Guide was thoroughly reliable. He did not speak during the entirety of their convoluted journey through the corridors of the Castle but did, at the arrival at their destination, wish Frank a cursory 'good day', before setting off once more, with a quick bow, like a rat into the sewer pipes.

'Yes?' said the secretary. 'Can I help you?'

She had long hair pulled back in a ponytail, stretching the skin of her face, and her eyebrows with it, upwards into a permanently surprised expression.

'Er . . . Palp. Frank Palp,' he replied. 'I have an appointment . . . with Mr Mandible.'

The secretary licked her lips, opened a ledger on her desk and ran her finger down a list of names until she reached Frank's.

'Here we are,' she said. 'If you'd like to take a seat, Mr Mandible will be with you presently.'

Frank looked round and saw that there was a sofa and chairs with a small, round coffee table. Sitting down, he picked up one of the many Ministry magazines on offer, but before he had even opened it, the secretary called to him.

'Mr Mandible will see you now,' she said, looking over the top of her glasses.

By the time Frank had got to his feet, she was typing again. The door was already open and Mr Mandible beckoned him in.

'Come in,' he said. 'Sit down, sit down.'

Mr Mandible was a stout man, a little shorter than Frank, with thin, straggly hair scraped forward and curling up slightly as it reached his forehead. There was a drift of dandruff on his collar. He sat down behind his desk and invited Frank to sit in the empty chair opposite.

Frank sat down and Mr Mandible looked at some papers on his desk, humming to himself. Frank assumed they were his school records, although he was surprised at the amount of material. How on earth had they found so much to say about him?

'I've looked through your application, Mr Palp,' said Mr Mandible. 'It all seems in order, and your school reports don't seem to hide any dark secrets. Or are they just well hidden?'

Here Mr Mandible looked at Frank with a slightly conspiratorial expression as though he was inviting Frank to confess to something more interesting.

'No, sir,' said Frank. 'No dark secrets.'

Frank realised with a touch of sadness that this wasn't even a lie.

'Good, good,' said Mr Mandible, in a vaguely disappointed voice.

He picked up a piece of heavily typed pink paper, held it up to his face and then put it back on the desk.

'Your exam results,' said Mr Mandible, 'are not, shall we say, spectacular.'

'No, sir,' said Frank.

'No matter,' he said. 'They will more than suffice.'

'Sir?' said Frank.

'School is over now, Mr Palp,' said Mr Mandible. 'You'll find that it doesn't matter much what exam results you got, it's how you apply yourself to your life here once you start. It's a new beginning.'

Frank smiled.

'Does that mean I have a job?' said Frank.

Mr Mandible looked at him.

'Let us say that someone seems to have taken a special interest in you.'

'Really?' said Frank.

Mandible waved his hands.

'I should not have said. Ignore me, Mr Palp. You're perfectly well qualified and your father is a very valued employee – and a war hero.'

Frank shrugged. Mr Mandible frowned.

'I hope that you do not undervalue your father's contribution to the Ministry or to history, Mr Palp,' said Mr Mandible.

'No, sir,' said Frank, sitting up straight. 'I'm very proud of him. We all are.'

Mr Mandible smiled, placated.

'Excellent,' he said. 'And we are enormously proud that he has been chosen to play such an important role in the Big Day. You must be very excited. Your family will be invited, of course. You will have very good seats, right here, in the Castle.'

'Yes, sir,' said Frank, trying his best to sound excited.

'Have you ever seen the King?' asked Mr Mandible.

'No, sir,' said Frank.

'I have,' said Mr Mandible, resting back and half closing his eyes. 'Many years ago. It is quite something, let me tell you. He had this kind of . . . how can I put it . . . an aura about him.

'I used to travel with the Ministry in those days as a courier, and I had been employed to take a very important message from the Ministry to the King's country retreat.

'It was a long, tiring journey but, as ordered, I took the message and delivered it into the King's own hands and he read it right there in front of me.'

'What did it say, sir?' asked Frank. 'The message?'

Mr Mandible looked taken aback.

'I have no idea!' he said. 'The King wasn't about to share a private message with a lowly Ministry courier. The idea!'

'What did he say to you then?' said Frank.

'He didn't say anything to me,' said Mr Mandible. 'He did nod – I distinctly remember that. You don't forget a thing like that. Then he walked away as though nothing had happened.'

Nothing *had* happened, thought Frank. He waited for the anecdote to take a more dramatic turn but he could see that the story was over. Frank looked around as Mr Mandible's attention drifted away to his memory of that momentous meeting.

'He was younger then, of course,' said Mr Mandible eventually.

'Yes, sir,' said Frank. 'I imagine he was.'

'Well, we all were,' he said.

'Yes, sir.'

Mr Mandible leant back and studied Frank for a while, making Frank shift uneasily in his chair.

'I want to say how pleased I am that you chose to use your father as your introduction to the Ministry,' he said. 'So many others would have used any influence they might have – if you take my meaning – but you have understood that we rate family ties very highly at the Ministry. If you think of the Ministry as an extension of your family you will be very happy here – and you will do very well.'

'Yes, sir,' said Frank. 'Thank you, sir.'

Frank was absolutely positive that he did not want to think of it as an extension to his family. Anything but, in fact.

Mr Mandible nodded.

'We usually write a letter of confirmation,' he said, winking at Frank.

He flattened out Frank's application form with one hand and then lifted up a stamp with the other, hammering down with a bang. The word ACCEPTED was printed in a box at the bottom.

'But I see no harm in saying,' continued Mr Mandible, standing up, 'that we will expect you first thing a week on Monday, Mr Palp. Welcome to the Ministry. Don't be late.'

'No, sir,' said Frank, shaking Mr Mandible's outstretched hand. 'And thank you.'

Chapter 30

Frank spent the last days before starting at the Ministry at home. Just that hour or so in the Castle had made him see that it was a place in which he could reinvent himself. School and every petty slight and annoyance associated with it ended at his entry through the Great Arch.

Frank felt less like he had changed than like he had been reborn. But he still cringed every time he thought of himself cycling past Olivia's apartment, despite the fact that no one really knew except Dawn.

The secrecy didn't stop it being embarrassing – it actually seemed to make it worse. He just wanted to hide away inside and forget about it, if that was possible. The sooner he started at the Ministry the better. All memories of Olivia would be expunged there, surely.

At first Frank stayed in his room, but he soon found that this was not a good idea. His room had been the epicentre of his fixation on Olivia. He had brought her there in his imagination so many times.

Frank found that he could not clear his head enough to read, and neither did he seem to be able to write. When he tried, he simply sat, fingers poised over the typewriter keys.

But nothing came – nothing at all.

It was not just that he could not think of anything to write – that happened all the time. Not being able to write was one of the signs of being a true writer. No – it felt more like he had forgotten how. The typewriter was an instrument he had forgotten how to play, or at least how to make music from.

So, reluctantly, Frank gravitated towards the lounge and the company of his parents where he sat with them and the Student and watched television. To his great surprise, this now felt less odd than sitting alone with the typewriter and the blank sheet of paper.

He didn't enjoy the dull parade of Ministry programmes any more than before, but they served a purpose – they were just interesting enough to stop his mind from wandering. He began to understand their appeal.

Petra spent more and more time at the apartment and often stayed over – as she did on the night before he was due to start work. If it hadn't been for the Student, thought Frank, it would have been like the old times before she married the dreadful Ralph.

What Petra saw in that man was a mystery to Frank and whilst no one was allowed to voice such thoughts, he knew his parents felt the same. Petra was too good for him. She deserved better.

'I saw Dawn the other day,' said Petra one evening as they all sat together watching the news.

'Oh?' said Frank.

'She was asking after you.'

'Was she?' said Frank.

'I got the impression that you and she had had a bit of a tiff,' said Petra.

'Shhh,' said their father.

'We have not had a tiff,' whispered Frank. 'You have to be . . . I don't know . . . But in any case we haven't had a tiff.'

'If you say so,' whispered Petra.

'I do,' whispered Frank.

'Will you both please be quiet and let me watch the news!' pleaded their father.

They both registered the beginnings of anger in their father's voice and took the hint to be silent.

'I like Dawn,' said Petra later when their parents had gone to bed and she was alone with Frank and the Student, sorting out her bedding.

'Would you like any help?' said the Student.

'No. Thank you,' said Petra.

Frank and the Student both knew not to ask twice. Petra was very sensitive about any attempt she saw to treat her as an invalid.

'I like Dawn too,' said Frank. 'It's just that . . .'

'Just that what?' said Petra.

'We're just going our different ways,' said Frank. 'You know.'

The Student started writing in his notebook.

'Must you?' said Frank.

'Oh, leave him alone, Frank,' said his sister.

Frank sighed.

'It's not like we're saying anything bad,' said Petra. 'Or secret.'

'It's not that,' said Frank.

'Anyway,' said Petra, 'let's not get stuck on one of your rants about the Student. I'm not in the mood.'

Petra folded out her bed and started putting the bedding on it.

'Actually,' said Frank, 'the Student and I get on a lot better now. Don't we?'

'We do,' said the Student. 'Frank has been very kind.'

'He has?' said Petra.

Petra stared at her brother.

'What?' said Frank. 'You'd think I was some kind of a monster.'

'Sorry, Frank,' she said. 'I'm glad.'

'Good.'

'But maybe you could learn to be a bit kinder to Dawn.'

'What is this about Dawn?' said Frank.

'I like –'

'You like her, I know.'

'We were friends,' said Petra 'In the old days. Remember?'

Frank wondered for a split second what she was talking about because whenever he reminisced about the days in the playground with Dawn and the other kids, he always forgot that, for a while anyway, Petra was there too.

Petra was the oldest by some way and so she took on a kind of maternal role in all their games. The younger children especially adored her and followed her about and she was endlessly kind and patient, indulging them in all their childish requests and stepping in to adjudicate in the many disputes that sparked up around the playground.

Petra and Dawn were closer in age but there was still a large gap. Their relationship was more like a younger and older sister. In many ways they were closer than Frank and Petra – or Frank could remember being stung by Petra sometimes taking Dawn's side over him, at least.

Dawn missed Petra when she finally put aside these childish things and started dating Ralph, her future husband. Dawn said that the playground was never the same again after she stopped coming, and Dawn was probably right.

'I loved those days,' said Petra. She gazed off, smiling to herself. 'Do you remember that time when you threw a stone at Dawn?'

Frank's hand went straight to his scarred lip.

'Yes,' said Frank.

'Dawn's had a tough time,' she continued.

'I know,' said Frank.

'That mother of hers,' said Petra.

'What about her father?' said Frank.

They both mechanically looked up to the ceiling and followed the audible trace of footsteps going from one corner to the other, followed by muffled voices and then something being dropped.

'How did those people ever produce someone as lovely as Dawn?'

'Same could be said of you,' said Frank.

She slapped him hard on the leg.

'Hey!'

'Don't you dare compare our parents to those . . . those . . .' said Petra.

'It was a joke,' said Frank, frowning and rubbing his leg.

'It wasn't even remotely funny.'

'It's all right for you,' said Frank. 'You don't live here any more. You –'

Frank stopped as Petra collapsed into sobbing and sank onto the bed. Frank got up and put his arms around her. The Student got up, putting his notebook away.

'I should leave you alone.'

'I'm all right,' said Petra, wiping her eyes. 'Really.'

'Even so,' said the Student. 'It is late. Goodnight.'

'Petra?' said Frank when the Student had gone. 'What's the matter?'

'Why do things never get better?' she said. 'Everything just gets worse. Things rot, things fade, decay . . .'

'God,' said Frank. 'You sound like me!'

Petra laughed, sniffling and hunting for a handkerchief in her cardigan pocket.

'I'm all right, Frank,' she said. 'Honestly.'

'Are you sure?'

'Yes,' said Petra. 'I'm tired. I'm just tired.'

Frank embraced his sister and she held on tight to him for a few moments. When she released him she almost looked like her old self.

'Off you go,' she said. 'It's a big day tomorrow.'

'I suppose it is,' said Frank.

'Don't pretend you're not excited.'

Frank shrugged.

'See you in the morning then,' said Frank.

'Yes,' said Petra. 'Sleep well.'

'You too.'

Chapter 31

Frank was surprised to find that he was actually excited about starting work and found it hard to get to sleep. When he woke up he was filled with a kind of nervous exhilaration, fumbling his attempt to switch off his alarm clock and dropping it to clatter across the floor. For the first time he could remember he was out of bed before the Student, who squinted up at him as he got dressed.

'How are you feeling?' said Frank.

'Not too bad,' said the Student. 'Thank you for asking.'

'You do look better,' said Frank as he pulled his trousers up and buttoned the fly.

'The suit looks better on you than it did on me,' said the Student.

'I had it cleaned,' said Frank. 'No offence.'

'None taken,' said the Student.

'I'd better get going, I suppose.'

'Good luck.'

'Thanks.'

Frank's Guide seemed to walk even faster than the one he had on his interview day and he yelled at him to slow down, more than once, but was ignored. He arrived breathless at the desk of Mr Mandible's secretary, sweat dripping saltily into his eyes.

'Frank . . . Palp . . .' he panted. 'Starting work . . . today . . .'

She looked surprised to see him.

'Good morning, Mr Palp,' she said, looking at her watch and writing his name neatly into a ledger. 'Mr Mandible is expecting you. He won't be a moment.'

Almost before she had said these words, Mr Mandible emerged from his office and stepped forward, nodding.

'Excellent,' he said, pointing at the clock on the wall. 'On time. But you need to be on time every day, Mr Palp. Every day. No exceptions.'

'Of course,' said Frank.

'Miss Petiole,' he said. 'Could you show Mr Palp to his cubicle and set him to work?'

'Yes, Mr Mandible,' she said, getting up from her seat and straightening her skirt.

'Welcome aboard, Mr Palp,' said Mr Mandible.

'Thank you, sir,' said Frank.

Mr Mandible did not move and was standing in a position where, to get past, Miss Petiole had to squeeze herself between him and her desk. It was a difficult manoeuvre and it took her two or three shoves, planting her hands on her desk to give her leverage. Mr Mandible remained doggedly in place, only a slight tremble in his upper lip acting as any clue to the effect her passing had upon him.

With one last sideways thrust of her hips she escaped, almost falling to the carpet in the effort.

'This way,' she said, composing herself.

Frank looked back at Mr Mandible, who stood smiling, his eyes half closed. Miss Petiole walked ahead, taking him through a maze of corridors until they arrived at a long corridor that trailed off into the distance.

Or so Frank thought. When they started to walk down the corridor, Frank realised it was not actually as long as it appeared at first, but was getting smaller, the floor, walls and ceiling angling in.

When they arrived at a door at the end of it they had to bend over double to squeeze through it, and stepped awkwardly into a large room with a ceiling so low that Frank had to stoop slightly to avoid hitting his head on the light fittings.

The room was divided into a series of tiny cubicles, in each of which was a man sitting at a tiny desk on which was a number of books and a telephone. Miss Petiole brought Frank to an empty cubicle and pointed to the chair.

'Here we are,' she said in a bored, sing-song voice. 'This is you.'

'Oh,' said Frank. 'Right . . .'

'Please do not use the telephone for personal calls,' said Miss Petiole. 'That will lead to instant dismissal.'

'What exactly am I doing?' asked Frank, genuinely concerned that no one was actually going to tell him.

'On the desk you will find a Ministry directory,' said Miss Petiole, in the monotone voice of someone who had made this little speech too many times. 'You will go through the directory, ringing each number in turn. When it is answered, you will check that the information in the directory matches the person who is answering the phone.'

Frank picked up the directory and opened it.

'But it's massive,' said Frank. 'There are thousands of numbers here.'

'Everyone says that,' said Miss Petiole with a smile.

Frank peered over the screen and looked at the other cubicles. There seemed to be over a hundred of them.

'What's everyone else doing?' he said.

Miss Petiole furrowed her neatly plucked eyebrows, as much as her stretched-back forehead would allow.

'The same, of course,' she said.

'What?' said Frank.

'They are doing the same as you,' she said with a smile.

'What's the point of that?' said Frank.

She cocked her head.

'I suppose you think we should just trust you to check this information,' she said loudly.

There were a few sniggers from nearby cubicles. Frank blushed and sniffed.

'I'm not saying that, but –'

'Let's see how you get on,' said Miss Petiole – again loud enough for everyone to hear. 'And then maybe we can let all these others go.'

Frank frowned and sat down as more sniggers erupted from the other side of the screens. Miss Petiole set off back to Mr Mandible's office.

Frank sat down, picked up the directory and turned to the first page.

AAAA – Association of Abattoirs and Abattoir Attendants.

He picked up the phone and dialled.

'Hello?' said the voice after a few rings.

'Ah, hello,' said Frank. 'I'm calling from –'

'I'm afraid I'll have to ask you to speak up,' said the voice at the other end.

'Sorry,' said Frank, a little louder. 'I'm calling from the Ministry.'

'Good,' said the voice. 'When will those spare parts for the incinerator arrive? We ordered them two weeks ago.'

'No,' said Frank. 'I'm calling to –'

'It's all right for you pen-pushers up there, but we need deliveries to arrive on time. You will be the first to come down here and shut us down if we don't meet our quota. It's not good enough. There is no point in –'

Frank put the phone down.

By lunchtime Frank was exhausted. Somehow the thought that everyone in the room was echoing his work made the task feel more taxing, as though he was dragging all those other workers with him, or that he was having to hold them at bay while he spoke to the office in question.

Many attempts to check failed initially because the phone line was engaged and though they might have been engaged on other business, Frank was convinced that someone else from another cubicle was tying up the line. Frank even stood up at one point to try to listen to the people nearby but he could not pick out individual conversations from the constant whisper of voices, dialling of numbers and flicking of pages. It was a perpetual background white noise.

The room was airless. Frank was breathing in the stale exhalations of all these unseen co-workers. He could smell it, taste it. It caught in the back of his throat.

'I thought it was you,' said a voice nearby.

Frank turned round but there was no one there.

'Here,' said the voice again.

Frank looked up and saw the top of a head peeking over the screen of the adjoining cubicle, turned sideways, squeezing between the top of the screen and the ceiling.

'Hello?' said Frank.

'It's me – Scape.'

Frank saw that now.

'You look different,' said Frank, coolly.

'Look who's talking,' said Scape. 'I wouldn't have recognised you. But that whiny voice – now I'd know that anywhere.'

Scape chuckled.

'Well,' said Frank, picking up the phone. 'I've got to get on.'

'Because the Ministry will grind to a halt if you don't, right?'

Frank smiled despite himself.

'Anyway,' said Scape. 'Good to have a familiar face in this dump.'

Frank said nothing. Scape's head disappeared behind the screen and Frank stretched, almost bringing the fluorescent light down with his fist. Scape suddenly appeared at his side.

'Come on,' he said. 'Let's go and grab some lunch.'

Frank looked at him, baffled.

'What?'

'Lunch,' said Scape. 'You have to eat.'

Frank stared at him. Why was Scape even talking to him? They weren't friends. They weren't anything. Lunch?

'Well, don't just sit there,' said Scape.

Frank could not bring himself to just tell Scape to go away, so got up from his chair and followed Scape out of the room by a different door, which led to a stairwell. They climbed two floors and Frank followed Scape through a door into a low, vaulted refectory.

'We've gone up, but it feels like we're in a cellar,' said Frank.

'Yes,' said Scape. 'I know. We're standing on a false floor – one of many false floors in this place. We're up near the ceiling of what used to be a huge hall. Or so the woman on the till told me anyway.'

Frank stared at the finely moulded ribs of the arches and the delicate carved-stone faces and decorations in the corners.

'It must have been incredible once,' he said.

Scape looked up and shrugged.

'I suppose it must have been,' he said, picking up a tray and handing it to Frank. 'The food isn't that bad here. Better than my mother's anyway.'

The food was poor – so poor that Frank wondered just how bad Scape's mother must have been as a cook. But he was so hungry he ate it all. Scape ate all of his too, whilst talking constantly.

Frank tried to remember whether Scape had always been this chatty or whether it was an effect of leaving school and not having a crowd of attentive listeners gathered round him.

Frank was enjoying the idea that Scape was a nobody at the Ministry, so lonely he had to talk to Frank, but it soon evaporated as every person who walked past seemed to say hello or pat him on the back. A beautiful young woman, two or three years older than they were, even sat on the edge of the table and chatted for a few minutes, casting the odd curious glance towards Frank.

'She liked you,' said Scape after she'd gone.

'What?' said Frank. 'No, she didn't.'

Scape shrugged.

'OK,' he said. 'But she did. You can always tell.'

Can you? thought Frank. How?

The lunch break was over and Scape got up. Frank followed him back downstairs. They didn't say a word the way until they reached Frank's cubicle, when Scape slapped him on the back.

'Well, Frank,' he said, as though about to impart great words of wisdom, 'suppose we'd better get back to work. What are you doing when they let us out of here?'

'Me?' said Frank. 'Oh, I have to . . .'

'Have to what?' said Scape. 'Iron your socks? Come on. You're going for a drink with me.'

'Oh, I don't know,' said Frank. 'I really do have to get back.'

'Nonsense,' said Scape. 'See you later.

Frank left as soon as the siren sounded, determined to avoid Scape, and got himself lost in the process. In the end he had to pay a passing Guide twice the going rate to lead him out of the Department of Agriculture offices and to the main gate, by which time most of his shift had already dispersed.

He almost ran down the Old Steps, stopping halfway to laugh at the ridiculousness of running away from Scape. For years Scape had ignored or patronised Frank – now Frank was actually having to hide from him. There had been a shift in the fabric of things and it felt good.

Frank didn't walk straight home. He wanted some time to himself before he fielded the inevitable questions from his mother about every minute of his day.

Frank needed some time to assimilate this change in his life and wandered aimlessly through the streets. Only a year ago he would have seen it as utterly inconceivable that he would find

himself working in the Castle – working for the Ministry – and yet here he was, strolling through the streets after his first day at the centre of the Grey.

Part of him tried to feel bad about it, but no matter how hard he tried, he could now only see the Frank of before that day as a little boy – a little lost and foolish boy. Real life was full of compromises. He understood that now. Work was just a means to an end; a way of paying the rent. The Ministry could have his mind but that didn't mean they could have his soul. Frank was still Frank. Hell, he was more Frank than he'd ever been before.

He walked down to the river and stood a while watching the river barges go back and forth loaded with freight. He waved a couple of times but no one waved back. Then he saw something glinting at the river's edge near to a collapsed pier.

Frank knew what it was as soon as he glimpsed it. He thought about it later and wondered how he had been so sure, but he was – as sure as he was sure about anything in his life to that point. He ran down the stone steps two at a time.

An old man walking his dog eyed him suspiciously but Frank ignored him, determined to keep the diamond twinkle in his line of sight. The dog snarled at him as he passed and barked at Frank's back.

Frank squatted down, panting. It was a Liberation Beer bottle, green and with the Ministry Brewery label on it. The beer was gone and the metal top had been forced back on. Instead of liquid inside there was a piece of paper.

Frank's heart raced. He took it over to the steps and smacked the metal top off. The paper was a bit more difficult to extricate, but he managed it using a twig he found among the litter on the riverside.

It took patience and he almost gave up and smashed the bottle instead, but he managed to ease it out until the end of the folded-up piece of paper emerged from the mouth of the bottle and he could grab it and pull it free.

Frank took a reverential breath before opening the note and reading the wish written on it. Each letter was written in a different coloured pencil – *a different coloured pencil!* – and it shone like a jewelled casket in the grey of the river beach, flickering across his pale face like a firework display at dawn. It said:

ANYTHING
THAT
ISN'T
THIS.

Chapter 32

Frank got back to his apartment block in a daze without even remembering how he got there, the folded paper in his inside jacket pocket close to his heart. He could feel it there. It was warm.

He walked past Mrs Cremaster's door, heading for the lobby. There on her doormat were little bowls of food and water. Maxilla hissed and ran away as Frank approached. Mrs Cremaster opened the door a fraction and Frank said hello. She nodded and closed the door again without a word.

Frank reached the lobby and was just crossing to the stairs, still half looking at Mrs Cremaster's door when he walked straight into Dawn, nearly knocking her over.

'Sorry,' said Frank.

'No harm done,' said Dawn.

She started to walk away but Frank grabbed her arm.

'Where are you off to?'

'Just nipping to the chemist for my mother,' she said. 'You're in a bit of a brighter mood.'

'Listen, Dawn,' said Frank. 'About the other day. I didn't mean to –'

'It's not a problem, Frank,' she said. 'You were upset. We all need to let off steam every now and then, don't we?'

'Sit with me for a minute,' he said.

Dawn nodded and they walked over to the bench and sat down.

'Things were getting on top of me a bit.'

Dawn waved his words away

'It's forgotten.'

'Friends then?' said Frank.

'Always.'

Frank scratched his head, unsure of what else to say – or whether to say anything at all.

'Do you remember all the cats?' he said.

'Yes,' said Dawn. 'Hardly any left now. Where have they gone, do you suppose?'

'I don't know,' said Frank. 'But at least old Mrs Cremaster feeds them.'

'I know,' said Dawn. 'I think she only talks to the cats now. I haven't managed to get a word out of her for months.'

'Me neither.'

'Petra tells me you're working at the Ministry.'

Frank smiled sheepishly.

'You must think I'm mad.'

'No,' she said. 'We do what we have to do. I just thought –'

'I should have told you,' said Frank. 'I don't know why I didn't. I should have come up and told you.'

Dawn shrugged.

'You don't have to tell me anything,' she said. 'I was just a bit concerned when Petra told me – because I know how you've always hated the idea. But you don't seem too downhearted.'

Frank smiled.

'In fact, you look positively pleased with yourself,' said Dawn with a crooked smile. 'For someone who is working at a place they'd always sworn to avoid like the plague.'

Frank laughed.

'What?' said Dawn. 'Come on.'

'Do you believe that two people can be meant to be together?' said Frank.

'Yes,' said Dawn. 'Maybe. I think I used to. Why?'

'I found something today,' said Frank. 'Something amazing. I mean – really amazing.'

'Oh?' said Dawn. 'Are you going to tell me what it was?'

'It was . . .'

Frank put his hand to his jacket, to his heart, to where the paper lay folded. He was about to take it out when he changed his mind. Something told him that it needed to be a secret. It was something between him and Olivia.

'Sorry,' said Frank. 'I don't think I should say.'

Dawn smiled.

'Can't?' she said. 'Or won't?'

'Not just now, anyway,' said Frank. 'One day.'

'I'm intrigued,' she said.

'I shouldn't have said anything,' he said. 'I don't want to sound all mysterious.'

'Don't worry about it,' said Dawn. 'I find loads of amazing things I don't tell you about.'

Frank grinned at her.

'I just worry it might break the magic, you know,' said Frank.

'Magic?' said Dawn, eyes widening. 'Good grief. This isn't like you. What have they done to you up in the Castle?'

Frank shrugged, smiling.

'I know,' he said. 'I sound like an idiot. Sorry.'

'If you can't talk like an idiot to me, then who?' said Dawn. 'We've known each other our whole lives.'

Frank nodded.

'I'm glad,' he said. 'I'm glad we have.'

'Me too.'

Frank took a deep breath and stood up, rubbing his hands together.

'I ought to . . .' he said, pointing to his apartment.

'Of course,' said Dawn, getting up herself. 'I better get off myself.'

'Night, Dawn.'

'Night.'

She walked away, heading for the street. Frank walked to the lobby to see Mr Spiracle stepping out of the shadows. His rogue eyebrows were arched high on his forehead as though in surprise.

'Hello,' said Frank, trying to sound casual.

Mr Spiracle moved towards him with surprising speed.

'The lift is locked,' he said, his eyebrows wandering drunkenly across his forehead.

'I know,' said Frank. 'I wasn't –'

'As it should be,' he said, tapping the side of his nose. 'As it should be.'

'Well, then,' said Frank. 'That's good.'

Mr Spiracle stared at him for a while and then stepped backwards into the shadows. Frank hurried up the stairs and into his apartment.

He fielded all his mother's questions with a good humour that surprised everyone, including himself, but eventually he went to his room and took out the piece of paper, flattening it out on his little desk next to the typewriter.

Frank was sure he didn't believe in signs and portents and yet surely that's what this was. What were the chances of him finding Olivia's wish? And it had to be hers – with each letter a different colour. Who knew how many bottles were thrown off that bridge? Why wasn't it washed away downstream?

Not just the finding of it but the wish itself. It could have been his. Finally – there was someone in this dull, dull world who thought the same as he did. All the doubts he'd suffered in his darker moments – they were gone now. Tears sprang to his eyes.

Olivia really was the one. The only one. He knew it. He had always known it. He hadn't been deluded. He had been deluded about being deluded. He had lost faith but now his faith was returned to him, multiplied a thousand times.

He had been trying to put Olivia behind him when what he needed to do was just grow up and understand that he was never going to win the heart of a girl like Olivia by hanging around outside her apartment like an idiot.

Frank had started a new life at the Ministry. He had a job now. He wasn't a child any more and whoever he had been at school didn't matter at all now. Even Scape was talking to him, choosing to talk to him. If that could happen, surely anything could?

But this had to mean something. Frank refused to believe it didn't. The Ministry – the Grey – wanted nothing to have significance, but Frank didn't have to go along with that. He may work at the Ministry, but that didn't mean he couldn't keep his heart free. They couldn't own his desire.

Chapter 33

Frank took Olivia's wish with him to work. Ideally he would have liked to stick it up on his cubicle right in front of his face. Then he could gaze at it all day long and remind himself how close the Grey had come to crushing his spirit, but he didn't want anyone asking about it. Especially not Scape.

So Frank would surreptitiously take it out when he was sure he was alone and just take a brief peek at it. That was enough. The burst of colour was so dazzling, so electrifying, it made him gasp every time he saw it.

Even back in his pocket, the wish dominated his thoughts. He saw how easy it would have become to regard working at the Ministry as normal – perhaps he already had. But now he had this talisman to rouse him from his stupor.

Olivia had once given him a sense of purpose at school when life seemed purposeless – however misguided and childish the form it took – and now she was doing it again. Frank had still not quite worked out what to do about it, but he would. He had plenty of time.

'Do you have any idea what day it is?' said Scape.

Frank looked at his calendar – his mother had given it to

him. It was the only thing he had on his cubicle walls. He shook his head.

'No – enlighten me.'

Scape grinned.

'Pay day, my friend. That's what day it is.'

'Oh?' said Frank.

He had actually completely forgotten about being paid. Scape seemed to guess this and shook his head.

'You crack me up, Palp,' he said.

'Glad to be of service,' said Frank.

'Well, come on, you enormous tart,' said Scape. 'Let's get our money. We've earned it, haven't we?'

'I suppose we have,' said Frank.

Frank could see that there was nothing for it but to give in to Scape, so he followed him down a series of corridors and staircases until they arrived at a small courtyard that appeared to be sitting on top of one of the flying buttresses.

The courtyard was surrounded by a low and crumbling wall and Frank kept well away from the edge after catching sight of the precipitous drop. A raven croaked by, flapping untidily into the teeth of a stiff breeze.

'Amazing view, huh?' said Scape, shoving Frank towards the end.

'Aaargh!' said Frank. 'Don't do that!'

Scape burst out laughing.

'Your face!' he said. 'Do you really think I'd push you over?'

Yes, thought Frank. Yes I do.

'No,' he said. 'I'm just not great with heights.'

'Ah,' said Scape. 'Sorry.'

That didn't stop him having another bout of laughter.

'Anyway,' said Frank, 'where the hell are we?'

'We're getting our money, of course,' said Scape.

Scape beckoned him over and Frank realised that there was a small window in the side of the castle wall. The window was so low, Scape had to bend over to rap on it.

The window suddenly slid sideways and a woman's face appeared in the gap. The gap was small and the face was only partly visible. She peered at them both suspiciously.

'Names?' she said.

'Scape.'

'First name?'

Scape cast a swift glance towards Frank.

'Timothy,' he said.

Frank grinned.

'You?' she said.

'Palp,' said Frank. 'Frank Palp.'

The woman disappeared. Frank could hear her retreating footsteps becoming fainter and more echoey. Then there was silence apart from the breeze in his ears and the distant sound of barges on the river.

'Where has she gone?' said Frank.

'Who knows?' said Scape. 'Somewhere in the bowels of the tunnel system where they keep the loot.'

'Then why have the window out here?' said Frank.

Scape shrugged.

'Who knows why the Ministry does anything?' he said. 'Best not to even think about it.'

Frank nodded. He looked up at the Castle's silhouette above, all pointed turrets and spiked pinnacles, looming like a gigantic crown of thorns. Frank had to look away. It was more dizzying than looking down. To his relief the woman's face reappeared at the open window

'Scape!' she said, and poked a brown envelope through the gap.

Scape took the envelope and Frank did the same when his name was called. As soon as the envelope was in his hand, the woman slammed the window shut and Scape tapped him on the arm and they went back inside the Castle.

Once inside, Scape opened his envelope and flicked through the notes.

'It's a pittance,' he said. 'But I still get excited every time I see all those notes.'

Frank smiled. He knew what Scape meant because he was pretty excited too as he let his thumb stroke the edge of the wad of banknotes. He had never seen so much cash before.

'What are you going to spend yours on?' said Scape.

Frank shrugged. He'd given this no thought whatsoever.

'I don't know. What about you?'

'Well,' said Scape, 'beer might be bought and drunk. But mainly I'm saving up for a motorbike.'

'A motorbike?' said Frank. 'Why?'

'To ride,' said Scape. 'What do you think I want it for? It's better than that stupid bike of yours.'

'A bike is all you need in the city,' said Frank. 'It's cheap and –'

'Boring,' said Scape. 'Yes, I know. I don't want a motorbike to ride around the Old Town. I want it to get away from the Old Town – out of the city completely. You know, head off into the country.'

'Sure,' said Frank. 'You can't go anywhere without travel permits. There are road blocks every twenty miles or so.'

'Like you'd know,' said Scape. 'Have you ever set foot out of the city?'

'No, but –'

Scape dropped his voice and looked round before continuing.

'My uncle says there are roads out there – minor roads – that don't have a road block on them. He says if you're careful you can get right up into the mountains. Imagine that? The mountains, my friend. Imagine breathing in that fresh air, Frank? Huh?'

Frank had to admit it did seem appealing. Scape slapped him on the back and they returned to their cubicles. Frank sat down and opened the directory at where he had marked it before they left, and picked up the phone.

But Frank found it hard to concentrate. He had been a little taken aback by hearing that Scape was actually saving up for something – that he had a plan, of sorts. He took the paper out of his pocket and bathed in the multicoloured wish for a few minutes.

At the end of the day, Scape appeared and grabbed him by the arm.

'Come on,' he said.

'What?' said Frank.

'You've got to have a drink on pay day,' said Scape. 'It's the law.'

Scape knew a bar at the foot of the Castle Steps. It was downstairs in an old warehouse, cave-like and bustling with people, mostly from the Ministry. It had no doubt once been full of atmosphere but was now as functional and anonymous as a hospital waiting room.

'Two beers,' said Scape to the barman, who nodded and grabbed two long glasses from the shelves behind the bar.

'You've been here before,' said Frank.

It was a statement rather than a question, but Scape smiled and nodded.

'Once or twice, yes,' he said. 'My father brought me here when I was a kid after school. He used to let me finish his drinks.'

Scape's smile faded as he fell back into his memories for a moment.

'Does he work at the Ministry, your father?' asked Frank.

'Not really,' said Scape, shaking his head. 'He's dead.'

'Oh,' said Frank. 'Sorry. I didn't know.'

Scape slapped him on the back as the beers arrived.

'I know that,' he said. 'Why would you? He died years back.'

'How?' said Frank. 'How did he die?'

'He fell in the river. You know, from the railway bridge. Right where they drop empty beer bottles with wishes in them. Ironic really, given that he was full of beer most days. You know where I mean?'

Frank nodded.

'Drunk, of course. They found him washed up on a river beach near the border.'

'I'm sorry,' said Frank.

'Don't be,' said Scape. 'He was a miserable bastard unless he was drunk – and then he was a cruel bastard.'

Scape broke into a grin, dispelling the gloom he had created.

'Cheers,' he said, clinking his glass against Frank's.

'Cheers.'

'Do you ever see anyone else from school?' said Scape.

Frank shook his head. He hadn't noticed anyone else from school at the Ministry. Which was odd, given that was surely where most of the pupils had ended up. It was like they had been absorbed into the fabric of the place.

But that was the Castle for you. It swallowed people up – people, ideas, history, time. It swallowed everything and passed it down into its tunnelled bowels, never to be seen again. Maybe that's what happened when you retired, thought Frank. They just sent you down into the tunnels, never to return.

'I saw that fat kid – the one who was always going to the toilet,' said Scape.

'Oh?'

Frank had no idea who he was talking about. Scape chuckled to himself.

'There was this time,' he said, 'we –'

But Scape suddenly stopped, having second thoughts about finishing the anecdote. Whatever cruelty he was about to describe it was in the past now and better to stay that way. Scape understood, just as Frank did, that school was a taboo subject if they wanted to be friends. It had happened to two other boys, not them.

'What about your father?' said Scape.

'What about him?'

'Does he drink? Did he ever beat you? Does he knock your mother about?'

Frank shook his head.

'No,' he said. 'None of those things, actually. He's never hit me – yet.'

'Yet?' said Scape. 'He's hardly going to start now, is he?'

'I don't know,' said Frank. 'He wants to sometimes – I can see it in his face. Sometimes I wish he would. He gets into these terrible moods and everyone just has to put up with it because they are so frightened of pushing him over the edge. But it just means he always gets his own way and we live inside this thunderstorm. I hate him sometimes.'

Frank had never said that out loud and he immediately regretted it. He felt he was being disloyal – not to his father especially, but to Petra and to his mother. Scape just nodded.

'At least your father did something,' he said. 'I mean, him and his men are part of history. It's more than either of us will ever be, let me tell you.

'Those men saved the King and saved the Castle and stopped an army. Imagine that. Imagine making a difference. Say what you like about your father, he was brave when it counted and he's made his mark. What the hell is either of us ever going to do?'

Frank felt more than a little uncomfortable with the idea of Scape defending Frank's father.

'I know,' said Frank. 'But –'

'And everyone's going to be watching him on the Big Day,' said Scape. 'Everyone. You know how rare it is for anyone to get made a fuss of by the Ministry?'

Frank nodded.

'You're right,' he said. 'I know. It's amazing.'

Agreeing with Scape always confused him long enough to change the subject. Frank was wondering how he was going to get away but it was Scape who called an end to their evening by telling Frank he had a date and best be on his way. They parted on the street and Frank headed home, a head full of swirling, multicoloured letters.

Chapter 34

Frank caught sight of his reflection in a shop window. He almost didn't recognise himself. It wasn't just the suit, or the new haircut. Only a short time at the Ministry seemed to have changed him entirely. It was troubling and exciting in equal measure.

He looked serious – intense, even. If he had passed this version of himself on the street a few months ago, he would have stepped aside, intimidated. This was New-Frank and he liked it. He smiled and he liked the new, assertive smile that reflected back at him.

He was about to walk on when he noticed Dawn some way off down the hill. She didn't see Frank and he stepped back into a doorway to make sure that didn't change. She was with someone. A man. A boy. A young man about his own age. He had his back to him so Frank couldn't see his face until they both walked up the hill laughing. It was Roland.

Frank wasn't sure what bothered him more – that Dawn was seeing Roland, whose curdled friendship Frank would rather not be reminded of, or that Roland was seeing Dawn and somehow moving closer to Frank's life. Would he come to the apartment block? Would Frank have to walk past them in the courtyard, buried in each other's faces? They walked past without even glancing in his direction

Frank quickly regained his equilibrium and told himself that none of that mattered. He crossed the street and headed through the doors of the Pulvillus Clothes Store.

Frank found Olivia next to a display, folding a mohair jumper. She looked stunning. He almost lost his nerve completely. The Frank of a month ago would have turned back.

Instead, he took a deep breath and walked straight forward, bumping into Olivia. He hit her harder than intended and she would have fallen had he not quickly grabbed her. As he steadied her, he looked into her face.

'Olivia.'

'Do I know you?' she said, stepping back out of his reach and looking down her long, beautiful nose at him.

Frank could not help himself from laughing. Olivia did not appreciate this and scowled. She looked so beautiful.

'Frank,' he said. 'Frank Palp.'

She shook her head and shrugged. Frank chuckled again.

'I sat near to you in History,' he said. 'In another lifetime.'

'Did you?'

She was peering at him, clearly trying to decide if he was joking.

'Yes,' he said. 'Next table. I'm sorry – I should have been looking where I was going.'

'You should,' she said, returning to the jumper.

She began to walk away. Frank surprised himself by speaking up.

'Although,' said Frank, 'if I had been, I might not have bumped into you, so I'm glad. In a way.'

Olivia turned and studied him. Then she smiled. Frank took a gulp of air. She actually smiled.

'I remember you now,' she said, taking a step back towards him. 'But you look different.'

'Haircut,' said Frank.

She nodded, pointing to his head.

'Oh – yes, you used to have that mop of curly hair. We all used to call you . . .'

'Yes?' said Frank.

'It doesn't matter,' she said, blushing a little.

'I suppose not,' said Frank.

'You work at the Ministry now?'

Frank nodded.

'Anyway,' she said, stroking some stray hairs from her face. 'Be more careful next time . . .'

'Frank,' he said.

She nodded and started to walk away. Frank turned and was about to set off in the other direction when he suddenly clapped his hands together and turned back.

'Wait!' he said, loudly enough for a woman nearby to gasp and back off a little.

'Yes?' said Olivia.

Frank's courage was dissolving rapidly.

'Look . . . I mean . . . the least I can do is buy you a coffee,' he called.

'You don't have to,' she answered. 'People bump into me all the time. Thanks anyway.'

She moved away again.

'No!' he shouted.

The woman nearby tutted loudly.

'I want to. You see –'

'All right,' she said, smiling.

'What?'

Frank knew what she said.

'I said all right.'

'Sure,' said Frank. 'Absolutely.'

She shook her head and smiled again.

'When?'

'Erm – I don't know. Now?'

'I can't now,' she said. 'I'm working.'

'Of course you are. Idiot. Tomorrow, then?' said Frank.

'Tomorrow,' she said. 'What time?'

'Eleven?' said Frank.

'Eleven it is,' she said. 'I'll meet you here.'

Frank stood for a moment, a wide grin frozen to his face.

'All right, then,' he said. 'See you tomorrow.'

Then he turned and walked straight into the corner of a large table covered in neatly folded underwear. It was painful, but he limped away without looking back for fear of spoiling the moment.

Frank was in a joyful daze for hours and arrived at his apartment block without really remembering how he got there. Mr Spiracle was standing in the shadows by the lift but Frank ignored him and if the old man said anything, Frank didn't hear it.

He took the stairs two at a time, skidding to a halt outside his apartment door and calming himself before slowly opening it and greeting his parents. His father was at the table reading the newspaper. His mother was getting dinner ready. The Student was nowhere to be seen.

'Good evening,' said Frank breezily. 'Mother. Father. Where's the Student?'

'He's at the Ministry,' said his father. 'You probably passed him on the way.'

Frank rewound through his memory searching for any sign that the Student had been near him when he left the Pulvillus Clothes Store but saw nothing. Although he had to admit an armoured elephant might have thundered past and he would still have only noticed Olivia.

'You look cheerful. How was work?' said his mother. She chuckled to herself. 'It still sounds so funny,' she said. 'Asking you about work.'

Frank smiled. He would normally have found this irritating, but he could see how proud she was and he enjoyed it.

'It was fine, Mother.'

Frank was both desperate to tell someone about Olivia but also acutely aware that he did not want his parents to know anything about her. But it was an effort of will to prevent the news from simply blurting out.

'And it only seems a moment ago that . . .'

She waved her hands in front of her face.

'He's only gone to work,' said Frank's father. 'He hasn't died.'

'I know,' she said. 'I'm being silly. I'm just so proud.'

Frank's father shook his head behind his newspaper. His mother walked up to Frank and gave him a rib-crushing hug. Then she blew her nose on a handkerchief and went back to her cooking.

'Did you eat?' she called.

Frank sat down at the opposite end of the table to his father and looked towards the balcony door. He saw Olivia standing there, holding her arms open, her lips slightly parted.

'Yes,' he called back dreamily. 'I had lunch with the kid I told you about – the one from school.'

'Oh,' said his mother. 'That's nice, isn't it? You already have a friend at work.'

'He's not really a . . .' began Frank. 'No – you're right. It is nice.'

Olivia smiled at him. She licked her lips.

'Is it that Roland you used to be so friendly with?' asked his mother.

'No!' said Frank. 'I wasn't that friendly with Roland. I don't know where you get that idea from.'

'Of course you were,' she said. 'You were always playing with him at one time. You were inseparable.'

Frank frowned.

'Well, I haven't been friends with him for years,' said Frank.

'Oh,' said his mother, putting a plate of food in front of Frank and his father. 'Did you fall out about something?'

'No,' said Frank. 'Why are we talking about Roland anyway?'

'Who was it then?' said his mother, returning with her own food. 'This friend at work.'

'No one you know,' said Frank.

'Oh?'

'Does it matter?'

'No, I just –'

'His name is Scape. Happy now?' said Frank.

'What did they have you doing?' said his father, who seemed not to have even noticed this conversation and was chasing a potato round his plate.

Frank was happy to change the subject and told them once again about the directory and about phoning up to check details and was struck by how they seemed – again – to miss how dull and pointless the task was.

'You have your own cubicle?' said his mother, wide-eyed. 'You never told us that.'

'I did,' said Frank. 'Of course I did.'

Frank smiled. She made it sound so impressive. Frank skewered a piece of meat with his fork and put it in his mouth.

'And using the phone all day,' she said, in a tone of wonder as if he had told her that he was fashioning jewellery from unicorn teeth.

'That's a very responsible job,' said his father, noisily chewing on his food. 'I hope you're doing it properly.'

Frank laughed.

'A child could do it,' he said, opting to swallow the mouthful whole and almost choking.

His father's smile weakened. He put his knife and fork down. The electrical hum began to pulse. The lights faded in and out.

'You'll learn soon enough, I hope,' he said, sitting back in his chair, 'that whatever job you're given, it's worth doing it well. Not enough people understand that.'

Frank coughed, massaging his throat.

'You'd have to be an idiot to do it badly,' he said. 'It's just ringing people up to check information. You have to be able to read and speak. That's pretty much it.'

His father stared at him for a moment.

'Nothing's good enough for you, is it?' said his father.

'What?' said Frank. The meat seemed lodged somewhere in his chest en route to his stomach.

'Who do you think you are?'

'Eh?' said Frank. 'What's that supposed to mean? What's the matter with you?'

His father slammed his hand down on the table. The air was fizzing. There was a white noise in Frank's ears and his heart was fluttering. The meat pressed into his chest as though it was expanding.

'Don't you talk to me like that!' he yelled.

Frank pinched his lips together. He thought that going out to work would make him feel stronger in these face-offs, but it didn't. Nothing had changed. Would it ever?

His father's pent-up rage grew and grew in the room like an inflating balloon and Frank was pushed to the edge, pinned up against the wall, gasping for breath.

He longed to see that balloon punctured, to see his father deflated and belittled as Frank had so often been deflated and belittled by him.

One day.

One day.

Chapter 35

Frank was half an hour early for his date with Olivia. He walked back and forth, occasionally coming to a halt to rock from heel to toe and look at his watch to check it wasn't broken.

Olivia arrived wearing her tight black leather jacket, a pale yellow scarf at her throat. She behaved as though this date was the most usual thing ever when to Frank it was as extraordinary and momentous as the birth of the universe.

Frank almost took her to Café Labrum – an old haunt of his in the Old Town – but he had decided he would never go there again. It was a café with a rich history. A writer's café. But that Frank – that silly, deluded, pseudo-intellectual Frank - was gone. This was New-Frank and New-Frank had decided to be happy. He had wanted to be an intellectual, the way another child wanted to be a pirate or an explorer. With as little sense of what it might actually mean. Time to put all that away.

He took her instead to the Café Paraglossa in the Old New Town and they took a window seat overlooking the river. The cloud was thick but occasionally broke to allow a burst of sunlight through to make a filthy spotlight on the river and the Old Town crowned by the Castle.

Frank had rehearsed several conversation openers but now that he sat opposite her, none of them seemed adequate to the task. It was Olivia who spoke first.

'Did you pick up your results?' she asked as their coffee arrived. 'From school?'

Frank nodded.

'Mine were terrible,' said Olivia, grimacing.

'Does it matter?' said Frank.

'There speaks a clever person,' said Olivia, smiling and wrinkling her nose.

Frank sighed.

'Not really,' he said.

She frowned.

'But you are,' she said. 'You know you are.'

Frank shrugged.

'My results aren't exactly those of a genius,' he said.

'Pah!' said Olivia, swiping the air. 'Who cares about school? I mean, you're clever in the way you think. You can just tell. I know enough stupid people, Frank, to know a smart one when I see one. Remember when you were talking about Time at school . . .'

'You remember that?' said Frank.

'Of course,' said Olivia. 'I couldn't get it out of my head all day. The idea that the future isn't there at all – that we are heading into nothing, making it up as we go. It's kind of scary – although also kind of exciting.'

Frank gazed at her in awe.

'It was just an idea,' said Frank. 'I was just talking. I don't know that I'd say the same now.'

'Really?' she said. 'Why?'

'Maybe I was just saying that because the future looked so grim,' said Frank.

'But not now?' she said.

Frank smiled. The sun burst through the clouds and suddenly lit up Olivia's face.

'Maybe it's just about having something to look forward to,' he said.

Olivia laughed and the mole danced around on her pale throat. Frank took a sip of coffee and burnt his lip. He swore. She laughed again. Frank would have gladly taken a bullet from the Sniper to have died in that moment.

They talked. Well, Olivia talked mostly and Frank listened. He was surprised at how interested he was in hearing about the very people he had so recently despised, and had he been honest, still did.

It didn't matter what she was talking about. He could have watched Olivia's mouth open and close for ever and every time she was about to let Frank in on a particularly risqué secret, she would lick her lips and look sideways, and Frank had to stop himself from falling forward across the table.

After coffee they walked along by the river. She quizzed Frank about his family and home life and ordinarily he would have been irritated or embarrassed but on this occasion Frank was happy to answer any questions.

Olivia seemed so interested in his family that he found himself finding them interesting – or at least not as annoying as he usually did. They just seemed normal when viewed through Olivia's eyes. Maybe they were. Her genuine excitement about his father's role in the Big Day was baffling to Frank but infectious.

'How about you?' said Frank as they approached the weir. 'What does your father do exactly?'

'Well, my father and mother divorced, way back,' said Olivia. 'He lives up on the hill. He works at the Ministry but he travels a lot. My mother has remarried. I hate my step-father.'

She rolled her eyes. Frank grinned.

'He works at the Ministry too.'

'Doesn't everyone pretty much?' said Frank.

'Not me,' said Olivia.

'Oh?' said Frank.

'No,' she said. 'My mother runs a clothes shop and I'm working for her now.'

Frank nodded.

'I love clothes,' said Olivia.

'They look good on you, that's why,' said Frank.

'Flatterer,' said Olivia.

Frank blushed. He hadn't meant to flatter. It was genuinely the first thing he had thought. Clothes did look good on Olivia. He barely noticed what anyone else was wearing.

'The right ones would look pretty good on you, actually,' said Olivia, raising her eyebrows and looking him up and down. 'That suit . . . What is that suit?'

'What?' said Frank. 'Is it that bad?'

'It doesn't do you justice,' she said. 'You're earning now. You can do better. Much better.'

Frank nodded.

'I'll help you,' she said. 'I have a gift for shopping, my mother says.'

Frank picked up a stone and tossed it into the river. It entered the water with barely a splash.

'What do you do?' asked Frank. 'At your mother's shop.'

'She wants me to give it some new life,' said Olivia. 'It's very old-fashioned. She wants me to buy in some stock that will appeal to younger women. I used to work there on Saturdays but now I'm full-time I can give it my undivided attention.'

Frank smiled wryly at the thought of how many times he had cycled past her apartment on a Saturday with no hope of her ever appearing because she wasn't actually there.

'What do you do, Frank?' she asked. 'At the Ministry?'

'Too boring to even talk about,' said Frank.

He almost mentioned Scape but he didn't want him there, even in the conversation.

'What would you do if you could do anything you wanted?' asked Olivia.

Frank paused for a moment.

'I don't know. I always wanted to be a writer,' said Frank.

He regretted saying it the instant the words came out of his mouth. It sounded ridiculous. It sounded pretentious. He had ruined the moment – ruined the whole day. He was an idiot.

'Really?' she said. 'I can see that.'

'You can?'

He wasn't sure that even he could see that now.

'Definitely. Do you remember when Mr Nodus read your story out in class?'

Frank did remember. The thing he remembered most was Scape turning to face him with a look of cold outrage on his face that he was being made to listen to something Frank had written.

'But why did you say "wanted"?' asked Olivia. 'Don't you want to do that any more?'

Frank shrugged.

'It just sounds a bit crazy, doesn't it?' he said. 'Wanting to be a writer. It's like wanting to be a . . . I don't know, a . . .'

He couldn't think of anything it was like.

'I don't think so,' said Olivia. 'I think it sounds exciting. Maybe you'll be a bestselling author one day. I'd love to read something you'd written.'

'Really?' said Frank.

'Really,' said Olivia.

Frank opened his mouth to continue but Olivia leant forward and clamped her own open mouth over his, her nose momentarily colliding with Frank's. It was so unexpected for Frank that he almost pushed her away. Instead he found himself being pulled close as she slid her arms inside his coat and dug her fingers into the small of his back.

Frank had kissed before. He had kissed Dawn for a dare when he was ten, but that had been nothing like this and he was a little disturbed to be thinking about it at all as Olivia's tongue seemed to become detached and go swimming about inside his mouth like an eel.

He had closed his eyes as Olivia moved in but opened them now, startled to find Olivia also had her eyes open. He felt her take hold of his hand and place it on her breast. It felt like touching the soft feathers of a bird and now she closed her eyes.

Frank felt like this sensory overload was going to cause some sort of short circuit in his brain. Olivia clearly did not share his concern because she pushed her hips forward and pressed into him, increasing the intensity of her kissing. A barge sounded its horn. Frank let his hands drop to her backside and he squeezed and pulled her forward.

'You certainly know what you're doing,' she said, when their faces finally pulled apart and Frank gasped for air.

He had absolutely no idea what he was doing.

Frank and Olivia met many times over the next few weeks, walking along the embankment on the late summer evenings. Every time they kissed, Frank imagined he was going to wake from a dream and find himself back in his cold bed, the Student snoring nearby.

Frank was amazed at how quickly their relationship had become normal to him, considering how extraordinary such

an idea would have once seemed. His life had been so empty before that Olivia flooded in to fill it, and it was soon hard to even remember what he had done before.

If Olivia found it strange to be with Frank, she did not show it, but she did make it clear that she required a few changes from him – and Frank was very happy to oblige.

Looks were very important to Olivia and though Frank might have dismissed this as shallow in the past, the fact was he enjoyed her interest in the way he looked. He liked Olivia telling him what suited him and what didn't.

Olivia would take Frank on shopping expeditions in the Old New Town. Frank would follow behind her listening in fascination as she explained why such and such a button was stylish and another not.

Initially he had been shocked at the cost of things she picked out for him and confused as to why the best jacket or shirt or pair of shoes, seemed always to be by far the most expensive.

'You can't get quality cheaply,' she said to him and Frank agreed.

Olivia would take him round the shop, gathering up bundles of clothes and sit outside the changing room waiting to make her judgement – and her judgement was always sound. Frank looked good – he looked sharp. Even Scape started to notice.

Olivia liked the cinema and although Frank had always said he would rather push pins into his eyes than watch Ministry movies, he found that, with the right company, they weren't really that bad.

Mostly though, they would simply walk the river shore and find a secluded spot behind the piers of a bridge or some such place that Olivia always seemed to know. Then they would be a writhing tangle of limbs as clothes were unbuttoned, unzipped, hands and lips exploring.

But however wild and abandoned Olivia would seem – and she was wilder than Frank could ever have imagined – there was a point at which she made it very clear she would always stop and would never go further.

'I'm sorry, Frank,' she panted into his ear the first time he attempted to cross this line.

'What?' said Frank, fearing he had done something wrong.

'I can't,' she said.

They parted and rearranged their dishevelled clothes.

'I'm saving myself for when I get married,' said Olivia. 'That probably sounds silly, I know.'

It didn't sound silly at all to Frank. It was intensely frustrating, but not silly. In fact, it made Frank think of Olivia in a completely different way and of his relationship to her as more intense. Besides, when she had said she was saving herself for marriage, she had given Frank the strangest of looks.

He could wait.

Chapter 36

No matter how dull or ridiculous or pointless or annoying his work was at the Ministry, remembering that he would be seeing Olivia made the work relatively painless. That said, he had to develop an iron discipline not to think about her too much, because he then would get nothing done at all.

In fact, Frank was actually very productive. He surprised himself. Scape was amazed at how Frank would breeze through the day, getting further through the directory than any of the others in their sector. Despite having started weeks later than Scape, Frank had already overtaken him.

'You do know,' said Scape one day over lunch, 'I've heard that when we finish this directory we just start over again. Can you believe it?'

'Why would they do that?' said Frank.

'You work here, the same as me,' said Scape. 'Look around – why do they do any of this crap?'

Frank shrugged, not really listening, an absent-minded half-smile on his face. Scape stared at him.

'What is it with you?' he said. 'Why are you so un-botherable? You've been acting very peculiar – even for you.'

Frank shrugged again.

'I just think about what I'll be doing when I get out of here,' he said.

Scape cocked an eyebrow, leering lasciviously.

'Oh?' he said. 'Tell me more.'

For once Frank was happy to let Scape think whatever he wanted.

'Come on,' said Scape. 'Who is she?'

Frank blushed a little.

'Look, I've got to get back,' he said.

Scape grabbed him by the arm as he stood up. Frank protested, but in reality he was happy to let Scape wheedle the truth out of him. Why shouldn't he tell? How often had he had anything to show off about in his entire life?

Besides, he wanted to see the look on Scape's face. He had buzzed around her continuously at school but it was Frank she had chosen.

'Come on!' he said, leaning forward. 'It's a girl, isn't it? Is it someone from school? Someone from this place? Who? Do I know her?'

'Not here,' said Frank. 'I'll tell you later.'

'I'm actually intrigued,' said Scape as they headed off along the corridor, towards their cubicles.

Frank sat down, but instead of going back to his own cubicle, Scape stood over Frank, pleading with him to at least give him a clue.

'Have you finished the directory, Mr Scape?' asked Mr Mandible, stepping up beside them.

'No, sir,' said Scape. 'Sorry, sir. Palp was having a problem and he asked for my help.'

'A problem, Palp?' said Mr Mandible.

'Erm . . . yes, sir,' murmured Frank. 'But Mr Scape solved it for me.'

'Did he?' said Mr Mandible. 'Well, excellent work, Scape. Now back to your cubicle. Mr Palp must deal with these things himself. He can't go disturbing you every time he gets stuck.'

'No, sir,' said Scape. 'I was rather busy.'

'Try to deal with your own problems in future, Palp,' said Mr Mandible.

'Thanks a lot,' said Frank as soon as he'd gone.

Scape laughed.

'Old walrus,' he said. 'He doesn't care. As long as he can grope that secretary of his a couple of times a day, we could all disappear in a puff of smoke.'

Scape was leading Frank out of the building while the last note of the end of day siren was dying away. They skipped their way lightly down the Old Steps and into the gloom of the bar.

'So,' said Scape, taking a swig of his beer and leaving a foam moustache on his upper lip. 'Out with it. Who's the girl? Assuming it is a girl, of course.'

Scape chuckled.

'It is,' said Frank, ignoring the intended jibe.

'Well?' said Scape. 'I'd try to guess but honestly I can't think of anyone. No offence.'

Frank left a pause for dramatic effect.

'It's Olivia,' said Frank.

Scape leant back, peering at Frank.

'Olivia?' he said. 'Olivia who?'

'Olivia Pulvillus,' said Frank.

'What? Really?'

Frank laughed.

'Listen,' he said. 'No one's more surprised than me.'

Scape was still peering at him as though waiting for the punchline of a joke. When he saw it wasn't coming he slapped Frank on the arm.

'Good for you, you dog,' he said. 'Who'd've thought it?'

Frank blushed with pride a little.

'Who'd've thought?' repeated Scape.

A large group came into the bar – men and women. They were clearly Ministry workers too, although from another sector. Frank thought he recognised a couple of typists among the women, but he wasn't sure.

'Another two beers!' shouted Scape, draining his glass dry.

'Oh, I don't know,' said Frank who had barely started his first.

'Rubbish,' said Scape, slamming his glass down on the bar. 'Don't ever have just one beer. They need company like everyone else.'

Frank wondered whether this sage advice had come from Scape's drunken father, but still he smiled and nodded and drained his own glass, belching loudly as he put the glass down. Scape thought this was hilarious and slapped the bar, laughing uproariously, looking round at the other customers and pointing to Frank.

Frank found he was joining in, despite himself. Maybe it was the alcohol but he was starting to find Scape amusing rather than annoying. If he had met him now, without all the baggage from school, he would have to admit that Scape was all right.

He was so easy in his own skin. Maybe that was what Frank had found so hard to take at school – because Frank was so uneasy in his. Scape spoke without thought or doubt, as though the words were scripted for him and he just had to say them. Frank doubted everything.

They were an unlikely pair but after a couple of beers they seemed less so. Frank found himself laughing along with Scape rather than being laughed at. Frank had never laughed so much in one evening – or for some considerable time.

Frank had only ever drunk one beer at a time before – and had eaten nothing but bar snacks – so he felt woozy after three as he walked home. It would have been four, but he had managed to throw the fourth away while Scape was in the toilet. He was happy to take the withering look of the bartender.

'Come on!' said Scape when they finally left the bar, grabbing Frank by the arm.

'What?'

'I've got something to show you.'

'I really ought to –'

'It'll only take a few minutes,' said Scape.

Frank relented and followed Scape as he crossed the road and headed up an alleyway towards the river. They soon arrived at a shabby garage selling used cars, the stock locked up behind a chain-link fence, a scabrous dog growling in the shadows, tied up on a long chain.

'Look,' said Scape. 'Look at her.'

Frank thought for a minute he was talking about the dog, but he now saw the object of Scape's attention and clear affection: a powerful-looking motorbike, propped up near the wall.

'Isn't she a beauty?'

Frank knew nothing about motorbikes and cared even less, but even he had to admit this particular one did indeed seem beautiful, all lasciviously curved chrome and creased leather.

'I've almost got enough to buy it,' said Scape. 'And then . . .'

Scape made a revving noise and indicated with a sweep of his hand that he would be off to the mountains at the first opportunity. Frank laughed. He wasn't sure why. Scape joined in. They laughed and jumped up and down until Frank's head stopped liking that, and then they moved on back to the main road.

He said goodbye to Scape on the corner and set off home, finding that the ground was never quite where his foot was expecting it to be. His steering seemed to be malfunctioning too because he managed to walk straight into a tram stop he had made a specific and very deliberate effort to avoid.

Frank reached his apartment block and fumbled for his keys, trying several times to open the outside gate with the wrong key and dropping them more than once. He stepped into the courtyard and found Dawn sitting there in the dark.

'Dawn!' he cried. 'What are you doing here? It's night-time.'

'Just needed some air.'

She looked back towards her apartment, then at Frank.

'Are you drunk?' said Dawn.

'No!' said Frank, a little too forcefully. 'Shhh!'

Dawn chuckled.

'You are,' she said. 'You're drunk.'

'A little bit, maybe,' agreed Frank, trying hard to concentrate on the blurred Dawn and pull her into focus.

Dawn shook her head in wonder.

'Frank Palp drunk?' she said. 'What is the world coming to?'

'Just went for a drink with . . . with someone from work,' he said.

The effort of talking was making him feel a little queasy.

'Oh?' said Dawn. 'Of course. How is life at the Ministry?'

Frank shrugged.

'You know,' he said. 'Pretty stupid. But I don't care about any of that.'

Frank smiled.

'Oh?' said Dawn. 'That's a naughty smile. What are you up to?'

'Shhh. You wouldn't believe me if I told you.'

'Try me,' she said.

Frank sat down beside her on the bench.

'I'm seeing Olivia,' he said. 'Olivia Pul . . . Pulvillus. You know? Going out with her, I mean.'

Dawn's reaction was not the same as Scape's. His had been a kind of disbelief – amazement even. Dawn's was more dismay. Frank frowned.

'What?' he said.

Dawn shrugged and stared off across the courtyard as Maxilla crept past.

'So,' she said. 'Persistence finally paid off?'

'Yeah,' he said with a smirk. 'In a way.'

Dawn smiled. But only with her mouth.

'What's the matter?' said Frank.

'Nothing.'

'I know you don't like her,' he said.

'Do you?' said Dawn.

Dawn frowned. Frank got up and the courtyard seemed to have developed a slope and he staggered sideways, just managing to correct himself.

'So you do like her?' said Frank.

'I don't really think about her at all,' she said.

Frank winked at her.

'Are you a tiny bit jealous, Dawn?'

'Who of?' said Dawn, her face going red.

'I think you are,' said Frank with a grin.

'What? Why would I be jealous of . . . ? What are you –'

'Come on, Dawn,' said Frank. 'I know you'd like that money to buy paints and stuff.'

'Oh,' said Dawn. 'No, I'm not jealous of her money.'

'I'm just saying that I could see why you might be.'

'You can think what you like, Frank,' said Dawn.

Frank turned away. He didn't want to talk any more. He needed to sleep. Everything seemed to be moving and he was finding it hard to concentrate. Dawn called after him.

'Why does it make a difference what I think, anyway?'

'It doesn't,' said Frank without looking back.

Dawn nodded.

'Night then, Frank,' she called.

'Yes,' he said quietly, almost to himself. 'Goodnight, Dawn.'

Chapter 37

The alarm sounded like an explosion in a bell tower when it went off the following morning and the aftershock took some minutes to die down. Frank's brain cowered in the corner of his skull, whimpering to itself until he finally persuaded his body to sit upright and blinked his eyes open, peering into the morning light.

His mother's voice seemed unusually high pitched and shrill as Frank tried to eat breakfast and he had never before noticed how loud and annoying the rustling of his father's newspaper was.

'You didn't have much to say for yourself when you got in last night,' said his mother.

'Oh . . . Yes . . .' mumbled Frank. 'Wasn't feeling that well, to be honest.'

'You hardly touched your food.'

'Bit of a bug going round at work,' he said. 'Still not great.'

'Not trying to skive off work already, I hope,' said his father. 'You have to be at death's door for the Ministry to give you a day off, isn't that right, dear?'

Frank's mother put her hand to her son's forehead.

'He does feel a bit hot,' she said.

'Nonsense,' said his father. 'Stop mollycoddling the boy.'

It wasn't until Frank was walking to the tram with his father that he felt anything like his normal self. He and his father had taken to riding the tram together the three stops to the Castle. It seemed odd not to as they were both heading in the same direction at the same time, but Frank could tell that the arrangement did not suit his father any more than it suited Frank. Neither of them had much to say to the other and both would have preferred to be alone, particularly first thing in the morning.

The walk up the Castle steps was the worst part. Frank felt obliged to go at his father's slower speed for fear of looking as though he was racing him to the top, and by the same token his father was clearly climbing quicker than he felt comfortable with so as not to be outdone by his son. By the time they reached the sentry boxes, both of them were gasping for air – Frank with frustration, his father with exertion.

They passed through the sentries together but after a brief farewell, split up at the main courtyard – Frank heading towards one door, his father to another. They could both have entered by the same door, but this just felt like the place to part company for the day – before they actually entered the building proper.

'Have a good day,' his father said with the usual wave and a nod.

'You too, Father,' said Frank.

Upon entering the airless warren of the Castle, some of the symptoms of Frank's hangover returned and by the time he reached his cubicle he was sweating and feeling nauseous. Scape, however, seemed in even brighter spirits than normal, peeping over the screen with a demented look on his face that, even in Frank's foggy state, made him laugh.

At lunchtime, Frank was keen to get some air, and they took their sandwiches out to the King's Courtyard and stood at the east wall looking out to the far horizon: pale, blue-tinged and misted.

'Look at that,' said Scape. 'Look at that view. Miles and miles of stuff we'll never see.'

'Speak for yourself,' said Frank.

Scape snorted. 'What? You're going to travel, are you? I don't think so.'

'Why not?' said Frank. 'Some Ministry Men get to travel.'

'Not us, Frank,' said Scape. 'Not if the Ministry has anything to do with it.'

Frank frowned at the certainty – the finality – in Scape's voice and at that 'us' he had begun to use when voicing his many opinions.

'What about your motorbike?' asked Frank.

'Well, that's the point. That's why I'm buying it. Look at your father,' said Scape in the voice he used when delivering one of these worldly-wise speeches. 'A genuine war hero, for goodness' sake, and he hasn't moved an inch. He still lives where he was born. In a crappy apartment block. No offence. But am I wrong? What chance have you got?'

Frank couldn't see how the fate of his father was connected to his fate in anything but the most tenuous way, but had learnt from experience that arguing with Scape only encouraged him. The best way to combat him was to ignore him and move on.

'If you ask me, the only way we'll ever travel is –'

'Olivia wants me to meet her parents,' interrupted Frank, eager to change the subject.

That certainly grabbed Scape's attention.

'Really?' said Scape with a gasp. 'Well, now – it must be serious. I'm impressed. I'm honestly impressed. You know her father is some Ministry bigwig? Her step-father too, for that matter. Her mother is a hideous control freak, by all accounts.'

'Really?' said Frank.

'Absolutely,' said Scape.

'Hey – where's my other sandwich?' said Frank.

'It'll be the Invisible Lizards,' said Scape matter-of-factly.

'Oh, yeah?' said Frank, holding out his hand. 'Give it back.'

'Seriously,' said Scape. 'They are terrible for that, apparently.'

Frank arched a quizzical eyebrow.

'You believe in the Invisible Lizards?' said Frank incredulously.

'No,' said Scape. 'I don't "believe" in them, Professor. Believing is for gods and fairies and stuff like that. They exist. I know they do. I was bitten by one when I was a kid.'

Scape rolled up his sleeve and showed Frank a pale hollow in his forearm just above the wrist.

'What?' said Frank. 'They're invisible. How would you know it was them?'

'Well, what else is invisible and bites?' said Scape, shaking his head. 'You are stupid sometimes, do you know that?'

At the end of the day, Scape appeared at Frank's cubicle.

'Come on, Frank,' said Scape. 'Hair of the dog.'

'I don't know,' said Frank.

'Course you do,' said Scape, putting his arm round Frank's shoulder. 'Just one. I promise.'

Scape was more subdued in the bar. Frank had the distinct impression that telling him Olivia wanted Frank to meet her parents had annoyed Scape in some way. Maybe Scape just could not accept that Frank was fit for someone like her. Frank hoped in a way this was true. If Scape was jealous, that made it all the sweeter.

They did indeed have just the one drink, but that didn't stop Scape pleading with Frank to have another. Frank refused. They stood outside and said their farewells and Scape was just about to move away when he grabbed Scape's arm and pointed down the road.

'Hey, look,' he said. 'Isn't that the guy from school? Whatsisname?'

'Roland,' said Frank as a couple headed towards them, lost in conversation.

'Who's that he's with?' said Scape.

'Dawn Calypter,' said Frank. 'She lives in my apartment.'

Scape waved and whistled and yelled.

'Roland! Roland!'

Frank cursed as Roland and Dawn looked in their direction and Scape beckoned furiously. Neither of them looked any happier than Frank at this meeting. Only Scape was in high spirits.

'So!' he said. 'Roland. You remember Frank?'

'Yes,' said Roland coolly. 'How you doing, Frank?'

'All right,' said Frank. 'You?'

Roland smiled and shook his head.

'How's it going?' said Scape. 'Long time. And this is?'

'Dawn,' said Dawn.

'We were at school together,' said Scape, pointing at Roland.

'So were we,' said Dawn.

Scape frowned.

'Really?' he said. 'I'm sorry I don't remember you.'

'I'm not,' said Dawn, glancing at Frank, who refused to make eye contact.

'Listen, we've got to go,' said Roland. 'Good to see you.'

'Don't go,' said Scape. 'Frank's being boring and heading home, but he'll change his mind if we all go for a drink. It doesn't have to be here, we could –'

'Not tonight,' said Roland.

'OK,' said Scape with a shrug. 'Another time, then.'

They said their goodbyes, and Dawn and Roland moved on, engulfed by the shadows as they took a left turn out of sight.

'Well, well, well,' said Scape. 'Fancy that.'

Scape leant in towards Frank and dropped his voice to a whisper.

'Between you and me, I always thought Roland was queer.'

'Shut up,' said Frank.

'What?' said Scape.

'I said shut up.'

'What's the matter with –'

'So what if he is queer?' said Frank.

'All right,' he said. 'Calm down. Obviously touched a bit of a raw nerve there, lover boy. Didn't you two used to be best pals at one time?'

'No,' said Frank.

'Anyway, you might not care,' said Scape, stepping closer and dropping his voice, 'but the Ministry does. They round them up and send them to be chemically "realigned".'

'Maybe,' said Frank.

Frank had heard that too.

'It's true,' said Scape, his voice barely audible. 'It happened to someone in my block. And then the next time I saw him he was working as a Civil Servant. Not the ordinary ones – the mean ones. The ones who do the Ministry's dirty work.'

'So?' said Frank.

Scape shrugged.

'Just saying.'

'Time I was going,' said Frank. 'See you tomorrow.'

Chapter 38

Frank sat in Café Paraglossa the following Saturday waiting for Olivia to arrive. Olivia always kept him waiting, but he didn't really mind. He had always liked sitting in cafés on his own – which was just as well, all things considered.

He liked watching people. He liked to imagine lives for strangers and through them to imagine a life for himself. Frank was sure that this was what all writers were meant to do and he still habitually carried his little notebook around with him, although he found that he wrote in it less and less.

At first this realisation had troubled him, but he told himself that he was evolving, growing – and these changes must be accepted, not struggled with. He had been dissatisfied with

Old-Frank for so long, he was happy to let New-Frank have the benefit of the doubt for a while. If New-Frank didn't want to write, then that was fine.

He even began to wonder if his urge to write had actually been a symptom of his unhappiness or his sense of disconnectedness with the world around him. Maybe writing was actually a form of illness and now he was better – or at least better than he had been.

Frank still found other people fascinating – it was just that he did not feel the need to record these observations. After all, most people did not need to do it. Was writing actually some sort of neurosis, some kind of obsessive and deviant behaviour – spying on people, inventing stories about them? Wasn't this New-Frank just healthier – mentally – than the old one?

Frank was so engrossed in these deliberations that he didn't notice Olivia come in, and she had to wave a hand in front of his face to rouse him from his trance.

'Hello!' she called. 'Anyone there?'

'What? Sorry – Olivia!'

They kissed and Olivia sat down opposite him. She called the waitress with a raise of her arm and flick of her hand. Frank had been mortified the first time she had done this. Surely one just waited patiently for the waitress to appear? That was certainly what Frank had always done in the past.

But New-Frank had taken to this practice and now beckoned waitresses himself when he wanted to order, albeit awkwardly and self-consciously, ignoring their raised eyebrows and sour expressions.

They knew – even New-Frank knew – that Frank wasn't really the waitress-beckoning kind, just like a horse knew if you couldn't really ride as soon as you sat on its back.

One of the waitresses that was least disposed to pretend otherwise now came over and took Olivia's order, smiling warmly at her and then flaring her nostrils at Frank as she turned to leave.

'Did you see that?' said Frank.

'What?' said Olivia, taking off her jacket.

'That waitress,' said Frank. 'The way she looked at me.'

'You're so vain, Frank,' she said with a smile. 'Not everyone fancies you.'

Frank frowned at her. Vain? He wasn't vain.

'So,' said Olivia, 'I spoke to my mother and she'd be delighted.'

'About what?' said Frank.

'About you coming over for lunch, silly,' she said.

Frank was still looking at the waitress, who was now standing with two others. He saw them casting glances in his direction. One of them put her hand to her mouth to hide her giggles. Frank had a good mind to –

'Frank!' said Olivia. 'Are you even listening to me?'

'Of course I am,' he said. 'Lunch. Your mother.'

'Next Sunday,' she said. 'One o'clock.'

'I know,' said Frank. 'I remember now. I'll be there. Don't worry.'

She reached out and grabbed his hand.

'It's important to me, Frank,' said Olivia. 'I want them to like you. You want me to meet your parents, don't you?'

Frank choked on his coffee. His voice was thin and croaking when he replied.

262

'Of course. Absolutely.'

He could imagine few things worse.

'There's no food you hate or that you're allergic to or anything?'

He had no idea. He had only eaten about ten things his entire life. Besides, people in the Old Town didn't have allergies. His mother always said they weren't good enough for allergies.

'No,' said Frank. 'I eat pretty much anything.'

'And you will be smart, won't you?' said Olivia. 'My mother hates scruffiness.'

'I will wear my very best clothes,' said Frank. 'I'll even wash.'

Olivia slapped his arm.

'The pale jacket,' she said. 'The one I picked out for you last week. You look very handsome in that.'

'I do?' said Frank.

Frank smiled. The waitress brought Olivia's coffee.

'Yes, you do,' said Olivia when she'd gone. 'I'm sorry to nag, but I want it to go well. I want her to like you. She gives me such a hard time, Frank, I can't tell you. And even though he's a pain, I want my step-father to like you too.'

'Me too,' said Frank.

'I know it's a bore,' she said.

'No – I'm looking forward to it.'

Frank was not looking forward to it.

Chapter 39

Lunch was the big social meal in the city. The curfew meant that it was difficult for anyone to entertain in the evenings. Very few people could afford to entertain, in any case. Frank's family had never entertained. But then, Frank's parents never went out either. They seemed to have no friends at all. Not that it appeared to bother them.

Frank cycled most of the way to Perseverance Boulevard, but did not want to be seen arriving on a bicycle because he did not feel it really gave the impression he wanted. Although he wasn't entirely sure what sort of impression would be the right one.

The streets were full of posters for the Big Day, plastered over the shutters of empty shops and the back of tram stops – as well as the trams themselves – and every available wall and fence through the Old Town. They had been up so long they had already begun to fade and tear, as though they were but tattered remnants of the day itself.

Frank chained his bicycle up a couple of streets away and bought a bunch of flowers on the way. He had been shocked by the price and had seriously considered changing his mind but there was something about the attitude of the flower seller

that made Frank determined to go through with it. She so clearly assumed he could not afford it that he added a couple more sprigs and gave her a tip. He had hoped this might bring about a change in her demeanour, but it didn't.

Frank had to stop at the gate and pause before carrying on along the path to Olivia's apartment door. It seemed so incredible that he was finally going to get to see inside. He and Olivia had never met at her apartment block. The bare-breasted caryatids looked down at him over their pert nipples. He gave them a wink.

Frank ran his finger down the list of tenants and then rang the bell. A hoarse and slightly aggressive woman's voice hissed from the speaker on the entry phone and asked him what he wanted.

Frank had been preparing to hand over the flowers but quickly saw that the woman opening the door – the owner of the voice he'd just heard – was obviously the maid and lowered them again. The maid looked him up and down and asked him to come in and follow her.

She took him across a chequerboard tiled floor to a lift and they got in side by side. It was a small lift, but she made it a tighter squeeze by standing in the centre and forcing Frank into the space remaining.

She pressed the button and the lift rose smoothly, the staircase that encased it flashing by. At the fourth floor, the lift stopped, she opened both doors and stood to attention as Frank walked out.

'This way,' she said, closing the lift doors, and Frank followed her to Olivia's apartment.

'You must be Frank,' said Olivia's mother as he walked in.

'Mrs Pulvillus,' he said, shaking her outstretched hand. 'I'm very pleased to meet you.'

Mrs Pulvillus was as beautiful as Olivia, but with a relaxed assuredness her daughter did not yet possess. Frank handed her the flowers and she took them with a broad smile despite the fact that they had been slightly crushed in the lift.

'Well, isn't that lovely,' she said. 'How thoughtful. They're beautiful. Come through.'

Olivia walked forward and embraced him. It was the first time he had seen her nervous. This did not put Frank at ease.

'Sit down, Frank, please,' said Olivia's mother. 'Can I get you a drink?'

'No – thank you,' said Frank. 'Well, a glass of water, perhaps.'

Olivia's mother smiled and the maid went to the table and poured Frank a glass of water.

'Your father is playing a huge part in the Big Day, isn't he? Not long now. You must be very proud.'

'Yes,' said Frank. 'Of course.'

'How marvellous to have a man like that to look up to,' she said. 'A man of loyalty and integrity – of patriotism.'

'Yes,' agreed Frank. 'I suppose so.'

'There's no suppose about it,' said Mrs Pulvillus. 'You are a very lucky young man. I wish there were more like your father at the Ministry. More people who remembered who they are supposed to be serving.'

'Mother,' said Olivia, rolling her eyes.

'My daughter does not like me talking politics,' said Mrs Pulvillus.

Frank hadn't really registered that she had been talking politics.

'It's so boring!' groaned Olivia.

'I low about you, Frank?' said Olivia's mother. 'Do you find it boring? Politics?'

Frank looked between Olivia and her mother.

'I . . . I . . .'

Mrs Pulvillus laughed. Frank noticed that her laugh was almost identical to Olivia's, as was her long, arched nose.

'Frank doesn't know what to say, poor thing,' said Olivia's mother. 'He's not sure who it will be worse to offend.'

She reached over and touched his knee.

'Rest assured, it will be much worse for you to upset Olivia,' she said with a wink. Frank smiled.

'Mother,' said Olivia. 'What is that supposed to mean? And why are you grinning at Frank?'

Mrs Pulvillus got to her feet.

'Now I must go and see how lunch is progressing,' she said. 'If you'll excuse me.'

'My god,' said Olivia when her mother had left the room. 'Was she flirting with you?' She shuddered and made a gagging face.

'No!' said Frank. 'Why would you say that?'

Olivia giggled.

'Well, she definitely likes you,' she said. 'I can tell.'

'Do you think so?' said Frank.

Olivia nodded, leant towards him and kissed him on the lips.

'You are a very likeable young man,' said Olivia, sliding her hand between his legs.

'And you,' said Frank, grabbing hold of her and pulling her close, 'are a very –'

268

Olivia sprang backwards as her mother entered the room.

'Everything is in order,' said her mother. 'Now, where were we?'

'You were fondling Frank's knee, Mother,' said Olivia.

Mrs Pulvillus pursed her lips.

'Never mind my daughter,' she said. 'She can be very uncivilised. I think it must be something to do with those awful friends of hers.'

'Hey!' said Olivia. 'How do you know Frank isn't friends with them as well?'

Mrs Pulvillus looked at Frank.

'Well, are you, Frank?' said.

Frank took a deep breath, looked at Olivia and shook his head.

'Of course you aren't,' she said. 'I could tell from the second I laid eyes on you. I have no idea how you managed to meet my daughter, but I'm very pleased you did. You seem like a very sensible, level-headed young man.'

'Thank you,' said Frank.

Olivia rolled her eyes.

'And you've followed your father into the Ministry?'

'Yes,' said Frank.

'How are you finding the work?' said Mrs Pulvillus.

'Please, please, please,' said Olivia. 'Please don't let's talk about the stupid Ministry. It's so boring.'

'But Frank is our guest, Olivia,' said her mother. 'Don't be rude.'

'Frank doesn't want to talk about it either,' said Olivia. 'Do you, Frank?'

Again Frank was caught glancing between mother and daughter until they both laughed and Frank joined them. A bell sounded in the distance.

'Aha!' said Mrs Pulvillus. 'Lunch is served.'

Olivia smiled at Frank and they followed her mother through high glassed doors to another room with an enormous long table.

'Now, if you sit there, Frank,' said Mrs Pulvillus. 'Olivia, you can sit on the other side.'

They all sat down and the maid came through with a trolley.

'I'm assuming you like sckrupff, Frank,' said Olivia's mother as the maid placed a huge steaming object in the middle of his plate.

'Of course,' said Frank.

Frank had no idea what sckrupff was.

He waited for the others to be served, casting glances at the thing on his plate that was now becoming more visible as the steam cleared.

It was a large grey-brown lump, roughly spherical, about the size of a small cabbage head. It had a rough crust on it that was splitting, letting out more steam.

Frank noticed then that he had very odd cutlery: something resembling tweezers, a flat spoon with spikes on it, and a fearsome-looking cross between a knife and a saw.

Frank looked up to see that Olivia and her mother were waiting for him to start. They smiled encouragingly. Frank smiled back and looked down at the thing on his plate, then at his cutlery and then back to Olivia and her mother.

'Frank?' said Olivia.

'I think Frank is being polite,' said her mother, clearly realising Frank had never seen sckrupff before, let alone eaten one.

Olivia's mother slowly and carefully picked up the knife-saw, inviting Frank with her eyes to copy her movements – which he dutifully (and gratefully) did.

Frank sawed into the tough skin at one of the splits, releasing a gush of steam, a high-pitched whine and a curious aroma unlike anything Frank had ever smelt before.

'Have you ever gone sckrupff-collecting, Frank?' said Olivia's mother, knowing the answer before it came.

'No, I haven't,' said Frank.

'Oh, you should, if you get the chance,' said Olivia'a mother. 'It's fascinating.'

'I'm sure,' said Frank, copying as Olivia and her mother folded down the skin to reveal a pale, translucent globe.

'They have specially trained sckrupff-hunting cats,' said Olivia's mother. 'They go absolutely crazy when they find one in the woods. They are highly prized if they prove to be good sckrupff-hunters, because, of course, sckrupff is horribly expensive.'

'Really?' said Frank, looking at his plate, dubiously.

'Oh, Frank,' said Olivia, assuming he was joking.

Olivia and his mother had now picked up the spiked spoon, so Frank did the same, readying himself for what he was sure was going to be one of the most revolting food experiences of his life – and he had experienced many.

Frank looked up to see Olivia's mother giving him encouraging glances, so despite his lurching stomach, he dipped his spoon into the quivering mass, the spikes gaining purchase on the fibre running through it, and raised it warily to his lips.

'Frank,' said Olivia. 'Stop playing about!'

Frank looked to see that they were both using their spoon to pull the thing apart, rather than to eat it.

'You won't be laughing if you do eat some by mistake,' said Olivia.

Frank wasn't laughing.

'Olivia ate some when she was little and she was sick for days, weren't you, dear?'

Olivia shook her head at the memory.

'So don't joke about it,' said Olivia.

'Sorry,' said Frank, lowering his spoon and joined in with what appeared to be a search – although he had no idea what for. When the globe was reduced to a formless pile of jelly, Frank saw Olivia's mother pick up the tweezers. He did the same.

Olivia's mother leant forward, peering into the mass, and carefully extracted something about an inch long, black and shiny, like a tadpole. Like a tadpole, it squirmed when picked up.

'They really do look alive,' said Olivia's mother. 'Even though we know it's only a seed.'

This was clearly intended to reassure Frank, but it didn't work. To Frank's horror, he saw that this thing *was* to be eaten. Olivia's mother lifted the wriggling black comma to her lips and put it in her mouth. Olivia did the same. After a moment's pause, Frank reluctantly followed suit.

Frank did not know what to expect, but he certainly was unprepared for what did happen. The squirming creature exploded as soon as it was placed inside the mouth and released a burst of the most extraordinary flavours. It tasted like a sunny afternoon, birdsong – it tasted like joy. Then, moments later, it was gone.

Olivia's mother sighed. The maid collected the plates and the special cutlery and took them away. There was a kind of reverential pause as the three diners readjusted their emotions in the afterglow of the sckrupff.

The maid brought new plates and cutlery and the main course was brought through. After the sckrupff, a simple beef stew, rice and vegetables seemed rather dull, but it was delicious, as was the apple pudding that followed it. Frank had never eaten so well.

He had imagined the lunch would be awkward, but he felt more relaxed here than in his own home. Mrs Pulvillus was clever and very funny. She was easy to talk to. Frank almost forgot Olivia was there. He was actually disappointed when it was time for him to head off.

'Well, that went well,' said Olivia as she saw him to the door. Frank smiled.

'I'm glad,' he said. 'She's nice, your mother. I like her. I like her a lot.'

'She's not bad,' said Olivia. 'But you are seeing her in her best light. She can be a nightmare.'

'Really?' said Frank, raising his eyebrows.

'Really,' insisted Olivia.

'Well,' said Frank. 'I'll have to take your word for it. Goodbye. I'll see you soon.'

They kissed and Frank set off down the gravel path and away down Perseverance Boulevard to collect his bike. As he rode home, he belched a joyous bubble of undigested sckrupff.

Chapter 40

Frank finally reached the end of the directory. It happened at precisely eleven thirty-seven on a Wednesday morning in late September. It seemed worth noting, somehow. It was some kind of achievement after all, and he had reached the end before most of his colleagues – even the ones who had started ahead of him. Certainly ahead of Scape, who shook his head in disbelief.

Frank had been told that he needed to report back to Mr Mandible when he finished the directory so he headed off toward his office, not altogether sure that he remembered the way there.

It could not have been more than a few hundred yards and involved only one change in floors but now Frank could not remember whether Mr Mandible had been on a higher or lower floor. He knew he should just ask, but some sort of misplaced pride kept him going on, unaided.

Eventually he opened a door onto a huge room with a high ceiling and desk after desk of female typists. The collective noise of this orchestra of typists was deafening and horrible, like the crunching of a mountain of bones. Frank screwed his eyes, wincing at the needle-like impact of the *clicketty-clack* on his eardrums. The typists looked the same, all bobbing in time to the arrhythmic clatter, their eyes flicking left and right, their hands bouncing up and down.

Frank was about to turn back and put some distance between himself and the din when he saw his sister standing at a desk talking to a seated typist. Two men came by. One smacked her on the bottom, quite hard – although the sound didn't register above the din. Petra turned to face him and, as she did so, the other man grabbed hold of her and pulled her towards him, trying to kiss her. She arched herself backwards, smiling but avoiding his lips.

Frank was about to set off towards her when she slapped the man playfully on the shoulder and pushed him away, prodding him with her stick. Frank had thought she would be furious, but she was laughing and talking to these men as though this happened all the time. Maybe it did. He hardly recognised her.

Petra was always giving him lectures on treating women as equals and here she was letting herself be publicly disrespected. Frank left the room before Petra could catch sight of him, and eventually relented to ask directions to Mr Mandible's office.

'Excuse me. I've finished the directory,' said Frank.

Mr Mandible's secretary, Miss Petiole, nodded at him and rang through to Mr Mandible, who came out after a moment, smiling.

'That's excellent, young man,' he said. 'Excellent. Keep up the good work.'

Mr Mandible clapped his hands together, looked from Frank to his secretary and then back to Frank. With that, Mr Mandible went back inside. The secretary returned to her typing.

'Excuse me?' said Frank.

Miss Petiole jumped as though she had no idea he was still there.

'Yes?' she said. 'Can I help you?'

'What do I do now?' he said.

'Do?' she asked.

'Yes,' said Frank. 'What work am I supposed to do?'

Miss Petiole stared blankly up at him as though he was speaking a foreign language.

'I'm sorry . . .' she said. 'I'm afraid I'm very busy . . .'

She was looking in her desk drawer for something.

'But you haven't answered,' said Frank.

'I don't follow,' she said, taking out a stapler.

'I mean, what do I do now?' he asked.

'But you know what you are doing,' she said. 'You are checking the directory for errors.'

Frank took a deep breath before continuing.

'Yes,' he said, talking very slowly. 'But I've done that now, haven't I? I've finished.'

The secretary smiled and shook her head. She looked around for someone to share the joke with but the corridor was sadly deserted.

'A good job is never finished,' said Miss Petiole. She pointed to a Ministry poster on the wall. It said, 'A good job is never finished.' 'You clearly have a lot to learn.'

'But I have finished it,' said Frank. 'I've reached the end. It's finished. The job is finished. How can it not be finished if I've completed the task?'

'No,' she corrected. 'I'm afraid I would have to take issue with you there. You have reached the end of the directory. You have not completed the task.'

'How?' said Frank. 'How have I not completed the task? What more is there to do?'

'Dear me,' she said. 'Why, it's only the start. Your report on the directory goes to the printers and all errors you observed will be corrected.'

'There were no errors,' said Frank. 'Not one.'

'And then,' said the secretary, ignoring Frank's interruption and banging her hand down on the stapler. 'You check again. In case changes have been made since your last check.'

'Like what?' said Frank.

She waved her hands around.

'Perhaps a department might move buildings.'

'Why would they do that?'

'I couldn't say,' said Miss Petiole.

'It's ridiculous,' said Frank.

'Someone might have been promoted. Someone might have died,' said the secretary.

'Of boredom, perhaps?' said Frank.

The secretary peered at him and then returned to her typing. Frank remained where he was, staring at the top of her head.

'So I just go back and start from the beginning again?' said Frank. 'As though I'd never done it before?'

'That is correct,' said the secretary, loading her typewriter with fresh paper. 'I was worried I hadn't explained it properly.'

Frank stood for a moment longer but Miss Petiole was now studiously ignoring him, frowning with concentration as she typed, the skin of her forehead pulled so taut it looked like it might tear. He glanced at the 'A job is never finished' poster and then went back to his cubicle.

Chapter 41

Frank's work rate dropped after realising that Scape was right about the directory. It was hard enough to get excited about work so tedious but to feel that it was pointless as well was just too much.

Maybe the work really was just a way of keeping all the intelligent young people in the city occupied and distracted. Give them enough to do to exhaust them and to fog their minds; smother any revolution to death before it is born.

Days snailed their way by, one after another, one after another. Frank accepted it. What choice did he have? He thought no more about the hours that he spent in the Castle than a beetle thinks about the rotten wood it bores through.

A routine had settled upon Frank, as routines will. He became habitual in his telephone manner, seeing no reason to vary or embellish his conversation. Every day was, in almost every respect, identical to the last and to the one to come. If someone spilt a cup of coffee it was a major event.

Frank no longer had to discipline himself to keep all thoughts of Olivia at bay. He would occasionally reward himself with a lewd and fleshly thought but mostly he did not have the energy – or actually even the interest.

A pattern formed. Every day would feature lunch with Scape. Scape was now the person Frank spoke to most often – more often even than Olivia, whom he mainly saw only at weekends. Pretty much every evening, after work, Frank and Scape would go to the bar for a drink – or three. That was Frank's routine. That was already his life.

Frank surprised himself at how readily he accepted this new regime. He did not resent it. He did not fight against it. If anything, Scape was the one who seemed to find time to complain about it. For the most part Frank went with the flow. If stagnation can be called a flow.

Then one day, Frank was returning with Scape from the refectory, when Frank spotted someone he recognised coming up the stairs towards them.

'Mr Vertex,' said Frank.

Mr Vertex looked at him and smiled warmly, his neat moustache widening as he did so.

'We met some time ago,' said Frank.

'Mr Palp,' said Mr Vertex. 'Of course. I remember it well. So, you have finally given in to the lure of the Ministry? How are you?'

'I'm well, sir,' said Frank. 'How are you?'

'I'm likewise very well, thank you, Frank,' he said. 'But very busy.'

'Of course, sir,' said Frank.

Frank stood aside, but Mr Vertex stayed where he was.

'Was there something in particular?' said Mr Vertex.

'No, sir,' said Frank. 'I just saw you and thought I ought to say hello.'

Mr Vertex smiled, seemingly expecting more.

'I'll let you get on, sir,' said Frank. 'It was nice to see you.'

'Likewise, Frank.'

Frank and Scape walked on and when they had passed through a set of fire doors, Scape grabbed Frank by the arm, turned him around and stared into his face wide-eyed.

'You know Vertex?' said Scape.

'Well, I wouldn't say "know",' said Frank.

'But you've spoken to him,' said Scape. 'You've had a conversation with him. He knows who you are. He called you Frank, for crying out loud!'

Frank laughed.

'Are you all right?' said Frank. 'You look like you're about to hyperventilate.'

'But how?' said Scape, waving his arms about. 'How would someone like you – no offence – get to speak to a man like that?'

Frank shrugged.

'We were in a bookshop,' said Frank. 'He asked me about what I was reading. We chatted. He gave me his card. He said if I wanted to get in touch then . . .'

Scape leant against the wall, shaking his head.

'Then why the hell are you working in Mandible's sector?' said Scape. 'I mean, I get why you don't want to work with your father – but why would you do the mind-numbing crap we have to do if you already have a passport out?'

'Hardly a passport,' said Frank.

'Listen,' said Scape. 'A man like that gives you a card, he expects a call. Beg him for work if you have to.'

Frank smiled.

'And leave you on your own?' said Frank.

'You're insane,' said Scape. 'I'd drop you in a heartbeat if it was me. You wouldn't see me for dust.'

Frank knew it was true. He looked back towards the door they'd come through.

'Who's to say it would be any better in his sector?' asked Frank.

'Are you kidding?' said Scape. 'He's one of the top Ministry Men. They don't come much higher. You have a Student living with you too, right?'

'Yes,' said Frank.

'Well, that's who they report to,' said Scape. 'There's nothing that happens in this town that Vertex doesn't know about, let me tell you. You want to go to university, don't you? There's your ticket.'

'I don't want to be a Student,' said Frank. 'I don't want to spy on people.'

'And you want to do this?' said Scape. 'You'd only have to be a Student for a while. Most of the top guys were Students once. I thought you hated it here.'

'I don't know about hate,' said Frank.

'I'm telling you, I'd still be contacting old Vertex. More money for a start, my friend. Much more money. Not the Students, but the men who work in Vertex's sector.'

'How do you know?' said Frank.

'I got our Student drunk one night,' said Scape. 'He was very talkative. He was moaning about it. They are getting five times what he makes. Which mean they must be getting about twice what we make.'

'We make more than the Students?' asked Frank.

Scape nodded. Frank could see his Student didn't spend money but he assumed he was sending most of it home to his family.

'They get house and board, care of the host family, so it's not too bad,' he said. 'Plus it's a route to greater things. It all depends who you get landed with, he reckons.'

Frank wondered how his family ranked as a place to be billeted. Or Scape's.

'Imagine, Frank,' said Scape. 'You could end up in some house up on the hill with a beautiful daughter in the next bedroom. Think of it! It beats being stuck in a cubicle all day talking to dimwits on the telephone.'

'Maybe,' said Frank. 'But to spy on people? I don't know. You might be responsible for getting someone sent to a labour camp or worse. And I don't need anyone's beautiful daughter in any case, remember. I'm already taken care of in that regard.'

Scape took a deep breath.

'Your Student,' he said after a moment. 'Does he have anything much to report, do you reckon?'

'No,' said Frank. 'But only because we are the most boring family in the whole world.'

'Well, then,' said Scape. 'Same with mine. So if you have nothing to hide, there's no problem, is there? Mostly it must be the easiest job ever. And if you do end up with bad apples then you're doing everyone a favour.'

'Bad apples?' said Frank.

Scape chuckled.

'You know what I mean. Enemy agents. Insurgents. Terrorists. You know the Ministry are always foiling plots.'

'So they say,' said Frank.

'It can't all be made up. There are some bad people out there. Crazy people. Don't tell me you wouldn't want them caught. You'd be doing a public service. Something actually worthwhile. I thought that crap meant something to you.'

Frank sighed.

'Look none of this matters because I'm not going to talk to Vertex,' he said.

'Then you're even weirder than I thought,' said Scape.

'Maybe I am,' said Frank. 'But there we are.'

Chapter 42

Frank cursed as he caught his fingers in the latch of the gate and kicked out at the metal bar, cursing loudly.

'You are in such a terrible mood,' said Olivia. 'Are you sure you want to do this?'

'Of course,' said Frank. 'Sorry. I'm not in a terrible mood. I promise.'

'You seem like you are,' said Olivia. 'You're definitely making me feel tense. Please, Frank. I want to make a good impression.'

'Look at this place,' said Frank as they walked through the courtyard. 'You don't need to make any kind of an impression here.'

'Don't be silly,' she said. 'I don't care where you live.'

'Really?' said Frank, raising an eyebrow. 'You wouldn't even get the tram here. I had to come and pick you up, remember?'

Olivia stared wide-eyed.

'That is so unfair!' she said. 'If you're going to be mean to me, I'm going home.'

'Sorry,' said Frank. 'You're right. You're right. I'm teasing.'

He smiled and they embraced. Frank opened the door into the lobby and Olivia walked through, heading straight for the lift.

'We'll take the stairs,' said Frank.

Olivia raised a sceptical eyebrow.

'You can if you want,' she said. 'You're not wearing these heels. Come on, give me the key.'

'I don't have a key.'

'What do you mean?' said Olivia. 'Stop being horrible.'

'I don't have a key,' he repeated. 'We don't have a key. No one we know does, actually.'

Olivia stared at him, baffled.

'Then what's the point of having a lift?' she said.

Frank shrugged. Olivia muttered something under her breath.

'Look,' said Frank. 'This is how things are in the Old Town. I'm really sorry.'

Olivia scowled at him and then shrieked as she saw Mr Spiracle emerge from the shadows, both eyebrows over his left eye, one above the other.

'Ah, Mr Spiracle,' said Frank with a sigh.

Olivia retreated and ducked behind Frank.

'Stay away from the lift,' he said. 'Stay away.'

'We will,' said Frank. 'Come on.'

Frank ushered Olivia away towards the stairs.

'Who was that that revolting old man?' said Olivia as they climbed.

'Mr Spiracle,' said Frank. 'Our resident madman. Doesn't your block have one?'

'He's horrible,' said Olivia.

'He's harmless,' said Frank. 'I used to be really frightened of him.'

It was only then that Frank realised he no longer was. Olivia shuddered.

'He's so creepy,' she said.

'You get used to him,' said Frank. 'I feel a bit sorry for him, to tell the truth.'

Olivia shuddered again and cast a quick disapproving glance at the shabby stairwell as they arrived at Frank's floor and walked towards his apartment.

'I'm not sure I ever would,' she whispered. 'You should report him.'

'What?' said Frank. 'Why?'

'Grrr,' she said. 'Don't be annoying.'

Frank opened the apartment door. His family had clearly heard their approaching footsteps and the attempt to look surprised and also casual was farcical.

'Hello!' said his mother, rushing forward so fast Olivia flinched. 'Come in, come in. You must be Olivia.'

They kissed.

'Lovely to meet you,' said Olivia. 'Thank you so much for inviting me.'

'You are most welcome, I'm sure,' said Frank's mother in a curious Old New Town accent he had never heard before.

'Frank, darling,' she said. 'Why don't you take Olivia's coat?'

Frank raised an eyebrow. He would have laid money on his mother never having said 'darling' in her entire life and certainly not to Frank. His father was also behaving very oddly. He was grinning.

Frank's father did smile – not often, but he did – but he never ever grinned. Never. Except that now he was. Frank took Olivia's coat and let his mother shepherd her towards his father, who greeted her with a warmth that Frank had never seen him display before.

Frank felt like he'd walked into a dream, where his family had all been replaced by unconvincing copies. Even the Student seemed to be making a special effort. Petra alone seemed to be authentically Petra, embracing Olivia warmly and leading her towards a seat.

'You probably don't remember me,' said Petra.

'No, I . . . I do,' said Olivia. 'You were two years above me. You were always in the library.'

'You were?' said Frank, looking at Petra.

'Frank thinks he's the only one who can read,' said Petra.

Olivia laughed and nodded.

'That's so true.'

'So, Olivia,' Frank's mother was saying. 'You live in the Old New Town?'

'Yes,' said Olivia. 'On Perseverance Boulevard.'

'I go past your apartment in the tram on the way to the market,' said Frank's mother.

'Isn't there a market in the Old Town?' asked Olivia.

'There is,' said Frank's mother with a sniff. 'But it's very . . . Well, let's just say one meets a better class of person at the market in the Old New Town.'

Olivia smiled and looked at Frank, who shrugged apologetically.

'You must be very excited about the Big Day, sir,' said Olivia.

'Yes,' said Frank's father, puffing out his chest. 'It will soon be upon us. Will you be going?'

'Oh yes,' said Olivia. 'My mother has tickets to the King's Courtyard.'

'Really?' said Frank. 'You never said.'

'You never asked,' said Olivia.

'Frank isn't much interested, Olivia,' said his father. 'He thinks it's a lot of fuss about nothing.'

'I've never said anything about it, Father,' said Frank with a frown.

'Well, I think it's marvellous,' said Olivia. 'I can't wait to see the King. I can't imagine what it must be like knowing you're really going to meet him.'

'Well . . .' said Frank's father.

Frank stared at him. Was he actually blushing?

'I think it's amazing what you and those other men did, sir. No one can believe Frank's your son, can they, Frank?'

'No,' said Frank.

'It's so good that they are making a big fuss of you after all this time.'

'You see, Frank?' said his mother.

'I've never said anything about it,' repeated Frank.

'Frank is a bit of a grouch, isn't he?' said Olivia.

'Oh, you don't know the half of it, Olivia,' said Frank's mother, shaking her head.

'I haven't said anything about it one way or another,' said Frank.

Everyone laughed. Except Frank.

The dinner wasn't nearly as bad as Frank had imagined it would be. The food was awful but Olivia didn't seem to mind, gamely working her way through the courses with an enthusiasm that Frank found disconcerting. Why did she feel the need to please his parents? Who cared what they thought?

Conversation was stilted, but Frank had expected that and

his mother eventually gave up on her posh accent, halfway through. Olivia made a very good show of not noticing.

In no time at all they were sitting drinking tea and the ordeal was almost over. Frank began to relax. Soon he would be heading back with Olivia and everyone could move on. But there was something he had to do first.

'I promised Olivia I'd show her my room,' said Frank.

Olivia looked a little confused, but did not resist as Frank took her hand and led her away. His parents exchanged looks and the Student took out his notebook.

'Don't be too long,' said Petra with a wink.

As soon as they were in the room and Frank had closed the door, Frank pulled Olivia close and eased her towards the bed. Olivia slapped him and pushed him away.

'What are you doing?' she said.

'What does it look like?' he said with a grin.

'Come on, Frank,' she said. 'Your parents are just down the hall.'

'I know,' he said. 'I just wanted to –'

He reached out and she slapped his arm again.

'Stop it,' said Olivia. 'It's weird.'

'Why?' said Frank. 'You're not like this at your place.'

'That's because my place is . . .'

'What?' said Frank.

She looked around the tiny room, screwing up her face.

'It smells,' she said.

'No it doesn't,' said Frank, sniffing.

'Yes it does,' she said. 'And you share a room with your Student?'

'Yes,' said Frank. 'We don't have a spare.'

'How awful for him,' said Olivia.

'For *him?*' said Frank. 'Thanks.'

'You know what I mean,' said Olivia.

'Not really, no,' said Frank.

Olivia ignored him and saw the typewriter.

'What's this?' she said.

'It's a type—'

'I know what it is, silly,' she said, slapping him. 'I mean, what's it doing here. Is it the Student's?'

'No,' said Frank. 'It's mine. You know I write. Well, I used to use it to write.'

'When are you going to let me read something you've written?' said Olivia.

'One of my stories? Well, I . . .'

'Please!' said Olivia.

'Sure,' said Frank. 'I suppose. Of course.'

Frank pulled out a ring binder and handed it to her.

'There's a few in there,' he said. 'You probably won't like them.'

'That's not the attitude,' said Olivia. 'You'll never be a bestselling Ministry author talking like that. I'm sure I'll love them. Come on, let's get back to your parents before they think that we're . . . you know . . .'

'Well, they'd be wrong, wouldn't they?' said Frank.

'Shut up, Frank.'

Frank nodded and they walked back to the lounge where they all pretended not to be waiting for them to return.

'What have you got there?' said Petra.

'Frank's letting me read some of his stories, sad Olivia.

Petra's smile wavered. She looked at Frank but he refused to make eye contact.

'Oh?' she said. 'I didn't think anyone was allowed to read them.'

Frank opened his mouth to speak but thought better of it.

'Well, I'd better be going, I suppose,' said Olivia. 'Thank you for having me.'

'You are very welcome,' said Frank's mother. 'I hope it won't be too long before you come back again.'

'That would be lovely,' said Olivia. 'Wouldn't it, Frank?'

Frank nodded dizzily, suddenly utterly exhausted. It was over. The world of Olivia and the world of his family had collided at last. Things would surely never be the same again.

'Frank writes stories?' said his father.

Chapter 43

Scape called for another two beers and smacked his hand on the counter when he got no immediate response. Frank saw the tired look in the eye of the barman and apologised.

'Don't apologise for me,' said Scape angrily when the barman left.

'I just –'

'Don't do it,' said Scape with some of the old threat in his tone of voice. Scape seemed to realise this and quickly broke into a smile.

'I just don't like people apologising for me,' he said, taking a swig of his beer. 'It make me . . . It makes me agitated.'

Maybe if you didn't do things to apologise for, thought Frank.

'So,' said Scape. 'How did it go? How did Olivia get on at your place?'

Frank shook his head and groaned.

'It was hideous,' he said. 'But at least it's over.'

'Over for now,' said Scape. 'Don't think it's going to stop there.'

Frank nodded. 'I suppose.'

'No suppose about it,' said Scape. 'You're hooked, my friend. She's got you in her web now. There's no escape.'

Frank smiled. It didn't actually sound so bad. If that was the worse that life had to offer then it wasn't terrible.

'Once you get parents involved, that's it,' said Scape. 'Believe you me.'

'You sound like you speak from experience,' said Frank.

'I speak from experience of avoiding it,' said Scape. 'I've never let my parents anywhere near any of my girlfriends. My father would have scared them away for a start. My mother thinks any girl I spend more than a day with is going to be my wife. Girls get that idea too, if they meet your folks.'

Frank shrugged. 'Well . . .'

'Look at you!' said Scape. 'You don't mind, do you? Mind you, I suppose you could do worse. There's a lot of money in that family.'

'That's got nothing to do with it,' said Frank. 'And anyway, the opposite is true for Olivia. There's no money in mine!'

'True,' said Scape. 'Remind me what the hell she sees in you again?'

Frank chuckled. Scape ordered another beer.

'Not for me,' said Frank.

'Oh, don't be such a misery,' said Scape.

'I'm not a misery, I just – oh, never mind.'

The beers arrived despite Frank having barely touched the previous one.

'Your round,' said Scape, lifting his up.

Frank frowned and paid the barman, who cast a quick glance at Scape before walking away to the other end of the bar.

'Do you never think about all that stuff then?' said Frank. 'Marriage?'

To Frank's surprise Scape nodded.

'Yes,' he said. 'I think about it.'

'Really?'

'I want to get married one day,' said Scape. 'Have a bunch of kids, the whole thing. Just not any time soon.'

'You?' said Frank. 'A family man?'

'What's so weird about that?' said Scape.

'I don't know,' said Frank.

He did know.

'I'd make a good father,' said Scape. 'Better than mine anyway. Isn't that the whole point of life? Get married, knock out some kids?'

He took a swig of his beer. Frank said nothing.

'But the way I look at it,' said Scape, 'you have to enjoy yourself while you're young. You have to get it out of your system, you know? Then you don't have any regrets when you're married.

'I've been out with quite a few girls in my time. Some of them have really got to me – but I've always been too curious about the next one. My father married the first girl he went out with. I think that's why he drank. He was riddled with regrets. Though he was lucky to find anyone who'd have him.'

'Is this about me?' said Frank.

'What?'

'Is this about me marrying the first girl I go out with?' said Frank.

'Firstly,' said Scape, 'I had no idea Olivia was your first but that's hilarious.'

He allowed himself a throaty chuckle before continuing.

'Secondly, it's different for you, Frank. If you've managed to get your hands on a girl like Olivia – rich, beautiful – then you need to count your blessings and go for it. It's not likely to happen twice.'

Frank frowned, but in his heart he knew Scape was absolutely right. This was as good as it was ever going to get for him and a lot better than he had ever had a right to expect.

'My advice is ask her to marry you,' said Scape. 'Do it now – as soon as you can. Before anything goes wrong. If she says yes, then you're home and dry.'

'And if she says no?'

'Better to find out, isn't it?' said Scape. 'I bet her mother loves you, doesn't she?'

Frank smiled.

'I think she does like me. She called me level-headed.'

'Well, then,' said Scape. 'That's good. I suppose.'

'But what if it's too fast?' said Frank. 'What if I frighten her off?'

Scape leant forward and rested his hand on Frank's shoulder, looking him straight in the eyes.

'The only thing that will frighten Olivia off is you being a wimp. You need to grow some balls.'

Frank nodded. Ordinarily he would assume Scape was wrong about anything that might come up, but Frank had to admit that Scape knew about women and he knew about Olivia.

'You're right,' said Frank.

'Of course I'm right,' said Scape.

Frank walked home. A crack of thunder signalled a torrential downpour of rain and Frank sheltered under an arcade supported by stone giants, naked except for a carved fig leaf.

Frank stood under the buttocks of one of the giants as water cascaded from a down-pipe nearby, flooding into the gutter and away down the street. Old Towners ran by, mirrored in the wet streets, some with umbrellas, others with their collars turned up. Lightning flashed and Frank looked up from under the arcade to see it strike the Castle high above him. The crack of thunder made him flinch and seemed to split the air like a whip.

He was suddenly struck by the full significance of his talk with Scape in the bar. Marriage. Was he really ready for that? To his surprise he felt that he was.

Frank didn't know if there was a point to life, but if there was, then Scape's notion that it was to get married and 'knock out some kids' was as likely as anything else.

Frank had always had some notion about it being something to do with fulfilment and self-expression but that was probably because he never saw himself ever being fulfilled through other people. He had always seen himself being essentially alone.

The storm passed over and rumbled away across the sky towards the mountains, lightning bursts illuminating the clouds as it did so. The rain gradually came to an end and Frank decided to take his chances and head off home.

Chapter 44

With his pay-day envelope in his jacket pocket, stuffed with notes, Frank set off through the maze of alleyways in the oldest quarter of the Old New Town in search of a jeweller Scape had told him about.

It amazed and baffled Frank how Scape just seemed to know everything about everything. Frank would have had no idea where to start looking for a place to buy a ring, and yet Scape – who had never actually bought one himself – knew straight away.

'There's a place near the cemetery,' Scape had told him. 'They get the best of the stuff the Ministry confiscates and they sell it for reasonable rates – especially if they know you're from the Castle.'

Frank was sure he was following Scape's instructions scrupulously but he still managed to get lost, and every time he got lost he had to walk back to the cemetery gates and start again, where Scape's instructions started. Each time he did so, he cast a furtive glance at the tree and his grandfather's grave, pricked by guilt for not having visited him for so long.

Eventually Frank gave up and asked a passer-by, who pointed Frank in the right direction. It turned out that he had walked past the shop half a dozen times, not even realising it was there.

Scape had said he had heard it was small, but Frank now saw that it was scarcely wider than the door, which itself was very narrow and at an angle. There was a thin window to one side in which, in tiny gilt letters, was painted 'Ootheca & Sons – Jewellers to the Ministry'.

Frank pushed the door and it opened with a high-pitched ping. He stepped inside and found that the floor was at the same acute angle as the door and he had to edge his way along the counter, stooped over to avoid the low ceiling.

'Hello?' he called.

The tiny shop was empty. There was a narrow counter, which was actually a long, thin glass case with glass shelves in it. On the shelves were little mounts holding various things – earrings and brooches, a rather grand-looking necklace. Frank couldn't see any rings though.

'Hello?'

'Yes?'

Frank jumped and banged his head on the ceiling as an ancient man appeared from behind the counter.

'Where? How?'

'I was down in the basement, sir,' said the man. 'I keep most of my stock down there. There is so little room up here – as you can see. Was there something in particular I can help you with?'

'I'm after a ring,' said Frank. 'An engagement ring.'

The old man beamed.

'Congratulations, sir.'

'She hasn't said yes yet,' said Frank.

'A formality, I'm sure,' said the old man. 'It is distasteful to talk of these things, sir, of course, but might I enquire as to what sort of figure you were thinking of in terms of price?'

Frank opened his mouth to speak but the old man put his finger to his lips.

'No, sir,' he said. 'I can't bear to talk of such things. I do this job for love you see. Love! Can you understand?'

'I suppose so,' said Frank. 'But –'

'I knew you would, sir,' said the jeweller. 'I saw it in your face. You're from the Castle, I imagine?'

'Yes, sir,' said Frank.

'Of course you are. And you want to get married and start a family and who can blame you?'

The old man clasped his hands together, smiled and nodded as though he was actually attending the ceremony or the birth of Frank's first-born child.

'Well, you have come to the right place, sir,' said the jeweller. 'Ootheca and Sons have been selling jewellery for centuries. We were in a bigger shop – in the Old Town – before the Revolution of course . . .'

The old man waved his fingers in the air and sighed. Frank was still a little unsure as to how exactly he would buy something if they could not talk about price.

'So how will we?' began Frank. 'You know. How do we –'

The old man winked at him and pursed his lips. He ripped a page from a memo pad on the counter.

'Here is a piece of paper,' said the jeweller, understanding Frank's meaning. 'And here . . . here is a pencil. Write the amount you were intending to spend and pass it back to me.'

Frank did as he was asked, writing the number and pushing the paper, face down, back across the counter. The jeweller smiled, winked again and picked up the paper. His smile instantly disappeared.

'I see,' he said, flaring his nostrils. 'Well, that does make things simpler. I have only one ring that answers your requirements, sir.'

The old man disappeared behind the counter and Frank leant over to see there was a set of stairs leading away downstairs. In no time at all, the man returned, holding a small red felt box. He placed it on the glass counter.

'Open it, sir,' he said.

Frank picked up the box and opened it. Inside was a ring – a plain silver ring with a single blue-white jewel held in a simple silver clasp.

'What is the stone?' said Frank. 'Is it a diamond?'

The old man made an almost indiscernible snorting noise.

'It is an ice stone from the Eastern mountains,' said the jeweller. 'They were very popular at one time. Touch it, sir.'

Frank did as he was asked and the stone really did feel like a piece of ice, freezing cold to the touch.

'Do you think that seems odd – giving someone an ice-cold ring as a love token?'

'I really couldn't say, sir,' said the old man.

'It's very plain,' said Frank.

The jeweller said nothing.

'It's perfect,' said Frank. 'I'll take it.'

Chapter 45

For one reason or another Frank's next date with Olivia was almost two weeks after her visit to his apartment – and days after buying the ring. They finally arranged to meet in the Winter Café.

Frank had never been so nervous. He rehearsed this meeting for days. He knew exactly what he wanted to say and how to say it. He had written it, rewritten it, edited and redrafted it a dozen times until every tiny detail was perfect. If he couldn't be easy-going like Scape, he could at least write himself a good speech.

He knew exactly where he wanted to sit for maximum effect. That was important, he was sure. This was going to become a memory they would share for the rest of their lives. It needed to be perfectly designed. But for the first time ever, Olivia was there ahead of him.

'I'll have a coffee,' said Frank when the waitress came over, a little put-out by this disruption of his plans, but still determined to make the best of it. 'Do you want another one?'

Olivia shook her head. She had barely said a word to him. Frank waited for their coffees to arrive and as soon as the waitress was a safe distance away, he leant across and held Olivia's hand.

'Olivia,' said. 'There is so much I want –'

'Don't,' said Olivia.

'Is there something the matter?' said Frank. 'It's just that –'

'It's over, Frank,' she said.

Frank sat back. He had been about take the ring box out of his pocket, but he left it where it was for the moment. There was a look he had never seen on Olivia's face. Or maybe not since school. A shadow of the haughtiness he had found so intimidating passed across the table.

'What? What's over?'

'Us,' said Olivia.

'What do you mean?'

He knew what she meant.

'We're over, Frank.'

'No we're not,' said Frank. 'Stop saying that. It isn't funny.'

Olivia closed her eyes. She couldn't even look at him.

'Don't make this harder.'

'Why?' he said.

'Why is it over?' said Olivia, opening her eyes, but not completely. 'Or why not make it harder?'

'Why is it over?'

'I just can't do this any more,' she said with a sigh. 'I'm sorry.'

'Do what any more?'

'This!'

Olivia had hissed the word with such venom that Frank actually flinched.

Frank hunted through his recent memories of their meetings. Had he done something, said something?

'Is this about my parents?' he said after a moment. 'Is it about my mother's stupid accent? Is it –'

'No,' said Olivia. 'It has nothing to do with your parents.'

'A bit of a coincidence though, eh?' he said.

Could she really be that shallow? Could one visit to the Old Town and to his crappy apartment block end everything?

'Even so,' said Olivia, wafting at a crumb on the table.

'I don't understand,' said Frank. 'Everything was fine and –'

'No,' she said. 'It wasn't fine. We were just pretending it was.'

'I wasn't pretending,' said Frank.

She tossed her head back as though talking to him was torture.

'I don't know what to say,' she said.

'There has to be some reason,' said Frank.

'I don't love you,' she said. 'That's the reason.'

The words hit him like a chop to the throat and he found it hard to speak.

'Why don't you love me any more?' he said. 'What have I done? Or not done? Tell me.'

She looked at him for a long time. Olivia reached down to her bag and pulled out the ring binder with Frank's stories.

'You should have these back.'

Frank had forgotten he'd even given them to her. He took them and stared out of the window. A tram rumbled past.

'Did you read them?'

'Yes,' said Olivia.

'What did you think?' said Frank, looking at her.

But he could tell what she thought wasn't good.

'I hated them,' she said.

'I see,' said Frank, picking up the ring binder. 'Thanks.'

He hadn't thought he would care but he could feel his heart fluttering. This was why he had never shown them to anyone before, he understood that now.

'I didn't . . . I didn't understand them,' she said, her voice sounded resentful and exasperated. 'They weren't even . . . They made me feel – I don't know, like you were telling a joke that was too clever for me.'

'Well, I'm sorry,' said Frank coolly. 'I'm sorry they made you feel stupid.'

'I'm not stupid, Frank,' said Olivia.

'I never said you were.'

'You think it though,' she said.

'That's rubbish,' said Frank.

He was getting angry now.

'Yes, you do,' she said. 'You'd rather be going out with my mother. She'd have loved these.'

'Would she?' said Frank. 'Maybe you should hang on to them then.'

Olivia closed her eyes.

'I don't want to fight,' she said. 'I just realised what I knew deep down when I read these: that we are not suited. We can never be suited. You're too . . . weird.'

Frank stared at her.

'Wait, you're breaking up with me because you didn't like my stories?' said Frank.

'In a way,' she said.

'That's mad.'

'Is it?' she asked. 'Are those stories not important to you, then? Are they not a big part of who you are?'

'Yes,' said Frank. 'But –'

Olivia folded her arms tightly across her chest and leant back in her seat.

'Look, I never loved you,' she said. 'I thought I would – I thought I could, but it turns out I can't. I'm sorry.'

If she had punched him in the face it could not have struck him harder or sharper.

'You're . . . sorry?' he said.

His own voice now seemed muffled and distant, as though it was coming from a cave.

'Yes,' she said.

Frank stared at her, unable to say anything. For the first time in his life there were no words in his head.

'I know these things don't matter to you,' she said, 'but I want to get married and have a nice apartment and travel. I earn as much as you, Frank. How many years will it take to ever get a decent job at the Ministry? You have no ambition.'

He shook his head.

'No ambition?'

'No,' she said. 'I heard that you know Mr Vertex.'

'Really?' he said. 'And I wonder who you heard that from?'

'Don't interrogate me,' she said. 'The point is you'd rather do your stupid job than go to him and grab a chance at being somebody.'

'Because I'm nobody now?'

'You see,' she said, raising an eyebrow. 'You *do* understand.'

Frank took a deep breath.

'To think I used to dream about you – about being with you,' he said.

'You can't blame me for that. But even then – you dreamt about me instead of doing anything about it. That's you all over. You're a dreamer, not a doer.'

Frank felt numb.

'I did do something. I used to cycle past your apartment every chance I got just hoping you'd come out,' mumbled Frank.

'What?' she said. 'You used to do what?'

Frank's heart sank further.

'I used to cycle past your apartment hoping to see you,' he said. 'Hoping to bump into you.'

'Why?' she said. 'Why not ask me out if you knew where I lived?'

'Because . . .' began Frank, the memory of it flooding back. 'Because I didn't feel worthy of you, if you must know. I thought you'd laugh in my face. So I wanted us to meet by chance. I wanted you to come out and we'd meet by accident.'

She peered at him with something like revulsion on her face.

'How did you know where I lived?' she said.

'I just knew,' said Frank.

'So you didn't bump into me at all that day?' she said. 'You'd been following me?'

'No,' said Frank. 'Well, yes. I can't explain. It was fate! Finding the bottle – finding the wish.'

Olivia stared at him.

'What are you talking about?' she said.

'Look – I'll show you,' he said.

Frank opened his jacket and took out the paper and unfolded it, smoothing it out on the table.

ANYTHING THAT ISN'T THIS

'What the hell is that supposed to mean?' she said.

Frank stared at her, then at the note, then back to her.

'Well, you wrote it,' he said. 'I took it to mean you –'

'Me?' she said. 'What are you on about? Why would I write that? I don't even know what it means!'

Olivia grabbed the paper, crumpled it into a tight ball in her fist and threw it on the floor.

'But it was your birthday wish,' said Frank. 'You threw it off the bridge. I watched you.'

'What?' she said. 'You are such a creep. You *have* been following me.'

She shuddered.

'Look,' he said. 'I don't get it. I –'

Olivia got up and slapped him hard round the face.

'I wished for a nose job!' she said.

'But . . . But I love your nose – it's the best thing about you!'

She slapped him again – harder this time – and stomped away, slamming the café door behind her as she left.

Frank's face was hot and stinging and his brain was still shaking from the shock of it. The waitresses at the far end of the room were giggling. Frank picked up the crumpled note, put it in his pocket, paid the bill and left.

Frank walked to the railway bridge in a daze and was halfway across before he even realised where he was. He stood and looked down at the river flowing by, took out the box with the ice-stone ring.

Frank opened the box and touched the stone with his finger. It didn't even feel cold any more. Frank snapped the box shut and dropped it into the water.

Chapter 46

Ravens croaked high above the sooty pinnacles of the Castle, as they had done for century upon century. They wheeled and dived and came to rest along a roof ridge, gazing idly down at the humans in the courtyard below. Frank heard them call but did not take his eyes off his Guide as they strode purposefully through the throng.

'Mr Vertex will see you now,' said the secretary, clip-clopping towards him as he approached.

Frank knocked on the door. There was no response so he knocked again.

'Enter.'

Frank opened the door and stepped inside, amazed to find that the ceiling of the office, unlike the low-ceilinged reception area and corridor outside it, was arched high above like the vaulting in a cathedral. It was just like in the refectory, but here the room was its true height.

It was in the oldest part of the Castle and had an enormous fireplace, tall enough for both of them to stand in had there not been a raging fire burning in the hearth. Mr Vertex was standing with his back to Frank studying something on his bookshelves. The bookshelves covered nearly all the walls. Frank had never seen so many books in all his life.

'Hello, Frank,' said Mr Vertex.

'Good morning, sir,' said Frank.

'Sit down,' he said.

'Thank you, sir,' said Frank. 'This is quite a library.'

'Yes,' said Mr Vertex. 'It certainly is.'

They both looked up at the bookshelves for a moment.

'I'm very glad you decided to come and see me, Frank,' said Mr Vertex. 'Do you mind if I ask if there was anything in particular that brought about this change of mind?'

'Well, sir,' said Frank, 'I think I just realised that the opportunities for advancement were few in Mr Mandible's sector. I suppose I'm ambitious. I want to do more.'

'I see,' said Mr Vertex. 'Good.'

'I'm not suggesting that the work I do for Mr Mandible is not important,' said Frank.

'Quite,' said Mr Vertex, looking through some papers on his desk. 'All the work of the Ministry has its own importance. We are all vital cogs in the greater machine.'

'Yes, sir.'

'I see that in your career interview at school you expressed an interest in working in the Ministry.'

'Yes, sir,' said Frank.

'Yet when I first met you, you seemed not at all sure of that as a career path. You only said that at school because your father and sister work here and you really hadn't any idea of what you actually wanted to do. Isn't that right?'

Frank eyed him suspiciously.

'Come, now,' said Mr Vertex. 'It's not a trick question. I'm not interrogating you.'

'Then yes, sir,' said Frank. 'I suppose that was how I felt then.'

Mr Vertex smiled and tapped the tips of his fingers together.

'Honesty,' said Mr Vertex with a smile. 'It's rarer than you think. Some people believe it is just a matter of saying the correct answer, but it's more than that – much more. It's a quality I value more than any other, Frank. Do you understand?'

'Yes, sir,' said Frank.

Mr Vertex nodded.

'Have you ever thought about becoming a Student?'

'No,' said Frank, a little quicker than he had intended.

Mr Vertex laughed.

'You see? Honesty is mostly about *not* giving the correct answer.'

Frank smiled, but shifted uncomfortably in his chair.

'Don't worry. It's natural,' said Mr Vertex. 'No one likes a Student, it's true.'

Mr Vertex winked at Frank.

'But don't dismiss it,' he said. 'It would only ever be a phase in your career. You would get to study at university. I know you want that.'

'You do?' said Frank.

'Well, of course I do,' said Mr Vertex. 'You are a thinker, Frank. It's clear from all these reports. It's clear from talking to you for five minutes.

'The school reports say you don't concentrate. But you don't concentrate because you are thinking. They don't understand that. They think intelligence is all about soaking up knowledge and spitting it out when required. But true intelligence – the intelligence that really counts – is the ability to interpret facts, to make them your own.'

312

'My teachers wouldn't agree,' said Frank.

'If they are so clever, Frank,' said Mr Vertex, 'why are they teaching in that dreary school?'

Frank smiled.

'I didn't really get the results necessary to go to university, sir.'

'Let me worry about that,' he said. 'Exams are a way of sorting through the great mass of the people. They are a sckrupff spoon and nothing more. They are only one way. They work well enough for the ordinary citizen, but in your case I am much more interested in my gut.'

Mr Vertex patted his belly.

'My gut has never let me down, and my gut tells me that you will fit in well here.'

Frank smiled.

'Does this mean I am coming to work for you, sir?'

'Yes, Frank,' said Mr Vertex. 'Although there is a catch.'

'Sir?' said Frank.

'You have to want to work for me,' said Mr Vertex.

'Yes, sir,' said Frank. 'Of course.'

'So let me hear you say it,' said Mr Vertex.

'Say what, sir?' asked Frank.

'Say that you want to work here,' said Mr Vertex

'You want to hear me say it?' said Frank. 'Out loud?'

'Yes,' said Mr Vertex.

Frank found his mouth suddenly dry.

'I . . . I want to work here,' said Frank. 'I want . . . to work for you.'

'There,' said Mr Vertex. 'That wasn't so hard, was it?'

Mr Vertex stood up. Frank did likewise.

'Frank,' said Mr Vertex, shaking him by the hand.

'Sir,' said Frank.

'Come this way,' he said.

Frank followed Mr Vertex out of his office and down a corridor, then up a flight of stone steps that looked like something that might have formed part of the original fortifications. At the top was a dark corridor and Mr Vertex stopped at the first door.

'Open it, Frank,' he said.

Frank did as he was told.

'Go inside,' said Vertex.

Mr Vertex switched the light on as he followed Frank inside. It was a small office with a desk and chair, a filing cabinet and a phone. It also, to Frank's amazement had a window, and he could not resist looking out.

He had not realised how high he was. The window was on the very outer edge of the old Castle walls, overlooking the Old Town and his apartment building. He tried to work out which rooftop was that of his family home but they all looked alike. Mr Vertex came and stood beside him.

'Whose office is this, sir?' asked Frank.

'It's yours,' he said.

'Mine?' said Frank. 'Really, sir?'

Mr Vertex smiled.

'Really.'

Frank looked around the room with different eyes now, taking it in anew, claiming it as his own. An office? An office!

'I have great hopes for you, Frank,' said Mr Vertex. 'You remind me of myself – or how I was when I was your age.'

314

'I'm flattered, sir,' said Frank.

'Don't be,' said Mr Vertex. 'Just reward my faith in you, Frank. Be what we both know you can be. Don't limit yourself. Forget everything you thought yourself capable of before you walked through that door.'

He pointed out of the window.

'That world is not for you,' he said. 'You've always known that. You just couldn't take the next step without my help.

'Friends and family will not understand your work,' he continued. 'Don't expect them to. They can't. They will not accept you for who you are – for who you will become. In our early lives, families nurture us and push us forward, but as we grow older, they hold us back. They do not want us to grow. They are chains, Frank. Shake them off.'

Frank said nothing. Mr Vertex leant across and touched him on the arm.

'Frank,' he said. 'I say these things with no unkindness intended. They are merely lessons learnt over years following a path not unlike the one I think you will find yourself on.'

On Frank's desk was a pile of small notebooks. Mr Vertex walked over and patted them. Frank recognised them instantly as the same grey Ministry issue notebooks the Student used. Mr Vertex picked one up.

'What I want you to do,' he said, 'is to read these notebooks.'

'Read them, sir?' said Frank.

'Yes,' said Mr Vertex. 'I want you to read them and to look for . . . patterns. Anything that might arouse your interest – your suspicion. Do you understand?'

315

For a moment Frank wondered if this was going to be another pointless task like the directory checking one with Mr Mandible, but he saw that it wasn't.

'I think so, sir,' said Frank. 'You want me to see if anything unusual appears.'

'No,' said Vertex, shaking his head. 'Not necessarily unusual. It may be completely usual. It may be the most usual thing in the world. But there may be something about its mundanity that leaps out at you in some way.'

'Yes, sir,' said Frank.

'We collect this information,' said Mr Vertex. 'We gather it up and see what we have. Much of it is useless. You are like a gold prospector, sieving for gold among the grit. It's a skill. It's one that I believe you may possess. Don't let me down.'

'I'll try not to sir,' said Frank.

Mr Vertex looked at him.

'Frank,' he said. 'One last thing. Do not do this work to please me. You are not with Mr Mandible now. You need to believe in this work. You have to make it your own. You wanted more from your career at the Ministry – well, then . . . make this your vocation.'

Frank nodded.

'Yes, sir,' said Frank.

'This work is the most important work the Ministry does,' he said. 'I'm not just saying that because it is my sector or to flatter your interest. This work is vital. It keeps your mother safe. It keeps your sister safe. We can't all be soldiers, can we? We can't all be that kind of hero.'

Frank nodded. Mr Vertex smiled. The reference to Frank's father was subtle and welcome. Frank felt a conspiratorial bond. Here were two intellectuals, using their brains instead of their brawn. Here were two men who loved books, using that trained mind for the good of the people. Heroes, just as much as any soldier.

Mr Vertex left, closing the door behind him. Frank looked around his office, taking in every detail, right down to the crack in the wall.

He walked round his desk and sat down in his swivel chair, swinging right and left, eventually banging his knee painfully against the desk leg.

He opened up the drawers. They were empty. He wondered who the last occupant of the office was and then suddenly wondered why they were no longer here. How long would he be here? he wondered.

Frank picked up one of the Student notebooks. Just as he did so, there was a tremendous shudder in the whole fabric of the building that sent books tumbling to the floor from shelves and sent his phone crashing into the waste paper basket.

Frank jumped up and ran to the door. There was another shudder and he was knocked sideways into the wall. There was a Guide coming towards him.

'What's going on?' said Frank in a panic, coughing on the dust raining down from the ceiling. 'Is it an earthquake?'

'No,' said the Guide as another shudder sent them both stumbling. 'It happens from time to time. You'll get used to it.'

'What is it?' said Frank, sceptical that he would ever get used to such a thing.

'It's the tunnels,' said the Guide. 'There are so many of them. They have completely undermined the Castle. Every so often –'

Another shudder seemed to drop the whole corridor down about a foot.

'Every so often,' continued the Guide, 'the Castle shifts and settles. That was the last one probably. You get to tell these things when you've seen as many as I have.'

They stood expectantly for a while but the Guide seemed to be right. After a couple of minutes he winked at Frank and carried on along the corridor as though nothing had happened.

Frank went back into his office, picked up the fallen books, replaced the phone on his desk, brushed the dust from his jacket, picked up a notebook and began to read.

Chapter 47

Frank had tried several times to broach the subject of Olivia and their break up with his parents but could not bring himself to do so. Any sense of embarrassment had long gone; he just didn't want to have the conversation. Finally, as they all sat together watching someone on the Ministry Talent Show juggling kittens, Frank blurted it out.

'I've split up with Olivia,' he said. 'Or rather, she's split up with me.'

His parents turned to face him with shocked expressions as the audience on the television applauded ecstatically. The Student made a note in his book, shaking his head.

'Why?' said his mother, getting up to turn the television off. 'What have you done?'

'Done?' said Frank. 'I haven't done anything.'

'Well, something must have happened,' said his mother. 'She seemed so keen when she was round here.'

'Have you been caught seeing someone else?' said his father.

Frank sighed.

'It's us, isn't it?' said his mother, pursing her lips.

'It's nothing to do with you,' said Frank.

'Well, I think it is,' said his mother.

'It's personal. It has nothing to do with you.'

'Typical Old New Towners,' said his mother.

'What's that supposed to mean?'

'We're not good enough for them,' said his mother.

'It's not about you,' said Frank. 'How many times?'

'I'll just say, so you know: I didn't like her,' said his mother. 'I didn't like her at all.'

'You said you thought she was lovely,' said Frank.

'What was I supposed to say?' said his mother.

'You were all over her when she was here,' said Frank.

'Neither of us liked her, son,' said his father, puffing out his chest. 'That's the truth of it.'

'Well, this is nice,' said Frank. 'And were you ever going to tell me?'

'She wasn't right for you,' said his father.

'Is that so?' said Frank.

'So what reason did she give?' said his father.

Frank wished he could work all day and night and never have to speak to his parents at all.

'Was it money?' said his father. 'She looked a bit high maintenance for you.'

'Can we drop this now?' said Frank. 'You never liked her, so what does it matter?'

'Do you want me to have a word with Mr Mandible?' said his father. 'He knows me. He's been happy with what you do – told me himself. Why don't I –'

'It's not money!' shouted Frank. 'Why won't you listen? It's nothing to do with any of that.'

His father sat back in his chair staring at him, his nostrils flaring, the electric hum building in volume.

'No need to shout, son.'

'Besides,' said Frank. 'I don't work for Mandible any more.'

'What?' said his father.

'Oh, Frank,' said his mother. 'Have you been fired? Oh, is this what it's all –'

'Will you listen to me?' yelled Frank, standing up and banging his hand on the table. The Student jumped, dropping his notebook. Frank's father got up at the same time and banged his hand down, glowering at him.

'Calm down and sit down,' he said. 'Before I knock you down.'

Frank stared back at him, his mother glancing between them. The Student held his pencil in a shaking hand.

'Please, Frank,' she said. 'Sit down.'

Frank took a deep breath and sat down. His father did the same.

'I don't work for Mandible any more because I work for Mr Vertex.'

Frank's father peered at him.

'What?'

'It's better money,' said Frank. 'Better work.'

'How did you meet Mr Vertex?' said his father coldly.

'I met him ages ago,' said Frank. 'In a bookshop. He gave me his card and said if I ever wanted to work with him to get in touch.'

'And were you ever going to tell us?' said his father.

'Of course,' said Frank. 'I just . . . didn't think it was important.'

'I don't like secrets, Frank,' said his father.

'It wasn't a secret,' said Frank.

'Working for Mr Vertex for five minutes and already you're telling lies,' said his father.

'I haven't told you any lies,' said Frank. 'I just didn't tell you I'd changed sectors. Oh, I'm going to my room.'

Frank lay on his bed, staring at the ceiling. Every time he closed his eyes he saw Olivia, so he kept them open and stared until tears dribbled down the side of his face and into his ears.

The Student eventually came in and Frank sat up, drying his eyes. The Student ignored him and slumped to the bed, his face white and clammy.

'You look terrible,' said Frank.

'It will pass,' said the Student, but in a voice so quiet, Frank had to lean forward to hear it.

'What's the matter with you?' asked Frank. 'I thought you had recovered.'

'I don't know,' said the Student. 'I seem to have these relapses – these periods of weakness. The doctors say there is nothing actually the matter with me. Maybe I've just read too many of your stories.'

This amused the Student greatly and he laughed and choked and coughed and laughed and choked and wheezed.

'You've read my stories?' said Frank.

'Of course,' said the Student, smiling awkwardly.

Frank knew he ought to have been annoyed, but in reality he was a little bit flattered.

'They are really rather good,' he said.

'You think so?' said Frank.

322

The Student coughed and spluttered, nodding his head.

'Oh yes,' he said. 'I like them a lot. I was surprised.'

'Surprised?' said Frank.

The Student rubbed his chin nervously.

'To be honest, I didn't think you capable,' said the Student. 'No offence.'

Frank sighed and smiled.

'None taken,' said Frank.

'But you do not write any more?' said the Student.

'I do,' said Frank. 'I've just been busy.'

'You have not written anything new in months,' said the Student, checking his notebook.

'Rubbish,' said Frank.

But thinking about it now, the Student was possibly correct.

'I've been busy,' repeated Frank.

The Student nodded.

'You have been in love,' said the Student.

Frank smiled.

'I suppose I have,' he said. 'But not now.'

'And it hurts?' said the Student. 'The lack of love.'

'Yes,' said Frank. 'Sometimes.'

'But better to have loved and lost,' said the Student. 'As they say.'

'Do they?' said Frank. 'Well, maybe they need to think again.'

'No,' said the Student. 'It is better, believe me. Even unrequited love is better than none.'

There was something in the way that the Student said this.

'You sound like you speak from experience,' said Frank.

'I do,' said the Student.

'You?' said Frank, trying, but not succeeding, to sound casual.

'Yes,' said the Student. 'Does that seem so unlikely to you?'

'No,' said Frank.

It seemed very unlikely.

'But how?' said Frank. 'I mean, is it a girl from where you live – back in your village?'

The Student shook his head.

'Then how? Who? You rarely leave this apartment and the only women you ever meet are my mother and . . .'

Frank stared at the Student.

'Petra, yes,' said the Student, softly, as though he was whispering it into her ear.

'You love Petra?' said Frank.

The Student nodded.

'Petra? Petra my sister?'

The Student nodded again.

'But she's married,' said Frank.

'I know,' said the Student. 'I shouldn't have said anything. I know nothing can come of it. But love will not be tamed, will it? It goes where it pleases. I just needed to tell someone.'

'But why me?' said Frank.

The Student slumped back.

'Who else would I tell?' said the Student.

'Not me,' said Frank.

'I thought you would understand.'

Frank put his hand to his face, closing his eyes and rubbing the eyelids with his finger. He thought of Petra and Ralph and he thought of Petra with the Student. He sighed.

'I'm going to get you properly better again,' said Frank.

The Student shook his head.

'I'm fine.'

'You're not fine,' said Frank. 'You're not eating properly. You're sickly. You need exercise. You need to get out of this place and get some air. And you need some new clothes.'

Frank took out his wallet and pulled out some notes, handing them to the Student.

'No,' said the Student. 'I can't.'

'Yes,' said Frank. 'You can.'

'It's your money.'

'I don't have anyone to spend it on any more. Take it. Use it.'

After a moment the Student took the money.

'Thank you.'

'And stop hanging around in this apartment all the time,' said Frank. 'Believe me, this place would depress a clown.'

'Why do you care?' said the Student.

'I don't know,' said Frank. 'I think I just need to do something good while I still can.'

The Student smiled.

'Maybe it's because if I die you'll lose your only reader.'

Frank smirked.

'You're not going to die.'

'Good,' said the Student. 'I don't think I want to die.'

Chapter 48

Frank sat with his back against a tombstone. A raven croaked high above him but he could not actually see the bird through the tangle of twigs.

He pulled his shoulders up and sunk his chin into his chest, hugging himself against the chill breeze that snaked between the graves. There was a whiff of winter in the air.

Frank hadn't been to the cemetery for weeks. He had thought about it often but never seemed to manage to find time. He missed his grandfather when he thought about him, but he didn't have the need for the stories any more.

He did not seem to have room in his life for fiction. He did not read or write – only Student notebooks and his reports.

He had almost given up at the gate because he could barely budge it. The hinges seem to have rusted up entirely since his last visit and it was painful to scrape through the tiny gap he managed to prise open.

'Grandfather?' he said.

Silence.

'Grandfather?'

Frank was about to speak again when he heard his grandfather stirring, although he still did not reply. Frank was about to get to his feet and leave when his grandfather finally spoke.

'I wasn't expecting you,' said his grandfather matter-of-factly. 'You haven't been for so long.'

Frank said nothing. His grandfather made a noise Frank could not quite make out. A sniff, perhaps.

'I did say that I was going to be working now,' said Frank.

'You did,' said his grandfather.

'Well, then,' said Frank. 'I'm sorry. I've been busy.'

'What is it like?' said his grandfather. 'Working?'

Frank shrugged.

'I don't know,' said Frank. 'I don't think about it much.'

'You find it unfulfilling?' said his grandfather.

Frank laughed.

'Does anyone find their work fulfilling?'

'If they believe in their work, yes,' said his grandfather. 'If they believe it has meaning.'

Frank sighed.

'Well, anyway,' he said.

'Do you see your father at work?'

'No,' said Frank. 'We aren't really in the same sector.'

'I see,' said his grandfather.

'I see a friend from school,' said Frank.

'I didn't think you had any friends at school,' said his grandfather.

'Neither did I,' said Frank cheerfully. 'We have become friends. The truth is, when he was at school I hated him.'

'What has changed?'

'Him, I suppose,' said Frank. 'Or me. Both, maybe. But in any case I don't really even see him now. I've changed sectors.'

'I see,' said his grandfather. 'It sounds like a lot has happened. Nothing much has changed here, as you may have noticed.'

'Tell me a story, Grandfather,' said Frank.

'Are you sure?' he said. 'Are you sure you haven't outgrown my stories?'

'Yes,' said Frank. 'I'm sure.'

His grandfather seemed to shift position under the earth as if trying to think of a suitable story. It was a while before he spoke.

'There was a peasant who worked a small plot of poor soil in the flatlands to the east,' began his grandfather, 'who was plagued by the attentions of a demon.'

'Sorry?' said Frank. 'He was what?'

'Are you even listening?' asked his grandfather.

328

'Of course I am,' he said. 'I'm just a bit distracted. I was thinking about work.'

His grandfather sighed dustily.

'Carry on,' said Frank. 'The demon. Tell me about him.'

After a pause, Frank's grandfather began again.

'Every time the peasant went to the field, the demon would be with him. When he ploughed the earth, the demon would infest the ground with rocks that would dent the blade.

'He would cripple the ox and breathe disease into the livestock. He brought drought until the earth was as hard as iron and then rained floods upon the fields that washed away the topsoil and the paltry crops.

'Plague and famine followed in the demon's wake and the farmer lost first his wife and then his children, one by one, until one day he fell to the ground at the demon's feet and beat the earth with his fists.

'"Why do you curse me so?" he yelled. "I am not a bad man. My sins are small. Why do you treat me so badly? Everything I try to do, you ruin. You have destroyed everything I love. Finish the job and kill me now!"

'But the demon remained motionless. The peasant looked up and was shocked to see the demon's normally fierce and grotesque face contorted into an expression of anguish, tears welling in his eyes.

'"Treat you so badly?" he said. "But you do not understand. I have done what I could to protect you."

'The peasant got to his feet and stared at him.

'"What?' he yelled. "In what way have you protected us?"

329

'"There is a demon at my shoulder whom you could not even bear to look at," said the demon. "If you but knew what he had planned for you. I have only managed to keep him away from you by these torments you complain of – but believe me when I say they are mild in comparison to those he would heap on you. Out of love, I have taken those torments myself, for he must be satisfied."

'The peasant took a moment to take this in.

'"It seems I have done you a disservice, demon," he said. "But tell me this – why does this other demon torment us both? What have we done to earn his bile?"

'"But you must not blame him," said the demon. "For he has another demon at his back – a demon whose attentions I could not endure for a moment."'

Frank's mind was filled with demons getting bigger and stranger stretching off into infinity.

'The girl I told you about a long time ago,' said Frank.

'Yes?' said his grandfather.

'The one I could never get the courage up to speak to?'

'Yes,' said his grandfather. 'I know the one. How many were there?'

Frank smiled.

'Just that one,' said Frank.

'Well?' said his grandfather.

'We went out together,' said Frank.

'Good for you,' said his grandfather.

'It's over now,' said Frank.

Frank was surprised at how much it still stung to say those words.

'I really loved her, Grandfather,' said Frank.

But even as he said it, Frank wasn't sure this was true any more.

'Sometimes I wish that I could just get on a motorbike and ride off into the mountains,' said Frank.

'A motorbike?' said his grandfather. 'I didn't know you had a motorbike.'

'I don't,' said Frank. 'I was just saying. If I did have one. I just feel like getting away from it all, you know?'

'I'm sorry, Frank,' said his grandfather. 'Truly. But there will be another love for you.'

'How can you know that?'

'Because I'm a writer,' he said. 'I know how these things work. Believe me. This isn't the end.'

Chapter 49

Frank didn't see much of Scape now. He wondered if he had ever bought his motorbike. He hadn't even told him about Olivia although he knew he would have found out by now. Olivia and her Old New Town friends would probably be having a good laugh at Frank's expense. He told himself he didn't care, but it burnt away at him every time he thought about it.

Frank didn't see the point of seeing Scape after work because he knew Scape would quiz him about what he was doing and Frank couldn't say. He didn't have to see Scape at lunchtime because the workers in Mr Vertex's sector had their own small cafeteria. People sat on their own, mostly. It seemed that the work encouraged a desire for solitude. The chatter of voices coming from the Student notebooks meant that lunch was a welcome break and the workers sat quietly, savouring the silence.

Frank would have welcomed some conversation himself. He found that the silence only allowed thoughts of Olivia to return. So Frank tried whenever he could to get a seat by the window and he would stare out at the rooftops of the Old Town and try as much as he could to completely clear his mind of everything.

The only place where Frank was content was in his office,

working. The truth was, much to his surprise, that Frank found this new work fascinating.

At first it was just the feeling that he was doing something that actually had some point to it, as opposed to his weeks in the cubicle checking the directory. But it quickly became more than that.

Frank had always been an observer. Some of this had been forced on him by his inability to fit in at school or at home, but however it had come about, it made him a natural for this work.

Looking at these notebooks was like standing in the room with the families they depicted. To read the notebooks was to be the Students – to stand in their shoes, notebook in hand – but to do more than they were allowed to.

Frank was allowed to use his imagination – something the Students were expressly forbidden to do. Frank was allowed to sift through this raw data and look for stories. The Students were only allowed to record the 'what' and the 'when', but Frank was allowed – no, actively encouraged – to look for the 'why'.

Wasn't that, in essence, what writers did? They absorbed all the raw data of the world around them, looked for patterns and then made their report. This job wasn't the same as being a writer, but it was closer than Frank had ever thought he would get and it certainly felt like he was being employed for an actual talent he possessed, rather than just being used like a machine.

Was it wrong for him to enjoy his work? Was that a crime? All it meant was that he would do it well and do it correctly. He would make sure that no one came under suspicion who did not deserve to be. It was just like Scape had said after they bumped into Vertex that day – he might foil the plans of enemy agents or terrorists. It was important work.

338

Frank was on his way back from lunch when he took a detour to pick up some new notebooks and once again saw Petra. She was standing at some secretary's desk and once again she was suffering the attentions of two men Frank did not know. They were pushing themselves against her, whispering things to her and laughing.

Again, Petra was laughing whilst also trying to back away. The laugh was small and fake and forced. Frank could see she was in difficulty. The secretary was frowning at the men but they were ignoring her. It was Petra they were interested in.

Petra edged along the desk, trying to put some distance between her and them, but she was running out of space as she started to back into a wall.

Frank heard her tell them to stop being silly, that she'd shout out, but they did not stop. Petra was now pinned against the wall, unable to get further away or escape. One of the men lunged at her, pulling at her clothes and trying to kiss her.

Frank strode up and pushed the man away. Petra turned, shocked to see him, and straightened her clothes. The man Frank had pushed was twice his age and thick-set. He squared up to Frank and moved forward.

'Do you know what these are?' said Frank, his voice weaker than he would have liked.

Frank held up the handful of Student notebooks. The man instantly stepped back, dropping his hands, unclenching his fists.

'So you do?' said Frank. 'Then you know who I work for.'

The second man muttered something under his breath.

'Why don't we all go and see Mr Vertex?' said Frank.

'OK, OK,' said the first man. 'No need for that. It was just a bit of fun.'

Frank said nothing.

'I think you were the only ones having fun,' said Frank. 'Apologise.'

'What?' said the man. 'I don't think so.'

'Frank,' said Petra. 'It's fine.'

'Apologise to her or Vertex,' said Frank. 'Or maybe I'll just find the notebook from your Student and write a report that will have you and your whole family in a labour camp by the end of the week? How about that, you piece of crap?'

The other man nudged his friend in the back and he turned on him, cursing.

'Sorry,' he snarled.

'Not to me,' said Frank. 'To her. And nicely.'

The man looked like he was about to change his mind and thump Frank after all, when he took a deep breath, muttered something and then looked at Petra and said, 'Sorry. That was wrong of me.'

Petra nodded with a tight smile. The man glared at Frank malevolently for a moment, and then the two men turned and walked away. Frank was shaking and his hands were sweating. He breathed a huge sigh of relief and turned to smile at Petra, who glared at him for a moment and then stormed off without a word.

Frank stood for a moment, staring after her in bafflement. He looked at the secretary and shrugged but she just looked away and got on with her work. Frank shook his head and headed back to his office.

He smiled to himself and even broke out into a chuckle. The look on the idiot's face when he realised Frank worked for Mr

340

Vertex. Priceless. It was the closest thing to heroic Frank had ever managed in his entire life and he was more than a little pleased with himself.

However scared he had felt at the time was more than made up for by the way he felt afterwards. The background toothache of Olivia-pain was morphined away in an instant. For the first time, for as long as he could remember – maybe ever – he felt good about himself.

This was another milestone, he could sense it. What had his grandfather said about job satisfaction? That people did feel fulfilled if they believed in what they were doing? Well, maybe they also felt fulfilled if the job made them more than who they had been before. It certainly felt satisfying.

The only fly in this ointment was Petra's attitude to Frank's rescue. Had he not deserved some thanks, at least? He could see that she was embarrassed, but that was no excuse. He was reminded of what Mr Vertex had said about family holding one back. He wouldn't let Petra spoil the moment. Maybe if she had stood up to them herself he wouldn't have had to step in.

Frank returned to his office and sat down at his desk. He put the Student notebooks down and opened the top one. It was the record of another unnamed family of a Ministry worker – they were nearly all Ministry workers. The family consisted of two small boys, the worker, his wife and the wife's mother who lived with them.

They seemed almost heroically dull and Frank struggled to concentrate as he read through the daily routine. He knew what Mr Vertex wanted, but he could not see any stories emerging from the pages – not even dreary ones.

They ate, they slept, they shopped, they slept. If they were up to anything subversive or even interesting, they were certainly managing to keep it well hidden. It made Frank feel a little better about his own family. Perhaps everyone's lives were equally uneventful.

It wasn't helped by the writing of the Student whose notebook it was. The script leant this way and that as if the letters were blowing in a breeze. It made Frank slightly seasick to read it.

He reached the end of seventeen notebooks and there had been not one single incident or statement worth mentioning. It the Student had been recording the life of a shrub it might have been more riveting. Mr Vertex had warned him of the dullness in the notebooks.

'The Students are windows, Frank,' he said. 'The skill of a Student lies in allowing us to look in on the family without any kind of editorial input. They make no comment. They do not give extra weight to one thing over another thing. The Students record, that is all. They are transparent. Do not expect them to hint at what you might find. That's not their job.'

Frank picked up another notebook and started to read, stifling a yawn. This work was much more exhausting than the directory work. It required far more concentration. He licked his finger and turned another page.

No one was ever named in the notebooks; the Students were always very careful in that regard. But as Frank started to read these particular notes, he began to get the distinct impression that he knew one of the people being talked about. When the Student detailed the manner of the father's death by drowning, Frank was sure: it was Scape.

Chapter 50

Petra's apartment was in the New New Town. The building was a charmless concrete block not far from the industrial docks that made Frank's own apartment seem positively inviting. Frank chained his bicycle to a railing nearby.

Frank hated the fact that Petra lived there and blamed her husband Ralph, who was as charmless as the apartment. Petra deserved better than this – and him.

Frank's relationship with Petra had changed subtly. Even though she was his big sister, he no longer felt she was older than him. Everything was relative. Since he started working with Mr Vertex, Frank felt as though he had aged ten years or more. He felt protective of Petra.

Frank had waited for Petra to mention the incident at work but she was clearly never going to do so at their parents' apartment so he had decided to come and talk to her about it in private.

Petra had barely spoken to him at all since it happened. Frank thought it best to simply come straight out with it and clear the air.

'Look, Petra – about the thing at work,' said Frank as she poured him a cup of tea.

Petra put the teapot down.

'What about it, Frank?'

Frank didn't like her tone of voice.

'Why do you let them treat you like that?' said Frank.

'What are you talking about?' said Petra, going back to the sink and her washing up. Frank frowned at her back as she carried on washing dishes.

'You know what I mean,' said Frank. 'I saw how those men are with you. And that wasn't the first time either.'

Petra stopped washing-up for a moment and a spasm quivered through her back.

'You don't know what you're talking about.'

'Yes I do,' said Frank.

Petra said nothing more, she just took some dirty dishes and put them in the sink.

'Why are you being like this, Petra?' said Frank. 'I saw them. It was disgusting.'

'Disgusting?' said Petra.

'Yes,' said Frank.

'Don't be such a child, Frank,' she said.

'Child?' he said. 'I stood up for you!'

'Did you, now?' she said.

'Yes!' said Frank.

'It looked more like you were showing off to me,' she said. 'Showing everyone how important you are. It's easy for you to just swan in and start threatening people,' she said. 'But I have to work with them.'

'You don't have to be groped,' said Frank.

She sighed.

'It doesn't matter,' said Petra. 'Forget it.'

Frank scowled at his cup of tea.

344

'I don't understand why you're annoyed at me,' said Frank. 'Why aren't you annoyed at them?'

Petra dropped a dish into the bowl with a splash and turned on him.

'Do you think you are the only one who has ever wanted to leave this place?' she said. 'To do something else? Be someone else?'

Frank stared at her. He didn't know what to say.

'Do you think I haven't wanted to pack a bag and leave a thousand times?'

'I don't know,' said Frank. 'Have you? You've never said anything to me about it.'

Petra closed her eyes and sighed.

'You're my little brother,' said Petra. 'What am I going to say to you?'

'I thought you were happy,' said Frank.

'No you didn't,' she said. 'You didn't think about me at all.'

'That's not fair,' said Frank.

Petra started washing the dishes again.

'I'm thinking about you now,' he said.

Petra stopped and turned slowly round, her eyes brimming with tears.

'Well,' she said, 'since you're interested, I'm not happy.'

'I'm sorry, Petra – really,' said Frank.

Petra took her rubber gloves off and came and sat down at the table. She took a sip of tea.

'Is it Ralph?' said Frank.

'Ralph's gone,' she said.

'Gone where?' asked Frank.

'He's left me,' said Petra, her voice faltering. 'Why do you

345

think I spent all those nights at your place?'

'What?' said Frank.

'He wants a divorce.'

'The bastard!'

'I don't care,' she said. 'I'd rather he was gone.'

'But why?'

'Why has he gone or why do I prefer it?'

'Both,' said Frank.

'He's gone because he's found someone else,' said Petra. 'Isn't that always why men go? And that is also why I'm happy that he's gone. At least he's not sneaking around under my nose and treating me like I'm an idiot.'

Frank shook his head. It seemed inconceivable Ralph would find one woman to put up with him – but two?

'Does Mother know?' said Frank.

Petra nodded.

'Father?'

'No. He knows there are problems but he thinks we're sorting them out.'

'You need to tell him,' said Frank.

'No,' said Petra. 'Father has the Big Day and Mother is so excited about it. I don't want to spoil it for them. You have to promise me you won't say anything.'

'But –' said Frank.

'Promise?'

'Yes, all right.'

'Promise!'

'I just said so, didn't I?' said Frank.

Petra's face suddenly contorted with the effort of trying not

to cry but the tears broke through anyway and she began to sob.
Frank got up and went over to her, putting his arm round her.

'It'll be all right,' said Frank. 'You'll find someone else.
Someone better.'

She shrugged him off.

'Look at me, Frank,' said Petra, pointing to her leg. 'No one
is going to want me now. No one will love me.'

'That's not true,' said Frank.

Petra got up, scraping her chair back and dried her eyes on
a towel.

'I might be able to help,' said Frank. 'With Ralph. I know
some people at work who –'

'What kind of people?' said Petra. 'Vertex? Really? What
are you doing working for a man like that?'

'So this is what it's all about?' said Frank. 'Is that why you're
angry with me?'

'I never took you for a hypocrite,' she said.

'I thought everyone wanted me to get a job,' said Frank. 'I
thought you all wanted me to settle down and be like all of you.'

'We wanted you to get a job,' said Petra. 'But you couldn't
just work at the Ministry, could you? Oh no – not you. That's
not good enough for you, is it? Because you're special, aren't
you? You have to work for Vertex.'

'You don't know anything about him,' said Frank. 'Or what I do.'

'I know enough,' said Petra. 'I'm not a fool. I've seen people
disappear because of him.'

'Maybe they deserved to disappear!' said Frank.

Petra gasped and put her hand to her mouth, staring at him.

'I think you'd better go.'

Frank picked up his coat. He started to walk out, then turned.

'What's wrong with wanting to be special?' he said. 'Why should I do some boring job to make you all feel better?'

'What about us?' said Petra. 'Do you ever think about us? Do you think Father wants to do a boring job at the Ministry? Or me? Do you think Mother wants to clean offices? Have you ever thought about that?'

Frank had never thought about that.

'What has that got to do with me?'

'Everyone makes allowances for you, Frank,' said his sister coldly. 'They always have. You've always been the special one. No one ever asked me what I wanted to do. You think you're strong because you're cynical. You think you're tough all of a sudden because you despise everything. Working for Vertex doesn't make you strong, Frank. It just shows how weak you really are. Is working for Vertex your way of getting your own back on everyone who ignored you? You'll show them, eh?'

Frank left, slamming the door behind him, pattering down the steps and walking across the patch of wasteland at the back of Petra's apartment. Two Civil Servants were frogmarching someone ahead of him, shoving him across a piece of waste ground. Frank turned and took another route back.

Frank walked to the railing where he had left his bike, but all that was there was the severed chain of his bike lock. He grabbed hold of the railing and burst into hot, angry tears. He stood like that, head bowed for a few minutes until the tears subsided, dried his face with his sleeve and set off in search of a cab.

When he got home, Frank watched television with his parents and the Student, eager to have something to block out his

troubled thoughts. Eventually his parents went to bed and
Frank was left alone with the Student.

'You seem a lot better,' said Frank.

The Student smiled.

'I think I am,' he said.

'Good,' said Frank.

'Thank you,' said the Student.

'Do you think I'm a bad person?' said Frank. 'You know me
as much as anyone. More, maybe.'

The Student peered at him.

'Bad?' he said. 'No. I don't think you are a bad person.'

Frank sighed.

'Honestly?'

'Truly.'

Chapter 51

Frank didn't really know why he had arranged to see Scape for a drink. He could not tell him about the notebooks. Even if Frank could convince himself they might not be overheard, he knew that Scape could not be trusted with a secret – even a secret involving himself.

No, Mr Vertex had made it very clear that under no circumstances must the subject of the notebooks be made aware of any information gleaned from the notebooks. Failure to adhere to that rule would mean instant dismissal or worse.

Frank was taking a risk even speaking to Scape at all. Perhaps Mr Vertex had given him Scape's notebooks specifically, as a test of loyalty. And yet he could not stop himself.

He wondered if he was meeting with Scape just to prove Petra wrong. Because if he was the man she said he was, surely he would have just handed the notebooks straight to Vertex and Scape would be damned by now.

He had known almost nothing about Scape and now he felt like he had been living in the same apartment with him for months. The Scape that emerged from the notebook was different. He wanted to see if he could detect that new Scape in the flesh.

But he couldn't. Scape seemed just as thoughtless and self-centred as always. The threads were subtle and they did not point to any particular place, but it did appear that Scape was more critical of the Ministry than he ever let on – and certainly cleverer than he appeared.

Even in the notes the Student had taken, there was nothing overt. It was a hint. It was just an undercurrent. A hint of an undercurrent. But it was there, Frank was sure of it. Whether it meant anything, whether it had any significance at all, Frank could not say.

And that was part of the whole dilemma that was forming in his mind. If he had spotted the story threads in another set of notebooks he would have taken then straight to Mr Vertex. But Frank had delayed because of Scape.

'Thought you'd dumped me,' said Scape when they'd ordered their drinks.

'Dumped you?' said Frank.

'Yes,' said Scape. 'You're different.'

'I'm not different,' said Frank.

'Yeah, you are,' said Scape.

'I've moved to a different sector, that's all. I'm busy.'

'You decided to work for Vertex and his goons.'

'There are no goons,' said Frank. 'And you told me to work for him, remember?'

'So?' said Scape. 'Since when did you listen to me?'

Frank shook his head. Scape was edgy. They were both edgy. Meeting had been a mistake, Frank saw that now. But it was too late.

'You know it's over between me and Olivia,' he said.

Surely Frank's failure in love was safe common ground. Scape would enjoy that.

'Yeah,' said Scape. 'I thought you'd be down. You don't seem too cut up about it.'

'Feels like it happened a hundred years ago, to be honest.'

It felt like it had happened the day before.

Scape nodded. He took a swig of beer and wiped his mouth with the back of his hand.

'Don't get me wrong,' he said, 'but I was never very sure you were suited, if you want my opinion.'

Frank was not entirely sure he did, but nodded again, hoping that this would convey a silent manly indication that Scape was to mind his own business and just listen. It didn't work.

'I mean, you and Olivia,' he said.

'I know,' said Frank. 'Shut up.'

Scape put his hands up in a mock guard as though Frank, who had not moved or raised his voice, was about to hit him. Frank laughed. Not because Scape was funny, but because he seemed so ridiculous. So much time had elapsed, Frank realised they were no longer friends. There was the old distance between them once more, except that now the power was all with Frank. Scape just seemed a little foolish, as did the thought of him being subversive. He did not have the wit to be a threat.

'All right, all right,' said Scape. 'I get the hint.'

Frank took another swig of beer. What a strange bond they'd formed. A more unlikely couple it would be hard to find but, as with Olivia, it was over – a thing of the past.

'At least you got to have a go on that lovely body,' said Scape, pursing his lips obscenely.

Frank smiled despite himself and sighed. He felt relaxed now. He had always felt like a boy tagging along after Scape, but no more.

'Not really,' said Frank.

Scape sat back and raised an eyebrow.

'What?'

Frank took a swig on his beer.

'She is "saving herself" for marriage,' said Frank.

Scape looked at him for a long time and then slowly leant forward. Frank thought he was about to throw up, but in fact Scape was laughing.

Frank frowned at him. Scape caught his eye and stopped briefly, but burst into laughing again, more enthusiastically than before. He roared and wheezed and slapped the bar.

The bartender looked over, frowning. People at nearby tables looked over at them, wondering what was going on. Scape was gasping for breath.

'Shut up!' hissed Frank.

Scape made an effort to control himself, sighing and slapping his thigh.

'I'm glad you find it funny,' said Frank.

'Is that what she said?'

'What's that supposed to mean?' said Frank.

Scape took a drink.

'Sorry, Frank,' he said. 'But she has nothing to save.'

Frank put his bottle down on the bar.

'What do you mean?' said Frank.

'Frank, my friend,' he said, reaching out and putting his hand on Frank's shoulder, 'Olivia – how can I put it? – is very fond of sex. She has had more men than you've had –'

'Shut up!' shouted Frank, standing up.

The barman walked over.

'Either calm down now or take it outside,' he growled.

Frank stared at Scape.

'Anyone who says that is a liar,' said Frank.

Scape raised his eyebrows and held up the palms of his hands in supplication, looking from face to face in the bar before returning to Frank's.

'Frank, I've tasted those delights myself,' said Scape with a half-smile. 'More than once, I'm pleased to say.'

Frank leapt at him but Scape was faster. So was the barman who grabbed him by the coat collar.

'Right,' he said. 'Out! Both of you.'

The barman led them both up the stairs and shoved them into the street.

'Don't come back!' he shouted, spitting on the floor. 'Not tonight. Not ever.'

The barman turned and walked back to the bar muttering something about the Ministry. Frank looked at Scape, who was straightening his tie.

'You're lucky I don't give you a beating,' said Scape. 'But I'll let it pass for old time's sake.'

Frank said nothing. He just stared at him. It was as if the whole past few months were a dream and he had woken up right back where he had been before. Nothing had really changed, he realised. Scape would always be Scape. Olivia would always be Olivia. It was a lie he had told himself, that was all.

'Anyway,' said Scape, 'if you have nothing more to say I think I'll be heading off.'

'I hate you,' said Frank.

'Do you?' said Scape. 'Well, that's not nice, is it?'

Scape chuckled to himself and walked away.

Frank stood at the window of his office the following morning. A fog was settling over the river like a long piece of filthy white fur, and a frost clung to the shadows on the roof tiles of the Old Town.

That frost seemed to have settled too on Frank's heart. He could feel its cold fire burning away inside him. He went back to his desk, sat down, and collected up the notebooks from Scape's Student. He picked up a pen, opened the first of the books, and began to make careful notes in the margin.

Chapter 52

A barge sounded its horn in the fog and Frank turned to the sound but could see nothing. The buzzer rang and the maid answered.

'I'm here to see Miss Olivia,' said Frank.

'Is she expecting you?' said the maid in a voice that made it clear she thought this very unlikely.

'Why don't you ask her?' said Frank.

The maid went away for a moment. Frank could hear her shoes clunking down the hall. Nothing happened for a long time and Frank was about to ring the bell again. Then the door suddenly opened. Olivia stood before him.

'Frank,' she said, her voice sounding tired.

'Olivia,' he said. 'You look beautiful, as always.'

'What do you want?'

Her voice was cold and although she did look beautiful, Frank also saw that she looked younger than he remembered, almost child-like.

'I wanted to talk to you,' he said.

'Talk?' she said. 'Really?'

'Yes,' said Frank.

She closed her eyes and made a strange moaning sound

under her breath as though just being in his company for this long was a gargantuan effort.

'I'll get my coat,' she said.

'I can come in,' said Frank.

'No,' she said.

They walked down to the river and along the embankment. A barge was moored nearby, smoke pluming up from its metal chimney. A small caramel-coloured dog barked at them until it was pulled away by a hunchbacked old woman who waved at them. Frank waved back, but Olivia stared sullenly ahead.

'I work with Scape, you know,' said Frank. 'We're friends.'

'Really?' said Olivia. 'You and Scape? I don't think so.'

'Why would I lie about a thing like that?' asked Frank.

'I don't know,' said Olivia with a sigh. 'Where is this going?'

'I loved you,' said Frank.

Olivia laughed.

'No you didn't,' she said. 'You wanted to screw me.'

'Well, fat chance of that,' he said. 'With you "saving yourself". As I said, I work with Scape, remember.'

Olivia licked her lips.

'Scape?' she said. 'What is it with Scape? You're twice the man he is, even with all the weirdness.'

'And that's supposed to make me feel better?'

'Yes, Frank,' said Olivia.

'Well, it doesn't. Would it have been so terrible?' said Frank. 'If we had screwed?'

Olivia closed her eyes and groaned.

'I just want to understand why,' said Frank. 'Surely I deserve some explanation?'

'You think it makes it worse that we didn't do it, but it doesn't,' she said. 'I knew it would be a big deal for you. If we could have screwed and just enjoyed it for what it was then . . . But I knew it wouldn't be like that for you. And the more time we spent together I knew it wouldn't be like that for me either. I couldn't hurt you like that.'

'Ha!'

Olivia looked away towards the railway bridge.

'Look,' said Olivia. 'Try for just a second to see my side of this. My mother was going to send me to the east to live with my aunt. Have you been to the east?'

'I've never been anywhere,' said Frank.

'Well, it's horrible,' said Olivia. 'There are only villages and farms, fields, mud and turnips. What would I do in a place like that?'

'Am I supposed to care?' said Frank.

'My parents didn't like the crowd I was with,' she said. 'Scape and so on.'

'Who can blame them?'

Olivia ignored him.

'It all came to a head that night. The night of my birthday. After I made my wish on the bridge, I got drunk and ended up at a party after curfew. It got raided by Civil Servants and my mother had to use all her connections to get the charges dropped.'

Frank stared at her. It was as if he had been looking at someone else the whole time.

'She gave me once last chance,' said Olivia. 'Either I clean up my act or I was going to end my days on a farm plucking geese.

'I was trying to figure out what to do when you bumped into me at the shop. Do you believe in fate?'

'Not now,' said Frank.

Olivia put her head back and looked up at the grey sky. The mole on her throat quivered.

'When you asked me out, I thought it must be fate,' said Olivia. 'The idea that you would ask me out. You, of all people. Weird Frank. It had to mean something. I mean, I knew you fancied me. That was obvious. But you'd never even spoken to me.

'I thought maybe you were the answer. If I went out with you there would be no temptations. You weren't going to get me into trouble. That's why I went out with you. Because you were –'

'Boring,' said Frank.

'Safe,' said Olivia.

'Isn't that the same thing?' asked Frank.

'You're not making this easy, are you?' she said.

'Why should I?'

'I started to think maybe we could make a go of it, you know,' she said. 'You were funny and kind and my mother thought the world of you. But – I can't explain it – sometimes you just can't pretend. Do you know what I mean?'

Frank knew exactly what she meant.

'But in any case, you weren't boring enough, Frank,' she said.

'Well, I'm sorry,' said Frank.

'Look,' she said. 'I didn't know you were some weird obsessive, did I? I didn't know you were hanging about outside my apartment. You've got a nerve, honestly.'

'I've got a nerve?" said Frank, wide-eyed. 'Listen to you!'

'If you've just come to shout at me, think again,' said Olivia.

Frank stared off into the distance.

'I just thought, if I could maybe have a normal boyfriend,' said Olivia, 'they might get off my back. That's all.'

Frank closed his eyes.

'You were supposed to be normal,' she said. 'You couldn't even be that.'

'Why should I be normal?' said Frank. 'To make your life easier?'

'What do you want me to say? When I read those stories I knew you'd never be happy with someone like me. Don't make it seem like the pretence was all on my part. Who were you trying to fool?'

'I loved you,' said Frank.

She stopped and pushed the hair away from her face.

'This is getting nowhere,' she said. 'You're better off without me.'

'I know,' said Frank.

Tears sprang to Olivia's eyes and instead of sympathy Frank felt a little kick of satisfaction. But it was short-lived.

'So are you being sent east?' said Frank. 'Are you going to be a farmer's wife?'

Olivia shook her head.

'No,' she said. 'I'm going to university.'

Frank shook his head, turned and walked away.

Chapter 53

Frank had intended to give the notebooks of Scape's Student straight to Mr Vertex as soon as he had marked them up. He had bundled them together ready to take them, more than once. But he never got past his own office door.

Frank was sure that he had been scrupulously fair in the way that he had annotated the notebooks. He had genuinely seen the patterns he noted. He had made nothing up, invented nothing. He was sure of it.

Yet he was still left with a sour taste in his mouth. The fact was, he did want revenge on Scape – and the wanting of revenge tainted his evidence if not his judgement.

If Frank handed in the notebooks and Scape disappeared, then he could not think other than he was responsible. He could not have Scape on his conscience, haunting him for the rest of his life. No, if Scape was a problem, someone else would have to detect it.

Frank put the notebooks in a drawer in the cabinet next to his desk and locked it, hiding the key under the carpet. He picked up another set of notebooks, opened the first and began reading. He had hardly started when there was a knock on the door and Mr Vertex walked in.

'Frank,' he said. 'How are you getting on?'

'Very well, sir,' said Frank, putting the notebook down.

'Good,' said Mr Vertex. 'We've all been very pleased with your work. You've settled in very nicely.'

'Thank you, sir,' said Frank.

'No problems? No issues?'

'No, sir,' said Frank. 'I can't think of any.'

Mr Vertex stood smiling at him as though waiting for more.

'I still don't have my name on the door,' said Frank eventually.

'Your name?'

'Yes, sir,' said Frank. 'Someone was supposed to come and put my name on the door last week. But they haven't.'

'Do you have the fellow's name?' said Mr Vertex. 'I will have him shot.'

Mr Vertex delivered this with such deadpan gravitas that Frank wasn't entirely sure it was a joke until Mr Vertex finally smiled.

'I'm afraid I don't know the man's name,' said Frank. 'Luckily for him.'

'Quite,' said Mr Vertex. 'Apart from that administrative oversight – all is well?'

'I think so, sir,' said Frank.

'Better than the life of Mr Mandible's dreaded cubicles.'

'Yes, sir,' said Frank.

'Our work is all the more important with the Big Day coming up,' said Mr Vertex. 'Destabilising forces are at work, Frank, as you know, and they will savour the publicity they would get from disrupting such an event. And we don't want your father's moment in the limelight ruined, do we?'

'No, sir.'

'Your father,' said Mr Vertex nonchalantly. 'Is he happy with you working for me?'

'I haven't asked him, sir,' said Frank.

Mr Vertex cocked his head.

'Do you and your father not see eye to eye?' he said.

'I'm sure you've read my Student's notebooks,' said Frank.

Mr Vertex smiled.

'Your friends then? How do they view you working here?'

'I don't really have any friends, sir,' said Frank. 'As I'm sure you know.'

'No romantic interest?'

Frank took a moment.

'Not any longer.'

'Good,' said Mr Vertex. 'You will find the business of this sector very demanding on your time and energy. I always feel that single men do best here.'

'Are you single, sir?'

Frank realised he had no idea about Mr Vertex's life outside of the Castle. Mr Vertex remained static, his eyes fixed on a point above Frank's head. He stood there for a while and Frank began to worry that he had had some kind of a seizure or that asking him about his marital status was a huge mistake.

'Sir?'

'Shhh.'

Mr Vertex reached forward and grabbed at the wall, his fingers stopping just before they hit the surface. Frank stared at him. It was such a peculiar thing to do. He then turned, his hand still fixed in the grasping position and headed towards the window.

Staring at his hand the whole time, Mr Vertex opened the window with his left hand, reached out with his right – opening his hand wide, quickly closing the window and walking to Frank's desk to get a tissue and wipe his hand. Frank saw his thumb was bleeding.

'Sir?'

'Oh, he'll be fine,' said Mr Vertex. 'They throw themselves off walls higher than that all the time. They seem to have the ability to arrest their descent and almost float. Quite remarkable creatures.'

'What do?'

'The Invisible Lizards, of course,' he said.

Frank stared towards the window.

'You do have to watch when you pick them up,' said Mr Vertex. 'They will bite.'

He shook his head.

'I must be losing my touch,' he said with a smile. 'Haven't let one nip me for a very long time.'

They were real. They were actually real.

'But I couldn't see a thing,' said Frank.

'Oh, you will,' said Mr Vertex. 'It's a matter of getting your eye in. You'll see.'

Frank shook his head.

'Frank?' said Mr Vertex.

'Sir?'

'I want to let you know that I intend to give you more responsibility. Don't get too comfortable.'

'No, sir,' said Frank. 'I mean, thank you, sir.'

'Careful what you thank me for,' said Mr Vertex.

Mr Vertex wandered back over to the window and stood in shadow against the milky glow. The outline of his mantis-like silhouette was smudged and blurred.

'The Ministry – our part of the Ministry – is run on suspicion, Frank,' he said without turning round. 'To be good at what we do, we have to be suspicious of everyone, you must see that.'

'Yes, sir.'

'Everyone, without exception.'

'Yes, sir.'

Chapter 54

It was the end of October when Frank saw his father looking out from the King's Courtyard towards the east and walked over to greet him.

'It's cold,' said Frank.

'Frank?' said his father. 'Yes. The wind has moved round. Winter is coming.'

Frank put his hands on the wall and looked over.

'Is everything going to plan?' said Frank.

'I believe so,' said his father. 'My part in the proceedings is at any rate. I just thought I'd come here and go through the details in my mind. But all I seem to be doing is remembering.'

Frank nodded.

'Tell me what happened,' said Frank. 'On the day.'

'Ah, you've heard it lots of times,' said his father.

He had heard it many times, but Frank had never really taken any particular interest. He wasn't sure why – maybe Petra's outburst in her apartment had pricked his conscience – but he wanted to listen now.

'I know,' said Frank. 'But even so.'

His father smiled and stared out at the mountains.

'The enemy had entered the Old Town,' said Frank's father.

'They had moved through the streets, killing or sparing anyone they found on a whim.

'Children were shot,' he said. 'Women were raped. Mr Spiracle – you know, the man who is always hanging about by the lift?'

'Yes?' said Frank, fascinated to hear Spiracle's name mentioned.

'His whole family were shot,' said his father. 'They told him to wait in the shadows and not to move and they took them down in the lift. They were all shot. Dumped like animals. His mind has never been the same since. He's younger than me, you know.'

'Really?' said Frank.

'Really. His hair went white overnight.'

Frank tried to absorb this new information about Spiracle.

'A lot of minds were broken that day in the Old Town,' said his father. 'A lot of people were never the same again. That's what war does. Everyone is scarred by it. Everyone. Even those who weren't there.'

Frank nodded.

'The enemy knew it had to take the Castle – take the King. We were ordered to fight till the last man to stop them. We decided to hold our ground here at the final courtyard.'

'How did that feel?' said Frank. 'To be ordered to die?'

His father smiled.

'We weren't ordered to die,' he said. 'We were ordered to fight.'

'It must have seemed like the same thing,' said Frank, looking towards the mountains of the east.

'But here I am,' said Frank's father. 'So . . .'

Frank smiled.

'Although many better men than me died that day,' said his father.

'Did you know about the reinforcements?' asked Frank.

'No,' said his father. 'We just knew somehow that if they captured the Castle then everyone would give up. We knew we had to stop them and if we could hold them off for long enough then help might come.'

'And it did,' said Frank.

His father nodded.

'The fighting was intense,' said his father. 'The enemy had bombed and shelled the Castle, of course, but they knew they had to take it with men if they were going to finish us off.

'That was our only advantage,' said his father. 'We knew this place. We knew those courtyards and arcades and mazes of corridors and alleyways and they did not.

'We placed snipers on rooftops and hid gunmen behind statues and columns and picked them off one by one. I killed a man right over there.'

Frank followed his gaze and could almost see the body lying there.

'I shot him in the face with my revolver,' said his father. 'I can still see him to this day. He looked so surprised. Then he fell.'

He licked his lips.

'But there were too many of them, of course. They had us pinned down here and no matter how many we killed, more of them came. The reinforcements were the real heroes that day.'

'But if you had not held out for so long, they wouldn't have come,' said Frank.

'Perhaps,' said his father. 'But they did come. They were like a wild animal, roaring through the Castle. I was terrified of them myself even though they were on my side – I could see the bloodlust in their eyes and wondered if they'd remember to stop when they reached us.'

Frank's father looked him in the eye.

'Vertex was among them,' he said.

'What?' said Frank.

'Vertex,' said his father. 'He was at the forefront, leading his platoon. It was the first time I saw him. I've never seen a man so hungry for death, so fearless, so heartless. I remember him coming to shake my hand at the end of the battle. His face was spattered in gore.'

'Vertex?' repeated Frank. 'My Vertex?'

His father nodded.

'Yes,' said his father. 'He may not be remembered in the stories, but he became a high-ranking Ministry Man on the back of that battle. Some people rise and some people don't, Frank; you'll learn that in time – and it has nothing to do with merit, let me tell you. Crap and cream both float, as they say.'

Frank shook his head. Vertex? He just couldn't picture it.

'But you got the credit,' said Frank.

'Pah,' said his father. 'They made a show of honouring us, but look at as now. They gave me this job at the Ministry to bury me.'

'Bury you?'

'Yes,' he said. 'I wanted to stay a soldier. Your grandfather had brought me into the Ministry but I'm not a pen-pusher, Frank – no offence.'

Frank frowned.

'The War made me realise that I was actually good at something – I was good at being a soldier, and I wanted to stay in the army. But they made sure that didn't happen.'

His father nodded in the direction of some Civil Servants.

'Why?' said Frank.

'We'd served our purpose,' said his father. 'They didn't want us getting above our station. You know that old Prementum the barber was in my unit? They tried to give him a job here, but he turned it down. He wanted to be a soldier too, but failing that, a barber. He lost his ear that day and never even noticed until it was all over. Hard as nails.'

'But they've put you in charge of the Big Day,' said Frank. 'That must mean something.'

Frank's father shook his head.

'It was the King who requested it,' said his father. 'It came from him directly. He's a good man. They couldn't deny him when he had made the request and made it publicly. They know how everyone loves him.'

'I don't really understand why,' said Frank.

'Well, your generation don't,' said his father.

Frank had grown very tired of hearing this.

'Explain it to me, then.'

His father sighed.

'The King was with us all through the War. Up there. He never left his private apartment in the Castle. He could have left anytime he liked. The people won't ever forget that.'

'Was he there that day?' asked Frank

'Of course,' said his father.

He pointed to a door in the wall at the edge of the courtyard behind a thick column.

'That's the door to his quarters,' said his father. 'That's why we chose this place to make our stand. If they'd passed us they would have taken the King.'

'So you saved his life?' said Frank.

'I don't know about that,' said his father with a shrug and an awkward twitch of his jaw. 'They'd have probably left him in place – as a figurehead.'

'Isn't that what the Ministry have done?' said Frank. 'In effect?'

His father peered at him.

'As I said, your generation don't understand,' said his father. 'You don't respect anything.'

'What's that supposed to mean?'

'Never mind,' said his father.

Frank took a deep breath, determined to avoid an argument. 'I often wonder what I'd have been like in a battle,' he said.

'You?' said his father.

'Yes,' said Frank. 'No need to say it like that.'

'Sorry, son,' he said. 'But I don't have you down as a fighter.'

'Thanks,' said Frank. 'But there must be lots of people who have never fought in a war and then –'

'Not you.'

'You're saying it's impossible for me to be brave?' said Frank.

'Not brave,' said his father. 'No one knows whether they'll be brave or not when the time comes. No, I meant you could not be a soldier.'

'Because?'

'Because soldiers aren't brave, they follow orders. Soldiers do as they are told. They're not heroes. There are no real heroes, son. It just depends who is telling the story. Those men who tried to take the Castle – they would have been heroes to their families had they beaten us.'

'But you just told me how they killed children and raped women,' said Frank. 'You weren't the same.'

Frank's father smiled grimly.

'Do you think the same thing did not happen in the enemy's capital when our troops rolled in?' said Frank's father.

'No,' said Frank. 'You won't make me believe we are the same as –'

'But we are. We are men. Men do terrible things.'

'Not all men,' said Frank.

'All men have these things in them, Frank,' said his father.

Frank opened his mouth to speak but instead, he just shook his head and smiled wearily.

'I give up,' said Frank.

'What's that?'

'I just thought I'd try to . . . Never mind.'

They stood for a few moments in silence and then Mr Vertex appeared and began issuing instructions to Civil Servants in the arcade by the King's Door. Frank's father bristled.

'I need to get on, Frank,' he said. 'I'll see you at home.'

Frank watched him go, shaking his head.

'Everything all right?' said Mr Vertex.

'Yes, sir,' said Frank. 'I was just . . . My father . . .'

'You must go easy on your father, Frank,' said Mr Vertex. 'He's under a lot of pressure.'

'I know, sir,' said Frank.

Mr Vertex smiled and started to move away.

'He was just telling me about the day of the attack, sir,' said Frank. 'I hadn't realised you were there that day.'

Mr Vertex stopped and turned back slowly.

'And what did he tell you?'

'He said that you and your platoon were the real heroes that day,' said Frank.

'There are no such things as heroes,' said Mr Vertex.

'He said that too,' said Frank.

'You must forgive me, Frank,' said Mr Vertex. 'I have much to do.'

Frank watched him go, melting into the shadows. How strange to hear his father and Vertex singing the same song. He had thought them to be in two opposing camps but now saw they were essentially cut from different parts of the same Grey cloth.

They might make a fetish of following orders and being a cog in a machine, but Frank would be his own man. If he had to work there, then he would work there on his own terms. He refused to accept that the Frank he had once been had to be smothered in order to get through the day.

He did not have to be that cynical Dead-Frank the Ministry wanted of him. He certainly did not have to be bad. He could have condemned Scape out of spite but he didn't. He saw now that he had an opportunity to do some good there – to work with some kind of humanity. The Ministry did not own his soul.

Chapter 55

Frank sat contemplating this new plan and the more he thought about it, the better it seemed. He would quietly and subtly undermine the oppressive tendencies of the sector, day by day. He would report to Vertex only when he saw clear signs of intent to harm in the notebooks. He would be a secret force for good at the heart of the Grey.

Frank was excited. He wished he could tell Petra about his plan. But it was dangerous and the fewer people who knew the better.

Frank had just opened a Student notebook and started to read when there was a knock at the door and Mr Vertex walked in.

'Hello, Frank,' he said. 'Are you busy?'

'Yes, sir,' said Frank.

Mr Vertex smiled. Frank shifted uncomfortably in his chair.

'You misunderstand me,' he said. 'I am not checking up on you. I am asking you if you have a moment to spare.'

'I see, sir,' said Frank, still a little confused as to the answer he was supposed to be giving.

'Well?'

'Oh,' said Frank. 'Sorry. Then yes. I suppose so.'

'Excellent. Come along with me,' said Mr Vertex. 'I have something to show you.'

Frank got up and followed Mr Vertex out of the office. Wherever they walked, an eerie silence surrounded them as workers grew quiet and alert at Mr Vertex's passing, like rabbits at the passing of a hawk.

Frank followed Mr Vertex into a large room – much larger than the door had suggested. A portly man looked up as they approached and hailed Mr Vertex. He was standing beside some kind of machine and there were dozens – possibly hundreds – more at regular intervals in the cavernous room, a light bulb suspended over each one.

'You really ought to take a lot of credit for this, Frank,' said Vertex. 'I have been working on it ever since we had that conversation in the bookshop.'

'I don't understand,' said Frank, standing alongside him and looking at the machines. 'What have I to do with these? What are they?'

'Don't you remember?' said Mr Vertex. 'Our conversation about books, about reading?'

'Yes, sir,' said Frank.

Although it did seem an awfully long time ago.

'Oh, we have tried redacting before,' said Mr Vertex. 'But just covering up a few words doesn't work. Readers skim over them or guess what the word is from the context. That's why we took to taking out the last pages, assuming that this would so ruin the enjoyment of the reading experience that readers would be driven away from those books and into the Ministry's publications.'

Frank stared at the nearest machine. It was like some weird cross between an enormous typewriter and a loom.

'You simply put the book here,' said Vertex, pointing into the works and picking up a book. 'Fix it into place using the clamps – like so. There is a very precise set of attachments depending on the size and format of the book, so the most important thing is to make sure, before you begin, that you have chosen the appropriate template.'

Frank watched in bafflement as Mr Vertex pulled various levers.

'Then, when everything is in place, one tightens this, and pulls this, and then . . .'

The machine lurched into action, causing a flurry of page turning and a flicker of metal arms. It was over in seconds. Frank stared bemused, unsure of what had just happened.

'And there we have it,' said Vertex. 'It's all done.'

The machine had moved so quickly and efficiently that Frank did not see what had been done. The book sat there, closed once more, seemingly unaltered. Frank was about to ask what had happened, when Vertex unclipped the book and handed it to him.

Frank opened it up and flicked through the pages. Every page was covered in thick black lines of redactions so that now only fragments of sentences appeared.

'Let's see someone get enjoyment out of reading that!' said Vertex.

'But this is crazy,' said Frank. 'Why not burn it?'

'You don't seem to understand, Frank,' said Vertex, taking the book from him and leafing through it. 'Of course it is crazy. It is obscene. It is ridiculous,' he said. 'These are the tools we have. What better way to attack the persistent reader than by arbitrary interruption? What better way to derail the story-monger than to make the story frustrating? Imagine if you were trying to tell someone your theory about Time say, and every time you tried you were interrupted?'

Frank stared at Mr Vertex.

'Don't you see?' said Mr Vertex with a grin. 'This is so much better than destruction. This is better because it offends. It achieves two goals – it prevents the books from being read but it also demoralises simply by being so cruelly pointless. Do you see?'

'But how can a man like you allow such a thing, sir?' said Frank.

'I don't follow,' said Mr Vertex, leaning towards him as though Frank was five years old.

'A man who loves books, sir?' said Frank.

'Oh, I think you must have me confused with someone else, Frank,' said Mr Vertex.

'But all those books in your office?' said Frank.

'Yes?' said Vertex. 'What of them? I inherited them from my predecessor. That was one of the reasons I replaced him.'

'Oh,' said Frank.

Mr Vertex peered at him.

'I see,' he said. 'You thought that I was a reader of fiction, like you. You saw us as linked in that way?'

'Yes, sir,' said Frank. 'I suppose I did.'

'I'm sorry, Frank,' he said. 'No subterfuge was intended, I assure you.'

'No, sir,' said Frank.

'My interest in those books is purely professional,' said Mr Vertex. 'I have kept them as a microbiologist might keep a sample of the plague.'

377

'Yes, sir,' said Frank cooly. 'I understand. Is that all, sir?'

'Yes,' said Mr Vertex. 'Thank you.'

Frank turned to walk away. Suddenly there was uproar nearby. A man was calling out. At least he called out to begin with, but soon those cries turned to screams as his sleeve, caught up in one of the redacting machine arms, dragged him sideways.

Someone grabbed him, trying to pull him free, but they were too late. The sleeve ripped and the man was pulled into the centre of the flailing mechanical arms and they rained down on him, pummelling his face, his neck, his chest.

Frank, along with everyone else, was spellbound by this for a few moments. The machine seemed to have a sentient malevolence to it, as though it had been waiting to ensnare a human being all the time.

Mr Vertex was the first to snap out of the spell, stepping forward to pull on a lever so hard he wrenched it free. The machine shuddered and groaned and came to a halt, like a dying spider, its arms dangling horribly.

Its victim was carried free and laid on the carpet where, after a few spasms, he exhaled a last gasping breath, his body covered in blocks of black ink.

'Get him cleaned up and inform his family,' said Mr Vertex. 'Sorry, Frank – we'll speak later.'

Frank returned to his office and sat in his chair. He held his head in his hands. All illusions about being a benign influence in that place evaporated in an instant. It was a delusion. He saw that now. The Grey had caught him. He was trapped now, like a fly, wrapped up and injected with venom, waiting in a coma to finally be finished off.

But in reality, he knew he was already dead.

Chapter 56

There was a knock on Frank's bedroom door and Petra walked in.

'Hope I'm not disturbing you,' she said.

'No,' said Frank. 'I'm not doing anything.'

'I thought you might be writing.'

He shook his head.

'I'm just off. Listen, I wanted to say sorry about when you came over.'

'No,' said Frank. 'You've got nothing to say sorry about. You were right. I was showing off when I stepped in that day at work. I liked how it felt.'

Petra smiled.

'It's forgotten.'

'And Ralph?'

'One day he too will be forgotten, I hope.'

'I never liked him,' said Frank.

'I know.'

Frank smiled.

'Are you all right?'

'I will be.'

She kissed him.

'I've got to go. Friends again?'

'Always.'

Frank told his parents he needed some air and went downstairs to sit on the bench in the courtyard. He looked in vain for Maxilla the tomcat. Or indeed any other cat. The courtyard seemed utterly devoid of life. He saw the Grey clearly again now.

It was cold and damp. Frank's breath rose up in wisps like smoke. Dead leaves were tumbling slowly through the air to land on the ground near his feet. One even landed on his knee and as he brushed it off, Dawn appeared beside him.

'Frank?' she said with a weak smile. 'Haven't seen you here for a while.'

'No,' he said. 'I've been busy with work, you know.'

She nodded. There was an awkward few moments when neither of them seemed able to find a way to continue the conversation.

'You look worried,' she said.

'Worried?' he replied. 'No – tired. A problem at work. I can't really talk about it, I'm afraid.'

Dawn nodded.

'Sorry, Frank,' said Dawn. 'We haven't really been getting on, have we? Not like we used to.'

'Sorry?' said Frank. 'You've got nothing to be sorry about. It's me who should be saying sorry.'

'Doesn't matter,' said Dawn.

'It does. That night I saw you with Roland. With Scape. I was acting like an idiot. I do that a lot.'

'Yes,' she said. 'You do.'

Frank smiled. Dawn laughed and sat down next to him.

'I have to say it was a bit of a surprise seeing you out with Scape,' said Dawn. 'He was always so mean to you at school. I thought you hated him.'

Frank shrugged.

'Well, we're not friends any more. I was just as surprised to see you with Roland, for that matter.'

'Why?' said Dawn, frowning. 'We've always been friends.'

'It's none of my business anyway,' said Frank with a shrug.

'Spit it out, Frank,' said Dawn. 'What's none of your business?'

'I saw you together before that night,' said Frank with a sigh.

'And?' said Dawn.

'Look, forget it. I shouldn't have said anything.'

'I wish I knew what the hell you were talking about,' said Dawn.

'I just don't see why we can't be straight with each other,' said Frank. 'We've all grown up and moved on. If you and Roland –'

'Roland is gay,' said Dawn. 'If that's what you're babbling about.'

'What?'

'Shi—' said Dawn, clamping her hand over mouth. 'I especially promised not to tell you.'

'He's not gay,' said Frank.

'He is,' said Dawn.

Frank frowned, searching his memories for some sign that this might be true and finding only a brief glimpse of Roland's penis in the toilets at the dance.

'No!' said Frank. 'Really? But . . .'

'It's OK,' said Dawn, frowning. 'It's not catching.'

Frank shook his head, trying to assimilate this new version of Roland.

'You mustn't say anything, Frank,' said Dawn. 'Especially not to Scape.'

'Like I said, I'm not friends with Scape any more,' said Frank. 'I don't even see him now.'

'Oh?' said Dawn. 'How come?'

'I moved departments. He's not in my sector.' Frank sighed. 'Actually, the truth is, I realised I'd made a mistake being friends with him at all.'

Dawn smiled.

'I've made a lot of mistakes, come to think of it,' said Frank.

'Hasn't everyone?' said Dawn.

'I don't know,' said Frank. 'I don't know that many people.'

'They have, I promise you,' said Dawn. 'In art they say you learn more by your mistakes than you do by the things that actually work.'

'That's a nice idea,' said Frank. 'I should be a genius by now then.'

'It's true,' said Dawn.

'For art, maybe,' said Frank. 'Not for life. I don't seem to learn from any of my mistakes.'

'I'm sure that's not true,' said Dawn.

Frank shook his head. 'Honestly,' he said. 'Every time I think I have things sorted, it turns out I was wrong about everything. Still, at least I have plenty of time to think about it, stuck in the Ministry. I used to wonder why my father was always so angry. Thirty years from now that'll be me.'

'You're not your father, Frank,' said Dawn.

Frank closed his eyes and sighed.

'Look, I won't say anything about Roland. I promise.' Frank smiled weakly. 'You know that things didn't work out with me and Olivia.'

'I'm sorry,' said Dawn. 'Really.'

'Thanks,' said Frank.

'Anyway,' said Dawn, standing up. 'It was good to see you.'

'I really loved her,' said Frank as Dawn turned to walk away. 'Although I'm not sure she loved me. In fact . . .'

Frank hung his head. Dawn stopped and turned back. She opened her mouth to speak but then waved her hands and shook her head.

'What?' said Frank, looking up.

'I shouldn't,' she said. 'It's none of my business. And I don't want to fight.'

'No,' said Frank. 'Say what you were going to say. There's no fight in me.'

Dawn remained silent.

'Please,' said Frank, reaching out towards her.

Dawn sighed.

'I'm not sure you can really love someone if they don't love you back,' said Dawn.

'Really?' said Frank.

Dawn took a few steps closer.

'I think love is the combination of feelings,' said Dawn. 'You know – one person brings the flour and the sugar, the other brings the eggs and the butter. Love is the cake.'

'So what is it, then,' said Frank, suddenly feeling tired and tearful, 'when you're crazy about someone and they don't care about you?'

Dawn stared at him for a long time before replying.

'It's just flour,' she said, tears just springing to her eyes.

'Dawn?' said Frank. 'Are you OK?'

She wiped a tear from her eye.

'Sorry,' said Dawn. 'I'm tired.'

'Sit back down,' said Frank, patting the bench.

She smiled weakly and sat beside him.

'Look at us,' said Frank. 'Maybe we ought to throw a wish off the railway bridge.'

Dawn laughed and shook her head.

'It doesn't work,' she said.

'You've done that?' he said.

Dawn nodded and blushed a little.

'I followed Olivia and her friends one night,' said Frank. 'To the railway bridge. It was Olivia's birthday. I'd overheard them talking and I knew she was going to make a wish. I wanted to be there. I don't really know why now.'

Dawn nodded, peering at him.

'I watched her drop the bottle and then they all went off to a party or whatever. I thought no more about it until a while later.'

'And?' said Dawn.

'Well,' said Frank. 'You'll never believe this, but I was walking along by the river when I saw it.'

'What?' said Dawn. 'Olivia's bottle? With the wish in it?'

'I know,' said Frank, shaking his head. 'It's incredible, I know, but it's true. It was on the shore. It must have been circling round in the currents for all that time. I couldn't believe it. It's one of the things that made me feel like it was fate, you know?'

He smiled, lost in that moment of discovery. Dawn said something but he didn't catch it.

'Sorry?' he said.

'How did you know the bottle was hers?' she asked. 'I mean, if it was a long time after she threw it? She's not the only person throwing bottles off the bridge. Was it something about the wish?'

'Yes,' he said. 'The wish – and how it was written. You know – each letter a different colour, just like she always used to –'

'What was the wish?' asked Dawn.

Frank reached into his jacket pocket and brought out the crumpled piece of paper, flattening it out on his thigh. Even after all this time, the colour sang out and lit up their faces as though they were looking through a stained-glass window. Dawn shook her head and put both her hands to face. She looked away and then back in disbelief. Then she laughed.

'What?' asked Frank.

'You won't believe me,' she said.

'I will,' he replied.

'That's mine, Frank.'

'What?'

'It's my wish,' she said. 'I threw it off the bridge on my birthday. It didn't get far, did it? And it sure as hell didn't work!'

Frank looked at the note. He felt confused, as though he might wake at any moment from a dream. He looked at Dawn and she at him.

'If that's supposed to be funny, Dawn . . .' said Frank.

386

She shook her head. Her eyes were glistening.

'No, Frank,' she said. 'I promise.'

'I don't understand,' said Frank.

'It was my birthday,' said Dawn. 'Things had been getting me down. My parents arguing all the time. One thing and another.'

She looked away and a slight shudder passed through her as if she was trying to control herself.

'I know it's stupid,' she said, turning back. 'You're right. But I needed something and so . . . so I went onto the railway bridge with my wish and dropped it in. I'm guessing it would have been the night before you found it.'

'But the colours . . .' said Frank.

'I borrowed them,' said Dawn. 'That day in the library – you remember? I used them while Olivia was out of the room. I just thought it would make the wish more . . . I don't know, more likely to come true!'

She chuckled grimly at this thought. Frank put his face in his hands and tried to absorb all this new information, but it was like grinding gears. It was crunching through what he thought he knew of the last few months.

'I'm sorry, Dawn,' he said eventually. 'I've messed up.'

'Who hasn't?' said Dawn.

He put his hands in his lap and looked at her.

'What an idiot you must have thought I was. Think I am.'

She shook her head.

'No,' she said. 'Never that.'

'Bastard then?' he said. 'I've ruined everything.'

'Not everything,' she said.

'How can you still want to be my friend?' he said. 'When

I've been so stupid and so useless.'

'Because I love you,' she said. 'I've always loved you. But you are such a bloody idiot, you never knew.'

Frank stared at her.

'Dawn,' he said. 'I don't know what to say.'

'Then don't say anything,' she said.

'I'm sorry,' he said.

'Stop apologising,' said Dawn. 'For crying out loud.'

'Dawn.'

Frank reached out for her but she shook her head.

'Don't . . .'

Dawn turned and walked away. Frank called after her but he could already hear her running up the stairs to her apartment.

Chapter 57

Frank did not sleep well and woke from a night of troubled dreams to find the Student sitting up watching him.

'You look terrible,' he said.

'Thanks,' said Frank.

'Seriously.'

Frank staggered to his feet and looked in the mirror. The Student was right. He did look terrible.

'I thought I heard you talking to Miss Calypter in the courtyard.'

Frank smiled at him.

'Oh, did you now?'

The Student held his hands up in protest.

'I heard nothing specific, I promise you. But I thought you would arrive at the apartment and you did not – not until just before curfew. Is everything all right? I ask as a friend, not as your Student.'

'My friend?' said Frank. 'Is that what you are now?'

'I could be,' said the Student.

'Well, my friend,' said Frank, 'if you want to know the truth of it, my whole life has turned to crap.'

'I'm sorry to hear that,' said the Student.

'Well, there you are.'

'It's none of my business, of course . . .' began the Student.
'Isn't everything your business?'

The Student nodded. 'Mr Vertex would say so,' he replied.

Frank looked at him. He was about to reply when he remembered the words of Mr Vertex himself. 'Be suspicious of everyone.' Frank clapped his hands. 'Anyway,' he said. 'Can't stand here talking. Must get up to the Castle.'

'Have you and Miss Calypter had a falling out?'

'We haven't had a falling in,' said Frank. 'Wait a minute. Why would you ask that?'

The Student looked at the floor.

'Are you spying on her too?'

'Forgive me,' said the Student after a moment. 'I met Miss Calypter's Student.'

'What?' said Frank. 'And you talk about us to each other?'

'No. It's not like that at all. I didn't know he was the Student upstairs. As chance would have it, we have never met in the building. I met him at a Ministry function and he was talking about the girl of the family he was with and how she liked to paint and how she was . . . how she was in love with the boy downstairs.'

Frank cursed under his breath.

'As soon as I realised that I knew the subject he was speaking about I ended the conversation, I promise you.'

'And you never thought to tell me?' said Frank. 'Some friend you are.'

'You know how it is. I shouldn't even be having this conversation. Don't pretend you do not hold secrets. We both know that you do. No one could work for Vertex and not.'

390

Frank thought of Scape and the notebooks and looked at the floor.

'Frank!' called his father on cue. 'Are you coming?'

'Got to go,' said Frank.

When Frank arrived at his office there was a young woman sitting outside, behind a desk placed next to his door. She smiled and stood up as he approached.

'Mr Palp, sir,' she said, flattening her skirt with one hand and shaking Frank's hand with the other. She was very pretty.

'Miss?'

'Miss Elytra,' she said breezily. 'I'm your new secretary.'

'Mr Vertex sent you?'

'Why . . . yes – yes, he did,' she replied.

'Well, that's good of him,' said Frank. 'Is there anything you need?'

'No, sir,' she said. 'I have everything here. I will take your calls. Make sure you aren't being bothered by anyone you don't want to be. Can I get you a cup of coffee?'

'No – thank you.'

'Tea?'

'Nothing, thank you,' said Frank.

'Very well, sir,' she said. 'If there is anything I can do for you – anything at all – just call.'

'I will,' said Frank.

Frank closed the door behind him and sat down in his chair, staring in the direction of the secretary. Vertex was keeping an eye on him. And if he was keeping an eye on him, that meant he suspected something.

Frank cursed and kicked out, sending a waste-paper bin across the floor. The door opened and Miss Elytra poked her head through, looking concernedly at the bin and the scattered waste paper.

'Is everything all right?'

'Yes,' said Frank. 'An accident.'

'Shall I – ?'

'No,' said Frank, more sharply than he had intended to. 'Thank you. I can manage.'

'Very well, sir.'

Miss Elytra disappeared, the door closed and Frank tidied up and then returned to his desk. He had to keep working. He had to carry on as though everything was normal. It was vital.

Frank went over to his shelves and gathered a set of Student notebooks. He placed them in a neat pile, took the top one off, opened it up, flattened it out and began to read.

Miss Elytra had interrupted him twice before he reached the third notebook, but already he was beginning to see a pattern forming through the Student's notes.

It was clearly an Old Town family, but no one Frank felt he knew. The father worked in the taxation sector at the Castle and it seemed he was cheating on his wife with a secretary from the transport sector. None of this was explicit in the notes, but it was there if you looked hard enough.

But Frank wanted the man to be committing some actual crime so that he could send the notebooks to Mr Vertex. Maybe if he was able to bring a truly dangerous agitator or radical to the attention of the Ministry, Mr Vertex might regain his confidence in him. Vertex surely couldn't believe Scape was actually a serious threat. Scape didn't want to overthrow the

Ministry – he just wanted to get on his motorbike and head for the hills. They'd be doing everyone a favour if they just let him.

Frank looked in his jacket pocket for a pen and found a folded piece of paper. Taking it out he saw that it was the wish – the ANYTHING THAT ISN'T THIS wish – the wish he had thought was Olivia's but that he now knew was Dawn's.

It was creased and ragged, having been carried round for so long and having been folded and flattened out so many times – as well as having been crumpled into a ball by Olivia.

But the colours still sang out, even after all this time. Somehow they sang out more, knowing that it was Dawn who had written the words. Frank didn't really understand why that was true, but it certainly was.

The note reminded him of Olivia and that last meeting with her. It reminded him of Scape too and of his anger at both of them. But those images quickly died away and were replaced by others: a long sequence of vivid moments from his life, right back to his earliest memory – and Dawn was there in every one.

Frank banged on the door. After a moment, Dawn's mother appeared. Her eyes were puffy and half-closed.

'Mrs Calypter,' he said. 'It's Frank from downstairs.'

'Frank?' she said. 'I don't know any Frank.'

'Of course you do,' said Frank. 'Frank Palp. You know my mother.'

'Who are you to come here and tell me who I know and who I don't know?' she said.

Frank hung his head and sighed.

'Could you just tell Dawn I'm here?' said Frank.

'What do you want with her?' she said, eyeing him suspiciously.

'I'm a friend,' said Frank. 'From downstairs.'

'What do you want?' said Dawn from behind her mother.

'You,' said Frank.

'What for?'

Frank smiled.

'Do you think we could talk without your mother between us?' he said.

'No,' said Dawn.

'Who is this, Dawn?' said her mother.

'All right, then,' said Frank, taking a deep breath. 'I just came to say that I think I love you, Dawn.'

'What did he say, Dawn?'

'He says he thinks he loves me,' said Dawn.

'Well, don't he know?' said her mother.

'Apparently not,' said Dawn.

'I've had enough of this,' said Dawn's mother, and she started to close the door.

'No!' said Frank, shoving his hand against it. 'Look, Dawn,' he said. 'The fact is I don't know anything any more. I thought I did. Once. But everything I've been sure about has turned out to be wrong.

'All my life I've tried to know things – to believe as little as possible. I thought it would protect me from lies but it hasn't. So I don't want to know that I love you because I'm scared that will turn out to be wrong too and I couldn't stand that.

'I'm going to have to start again – question everything I thought I was sure of. Everything is swirling about in chaos, Dawn – until I look at your face. You're the only fixed point I have . . . You're the only truly good thing.

394

'I know there's no reason why you should listen to anything I have to say, but –'

'Stop talking,' said Dawn, barging past her mother and throwing her arms round Frank.

'I know I love you,' she whispered in his ear. 'That'll have to do for both of us.'

They kissed. Their faces pressed together and as they both leant to one side to avoid each other's noses, the scars on their lips married up exactly. They both felt the touch of that bare flesh and a tingle ran through their whole bodies; a place untouched, now touched, a place that was previously unreached was finally discovered.

'So who is he?' said Dawn's mother.

Chapter 58

Suddenly everything was different with Dawn. It just seemed natural. Frank had thought it would feel awkward but it didn't at all. They seemed to make the move from friends to lovers seamlessly, effortlessly.

But Frank had learnt one lesson from his experience with Olivia: he was not going to involve his parents. They didn't need to know. Besides, they seemed to have no room in their lives for anything other than the impending visit of the King.

So there would be no more sitting on the bench in the courtyard. Neither of them wanted to suffer the attentions of their parents if they happened to pass by. No, they would take to the streets together.

The first time they went out together like this, leaving the apartment separately and meeting on the corner of the next block, Frank suddenly realised something about Dawn he had never seen before.

'Wait!' he said. 'You're not –'

'Hunched over like an idiot?' said Dawn. 'No.'

'You don't believe in the Sniper?' said Frank. 'I mean, I'm not sure I do, but –'

'I don't know whether I do or not,' said Dawn. 'What I do

know is that believing or not believing is going to make no difference. Neither is walking around bent double.'

Frank smiled at her and slowly, wincing as he did so, stood up straight. It was terrifying. He felt sure that this was just what the Sniper had been waiting for and clenched his teeth, waiting for the shot. But it didn't come. Dawn chuckled.

'There,' she said. 'Isn't that better?'

Frank had to agree. It was better. He could breathe now and his view of the Old Town seemed to have changed entirely. Everything looked different standing upright.

Frank slowly spun round taking the whole street in – the cold, grey cobbles, the snaking tramlines, the buildings black beyond the reach of the streetlamps. Their giant shadows painted across the office blocks. He looked at the roofs and felt the fear ebb away the more he looked.

'You're amazing, do you know that?' said Frank.

Dawn smiled.

'Yes,' she said. 'On good days.'

'Do you mean on good days you're amazing?' said Frank. 'Or that on good days you know it?'

'Both.'

They mostly kept to the Old Town, and walking the narrow streets and alleyways away from the main thoroughfares they both discovered places neither of them knew existed – little islands of the pre-War, pre-Revolution Old Town.

They walked past buildings still derelict from the Revolution, windows dead and doors barred and tattooed with faded graffiti and ravaged posters proclaiming old slogans, old dreams, old lies.

These streets were both poorly and harshly lit, so that half their length would be in shadow and the next half raked with light, their shadows growing and climbing up pockmarked walls as they walked along.

Behind columns, under arcades and inside tram stops, there were silhouetted couples – embracing lovers, street walkers negotiating with clients, all kinds of night peddlers warily engaged in their business. It all had a decrepit glamour to it, a visceral edge that was missing from the Old New Town.

Dawn and Frank kissed too, in the shadows, but although their hands searched each other out in the darkness, tracing the new contours of bodies they knew but did not know, there was not the frantic edge there had been with Olivia.

Perhaps Olivia had been right. Perhaps what he felt for her had only been lust and nothing more. Because there was a difference in the feelings he had for Dawn. Lust was certainly there, but it was a lust for *Dawn*, not simply for sex. It made his feelings for Dawn seem like some new species of love.

They found a café on the banks of a little offshoot of the river, next to a ruined mill. It was in an unremarkable building and to get to it they had to climb a huge staircase in the shape of a lopsided parallelogram.

There were hundreds of steps – and it felt like thousands – before they reached the door at the very top, knocked and were let into a café that was a rambling collection of different rooms, eccentrically decorated and untidily stocked with books, sculptures, old machines and paintings.

It was an extraordinary place, full of fascinating people

neither of them knew, as well as the obligatory Civil Servants sitting in the corner watching everything. Neither of them could understand how they had never come across it before.

Frank and Dawn talked for hours, pausing only to kiss, neither hindered nor embarrassed by the gaze of others. Yet at no time in these long talks did Frank ever feel it was the right time to tell Dawn exactly what he did at the Ministry or about Scape and the notebooks.

This was despite the fact that they had talked about the Ministry, just in the vaguest terms. Dawn assumed Frank thought it would be boring for her to hear about and so she was equally vague about her job at the paper mill.

Frank wanted to tell Dawn – he did not want to hide anything from her – but he did not want the ensuing problems overlapping with this new problem-free pleasure. Telling her would poison it, he was sure. There would be time enough for that. He just wanted to enjoy this while it lasted.

'You know that Roland is a Civil Servant now?' said Dawn.

'What?' said Frank. 'How?'

Dawn laughed as Frank glanced over at the Civil Servants in the corner.

'There are gays everywhere, Frank,' said Dawn. 'In every kind of job.'

'But Civil Servants?' he said. 'I thought the Ministry – what's it called? – "chemically realigned" them.'

Dawn shook her head.

'That's just what they tell people. Roland says there are loads of gays in the Civil Service,' said Dawn. 'And in the Ministry in general.'

Frank peered at her sceptically.

'Did he mention any names?' said Frank.

'No, of course not,' said Dawn. 'He's hardly going to blurt that kind of thing out.'

'I suppose . . .' said Frank.

'Actually,' said Dawn, 'to be honest I can't really remember the last time we talked properly. He's changed since he took that job.'

'How?' said Frank.

Dawn leant back and looked Frank up and down.

'You know,' said Dawn.

Frank nodded.

'I suppose.'

'Working for the Ministry does seem to smarten people up. Both of you are a lot better turned out these days.'

Frank smiled.

'But it's more than that,' said Dawn. 'He's . . . colder, somehow. I can't explain. I'm worried about him, actually.'

'The Ministry will do that to a person,' he said.

'But not you,' said Dawn.

Frank wanted to tell her everything – about Vertex, about Scape – but the bell in the café warned them it was close to curfew. The moment had passed by the time they were outside.

They walked back as the last trams headed past. A thin cloud sliced through a full moon. The streets were full of people heading home.

When Frank and Dawn arrived back at their apartment block, they stopped at the foot of the stairs. Neither seemed sure of what to do next and it was Dawn who moved first, pulling Frank towards her.

They kissed – a long-lasting kiss, increasing in passion rather than drawing to a conclusion. When they parted, Dawn grabbed Frank's hand and led him upstairs past his own floor.

'My father is away on business and my mother is at a friend's,' said Dawn. 'She will be drunk by now and won't come back till tomorrow. The Student is at some Ministry conference out of town. We're alone.'

Frank allowed himself to be led to Dawn's door and across the threshold. The layout was identical to his own apartment, but while his mother was fastidious and house-proud, Dawn's was a drunk. The difference was astounding and clearly showed on Frank's face.

'It's a bit of a mess, huh?' she said.

Frank didn't know what to say. It was more than a bit of a mess. It looked like the place had just been turned over by very inefficient burglars.

'Come on,' said Dawn, leading him by the hand again. 'My room's not like this.'

Dawn took him down the hallway and Frank realised that his own family's hallway lay directly underneath this one and his own bedroom beneath the room he now entered. Dawn seemed to be having the same thoughts.

'I used to hear you typing sometimes,' she said. 'When it was quiet.'

'Sorry,' said Frank.

'No,' said Dawn. 'I liked it. I would shut out the arguments next door and concentrate on you typing. It soothed me. I haven't heard it much for a while.'

Frank shrugged. 'I don't seem to be able to do it any more. I don't seem to have anything to say.'

Dawn's room was very different from Frank's, even though it was the same proportions. It was not so much that it was more feminine as that it was more personal – it felt like Dawn's room more than Frank's room felt like Frank's.

For one thing, there was just one bed. No female Student had been available and so when their student had been billeted on them, it was thought best that he slept in the lounge on a fold-up bed. Frank almost felt sorry for him. It can't have been easy with Dawn's parents and there can't have been much point to the posting either. He couldn't imagine that Dawn's parents ever did or said anything that would have been remotely of interest to the Ministry. Maybe it was Dawn they were keeping an eye on. The Ministry was always suspicious of artists.

And it was that art that made Dawn's room so personal – that made it feel like stepping into Dawn's mind – into her imagination, her soul. Frank had nothing on his walls at all.

The drawings were in black and white and shades of grey, and they depicted places Frank knew well – the Castle, the river, Fortitude Bridge, even the cemetery. But they were drawn and painted in such a way that it felt as though he was seeing them for the very first time. Frank felt that, if he leant in towards them any further, he might tumble into the picture, and had to shake his head to clear it and return to the now and to Dawn.

Little dramas were taking place among the shadows and it almost seemed to Frank that Dawn had been illustrating

Frank's life over the last few months. There was a lone figure climbing the steps to the Castle. There was another standing forlornly on the railway bridge. There was someone standing outside the cemetery gate. The effect was dizzying. Frank sat down on the edge of the bed and picked up one of the drawings that were lying in a heap on top of a low cupboard. It was a pencil drawing of a woman standing in the nude, her head cocked to one side so that her bobbed hair brushed against her shoulder. The face was more severe than normal, because of the concentration involved, but it was instantly recognisable as Dawn.

Dawn smiled at Frank's discomfort in seeing her naked body.

'It's more embarrassing than I thought it would be,' she said. 'To have you look at those.'

'They're really good,' he said, picking up some more.

Dawn chuckled.

'Is that an artistic judgement?' she asked. 'Or are you just looking at my tits?'

'No!' said Frank. 'I mean, it's hard not to. I mean, I have to. They're right there.'

'Sorry.'

'No – they're nice. I mean, I'm not *not* looking at them . . .'

Dawn laughed. Frank looked at the drawing, at the curves of flesh, the creases, the ins and the outs – then at Dawn, then back again. And as he did so, Dawn started to unbutton her clothes and let them fall, one by one, to the carpet, until she stood there naked.

Her nakedness was vivid and unexpected, perfect in its imperfections, and for the first time Frank's own physical shortcomings did not sting. So he stood up and did the same. Dawn reached out and switched off the light and the scene was plunged into cool shadows, lit only by the streetlamps outside.

Frank buried his face into Dawn's neck as she eased back towards the bed and let his body drop gently onto hers, the heat of their bodies glowing in the dark. That other mouth, drawing him in. It seemed as though the bed, the floor, everything in the world, just fell away and they were falling, falling, falling . . .

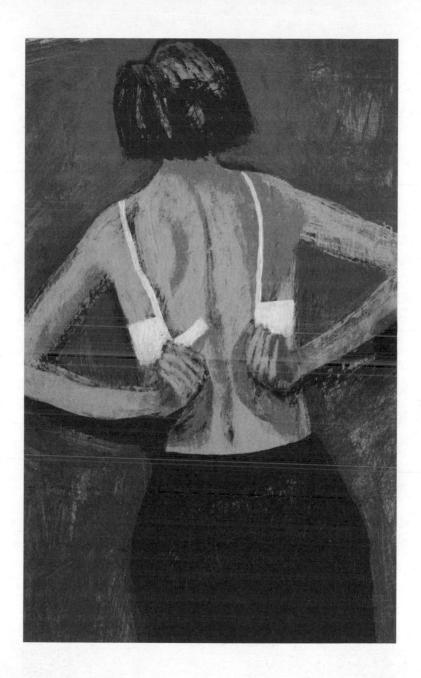

Chapter 59

The preparations for the Big Day were now almost complete. The King's Courtyard had been closed off behind screens whilst rehearsals took place in secret. Frank's father was behind them, drilling the survivors of his old platoon.

The Ministry Television Company arrived to plan their coverage. At lunchtime Frank watched the technicians going back and forth, and above the screens he could see them installing huge lighting rigs. When they tested them, it was a blinding burst of white light and Frank had to look away.

Frank was surprised to find himself a little starstruck too when he saw Davina Galea, the Ministry Television News presenter, walk past reading notes and chatting to a man Frank assumed must be the director.

Frank had been doggedly resistant to the idea that the Big Day was anything but an enormous waste of time, but he felt a little twinge of excitement as the day neared, and he smiled at the realisation. Maybe his relationship with Dawn was making him soft.

Frank was trying very hard not to think about Dawn at work, just as he had tried not to think about Olivia. But with Dawn it was more because whenever he thought of Dawn, he became re-sensitised to the whole issue of working at the Ministry

It was almost as if New-Frank wasn't really True-Frank, but just Old-Frank with a new skin – a skin that was now being shed – and the skin it was revealing was even more tender for being hidden over the past few months. That shared nakedness had changed something for good, Frank knew that.

Frank went back to his office and looked out of the window. The clouds were high but covered the whole sky, the light seeping through in varying degrees. It gave a strange mother-of-pearl sheen to the sky that was at once beautiful and unsettling.

Frank sat down at his desk but could not clear his mind to work. The issue of the notebooks – of Scape and of Vertex – was not going to go away. It was a problem that just became more intractable the more he thought about it.

Just as Frank was trying to make sense of it again, there was a knock at the door and in walked Scape.

'Mr Palp, I'm very sorry, I did say –' said Miss Elytra, frowning at Scape.

'That's all right, Miss Elytra,' said Frank. 'Thank you. Everything's fine.'

Miss Elytra gave Scape one last frown and then left, shutting the door behind her.

'Frank,' he said. 'So this is where you're hiding yourself away? Look at you – very smart suit. And a secretary! Not a bad looker, either.'

Scape was pacing up and down, looking this way and that. Frank had rarely seen him look so tense.

'You shouldn't really be here,' said Frank.

'Good to see you as well,' said Scape.

'Look,' said Frank, 'don't you remember that we didn't exactly part on good –'

'Water under the bridge,' said Scape, waving him away and walking over to the window. 'You've got a view! An actual view!'

Scape stood drumming his hands on the windowsill.

'You shouldn't be here,' said Frank. 'You know that. This sector is restricted.'

'Yes, yes,' said Scape without looking round. 'Are you going to report me, then?'

Frank frowned. Why shouldn't he report him? He didn't owe Scape a thing. He should have already gone to Vertex as it was. If Scape really was under suspicion, then what would it look like if he was seen in Frank's office?

'Was there something in particular?' said Frank, trying to sound as cool as possible.

Scape chuckled.

'Was there something in particular?' he parroted in a ridiculous high-pitched voice. 'You crack me up.'

'Do I?' said Frank.

Scape turned round. Frank saw for the first time how ragged he looked. He had lost weight and had dark rings under his eyes.

'I wondered if you wanted to go for a drink some time?' said Scape, suddenly adopting a friendly tone. 'For old time's sake.'

'I really don't think –'

'All right,' said Scape, his smile gone in an instant. 'Just a thought, that's all. Don't get yourself in a state.'

Frank sat back and looked at him. How had he ever been

409

intimidated by someone like this?

'Did you ever buy the motorbike?' said Frank.

'What?'

'The motorbike you wanted,' said Frank. 'Did you ever buy it?'

'Are you telling me to run?'

'Why would I be telling you to run?'

Scape chewed on his bottom lip.

'No,' he said. 'Weirdest thing, but just as I was about to buy it, the guy at the garage said it had been impounded by the Ministry. They wouldn't tell him why.'

'Well, then,' said Frank. 'I am quite busy. So . . .'

Scape lurched forward.

'If you knew something,' said Scape, 'if you heard anything . . . You'd tell me, wouldn't you?'

Frank swallowed hard.

'Like what?'

'I'm asking you as a friend,' said Scape.

'A friend?' said Frank.

'Of course you have so many, don't you, so you can be fussy?' said Scape.

'Like I said,' said Frank. 'I'm busy.'

'Listen,' said Scape, leaning across Frank's desk. 'I'll beg if you want me to, you fu—'

'Is everything all right?' said a voice behind Scape. Scape stood and leapt back from the desk.

'Everything is fine, Mr Vertex, sir,' said Frank.

Vertex peered at Scape.

'Scape was just passing,' said Frank.

'On the way to where?' said Mr Vertex.

'I . . . I . . .'

'He got himself lost, sir,' said Frank.

'Yes, sir,' said Scape. 'I was lost and then I saw Frank's name, sir, and so . . .'

Mr Vertex smiled benignly and nodded.

'I see,' he said. 'Well, then, I'll show you the way back to your sector.'

'There's no need, really, sir,' said Scape.

'I insist,' said Mr Vertex.

'Yes, sir,' said Scape. 'Thank you, sir.'

Scape straightened his tie and headed for the door, holding it open for Mr Vertex, who smiled and nodded at Frank as he left.

Frank let out a long breath as soon as the door closed and he was alone. He leant forward, elbows on the desk, fingertips on his temples, trying to think.

Scape knew. He must have realised his Student's notebooks showed him in a dubious light and he must also know that they might get into Frank's hands. How did he even know that? Maybe Scape was a spy after all. No, thought Frank. He was too stupid for that, surely? Too talkative, anyway.

And what about Mr Vertex? It couldn't have been accidental that he just happened to walk in whilst Scape was there. Miss Elytra had no doubt called him. Frank had put the notebooks away in a drawer in his desk. He fetched the key and unlocked it, pulling the drawer open and staring in, dumbfounded.

It was empty. Even though that was clear from a cursory glance, still Frank had to pull the drawer open wider and root around, and then open all the other drawers and then get

411

up from his desk and search his shelves, despite all the time knowing full well that he had put the notebooks in that first drawer and that was where they should be.

His heart raced. Someone had taken them. But who? Frank tried to imagine all the people who might do such a thing, but for one reason or another, he always came back to Mr Vertex or someone in his employ. Frank thumped his fist down on his desk. Miss Elytra's head popped through the open door.

'Is everything all r—'

'Get out!' yelled Frank, throwing a book at the door.

Miss Elytra squealed and disappeared, slamming the door. Frank slumped back into his chair. Now that Vertex almost certainly had the notebooks, he would see Frank's loyalty as being fundamentally compromised.

Chapter 60

The Big Day finally arrived. The whole city was given the day off and every household was provided with an assortment of flags and a map of the route with a politely worded message explaining that the Ministry expected them to attend.

But in fact no coercion was needed. The city was only too happy to come out and show their support for the King. He lived in his country residence and no one had seen him – except on television – for years.

Frank had assumed that it would only be the older generation who would get caught up in the occasion, but he saw that the excitement was universal. From grandparents to grandchildren, Frank had never seen so many smiles in the Old Town. He did not recognise his own, normally joyless, neighbours. So little happened. Didn't Frank always say that? Dawn had been right all along – it was better to enjoy whatever came along. Dawn was not invited to the Castle but she'd said she would be in the crowd on Resolution Avenue. Even her feckless parents would be there. The Ministry had draped bunting across the roads leading up to the Castle. Each pendant was pale grey with alternate designs showing the Ministry logo (the Castle in silhouette) with the Royal

arms (a raven holding a human eye in its beak). It was very festive, after a fashion.

Of course, the King would not be coming via the Old Steps. They were not going to make the King climb those. No, the royal motorcade would arrive at the foot of the rock at the western side of the Castle and he would take the royal funicular railway, built by the insane King Scutum III.

So, as Frank walked up the steps, a steady stream of people not invited to attend inside the Castle cascaded giddily downwards, heading for a vantage point along the processional route.

Frank allowed himself a smug smile in response to the suspicious and resentful looks he received by those heading downwards. That's right – he was invited to the ceremony in the King's Courtyard! For the first time ever he was getting some enjoyment out of being his father's son.

Frank walked past the sentries and through to the great courtyard. He thought he would visit the toilet before the event got started and was wandering down the corridor when he saw Mr Vertex standing talking to a group of men.

Frank only caught a glimpse of them. He didn't recognise the men but there was something a little intimidating about them, even from the back. They were all big, broad-shouldered and thick-necked. Plain-clothes security, presumably. Frank ducked into the toilets before he was seen. When he came out, the corridor was empty.

The courtyard had begun to fill up and the Ministry Band took their places. All the most senior of the Ministry Men were there, dressed in black, wearing hats and chests full of medals. Mr Vertex was right at the front.

There was a television crew with two cameras and bright arc lights shining down on the courtyard. Frank saw his mother and Petra taking their seats. He waved to them and took his place alongside his mother. She grabbed his hand, squeezing it so tightly it hurt.

'It'll be fine, Mother,' said Frank.

'I'm so nervous,' she said. 'Your father didn't sleep at all last night.'

'It'll be fine,' said Frank. 'You know Father. He will have rehearsed and rehearsed. Don't worry.'

The seats filled up and there was a restless fidgeting and whispering – a breathless expectation. The buglers blasted a loud volley of notes that seemed almost random at first but which, after a moment, turned into the national anthem.

Everyone got to their feet. Frank stood up with them, and with them he placed his hand over his heart. He was amazed at how uplifted he felt, by both the music and being part of this crowd and, for the first time ever, feeling part of its mood. He grinned as his father led the surviving defenders of the Castle out into the courtyard, all dressed in their best suits, medals shining in the arc lights.

Frank had never seen his father in military mode. He looked so different. He looked taller, younger. He led the group, barking orders. One of them was Mr Prementum, his tin ear glinting – possibly the only time Frank had ever seen him without his white barber's jacket on.

They came to a halt whilst his father carried on, stamping his shoes and turning to salute the veterans. They saluted back and Frank's father turned, stamped his feet, and they all came to attention facing the crowds, who erupted into a raucous applause.

Frank turned in his seat to look at the crowd. There was Mr Mandible clapping away. There was Olivia and her mother. She didn't see Frank, or if she did she didn't show it. There was Mr Vertex too, a benign smile on his face as though clapping children at a school play.

The King finally arrived to a surging wave of cheers that washed across the crowd and submerged Frank in its roar. He had never experienced anything like it. He had never even thought about the King and yet he felt it too – he felt something special in the air. It was the Grey being pushed away.

Frank had no interest in the King – and still didn't – and yet he was fascinated by this communal fervour the King's visit had inspired. This is what his mother had talked about all his life and he had just dismissed as tiresome nostalgia. But it was real. It was. It couldn't be denied. What a massive misjudgement it was for the Ministry to organise this showcase for the King – to reawaken this fellow feeling.

Frank had seen pictures of the King. Every shop, office and Ministry building had one. He still appeared on stamps. But it was always the same picture. He had never seen the whole of the King – only ever that stock head-and-shoulder shot in profile. So Frank was surprised by how tall he was – tall and slender, towering over the President, who was, by contrast, a very unimpressive figure who seemed to be walking twice as fast as the laconic King, just to maintain the same pace.

When the King reached Frank's father, the veterans saluted once again. Mr Prementum's tin ear lit up in the spotlight like a

beacon. Frank and the crowd watched in awe as the King spoke quietly to Frank's father. Frank could feel everyone craning forwards, trying to hear what was being said. Then Frank's father stood aside and began to introduce the men.

That was when it happened.

Four men stood up among the seated crowd and, yelling, threw things towards the King. Frank's first thought was that they were bombs, but they were balloons filled with white paint. One of them hit the King in the back, another in the side of his face. Frank's father stepped forward but was immediately hit in the face himself and blinded. He stood there, flailing, confused.

Guards leapt forward and grabbed the men, dragging them away. Frank's mother started crying and Petra comforted her.

The King was led away and Frank watched his father standing with the other veterans, paint dripping off his face, looking back at them.

'We need you to leave, now,' said a Civil Servant, ushering them from their seats. 'There may be more. We have to secure the area.'

Frank looked back over his shoulder and saw his father and the veterans being shepherded away by Civil Servants. Their proud demeanour of a few minutes ago had vanished and they looked like the old men they were.

'Who would do such a thing?' said his mother. 'Who would do such a terrible thing?'

'I don't know, Mother,' said Petra.

Frank and his sister helped their mother out of the Castle, protecting her from the disgruntled, jostling crowd. All good will had evaporated, Frank noticed. The speed of this reversal was astounding. The Grey had settled back on them. All was as it had been.

Or rather, it was worse than it had been, because although his mother did not seem to notice, those in the crowd who recognised them as being related to his father looked at them with a mix of pity and disgust, and Frank could hear them mutter as they passed. It seemed his father had gone from war hero to doddering old fool in the blink of an eye.

All the way down the Castle steps Frank could overhear people demanding to know who did it, speculating about who they might be – counter-revolutionary terrorists seemed to be favourite – and baying for their blood. They wanted them punished, and the more cruelly the better.

It took a long time to get to the foot of the hill and by that time they were almost carrying their mother. They had to walk home because the street was still closed to trams.

'Why would they do it?' repeated their mother faintly as they walked. 'Why?'

'There, there, mother,' said Petra. 'We'll find out soon enough.'

Frank looked back towards the Castle. He wasn't so sure they'd ever know. One of the attackers had been standing only a few feet way from Frank and had cursed loudly as he was taken away. Frank recognised him immediately as one of the men to whom Mr Vertex had been talking before the ceremony.

'Listen,' said Frank to his sister. 'You take Mother home. I need to go back.'

'Frank?' said his mother.

'Go home,' said Frank. 'I'll be back soon.'

Chapter 61

When Frank reached the sentry boxes he was astounded to find them empty. There were no guards in sight. Frank walked through the open gates and through the grand entranceway, under the mighty arch, and into the central courtyard.

It looked even more impressive empty and still and lit by the dying sun. He felt self-conscious about the sound of his footsteps chattering around the walls of the empty offices, echoing through back and forth. The Castle had taken on the air of a monastery and Frank felt as though he was intruding on the cloistered serenity.

He entered through the main door and was surprised to see someone sitting on the reception desk.

'Hello?' said Frank. 'I didn't think there was anyone here.'

The receptionist looked at him but said nothing. Frank took a few steps and then turned back.

'You know there are no guards at the gate,' said Frank.

'Oh?' she said.

'Should we . . . do anything about it?' said Frank.

'Do anything?' she said with a little frown of her thin, pencil-line eyebrows.

'About the guards?' said Frank. 'About them not being there?'

The receptionist looked very stern and reached into a drawer for a ledger.

'You wish to make a formal complaint,' she said, putting on the glasses that hung around her neck. 'It's Mr Palp, isn't it?'

'Well . . . I . . . No, I wasn't meaning . . .'

Frank didn't know what to say. The receptionist stared at him, her pen poised above the open ledger.

'Never mind,' said Frank. 'Forget I said anything.'

The receptionist shook her head and closed the ledger with a suddenness that made Frank jump.

'Very well,' she said, with an arch of the eyebrow. 'As you wish.'

Frank stood there for a moment, feeling as though he should say something but unable to come up with anything appropriate.

'Thank you,' he said finally.

But the receptionist was already looking away towards the door. Frank could see the contempt in her face.

'I'm sure the King is safe in any case,' she said. 'No thanks to some.'

Frank glared at her.

'If this is about my father,' said Frank, 'you weren't even there. That wasn't his fault. What was he supposed to do?'

'I'm sure I don't know what you mean,' said the receptionist coldly.

Frank ignored her and set off towards Mr Vertex's office. His secretary wasn't there, so Frank went straight to the door and opened it without knocking. Mr Vertex looked up as though he was expecting him.

'It was you,' said Frank.

'I'm sorry, Frank,' said Mr Vertex, looking at his pocket watch. 'I'm afraid I'm rather busy. Today's drama has created quite a stir, as you can imagine.'

'You sabotaged it,' said Frank. 'You sabotaged the whole thing!'

'Now why would I do that?' said Mr Vertex with a sigh.

'Because you wanted to embarrass the King,' said Frank.

Mr Vertex smiled and sat back in his chair. He leant back, lacing his fingers across his stomach.

'I saw you with those men – the ones who attacked the King,' said Frank. 'I saw you talking to them before the ceremony.'

Mr Vertex nodded.

'I see,' he said.

'You see?' said Frank incredulously. 'You see? Is that the best you can come up with?'

Mr Vertex slammed his hand down on his desk. 'What do you want me to say?' he said. 'Do you want me to burst into tears? So you've caught me. What are you gong to do about it? Who is going to take your word over mine?'

'You've made my father a laughing stock,' said Frank. 'He's a war hero. I thought the Ministry looked after its own.'

423

'War hero? If it wasn't for me, your father and all those men would be dead. You would never have been born. You owe your very existence to me, Frank.

'There are people in this country who have forgotten what it takes to defend the things you love and hold dear. They don't want to pay that price. They live in their nice apartments in the Old New Town and chatter away. They have gone soft. They have allowed themselves the indulgence of guilt. Guilt is a luxury, Frank – it is a form of decadence.

'Those paint bombs could have been grenades,' said Mr Vertex. 'What then? Your father, the King, most of the Ministry Men watching from the front row – they would all have been killed. I showed them a glimpse of what might have been. I showed the people what might have been.'

'Why did you try so hard to save the King in the War, then?' said Frank. 'What was the point?'

'Are you a Royalist now?' said Mr Vertex with a smile. 'Let me tell you about the King. He was a traitor to his own people.'

'I don't believe you,' said Frank.

'Ask your father,' said Mr Vertex. 'You have been told, no doubt, that he was there to protect the King.'

'He was.'

'From himself, perhaps. We discovered the King had contacted the enemy and agreed to accept their right to rule were they to ensure his safety after the coup and allow him to continue as monarch, thereby giving the new regime the credibility they needed.'

'So what was my father's job, then?' asked Frank.

'He was there to stop the enemy from capturing the King,' said Mr Vertex. 'Just as the story goes. We could not allow that. The major difference was that your father was under specific orders to kill the King if capture looked imminent. He was unlocking the door to the King's apartment as I arrived with my reinforcements. He would have killed him, be sure of that. Your father was a good soldier.'

Frank stared at him. Mr Vertex took a deep breath and his usual implacable calm returned.

'Was there anything else?' said Mr Vertex, picking up some papers from his desk. 'Because, as I mentioned, I am most awfully busy.'

Frank turned to go.

'I am very disappointed in you,' said Mr Vertex. 'I had hoped for something better. I saw you as a special project right from the start – right from when my men reported you hanging about in front of the apartment block on Perseverance Boulevard.'

'What?' said Frank, his stomach lurching downwards as though in a plummeting lift.

'When my men reported back that you were cycling up and down in front of an apartment block containing so many important men I was intrigued. Then I examined the details. Always three times in either direction – never more. I had to know why.

'The Civil Servants wanted to arrest you, of course. They wanted to bring you in and have you interrogated. They suspected you of being a terrorist or an assassin, but I knew you weren't. Besides, if you were planning to assassinate Mrs Pulvillus you'd have been doing us all a favour, if you get my drift.'

'Not really, no,' said Frank.

'She's a trouble maker,' said Mr Vertex. 'She is a typical bleeding-heart Old New Towner who thinks that the Revolution has been betrayed. She is an exemplar of all that is rotten in this place.

'It was the work of moments, of course, to discover you sat near her daughter at school, and footage from the classroom showed you were clearly in thrall to her. Of course I also had the notebooks from your Student . . .'

Frank said nothing.

'So I followed you to the bookshop where we had our chat and I was genuinely intrigued by you. There was no lie there. You'll find I rarely lie. I see no point in it. Truth will out. I truly thought I had finally found someone with the required combination of imagination and . . . moral neutrality . . . to be a great Ministry Man one day. I mean that, Frank – great.'

Again Frank said nothing.

'I realised that you were trying to force the hand of fate,' said Mr Vertex. 'That's what I found so compelling. Instead of simply ringing the doorbell and asking to see her, you were trying to bring about an accident. Tell me – do you still believe in chance?'

'Yes,' said Frank.

'You are saying that because you think it offends me,' said Mr Vertex. 'But I don't believe you.'

'I don't care what you believe,' said Frank. 'I'm going to tell my father what you did.'

Mr Vertex smiled.

'You must do as you see fit, Frank,' he said. 'Now – I must get on.'

* * *

Frank's shoes squeaked on the newly waxed floors of the corridors and the noise was the only thing that stopped him feeling like a ghost, or that he was in a dream, because nothing about this familiar building seemed familiar at all.

The corridors were always full of people going back and forth, usually in a hurry – or with the appearance of being in a hurry. To walk down the corridor was to undergo a series of minor collisions – from the faintest of cloth brushes to the painful – and avoidance of collisions. Constant swerving and dodging and occasionally coming to a full stop, apology and side step.

But to see it empty was like looking at a blank screen at the end of a movie. It was lifeless and forlorn and lacking. Frank had no love for this building when it was full, but empty it was even worse. Empty it was like some horrible machine.

The light was glowing from under the door of his father's office and Frank knocked once and walked in.

His father sat at his desk but turned away from it, facing the wall. A reading lamp was the only light in the room. The blinds were open and the windows were black.

His father sat there, white paint still flecked across his face, his jacket drying on the coat stand, damp from where he had tried to mop the paint off. His father was full of silent rage, like a minotaur at the centre of a maze. Frank did not come any closer.

'It was Vertex,' said Frank. 'Vertex hired those men.'

His father did not look at him.

'Father?' said Frank. 'Did you hear me?'

427

'Yes,' said his father quietly.

'Well?' said Frank. 'Did you already know? You don't seem surprised.'

'No,' said his father. 'I didn't know. But neither am I surprised. That is the kind of man you work for.'

'But there must be something we can do,' said Frank.

'We?' said his father.

Frank frowned at him.

'Yes, we,' said Frank.

His father closed his eyes and breathed in, his nostrils flaring.

'What exactly do you think "we" can do?' said his father.

Frank shrugged.

'There has to be something.'

'Grow up, Frank,' said his father. 'There is nothing we can do and he knows it.'

'But I told him I know,' said Frank. 'I told him –'

'Then you're a fool,' said his father. 'Now you'll be buried in here like I've been buried. If you're lucky.'

Frank stepped forward and reached out to his father but flinched back as his father turned, snarling.

'Don't you dare pity me,' said his father.

'I wasn't,' said Frank. 'I was just –'

'You think you're better than us, don't you?' said his father. 'That's what's at the root of all this. You think you're special.'

'No!' said Frank.

But he did. It was true. It had always been true. His father shook his head and sighed, staring down at his desk.

'Well, you were right to put some distance between yourself and me, son,' he said. 'The Palp name won't help you now.'

'Mother is worried about you,' said Frank. 'You should go home.'

'Tell her I'll be home presently.'

Frank could see that the conversation had come to a close. He would get nothing more out of his father. He turned and opened the door.

'If you've got any sense you'll try to get back into Vertex's good books, son,' said his father without looking up. 'You don't want that man for an enemy.'

Frank turned to leave and then looked back.

'What did the King say to you?' said Frank.

His father looked up at him.

'He said, "It's all over for the likes of us".'

Frank opened his mouth to say that he knew – that he knew his father had had orders to kill the King that day – but instead he said nothing and left, walking through the corridors at a faster and faster pace, eager to get away from that place and everything it represented. The receptionist said something to him as he passed but he didn't hear it. Within seconds he was running down the steps, as though pursued by demons.

He skidded to a halt, gasping, in the small square by the old market. A group of Civil Servants were standing under a light by the arcade. They all turned to look at him. Frank knew better than to make eye contact with them, and set off immediately for home.

Chapter 62

Frank's father came home later. He had washed his face but there was still white paint visible in the wrinkles of his skin, among the hairs of his moustache. His jacket was still damp and streaked with smears of paint.

They all froze, even the Student, as he walked in, fearful of the temper he might be in, but it was worse than that. He looked broken. Frank's mother moved towards him but he held up his hand and stopped her. Then without saying a word he went to run himself a bath.

Frank dreaded seeing his father return from it, but was amazed to find that when he did, he was almost his normal self. In fact, the only thing that was noticeably different was the fact that he was not so bad tempered as normal.

They ate together and although Petra and Frank exchanged puzzled glances, their parents talked as though nothing much had happened. No mention at all was made of the Big Day, the King or the attack.

So this was the famous wartime spirit Frank had heard so much about. They were erecting a fortress around themselves, moated and barred to all but friendly traffic. They decided what went in and what went out. They were going into a siege.

For the first time in Frank's memory, the television remained switched off – for fear, no doubt, that there would be extensive coverage of the event and particularly of the attack on the King. They would just lie low until it was all forgotten. It was not as though Frank's father had done anything wrong.

When he got the chance, Frank popped upstairs to see Dawn. Her mother answered the door, reeking of booze, and was clearly about to regale Frank with her thoughts on the whole Big Day fiasco when Dawn pushed past her, closing the door as she did so.

'Oh, Frank,' she said, embracing him. 'I saw it on television. Your poor father. It must have been awful.'

Frank nodded.

'They're just pretending it didn't happen,' he said.

'You can't blame them,' said Dawn. 'The news was not very kind to your father and the other veterans.'

Frank winced.

'What did they say?'

'Does it matter?'

'Tell me.'

'They said there wasn't much sign of their wartime bravery today.'

'What?' said Frank. 'Bastards. What did they expect them to do? They're just ordinary civilians now. Old men. They weren't armed. They didn't even have a chance to –'

'Whoa, Frank,' said Dawn. 'You don't have to convince me.'

Frank took a deep breath.

'Sorry,' he said. 'It makes me mad.'

Dawn put her arms round him.

'I know,' she said. 'But what can you do?'

431

Frank opened his mouth to tell her about Vertex and about Scape but he could not bring himself to do it.

'Everything will be OK,' said Dawn. 'You know how things go. The newspapers will be talking about something else before you know it. It'll blow over.'

Frank nodded.

'I better get back,' said Frank. 'I think I ought to be with them.'

Dawn nodded.

'Tomorrow, then,' she said.

'Tomorrow,' said Frank.

Petra was going down the stairs, heading home, as Frank came down from Dawn's floor. He ran down to catch her up.

'Petra!' he called.

She turned round.

'Frank,' she said. 'So you finally saw the light?'

'How do you know about Dawn?' said Frank.

Petra smiled.

'I saw the two of you together a few nights ago,' she said. 'I'm pleased for you, Frank. She's always had a thing for you, you know.'

'Was anyone ever going to tell me?' said Frank.

'Would you have listened?'

'Maybe not,' said Frank. 'But I've got something to tell you.'

'Oh?' said Petra. 'Something good I hope.'

Frank smiled.

'I hope you'll think so,' said Frank. 'The Student – our Student . . .'

'Yes?' said Petra.

'Well,' said Frank. 'The fact is – he's in love with you.'

Petra stared at him.

432

'Is this a joke, Frank?' she said. 'Because it's cruel if –'

'It's not a joke,' said Frank. 'He is. He's told me so. And I know you like him too, don't you?'

Petra blushed.

'He's got to be two – three – years younger than me,' said Petra.

Frank raised his eyebrows and smiled.

'I'm just the messenger,' said Frank.

Petra looked back up towards the apartment, going through the times she had come over, replaying all the glances she had exchanged with the Student and the times she had turned to find him standing beside her. She pulled Frank to her, hugging him, kissing him on both cheeks.

'Thank you,' she said.

'I hope he deserves you,' said Frank.

She kissed him again.

'I've not been a very good brother to you, Petra,' said Frank. 'I'm sorry.'

'Don't be silly,' she said.

'I always thought the world of you,' said Frank. 'Remember that.'

'What do you mean?' said Petra. 'Don't talk like that. You're worrying me.'

Frank put his arms around her.

'I hope you'll be happy,' he said.

He could see the exhaustion etched into his father's face when he returned to his apartment – the strain of trying so hard not to recall his humiliation. Frank was sure that some of that strain was evident in his own face.

They played cards for a while, but the initial enthusiasm quickly wore off. Eventually his parents went to bed. Frank was going to tell the Student he had told Petra but he decided that he had interfered enough in that affair and he would let Petra make a move if she wanted to.

The Student made his way to bed himself but Frank stayed in the lounge and stared at the dead television screen. He had no idea how long he had been doing this when his mother appeared beside him in her dressing gown.

'Frank?' she said. 'What are you doing?'

'I don't know,' he said. 'I was thinking.'

'Thinking? No one thinks about anything good in the middle of the night,' she said. 'If it's this business today, it will all blow over.'

Frank smiled weakly.

'It's not that,' said Frank. 'Or not just that, anyway.'

His mother sat down beside him and put her hand on his knee.

'What is it?' she said.

'I'm in trouble, Mother,' said Frank. 'If you want to know the truth of it.'

'What kind of trouble?'

'I can't tell you,' said Frank.

'Why not?' said his mother.

'I just can't.'

'Because you think I'm not clever enough to understand?'

'Because its not safe for you to know,' said Frank.

Frank saw his mother grow a little paler at those words.

'This is about that man Vertex, isn't it?' said his mother.

Frank said nothing.

'Why on earth did you get yourself mixed up with a man like that?' she said.

'I don't know, Mother,' said Frank. 'But I wish I hadn't.'

His mother got up without saying a word and went through to the kitchen, opened a cupboard door, rooted around at the back and then returned, handing him a large tattered brown envelope.

'What's this?' said Frank.

'Take it,' said his mother.

Frank opened the envelope. It was stuffed with bank notes. Frank stared at his mother.

'There must be thousands here,' he said. 'Have you robbed a bank?'

'I've saved it,' she said. 'For thirty years. My mother left most of it to me and I have put a little by when I could.'

Frank tried to hand it back but she would not take it.

'But you must have been saving it for a reason,' said Frank.

'I was,' said his mother with a sad smile. 'I was saving it for this. It should be enough to buy you papers and get you out of the country and away from Vertex.'

Frank stared at her. He felt like he didn't know her at all.

'What about Petra?' he said.

'Petra does not need it like you need it,' she said. 'If she were here she'd say the same thing.'

'I can't . . .'

'I always knew you would leave, sweetheart,' she said. 'I didn't know how or when, but I knew that some day you might need this.'

'How?' said Frank. 'Why?'

435

'I just knew,' said his mother, tears in her eyes. 'You never belonged here. I don't know why. Even as a baby you used to crawl away the second I turned my back.'

Frank smiled, eyes stinging with tears.

'I'm sorry,' he said. 'It wasn't because –'

'I hoped you might find somebody you loved here and settle down,' she continued. 'But I only ever wanted for you to be happy. I thought you might marry and that might make you stay. I even thought you might marry Dawn from upstairs – you seemed so close when you were young. Mothers have these silly thoughts.'

Frank got up and went to her, kissing her on the cheek.

'Not so silly,' said Frank.

Chapter 63

Frank could think of no one else he could trust. The Student listened quietly and nodded. He might be able to get the papers. He had a friend at the Ministry who owed him a favour. But it would be expensive. Frank handed him the envelope. The Student took what he needed and handed the rest back.

The next morning, Frank went to see Dawn but she wasn't in. He did not know how he was going to tell her or how he was going to bear to leave her behind. But he knew he couldn't endanger her. He was thinking clearly for perhaps the first time in his life. He borrowed his father's old bike and set off just like he used to and cycled over Fortitude Bridge.

Frank even turned on to Perseverance Boulevard and stopped, staring down the road at Olivia's apartment. He slowly headed past, watching her door. He thought he even saw her and her mother through the window and smiled to himself. He was shocked by his total lack of feeling for her now. Not even the sting of regret or embarrassment. There was nothing.

Frank cycled past the bookshop but when he stopped to look he saw it was closed and the shutters locked. It didn't seem to have opened for some time. Maybe Frank had been its only customer. Maybe Vertex had closed it down.

Eventually he ended up beside the black hill of the cemetery. The tree looked bigger, the graves more ramshackle. Frank chained the bike up and walked across the street. He stood looking up at the gravestones above his head, silhouetted against a grimy sky. He couldn't remember the last time he had visited his grandfather or heard one of his stories.

'Frank!'

He turned and saw Dawn walking towards him. He almost didn't recognise her, because she was out of the normal context. A lump caught in his throat. The surprise of her had unmanned him.

'Dawn?' he said. 'What are you doing here?'

'I was shopping for my mother,' she said. 'Then I saw you. How are you?'

'I . . . I came to see you – earlier – at the apartment.'

'Oh?'

'I needed to talk to you.'

'Well, I'm here now.'

'I thought I might visit my grandfather,' said Frank. 'I feel bad. I haven't been for a while. Why don't you come and meet him? He'd love that.'

Dawn smiled.

'All right.'

They walked forward and Frank saw that the cemetery gates were closed now and a big metal chain and padlock were laced through the bars, locking the gates together.

Frank grabbed hold of the gates and shook them angrily. They growled and rust flaked off in a shower.

'Frank?' said Dawn.

A man in a grey suit walked up to him. He said nothing but stood close.

'Why are the gates locked?' said Frank as another man stood beside him. They were Civil Servants.

'They are always locked,' said the first man.

'No, they aren't,' said Frank.

The second man just smiled at him.

'Let's go, Frank,' said Dawn.

'Why are they locked?' repeated Frank, kicking them.

'They have always been locked, sir,' said the man.

'No!' said Frank. 'That's a lie!'

'Always.'

'No!' shouted Frank.

He grabbed the man by the coat collar. Two more Civil Servants standing outside the bookshop started to walk over.

'Frank!' shouted Dawn. 'We need to go. Now!'

Frank looked at the man, then at the locked gate and then shoved him away.

'It's OK!' called Dawn as she pulled Frank away from the Civil Servants. 'He's just upset. We don't want any trouble.'

'It's all right,' said one of the Civil Servants. 'I'll deal with this.'

It was Roland. The other Civil Servants nodded and began to disperse.

'Roland,' said Dawn. 'Thank you.'

'Go home, Frank,' said Roland coldly. 'Or you'll get arrested.'

'But –'

Roland grabbed him by the lapels.

'Do it!' he hissed. 'Now!'

He shoved him back against the locked gates. Frank thought about retaliating but saw the blurred shapes of the other Civil Servants over his shoulder.

'Come on,' said Dawn.

They walked away, never once looking back. When they were far enough away, Dawn stopped and slapped him on the arm.

'Are you crazy? You'll get us arrested, Frank,' said Dawn.

'I don't care!' said Frank.

'Well, I do!' shouted Dawn.

Frank took a deep breath and nodded.

'Roland,' said Dawn. 'He just looked straight through me.'

'I just –'

Frank started to sob.

'I don't know what to do!' he said.

'No one does,' said Dawn.

Frank wiped his eyes.

'Buy me a coffee,' said Dawn.

Frank nodded.

They walked down to the embankment and walked into Café Paraglossa. It was almost empty and Frank deliberately sat at a different table to the one he had shared with Olivia.

Frank wondered if the waitresses would remember him and talk about the fact that he was here with a different girl. But if they did remember him, they did a very good show of denying it. They seemed utterly bored and formal, taking their order with detachment.

'Dawn,' said Frank. 'I'm sorry about everything.'

'Everything?' she said. 'Surely there must be something that isn't your fault.'

He smiled.

'Actually, it doesn't feel like that right now,' he said.

'I love you, Frank,' said Dawn.

'And I love you,' said Frank. 'Truly. But I have to leave.'

'What?' said Dawn. 'What do you mean? How can you leave?'

'I . . . I . . .' He shook his head. 'I have to. My mother has given me money.'

'Why then?' she said. 'Why are you leaving? Why are you leaving me?'

'I'm in trouble, Dawn,' said Frank.

'What kind of trouble?'

'It's better that you don't know,' said Frank. 'But you know I wouldn't go unless I had to.'

She stared at him and then closed her eyes, a tear rolling down her cheek.

'No,' she said, shaking her head.

Frank could think of nothing to say. He just reached across the table and held her hand and gripped it hard, as though he was a drowning man in danger of being swept away. Which is how he felt.

As they were heading home, someone lurched out from an arcade. They both stepped back, thinking they were being mugged or arrested, almost into the path of a tram, which honked loudly at them. In the bright lights as it passed, Frank saw that their assailant was Scape.

'Frank,' he hissed. 'You've got to help me.'

'What?' said Frank. 'Why would I help you?'

'You have to, Frank,' said Scape. 'I'm begging you.'

'Help you how?' said Frank.

He knew how.

'You work for Vertex,' said Scape.

He was drunk, wild-eyed. He looked like he hadn't slept for days and when he had it had been in his clothes.

'So?' said Frank, glancing at Dawn. Scape grabbed his arm and pulled him into the shadows.

'Something has been flagged up about me,' said Scape. 'I can tell.'

'What kind of thing?' said Frank.

'I don't know,' said Scape. 'That's the point. You know what it's like, Frank. It doesn't take much.'

'If you haven't done anything, you'll be fine.'

Scape stared at him.

'You bastard,' he said.

Then he strode off out of sight.

'Come on,' said Frank. 'We'd better move on. Just in case.'

They walked in silence for a few hundred yards and then Dawn stopped and stood in his way.

'What did he mean?' said Dawn. 'How do you know what it's like?'

Frank shrugged.

'He's drunk,' said Frank. 'And he looks pretty guilty too. So –'

'How could you help him?' said Dawn. 'Why would he think that?'

'I don't know,' said Frank.

'You are such a terrible liar,' said Dawn. 'What's going on? I thought you were friends.'

'That was before . . .'

'Before what?'

'We had an argument,' said Frank.

'About Olivia?' said Dawn.

'Why do you say that?'

'Was it?'

'Yes,' said Frank. 'What is this?'

'I don't know,' said Dawn. 'I thought you did some boring pen-pushing job at the Ministry – too boring to talk about. So, again – why would Scape think you could find out what they know about him?'

Frank licked his lips but could not look at her. Dawn stared and backed away.

'Oh my god,' she said. 'That's what you do, isn't it? That's your job. No, no, no.'

'Dawn, listen,' said Frank. 'I work in that department. We look for any sign of insurgency or terrorism or . . . If Scape really

443

hasn't done anything then he has nothing to worry about. I just read what the Students write. That's all.'

Dawn put her hand to her mouth.

'You've read what his Student wrote, haven't you?' she said. 'You saw something there? Did you report him?'

Frank sighed and shook his head.

'I can't tell you that,' he said.

'Frank, Frank,' she said.

They walked into the apartment block and into the courtyard.

'Can you help him?' whispered Dawn, grabbing his arm.

'I don't know,' said Frank.

'Are you to blame?' she said. 'Is this your doing?'

Frank didn't reply. Tears dripped from his eyes.

'Frank?'

He tried to embrace her but she put her hands up to stop him and turned and walked away towards the stairwell. There was a click and Frank turned to see Mrs Cremaster emerge from her apartment. She was heavily made up, her face encrusted in a white paste. She smiled and bowed to him very grandly and walked towards the courtyard.

She was wearing a long and extraordinary fur coat. It was made of many panels of differing fur – some grey, some black, some white. As she walked away, Frank saw the shape of a white heart in the centre of a long ink-black panel.

445

Chapter 64

Two days later the Student grabbed Frank's arm as he walked into the bedroom after work.

'I have your papers,' he said, reaching under his pillow.

Frank grabbed a bag and started to pack. Dawn wouldn't speak to him now. He'd screwed up again. He'd pushed away the only chance he had of happiness. But regardless of what Dawn thought of him, he had to prove to himself he wasn't that man.

'How can I help Scape?' said Frank.

'What?' said the Student, holding the papers out to Frank.

'You heard me,' said Frank. 'Scape. Don't pretend you don't know who he is.'

The Student stared at him for a moment.

'Vertex already has him,' he said. 'He is interrogating him.'

'No!' said Frank.

'Why do you care?' said the Student. 'I thought you hated him.'

'No,' said Frank. 'I suppose I did. Once. I don't know. I never wanted that to happen. Is he guilty?'

'Guilty?' said the Student.

'Yes,' said Frank. 'Is he guilty of something? His notebooks hinted at something but there was nothing concrete. What has Vertex found out?'

'I don't know,' said the Student. 'I promise you. But whether he finds something out or does not, it's all the same. I warned you about Vertex. That's why you need these papers. That's why you have to go.'

'Why are there two sets of travel papers?' said Frank, as he looked through them.

'I wondered if you might want to take Miss Calypter with you,' said the Student.

'It's too dangerous,' said Frank. 'I can't be responsible for her getting into this mess.'

'As you wish,' said the Student. 'Have you asked her?'

Frank shook his head.

'Why didn't Vertex know about Dawn?' said Frank. 'He has never once mentioned her, not even in passing.'

'I don't know what you mean,' said the Student.

'Yes you do,' he said. 'Why didn't you put her in your notebooks? Isn't that a crime?'

The Student took a deep breath.

'Don't be sure he does not know about you and Miss Calypter. But I have always tried to protect you, Frank,' said the Student. 'You and those you love and who love you. Always. Many Students do this. We give enough information, but not too much. It's not much, but it's all we can do.'

Frank shook his head.

'You're my demon,' said Frank to himself.

He laughed and covered his face with his hands.

'Sorry?' said the Student.

'Nothing,' said Frank. 'Just a story I heard once. Thank you. For my parents. Thank you.'

Frank took the papers from the Student. He suddenly felt very tired.

'I have to try to save Scape,' said Frank.

'That would be unwise,' said the Student.

'I have to do something!' said Frank. 'I have to.'

'Why?' said the Student.

'Because if I don't, then I'm no better than . . .'

'Than me?' said the Student.

'No,' said Frank. 'Than Vertex.'

The Student nodded.

'I can perhaps help a little,' he said.

Frank peered at him.

'You can trust me.'

'I know I can,' said Frank.

'I can get Mr Vertex away,' said the Student. 'Not for long. But maybe long enough.'

'But what will happen to you?' said Frank.

'I will be fine.'

Frank nodded. The Student smiled.

'When?' said Frank.

'It needs to be now or not at all,' said the Student.

Frank's mouth became as dry as dust.

'Now?' said Frank. 'I don't even know where he is.'

'He's closer than you think,' said the Student.

'What?'

The Student dropped his voice to a whisper.

'You know that the Old Town is riddled with tunnels,' he said. 'Well, it is also full of chambers designed for specific purposes – secret chambers. There is just such an interrogation chamber favoured by Vertex. It is directly below this apartment.'

They both looked down at the floor.

'Below this apartment?' said Frank. 'In the basement?'

'No,' said the Student, shaking his head solemnly. 'In the sub-basement.'

'What sub-basement?'

'It is only accessible via the lift,' said the Student.

Frank stared at him.

'Which is why we aren't allowed to use it,' said Frank.

The Student nodded.

'That's why Mr Spiracle is always hovering about beside it,' said Frank. 'It's where his family were taken. He was warning me.'

'Only Vertex and a handful of Civil Servants have the key.'

'Damn it,' said Frank.

The Student smiled.

'And one or two Students.'

Frank clapped his hands together but then looked up at the Student, frowning.

'Wait,' he said. 'Why do you need a key to that lift? Do you . . . interrogate?'

The Student shook his head.

'I have it only because Vertex wanted me to report to him directly – about your father and about you. So I need access. He is often down there.'

The Student's face became even paler than normal.

'I have seen Vertex at work,' he said. 'His real work, I mean.'

Frank thought about it for a moment. He was trying to keep the fear at bay.

'So you can distract him?' said Frank. 'You can get him away from Scape? Long enough for me to get him out of there?'

'I think so,' said the Student. 'I can come up with a believable reason for his being needed back at the Castle. I will leave the lift unlocked. Give me half an hour and then follow me.'

Frank nodded.

'But what will you do then?' said the Student. 'What will you do with Scape? If you bring him here you are endangering the lives of your whole family.'

'He can use the spare travel permit,' said Frank. 'There's enough money to get us both out.'

Frank sighed.

'I need to say goodbye to Dawn. In case this doesn't work.'

'No,' said the Student. 'Trust no one.'

'I've trusted you,' said Frank. 'I think I can trust Dawn.'

Chapter 65

Frank left the Student at the stairwell and wished him luck before they parted, the Student heading for the lift and Frank for Dawn's apartment. He rang the doorbell and Dawn's mother appeared.

'Doesn't want to see you,' she slurred.

'Dawn!' he called.

'Doesn't want –'

'No offence, Mrs Calypter,' said Frank, 'but shut up. Dawn! Dawn!'

Dawn appeared in the shadow behind her mother. Frank grabbed her by the arm and yanked her out of the door.

'Hey!' said Dawn, shaking herself free.

Her mother stood in the doorway, glaring at Frank.

'It's all right,' said Dawn, pushing her mother inside and closing the door.

'Scape has been arrested,' said Frank. 'He's being interrogated.'

'No!' said Dawn. She put her hand to her mouth.

'It's my fault,' said Frank. 'I've got to put it right.'

'But how?'

'I'm going to free him,' he whispered. 'Or try. My Student is down there now getting Vertex away.'

'Down where?' said Dawn.

'There's a torture chamber under this building, apparently. You can only get there via the –'

'The lift!' said Dawn.

Frank nodded.

'And Scape is in there now? He's being tortured? Right below us?'

'Yes,' said Frank. 'I think so. I've got to find out. I'm going to get him out if I can, but we'll have to run. I have permits. I just wanted to tell you. In case . . . In case something happens and –'

'Wait there!' said Dawn, running back to her apartment. There were voices inside and then she reappeared putting her coat on.

'Come on,' she said.

'No,' said Frank. 'Not you.'

'Shut up,' she said.

She grabbed him and pulled him close and kissed him on the mouth.

'I can't let you risk it,' said Frank.

'Yes, you can,' said Dawn.

'But –'

'Look, Frank,' said Dawn. 'If you're caught . . . If you die – I don't want to live. Do you understand? If these are the last hours we have then I want to spend them together. And if this is the way we die, then we will have died doing something – trying to do something. What better way to die? You've always wanted something to happen – to be special. This is your chance – our chance.'

Frank could barely speak.

'How did I waste so much time?' he said. 'I'm so sorry.'

'It doesn't matter,' she said. 'Don't let's waste any more.'

They kissed and went to the lift on the ground floor. Just as the Student had promised, the gates were open.

They stepped inside and slid the door into place. Frank looked at Dawn and then pressed the button for the basement. After a second's pause, the lift shuddered and then sank. Frank's stomach did the same.

But the lift did not stop at the basement. It kept going despite there being no further floors shown on the buttons. It came to a sudden halt and they were thrown sideways. A fluorescent light juddered to life and flickered outside, illuminating a dank corridor. The electrical hum that was always present in Frank's

apartment was here too – only much louder, and it throbbed and surged every few moments.

Frank pulled open the sliding grille and then the gate beyond and they stepped out. It was cold and the walls were damp and rancid. Water was dripping somewhere and there was an electrical fizzing and spluttering from the strip lights overhead.

The corridor turned to the right about twenty yards ahead and they hesitantly set off in that direction, like Theseus and Ariadne looking for the Minotaur. They rounded the corner and saw an open door at the end of another straight stretch.

'Is that you, Frank?' came a voice.

Frank recognised it immediately. They entered the room, blinking against the harsh strip lighting on the ceiling. Mr Vertex was standing in a white jacket, the kind that barbers wore. The Student was standing in the corner of the room, failing to find a shadow.

Strapped into a chair that may have been an old barber's chair, was Scape, some sort of duct tape wrapped round his face, covering his mouth. He stared wide-eyed at Frank.

Mr Vertex put something down on a metal trolley with a metallic clang. Frank could see they were electrodes of some kind, a blue lightning flash dancing between them. Vertex flicked a switch on the wall and the blue light flickered and disappeared and the hum died down. He turned to face them.

'And this must be Miss Calypter,' said Mr Vertex.

'How do you know who I am?' said Dawn, backing away.

Vertex smiled.

'Because its my business to know,' he said. He cast a glance towards the Student. 'In spite of any attempts to stop me.'

'Please let him go,' said Frank, staring at Scape. 'He's too stupid to be dangerous.'

'I tend to agree,' said Vertex, pulling a rubber glove from his hand with a snap and tossing it on the trolley. 'Sadly you have arrived too late with your request. I expected him to be stronger. But there we are.'

Dawn whimpered. Frank noticed that Scape had not blinked since they walked in. Frank dropped his bag on the floor and clenched his fists.

'Why?' said Frank. 'Why did you have to kill him?'

Mr Vertex shook his head and tutted.

'Well,' said Mr Vertex, 'this is the kind of unfortunate accident that happens from time to time in our line of business. You must not blame yourself.'

'I don't! I blame you!' said Frank.

Mr Vertex smiled.

'That is easier, I suppose,' he said.

Frank clenched his fists and stepped forward. Mr Vertex pulled a gun from his pocket and Frank stopped and backed off. Mr Vertex waved the Student over towards Frank and Dawn.

'Now, sadly,' said Mr Vertex, 'whilst Scape may have been stupid and even innocent of anything desperately important, you are neither Frank – nor is the Student. And Miss Calypter has seen too much, I'm afraid. Under different circumstances I would be full of admiration for your sense of initiative, Frank. But unfortunately I am going to have to kill all three of you.'

'No!' said Frank. 'It's my fault. You're right. These two are only here because of me.'

'Because of your sister more than you, I think, in the Student's case,' said Mr Vertex, pointing the gun at his face.

Frank stared at him. Was there anything this man did not know?

'I think it best that you disappear, just as you had planned.' Mr Vertex smiled. 'Well, not precisely as you had planned. In my version you will find yourself with a bullet in your head and at the bottom of the river.'

Dawn grabbed hold of Frank's arm.

'Isn't that lovely?' said Mr Vertex. 'Some of my special Civil Servants – you've met them, Frank, remember? – will be coming for you. They will take you for a romantic moonlit trip along the river. We will meet them outside in a little while. But first I will take the papers.'

Reluctantly, Frank handed them over. Mr Vertex ripped them up and threw them on the floor at Scape's feet.

'I will have to have a little chat to your Student, Frank,' said Vertex. 'I am intrigued to know where those papers came from. They were really rather good . . .'

Then he lurched forward and grabbed Dawn, putting the gun to her head.

'But that is for later. Move. Any attempt to do anything other than walk straight ahead of me and I will splatter her brains across the pair of you. She will die anyway but I'm sure if you ask the Civil Servants nicely they will kill you lovebirds together. Better that than watching the other one go first.'

Frank picked up his bag and he and the Student walked ahead with Dawn moaning as she was pushed along, the barrel of the gun against the back of her head.

'Sorry,' said Frank.

'No,' said the Student. 'Don't be sorry.'

'No talking!' said Vertex, shoving the gun forward and making Dawn cry out.

'Stop!'

They all turned in the direction of the voice. It was Mr Spiracle.

'What have you done with my family?' he said. 'What have –'

The gunshot boomed through the corridor and Mr Spiracle dropped to the floor. Dawn clamped her hands over her ears.

'No!' shouted Frank.

He made a move towards Spiracle but Vertex aimed his pistol back at Dawn's head and smiled. Then Vertex aimed the gun at Spiracle's head and fired again. The noise was deafening and dust cascaded down from the ceiling. Dawn turned away, crying.

'Bastard!' yelled Frank. He noticed one of Mr Spiracle's eyebrows wandering up the wall. Mr Vertex followed his gaze. He flicked the eyebrow from the wall and put his foot on it, grinding it into the floor.

'I'm disappointed in you,' Vertex said. 'I won't pretend I'm not.'

'Screw you!' shouted Frank. 'There was no need for that.'

'I'm sorry to find you a sentimentalist.'

'Is it sentimental to be sorry someone's dead?' said Frank.

'When you barely know them, possibly,' said Mr Vertex. 'When you actively dislike them, definitely. You don't feel sorry, Frank – you feel guilty. People often confuse the two.

'The truth is you would have been happy enough never to see old Spiracle's face again – it's just the manner of his departure that bothers you.'

'Of course it bothers me!' shouted Frank. 'You killed him.'

The ground lurched sideways and everyone in the corridor did likewise. Everything began to vibrate. The plastic casing on the strip lights jittered and jangled until it fell off and crashed to the floor.

A crack opened up in the ceiling and dust rained down as a low rumble grew in volume until it sounded like a train was about to come careering down the corridor towards them. Frank knew what it was.

'It's the tunnel system shifting,' he shouted to Dawn above the din. 'Maybe this is it. Maybe the whole thing is going to collapse on top of us. But if we're going to die anyway, then at least we get to take him with us. Who knows, maybe even the whole Castle!'

Frank saw a new expression pass over Vertex's face – if not fear, then something like frustration – and it felt good. Vertex saw the look of satisfaction on Frank's face and smiled. Then the rumbling stopped.

'Not today, Frank,' he said. 'The Castle will be here long after you have been forgotten.'

Frank moved towards Vertex and he pointed the gun at Dawn.

'Miss Calypter,' he said. 'If you'd be so kind.'

He indicated for her to turn round and he once again jammed the pistol into the back of her head.

Mr Vertex smiled. 'Move!' he said.

Frank and the Student got in the lift, followed a moment later by Vertex and Dawn. At Vertex's order the Student punched the button and the lift ascended to the ground floor. Vertex backed out with Dawn and waved at Frank and the Student to follow, before pushing them towards the courtyard and the exit gate.

It was after curfew so the street was completely deserted. Even so Vertex marched them along the road and then down a side street, where he stood all three against the wall and occasionally peered out, looking for the Civil Servants' car.

'You see?' said Vertex. 'Do you see how the Ministry works tirelessly on behalf of its citizens, pruning the apple tree so that only the healthiest fruit will develop? The Ministry ensures that only that which is supposed to happen – is *permitted* to happen – happens, and happens at the time and place allotted to it.

'In fact, that is one of the most important functions of the Ministry – to eliminate chance.'

'You can't eliminate chance,' said Frank. 'How can you? You aren't a god.'

Vertex looked down the street.

'This is why you are in thrall to fiction, Frank,' said Mr Vertex. 'You imagine that there are endless possibilities. You take comfort in that idea, but most people do not. Most people take comfort in predictability, in simplicity – in knowing there is only one possibility – and in believing they chose it, when in reality it was chosen for them by the Ministry.

'They don't want to feel there are other unconsidered possibilities out there, vying for their attention. That would only cause them to be dissatisfied. The Ministry does not want people to be dissatisfied. Dissatisfied people are angry people. Dissatisfied people are not good citizens. Dreamers are not good citizens. Fiction – wayward, pointless, self-indulgent fiction – is a danger to society.'

'People will always dream,' said Frank.

'Perhaps,' said Mr Vertex. 'But if we control their imaginations, we can control their dreams – or at least we control the scope of those dreams.'

'Or own them,' said Frank, 'and sell them back to them.'

Mr Vertex sighed.

'Very good. You see, Frank? You would have made such a great sector head – or even a Minister – one day, I still believe that,' he said. 'You have the right mind for it.'

Vertex smiled, lost in his own thoughts and Frank tried to work out how long it would take to bridge the gap between them and grab the gun.

'Ah,' said Vertex, clearly reading his thoughts. 'We are not in one of your stories. That is your one failing. You cling to hope when there is none. There is nothing left to chance

461

here – nothing the Ministry does not control. There is nothing –'

There was a bang from up on the roof of the building opposite. Vertex's head twitched and Frank saw the glint of the Sniper's telephoto lens.

When he looked back, Vertex was slumped on the ground, a hole punched into the stone of the wall above him, splashed with blood and more than blood. Vertex's eyes were open and staring at his shoes. He looked more alive dead. The gun was still in his hand.

After a couple of seconds they all ducked down a nearby alleyway, with Frank the first to peep out. There was no sign of the Sniper on the roof.

'Oh no,' said Dawn, noticing for the first time that the alleyway was a dead end. 'He can pick us off as soon as we leave.'

'And if he doesn't,' added the Student, 'then the men from the Ministry will kill us anyway. Perhaps the Sniper would be quicker.'

'I think we're safe,' said Frank, stepping back out onto the street. 'From the Sniper, at least.'

Dawn and the Student followed him out, cautiously. Frank looked at Vertex. A trickle of blood was making its way down the side of his nose and into his moustache.

'We need to move,' said Frank. 'The Ministry Men will be here any minute. They'll think we shot him.'

'What do we do?' said Dawn.

'Go and pack a bag,' said Frank.

'What?' said Dawn.

'Come with me,' said Frank, holding out his hand. 'Come with me.'

Dawn stared at him. She nodded.

'Yes.'

'Quickly,' said the Student.

Dawn ran back into the apartment block, leaving Frank and the Student.

'What will you do?' asked the Student.

Frank smiled.

'I don't know,' he said. 'But whatever it is it will be better for having Dawn with me.'

'Good luck,' said the Student.

Dawn arrived back, bag in hand. She dropped it and embraced the Student. Frank could see tears in his eyes as they parted.

'What about you?' said Frank.

'Don't worry about me,' he said. 'I will say that –'

The Student stopped in mid-flow and stared down the street behind them. Frank and Dawn turned to see a tram heading towards them, whining gently.

The lights from its windows lit up the darkened streets and made whirling shadows of lampposts and kiosks. Apartment windows glinted like golden tessera.

'The Ghost Tram,' said Frank.

'No,' said Dawn aghast. 'That's not possible.'

'Yes,' said Frank. 'Yes it is.'

'You've seen it before?'

She stared at him in amazement. Frank nodded.

'I thought it was just a story,' said Dawn. 'Just made up.'

'Maybe it is,' said Frank. 'Maybe everything is.'

'I'm scared,' said Dawn. 'I don't understand.'

'I'm not,' said Frank. 'For the first time in my life, I'm really not.'

'Frank?' said Dawn, staring at the advancing tram.

'If it stops for us I'm getting on,' said Frank calmly.

'But no one knows where it goes,' said Dawn. 'People say you're never seen again. It could go anywhere. It could end up in any place. It could be worse than the Ministry.'

Frank shook his head.

'No,' he said. 'It can't be worse than that. Than him.'

He nodded towards Mr Vertex.

'How do you know?' shouted Dawn.

The Ghost Tram was getting closer. They could clearly see that it was driverless now as it slowly rumbled towards them, electrical flashes sparking as it did so.

'I just know!' shouted Frank, grabbing Dawn by the shoulders and staring into her worried eyes. 'I know that everything I have done so far has been wrong. Everything I thought I knew I didn't. But this I know – that tram is an escape from this, not part of it. It may be the last thing the Ministry does not own. I know that it may be the last chance we have to get away from all this. And I know that I love you and I don't want to live without you.'

The Ghost Tram glided to a halt with one last burst of electrical light that lit them up like a flash bulb and tossed their shadows across the walls. A second later the doors opened. Inside was bright and clean and deserted.

'Dawn,' said Frank, holding out his hand. 'Come on.'

'It's your tram,' said Dawn, edging back, shaking her head. 'It stopped for you, not for me.'

'Come on, Dawn,' said Frank quietly. 'Trust me. It stopped for both of us.'

'I'm scared,' she said.

'I know.'

'I don't know what to do.'

'No one does.'

He held out his hand and after a long moment she took it, closing her eyes and letting him pull her close. As they were about to board, Frank turned to the Student.

'You could come too.'

The Student shook his head.

'No, Frank,' he said. 'Thank you. But I'm staying here. You know why.'

Frank nodded.

'But won't you come under suspicion?' he asked.

'When the Civil Servants come they will find a victim of the Sniper,' said the Student. 'That's all. My report will make no

465

mention of you. Mr Vertex will not be mourned or missed. Not even by them. That is his legacy,' he continued. 'He banished sentimentalism. He killed it. No one will ask why he died. As he said himself – people die every day.'

Frank shook the Student's hand, and he and Dawn stepped aboard the tram. No sooner were they inside than the doors gave a hiss and a groan and closed behind them.

Some of Frank's calmness and surety evaporated as they waved to the Student standing next to the fallen body of Vertex. The tram lurched forward and set off down the darkened street to who knew where.

They put their bags down and took their seats. The lights from the tram lit up the windows of the sleeping buildings and threw dancing shadows across the buildings they left behind. Dawn moved Frank's bag, groaning at the weight.

'What the hell have you got in here, Frank?'

'My grandfather's typewriter,' said Frank with a smile.

Dawn grinned.

'Any clothes?'

'A few.'

'Mine's full of paper and pencils,' she said.

They put their arms round each other, exhausted.

'Poor Scape,' said Dawn, her voice trembling a little.

'I know,' said Frank, hugging her tightly. 'And old Spiracle too. I feel like it's my –'

'Shhh! said Dawn, putting a finger to his lips. 'No more, Frank. It's over.'

Frank nodded and pulled her closer. She pressed her face into his neck and he could feel her breathing. The tram slithered through streets they knew and then half knew and then did not know at all, and as the tram rumbled on, they drifted into a deep sleep.

Chapter 66

Frank opened his eyes. He couldn't tell how long he had been asleep, but it was now daytime. Dawn was asleep beside him, her face pressed against his chest. The tram had come to a halt.

He squinted into the brightness outside his window. They were in a busy street. The pavements were full of people of every age and size and hue. Some wore grey but others wore clothes so bright and gaudy to Frank's colour-starved eyes that he had to squint to look at them.

Dawn awoke and she in turn marvelled at the view, her eyes full of questions her mind could not form into words. They got to their feet and stood gazing out at the people walking by, all seemingly oblivious to their presence.

'Something tells me we're not in the Old Town any more,' said Frank, holding Dawn's hand.

And then, with a whisper, the doors swung open.

Acknowledgements

A few years ago, a Czech theatre company called Divadlo Puls contacted me to say that they wanted to adapt one of my books for the stage. That's how I ended up in Prague – a city I had longed to visit – for the first time, as guest of both my Czech publisher, Argo, and Divadlo Puls.

Around the same time I found some old notebooks containing very, very short, fable-like stories – stories I had forgotten I'd written. I knew straight away that I wanted them to appear in a book, but had no real idea how. They would become the stories told by Frank's grandfather.

I came back to Prague again a year later to visit the Park Lane International School and had one day to look around. I met up with my new friend Petra Jíšová, whom I had met on my previous visit. We walked along the river on a beautifully sunny day, talking about all manner of things, and crossed at a railway bridge over the river. As we did so Petra told me a story about young people putting wishes in beer bottles and throwing them from the bridge into the water – just as the train passed over. I told her there and then that I would be putting that in a book some day . . .

Anything That Isn't This is not about Prague – although Prague lends a lot to the location. But I grew up in Newcastle-upon-Tyne in the 1970s and it has far more to do with my teenage feelings of needing to escape from what I felt was a life that did not, and could never, fit me. Art college was my escape.

I pitched the book first to Sarah Odedina when she was at Hot Key. Sarah had been the editor who brought me to Bloomsbury and was a guiding – and incredibly supportive presence – in all my work there. This is a chance to thank her for all that too.

But I need to thank Naomi Colthurst for easing the transition when Sarah moved on. I've been incredibly lucky with editors throughout my writing career and so it continues. Thanks too to Jenny Jacoby and Melissa Hyder who kept me on my toes as we honed the book in the latter stages.

I started out as an illustrator but it's been a while since I've had an opportunity to show that side of my work. I want to thank everyone at Hot Key for letting me illustrate the book and to Jet Purdie and Jan Bielecki (and Naomi) for being so enthusiastic when I came in to the office to show them half a dozen roughs. I need to thank them too for a superb cover.

Lastly, I need to thank all those clever, funny, warm and friendly people I met in Prague on both my visits. All the lovely folk of Divadlo Puls but especially my friend Lucie Radmerská. To Milan Gelnar and everyone from Argo, and particularly to my good friend Richard Klíčník for all his kindness and support on both visits. To Paul Ingarfield and the staff, parents and pupils at the Park Lane International School. Without these people, and the opportunity they gave me to visit their fantastic city, this book would never have happened – or certainly never taken the form it did.

Chris Priestley

Chris Priestley spent his childhood in Wales and Gibraltar, and his teens in Newcastle-upon-Tyne, before going to art college in Manchester. He moved to London and freelanced as an illustrator and cartoonist for twenty years before getting his first book for children published. He has written lots of books, fiction and non-fiction, has won awards here and abroad and been nominated for many others, including the Carnegie Medal. He now lives in Cambridge and spends a great deal of time looking out of the window . . . Follow Chris at http://chrispriestley.blogspot.co.uk or on Twitter: @crispriestley

HOT KEY BOOKS

Thank you for choosing a Hot Key book.

If you want to know more about our authors
and what we publish, you can find us online.

You can start at our website

www.hotkeybooks.com

And you can also find us on:

We hope to see you soon!